DEATH

BY TRADITION

B.M. ALLSOPP

DEATH
BY TRADITION

FIJI ISLANDS MYSTERIES 2

Coconut Press

First published in Australia in 2018
by Coconut Press
Copyright © B.M. Allsopp 2018
www.bmallsopp.com
Contact the author by email at bernadette@bmallsopp.com

Print book ISBN 978-0-9945719-3-9
Kindle ISBN 978-0-9945719-2-2
Epub ISBN 978-0-9945719-5-3

National Library of Australia Cataloguing-in-Publication entry (pbk)
Creator: Allsopp, B. M., author.
Title: Death by Tradition: Fiji islands mysteries 2 / B. M.
Allsopp.
ISBN: 9780994571946 (paperback)
Series: Allsopp, B. M. Fiji islands mysteries
Subjects: Detective and mystery stories.
Fiji—Fiction.
Dewey Number: A823.4

To all the people of Fiji

THE PRINCIPAL ISLANDS OF FIJI

Labasa

Rabi

VANUA LEVU

Buca

Savusavu

Taveuni

Yasawa Group

Nabouwalu

Koro

Ba

Levuka

Lautoka

VITI LEVU

Tanoa

Ovalau

Nadi

Nausori

KORO SEA

Suva

Gau

Navua

Sigatoka

Paradise

Delanarua

Beqa

Vatulele

Moala

Ono

PACIFIC OCEAN

Totoya

Kandavu

AUTHOR'S NOTE: The village of Tanoa is fictitious, as are Paradise and Delanarua islands. Other places on this map are real, but nearly 300 exquisite small islands are omitted.

Glossary and Guide to Fijian Pronunciation

bula – hello
moce – goodbye or goodnight
moce mada – see you later
io – yes
tanoa – large wooden bowl for ceremonial mixing of *yaqona* (kava)
ndina – true, indeed
vakalevu – very much
vinaka – thank you
yaqona – kava (applied to the plant, its roots, ground powder and drink)

Acronyms

DI – detective inspector
DS – detective sergeant
DC – detective constable
SOCO – scene of crime officer
NLTB – Native Land Trust Board

Spelling

The Fijian alphabet is based on English but it is phonetic, so each sound is always represented by only one letter, unlike English.

Vowels

a as in *father*
e as in *met*
i as in *Fiji*
o as in *or*
u as in *flu*

Consonants

Most consonants are pronounced roughly as in English, with the following important exceptions.

b = *mb* as in me*mb*er eg. **b**ula = **mb**u-la
d = *nd* as in te*nd*er eg. **d**ina = **nd**ina
g = *ng* as in si*ng*er eg. li**g**a = li-**ng**a
q = *ngg* as in stro*ng*er eg. ya**q**ona = ya-**ngg**ona
c = *th* as in mo*th*er eg. mo**c**e = mo-**th**ay

PROLOGUE

SATURDAY

Viliame used the torch on his phone to light his way. No reception here in Tanoa, but the torch was handy while the charge lasted. Kelera had left the spice gardens by the upper path and should be back home by now. Her eager embrace stayed with him as the evening air cooled. Her willingness to lie to her parents touched him. She deserved better than him; she deserved someone who loved her. But he wanted to protect her from village gossip. So he'd waited a while before taking a different path that skirted the nutmeg grove before descending to the village.

From Suva, it was a bit of a trek to get back home to Tanoa on Saturdays; over two hours on the bus followed by a truck from the market corner if he was lucky. If not, then he walked uphill for another two hours to the clusters of houses strung out above the river bend. He had to head back to Suva again after Sunday lunch. Still, it was enough time to build influence. Even some of the older villagers were starting to take notice of him, even to ask his opinion; not about village matters of course, but about the doings of the wider world. Despite their profound distrust and suspicion, they were intrigued by the modern world. His people were tough and enduring, but more were now ready to welcome a modicum of comfort and convenience. Electricity would give them that.

He entered the fallow garden site invaded by morning glory and lantana. As he brushed against the leaves, a sharp scent assaulted his nose. Why didn't the farmers root the lantana out when it appeared instead of shrugging helplessly once it had taken over? But that was just one of his many frustrations with village thinking.

As the path widened, he heard a rustle to the left. He pointed his dimming phone torch towards the noise, but saw nothing. Probably a mongoose returning late to its burrow under the protective lantana brambles. Now there was an animal with purpose and energy. If the villagers had a mongoose's sense of mission, their lives would be very different.

A brittle lantana cane snapped beside him. He turned, recognised the face in the faint glow of his phone. 'What…'

Two burly arms drove the weapon into Viliame's skull. His body crashed through the lantana and fell to the ground.

SUNDAY

1

Detective Inspector Josefa Horseman watched the game with increasing concern. The first match of the Suva Shiners was not going their way. They'd been unlucky to come up against Marist Brothers High School, one of the strongest rugby teams in the Suva district. None of the Shiners had made it to any high school; most eked out a meagre living as shoe-shine boys on Suva's streets. Their lack of discipline equipped them poorly to survive the Marists' attack. And that was just the psychological aspect.

Their physical fitness was another matter. Most were undernourished, their rapidly growing teenage bones straining against their skin. Dr Pillai, Horseman's right-hand man through four months of Shiners' training, stood beside him now. He looked up at Horseman, his brows drawn together in anxiety.

'I did have my doubts about Mosese, Joe. Look at him now.' He pointed to a lanky lad who was bent double, hands on knees, back heaving.

Horseman looked at his watch. 'Four minutes to half-time. Can he make it or do you want to pull him off now?'

Noticing he was the focus of attention, Mosese straightened and gave them the thumbs-up.

'My goodness, that boy could do four minutes more on willpower alone,' Dr Pillai said. 'Look, the forwards are getting themselves in something like a line now. Mosese!' he yelled. 'Line up!'

It seemed like a miracle—the much-practised manoeuvre

unfolded before Horseman's eyes. Scrawny Tevita threw himself at
the bigger Marist boy, who lost balance and toppled, the ball slipping
through his hands. Pita scooped it up, sped down the field, passed
it to Simeone just as a Marist blocked him. The forwards kept level
with Simeone, who passed to Livai a split second before two Marists
brought him down. Livai fumbled the ball, but managed to hold on
and ran like the wind. Suddenly the Marists were all behind Livai,
the team clown, who stopped dead just before the line and placed
the ball gently on the other side. The Shiners erupted in triumph,
the roars of Horseman and Dr Pillai surpassing even those of the
team. No matter that the Marists already had three tries and three
goals, this was the Shiners' first. Ever! The referee blew his whistle.
Could Paula, the Shiners' best kicker, now convert the try for two
extra points? Yes, the ball arced between the posts. More eruptions
of joy interrupted the whistle blowing for half-time.

Dr Pillai rushed to the team's resting spot beyond the sidelines.
The boys cheered as he joined them. The reserves handed out water
and hands of bananas.

Horseman limped after Dr Pillai, elated. On duty four months
ago, he'd set back his slow rehabilitation from knee surgery. A year
earlier he'd shattered his knee on the rugby field playing for Fiji. But
he didn't need the crutch any more, nor the stick. In time he would
play for Police again and maybe the national team. He knew most
people were sceptical of his ambition, believing he was washed up
for good.

During the break Horseman laid out the strategy for the second
half. The referee blew the whistle, pitched in the ball and the game
was on. His phone vibrated in his pocket. Damn, he'd forgotten to
switch it off. He couldn't tolerate any interruptions now. It was
Sunday, he was off-duty, and it was the Shiners' first game. But
perhaps it was his mother or one of his sisters. He'd better check.

Horseman regretted this decision when he saw the call was from
Detective Superintendent Navala.

'*Bula*, hello, sir.'

'*Bula*, Joe. Bad news, I'm afraid. Murder up in the hills. Tanoa village. A young man found dead in the church before morning service. Viliame Bovoro. Bludgeoned. This one's clear cut, according to Dr Tavua in Nausori. Definitely murder. You're the Investigation Officer.'

'Me, sir? Surely that's Korovou district?'

'Theoretically, Joe. Their inspector's on leave. They've only got one sergeant; they simply haven't got the resources. And Viliame, the victim, actually lives in Suva. He was home for the weekend. You might think we're short-staffed here, but you know we're the best-resourced district in Fiji. We're expected to be generous with our help.'

'*Io*, yes, sir.'

'Get in to the station soon as you can. It's too late to get a team up to the village today. Pity. Viliame's body is on the way to Suva. Dreadful business. His family…terrible.'

'*Io* sir. It's a shame they couldn't leave him there.'

'Dr Tavua made that decision. He must have had his reasons. We do have photos, however.'

'Okay. Is forty-five minutes alright?'

'Sure, it'll take me that long to get there myself.'

'Sir, have you given any thought to the team? I wonder if Detective Sergeant Singh would be available.'

'My thought exactly, Joe. See what I can do.'

Horseman put the call behind him and gave his full attention to the second half. The Shiners showed more courage, scored a penalty goal, and ten minutes later, another try. After that, the superior fitness, size, and experience of the Marists prevailed. For the final five minutes, the Shiners pushed themselves beyond their limits, but failed to stop the Marists scoring again and again. A lump came to his throat when he saw the street kids giving their all. He glanced at his watch. He couldn't leave before speaking to the boys, even though he'd be late for the super's briefing.

The boys clustered around him, slumped with fatigue, faces

expectant. 'Shiners, how proud I feel at this moment. Your first competition game, and you scored two tries off Marists, the strongest team in third grade!'

'We lost, Joe,' Tevita said gloomily. 'No hope against Marists.' Others muttered in agreement.

'Tevita, we've got those two tries to build on now. Look at the Marist coach over there. He's blasting those boys!'

Tevita stood up to look and grinned at the semicircle of boys, whose heads hung while their coach let them have it.

'He expected you not to score a single point!' Horseman smiled. 'Be happy, boys, you've done well. Let's celebrate the Shiners' first tries and goals. Give yourselves three cheers, you all deserve it. Hip, hip...'

The first cheer was subdued, the second stronger, but with the third, the boys shed their disappointment and roared happily.

'Shiners, one of my great pleasures as coach is to select the Man of the Match.' Horseman continued. 'Today it's Livai, who scored both tries, the first ever for the Shiners. Livai, let me shake your hand.'

Livai came forward, bowed, and grasped Horseman's hand. 'Three cheers for our coach, Shiners!' The full-throated response was deafening until the smell of grilling sausages demanded their attention.

Horseman announced, 'Dr Pillai is providing a special meal today, Shiners. Let's go.' The boys cheered again. Dr Pillai raised both hands, grinning.

There was a race to a portable barbecue set up near the grandstand where Detective Constable Tanielo Musudroka was turning sausages while two other police volunteers were unpacking loaves of sliced bread, tomato sauce, and cartons of milk on a trestle table.

Horseman had to get away, but he had another supporter to thank first. As Sunny Khan, the proprietor of Khan's All Sports Emporium, approached them, Horseman clapped his hands for attention. 'Shiners, how do you like your new jerseys, donated by your sponsor Mr Khan?' The boys sported tan jerseys with black collars and trim, shoe logo on the left breast, and the sports store's name emblazoned in large white lettering across the front. Spontaneous cheers broke out as Sunny Khan reached them.

'*Vinaka vakalevu*, thank you very much, Mr Khan. Your beautiful jerseys made the boys a team today. In your jerseys, the Shiners took twelve points from Marist Brothers this afternoon.'

Horseman interrupted the cheering so Sunny Khan could speak.

'Boys, boys, when your coach first asked me to sponsor your new team, I was doubtful. But Fiji's great rugby star, Josefa Horseman, is persuasive, isn't it? My, my, I couldn't say "no" in the end. You've made a good start today, boys. I look forward to you climbing the ladder as the season progresses. You've got the best coach and the best jerseys, so you've got everything going for you, isn't it?'

Their energy recovered, the boys jumped around, cheering and clapping, delighted with themselves. Only Tevita was subdued, and Horseman knew why. Sunny had not supplied them with rugby boots, Tevita's greatest desire. Of course they were expensive. Why should Sunny spend such a sum? It wasn't as though the Shiners would bring him any business. The jerseys had been purely a favour to Horseman. So the boys played barefoot, as did Marists and most of the junior teams. No shame in that, but one day Horseman would get boots for them.

He really did have to go. 'I'm off to work now, boys. See you all on Tuesday. Four o'clock. Don't be late now.'

Horseman strode off among more cheers, almost managing not to limp.

2

'*Bula*, hello, Joe, come in. How did your pet rascals go this afternoon?' Superintendent Navala asked.

So the super knew why he was late. 'Sorry, sir. I just couldn't walk out on the Shiners during their first game. They'd see it as desertion.'

'Never mind, Joe. We all admire the work you're doing with the street kids. Not all of us can share your optimism about the saving power of rugby, that's all.' One corner of the super's mouth turned up in an ironic curve, which was as close as he usually came to a smile. 'At least we know the boys in the team have alibis for any petty thefts this afternoon.'

Horseman chuckled. 'True sir. I don't think they'll get up to any mischief tonight, either. They're zonked, wrecked. Two tries, two conversions, and a penalty against Marists this afternoon. Their first game! Who'd have thought it possible, even a month ago?'

'You did, Joe. You've done well. Musudroka and the other volunteer officers too. I hope the rascals are grateful and don't pick your pockets.'

Horseman obliged the super with a chuckle again. 'What have we got then—a murder in a highlands village? How unusual is that?'

'Highly unusual, Joe. No pun intended.' Horseman grinned. He didn't mind indulging in puns himself, when they occurred to him.

'*Io*, yes, Tanoa is at the end of the road, or beyond the end of the road. Only four-wheel drive vehicles can get there, and even they have to stop across the river. Never been there myself, but I hear it's one of those old-fashioned places where they keep modern evils at bay. The parking bay, in the case of trucks. I guess many isolated places are the same. Bound to be conflict there. But murder? Your job is to find out who and why. The how's more straightforward this time.'

'That's something. Tell me, sir.'

'Fortunately, one of the villagers is a retired cop, a constable his entire career. The pastor discovered the murdered man in the church when he was preparing for Sunday school before nine this morning. Tomasi, our cop, advised the pastor about preserving the crime scene, rustled up a camera, took photos, and got someone to drive to the nearest police post at Kumi. Kumi post sent their entire force of two constables and Korovou station sent Dr Tavua. The doc certified death. He expects the PM to confirm death by a blow to the head with the proverbial blunt instrument. In church!'

'Any crime scene officers been there yet?'

The super shook his head. 'No SOCOs today, but I'll get a couple up there in the morning. In the meantime, there's a uniform from Kumi police post and Tomasi sharing guard duties.'

'Tomasi's not ideal, sir. The murderer's got to be a villager, don't you think?'

'Not so fast, Joe. *Io*, less than ideal. You can hardly expect the uniform to stay awake all night. Relief wasn't available.'

'*Io*, understood. Who have you lined up for me?'

'Take Musudroka with you. He seems to be a good choice after all, eh.'

He remembered taking issue with the super about assigning the raw CID transfer, Tanielo Musudroka, to his team back in January. Embarrassing. All Horseman had achieved was to expose his own lack of confidence to the perceptive super. But Musudroka proved keen to learn and would do well in time.

'*Io*, sir. Glad to have Tanielo. He's not ready for solo interviews yet, though. Can anyone else be spared?'

One corner of the super's mouth turned up again. 'As you know,

Sergeant Singh's still on leave at her home in the west. But as she's due back on Wednesday, I sent her a message asking if she'd like to resume a day or two earlier. I'm waiting for her reply. She's in the backblocks, too, but much more accessible than Tanoa. An officer from the closest police post has already taken the message to her parents' farm.'

Horseman's spirits rose. 'I don't think Susie will refuse an early return to work, sir.'

'*Dina*, true Joe. You made a good team on your double murder.'

Horseman nodded. 'Any chance of Kelepi Taleca?'

'As you know, Taleca was finally promoted to sergeant so he could join Training Division. He's an asset there. You hardly need two sergeants at this stage, Joe. Let's see how it goes, eh. I've booked the vehicle for six thirty. Call in at Nausori station on the way, find out what you can there, then head for the hills.'

'*Vinaka*, sir, this will be a change of scene for me. Looking forward to it. I'll start on background computer work now.'

Again, the super's mouth turned up at one corner. 'Just before I go, I haven't forgotten you go on recreation leave next Friday. I suppose your visitor from the US is still coming?'

'*Io*, sir.' He felt helpless. Melissa would land in the middle of a round-the-clock murder investigation.

'Let's pray this one's straightforward, then. I'll do what I can to enlarge your team. However, you're aware all leave is cancelled for IOs in serious crimes like this.'

'*Io*, sir.' What an incentive!

***

How could this work? He'd been trying to get Melissa to Fiji ever since he'd left Portland, Oregon, over four months ago. She'd be here in just five days. He hoped their reunion would lead to something, maybe even a decision about their future together. But now?

This murderer had cheated him, snatched his hope away. Hardly likely that they'd crack the case before Friday! But it was possible; he'd cling to that small chance and make it his private deadline.

He had to be rational though. It might be better to postpone Melissa's trip until this case was solved. But his job was unpredictable. This very situation could happen again next time. He had to talk it over with her, and now. Sunday at six o'clock in Fiji was eleven on Saturday night in Portland, Oregon. He texted her two words: 'News. Skype?' He set up his laptop, logged in to Skype, and waited. Within a few minutes, the computer pinged and she was there, a towel round her neck, her short hair wet, her mouth and eyes smiling.

'Ciao, Joe, can't see you yet. Ah, here you come now. As you can see, I was in the shower when you texted. I sure could use some Fiji sun! What's your news, honey?' She rubbed her hair, put the towel aside.

'A murder up in the hills today, a few hours' drive from Suva. I'm IO, heading the enquiry. I'm going up first thing tomorrow. No clue at this stage. It could complicate our plans for your trip. Quite easily, actually.'

Melissa's happy smile vanished. 'Sure, I can see that. What are you thinking?'

'Darling, I want you to come on Friday. I just need you to be prepared. If we haven't arrested the killer before then, I won't have any choice but to be working flat out on this case. My leave will be cancelled.'

She gazed at him, her blue eyes thoughtful. 'Do you think I should postpone my trip? It shouldn't be a problem at the hospital. I bought the flexible ticket, cancelling and rebooking will cost me zilch.'

The scatter of freckles over her nose and cheeks made him want to kiss her. He sighed. 'I don't know. The trouble is, a detective's caseload is unpredictable. If you postpone, it could easily be the same scenario later.'

'Oh no, I might never get there! You know what? Let's hope for the best, not decide yet. Who knows, you might go up to the hills tomorrow morning and return with the culprit in cuffs by dinner!' She smiled.

Positive thinking never did any harm. 'Let's talk again Monday evening when I get back to Suva—your Sunday night. But it could be too late for you, darling, maybe even after midnight.'

'No, just call when you can. I'll stay up. I won't be able to sleep.'

'Okay, I will. Got anything planned tomorrow?'

'Lunch with the folks. Maybe a walk with Dad later. He's gotten inactive the last few years, I want to encourage him.'

'Good. Give your family my greetings. Go easy on your father.'

'Good luck with your case, you gotta wrap this one up quick, honey!'

'Believe me, I'll do my best. But we'll make your trip work, Melissa, whatever happens. See you tomorrow.'

'Sure, honey. Can't wait. Sweet dreams!'

As she clicked off, he caught a fleeting glimpse of a worried frown replacing her smile.

MONDAY

3

The road inland from Nausori skirted the broad Rewa River and a bright patchwork of traditional root crops and fruit trees. To meet the demands of the growing number of tourists, enterprising farmers now grew previously unknown crops: lettuce, bok choy, capsicum, all shapes and sizes of tomato, and more.

'It's a picture, sir, isn't it?' Detective Constable Tanielo Musudroka gazed at the flourishing farmlands from the Land Cruiser's front passenger seat.

'It sure is,' agreed Horseman. 'You've not been along this road before?'

'Never had call to. I've heard about it, though. The farmers around my place near Ba say how good the ground is here, how easy the farmers have it.'

'A lot of hard labour goes into this pretty picture, too. Speaking of pictures, what do you make of the photos of the victim?'

'Strange, sir.' Musudroka took the A4 prints from the envelope on his lap and looked at them again. 'He's flat out, arms outstretched, his head towards the cross at the front of the church. It's kinda like a crucifixion position.'

He shuffled the pictures. 'In this one, I can see matted blood in his hair, so probably a head injury, but no cuts and bruises to his limbs. The mat he's lying on looks straight and clean, not like there's been a fight.'

'*Io*, he must have been taken by surprise and the first blow knocked him out, if not killed him. Dr Tavua said that there was hardly any blood, so it seems he was killed somewhere else and brought to the church, deliberately arranged like that. It might be a crucifixion position or possibly a submission position.'

Musudroka was silent for a bit. 'What does that tell us, sir?'

'Good question, Tani. It tells us that the murderer didn't want to hide his crime. He wanted to display it, while keeping his own identity secret. He's arrogant, and is probably among the villagers right now, acting shocked and grieving and enjoying his anonymity. He also wants to make a pronouncement. If the victim is presented as being crucified, then presumably the victim is the sacrifice, but for what?'

'And if it's submission?' Musudroka asked.

'That could mean the murderer is making the victim submit, maybe he saw him as a sinner who needed to be brought back to God. But what was Viliame's sin?'

'And who thinks he's God, judging and punishing?'

'Excellent question, Tani. You'll make a detective yet! Remember, those who like to act as judge, jury, and especially executioner rarely have any respect for the police. When we visit the village, we're likely to meet natural resistance that more isolated people always have to uninvited authorities. If the murderer's still there, he will not only try to outwit us, but he could amuse himself by turning the community against us.'

Musudroka looked alarmed. 'I'm used to people wanting to keep their business to themselves, but…'

'But this is different, Tanielo. A murderer who goes to a lot of trouble to display his handiwork in public, especially in a church, is different from one who hides his victim's body. This one will delight in discrediting the police, possibly by showing us up as fools or as crooked. We need to be extra careful to do everything by the book, and to show courtesy to everyone we speak to.'

'Of course, sir. Goes without saying.' Musudroka sounded a bit offended.

Horseman turned left onto a winding gravel road which climbed steadily. The commercial farms gave way to smaller plantations providing subsistence for the villagers who owned and worked them. Here and there were cleared paddocks, where brown cattle grazed the rough tussocks, constantly swishing tails and shrugging skin to rid themselves of biting insects.

They could hardly miss the final turn-off. This steeper track was deeply rutted where the gravel had been washed away. They were in the highlands now. The villages and plantations were smaller and further apart, the forested patches larger and lusher. Horseman slowed as two men on horseback approached, leading two pack horses laden with bulging sacks, bunches of bananas, and nets of root crops. The officers returned the men's friendly waves and shouts of '*Bula, bula.*'

Horseman idly wondered if the horses were descendants of the horse shipwrecked with his own ancestor in the early 1800s. That horse, the first in Fiji, had saved his ancestor's life when a chief instantly set his heart on the beautiful beast. Never having clapped eyes on an animal bigger than a pig, the chief had no idea how to handle the horse, so Horseman's ancestor was saved from the ovens, became the chief's groom, and lived to found a lineage. The ancestor became known as 'horse-man' by the Fijians, and the name was passed down through the generations.

'What's that dark green crop—the bushes over there?' Musudroka suddenly asked, disturbing Horseman's reverie. He pointed to an orderly plantation of small, dark trees stretching up the slope.

'Coffee Arabica bushes. They only do well at this height and higher. The best coffee in the world. Well, maybe just a bit behind Colombian. Fiji's isolated from diseases that periodically strike the large suppliers and raise the price. We don't have the volume yet to supply the major buyers, but the single-source coffee merchants want our beans, and pay top prices.'

'What are you talking about, sir? You're a walking encyclopaedia.'

Horseman chuckled. 'No, Tani, just a coffee obsessive and a patriotic one, too.'

'I don't even like coffee. Give me a good, sweet cup of tea any day.'

'Ah, that's because you've never smelled and tasted the good stuff. I'll have to educate you about coffee at the Arabica in Suva.'

Horseman was now forced to slow right down as the gravel disappeared into red clay mounded into even deeper ruts. These were a challenge even for the Land Cruiser, which often lurched, shaking the two men. The forest was thick and tall in the gullies now; mahogany trees festooned with epiphytes, the giant gingers drooping under the weight of their heavy red or creamy flowers. The track curved and descended into the misty forest. Horseman switched on the headlights. They heard the tumbling river again, and around the next bend a barrier of logs showed up in the headlights. A hand-painted sign instructed 'No Vehicles Beyond This Point—Pedestrians Only' in Fijian and English. Beyond the barrier was a timber footbridge. In a cleared area of muddy grass to the left stood a battered red truck, a couple of old bikes and a quite new-looking cream twin-cab utility vehicle. A few wheelbarrows were upended near the car park entrance.

'This is the car park the super mentioned. Literally the end of the road.'

'Tanoa's a funny name, isn't it? A *yaqona* bowl?'

Horseman shrugged. 'I don't know how the name came about. Maybe it was the landscape. We're surrounded by hills, could be like the bottom of a *tanoa*.'

Mist shrouded the river, thinning as it rose to the hilltops. The hazy river bank opposite curved to the point where the bridge crossed.

To the right stood clusters of houses and a church. Further up the slope was a terrace with a school and a grassed rectangle with bamboo posts at either end. This would be the *rara*, the ceremonial space that in small villages doubled as a rugby field, both functions equally vital. Here and there were washing lines and small sheds. At the beach below the bridge, women washed clothes, slapping them rhythmically on the smooth river stones. Others tended fish traps, watched closely by a couple of thin dogs. A typical backblocks village—picturesque, placid, dull. But this one harboured an unusual and dangerous killer.

To the left of the bridge, the land rose steeply to a high outcrop of rock, a near-vertical cliff. The stone at the top had been shaped, maybe boulders hauled up to increase the height. Horseman recognised the ruins of a precolonial hill fort. His hackles rose as he gazed through the mists of time at bloody battle scenes. Rough battlements would have protected the Tanoa defenders hurling spears, shooting arrows, throwing missiles with deadly accuracy. What better site to spot attackers from down river? What better site from which to repel them?

***

A middle-aged man strode forward to meet them as they crossed the bridge. He wore a short-sleeved blue shirt and pocket *sulu*, the formal version of the simple wraparound cloth worn in villages by both sexes. Horseman presented his police ID, introduced himself and Musudroka.

'*Bula vinaka*, officer. You're welcome. Of course, it's a pleasure to meet our rugby legend. I am Joni Tora, the Methodist pastor here. It was I who discovered our brother Viliame dead in our church yesterday morning. I can still hardly believe what has happened. Such evil, here, where life is so peaceful.'

'*Vinaka vakalevu*, Pastor Joni. We are very sorry you have lost one of your precious young men and apologise for intruding on your grief. It is clear that Viliame was murdered, so it is good that we find his killer. I'm afraid you will have to put up with a team of police troubling you until we do.'

'I understand, and so will Viliame's family. It is God's work you're doing here. Our chief is not here in the village today, but his headman, Ilai, is here. Come along to my house and have some refreshments. You must be tired after your long drive. Have you really come from Suva this morning? You must have left very early.'

Most of the houses were built of traditional plastered reed walls and palm thatch, others with painted weatherboards and corrugated iron. As they walked along, the sun broke through the oppressive cloud cover, cheering the scene. A minute later, women hauled rolled pandanus mats out of the houses and spread them on convenient hibiscus bushes.

'Ah, sunning the mats—such a pleasant sight,' Horseman said.

'And a job that's never done,' the pastor replied. 'It's often cloudy here in the hills. The women are constantly alert for the sunshine and act immediately.'

Pastor Joni led them past the white-painted church to the house next door, larger, more elevated, and more recently painted than the others. Bright green with a red door and window frames. 'Welcome to my humble home, officers. Please take a seat at our table. My wife, Mere.'

Horseman and Musudroka shook hands with Mere, a small plump-faced woman with a beaming smile. 'Mere is a huge rugby fan,' Pastor Joni explained.

They sat at the table, already covered with a yellow plastic cloth and set with glasses of water, teacups and saucers, a jug of milk, and a bowl of sugar. Mere brought a large aluminium teapot to the table and poured tea, then brought sandwiches and a basket of scones wrapped in a checked tea towel.

'You know exactly what we need Mrs Tora. We should be in top form after this wonderful morning tea.' Horseman dutifully ate a few tinned meat and tinned fish sandwiches and drank a cup of tea while eyeing the scones. Mere unwrapped the bundle, releasing the comforting aroma into the air.

'Do take a few, Inspector Horseman. We have butter, too.' She fetched a tin of butter from the open-shelved pantry and passed it to her husband who reached a knife from his *sulu* pocket and opened the tin. Horseman did not want to eat into his hosts' tinned supplies, but the tin was open now and scones were definitely better with butter. So he cut a scone in two, spread each half sparingly with butter while Mere poured him another cup of tea. Musudroka followed his example.

Suddenly Mere jumped up again. 'Silly me, I forgot the jam! Banana and passionfruit, I only made it last month.' She stood on a stool to lift a jar from the top shelf and set it on the table with a flourish. 'The passionfruit does give it a nice tang, if I say so myself.'

'Mere is a champion jam-maker, officer. This one is extra special,' the pastor said. They each had another scone, this time with Mere's jam.

Horseman never liked to rush village people, who considered haste very rude. However, it was time to be about their duties. 'Pastor Joni, can you tell me about your discovery of Viliame in the church yesterday?'

The pastor sipped his tea before he spoke. '*Io*, I went across well before nine o'clock, when Sunday school starts, to get things ready. It must have been around half past eight. I went first to the windows, opened a few wooden shutters and the light flooded in. I glanced around and immediately saw poor Vili, lying face down on the mats, arms outstretched. For a moment I thought he might be praying, although it is not our custom to prostrate ourselves in church, but still… then I noticed how still he was, then the blood on his hair.'

'Did you touch him, Pastor?' Horseman asked.

'*Io*, I got down on my knees and felt for a pulse in his neck. I raised his shoulder and felt for a heartbeat. His skin was a bit cool. I'm no expert, but he seemed dead to me and by another's hand.'

'What did you do then?'

'I went to his house, broke the news to his parents, and brought them here. Then I rang the bell outside to gather everyone so I could tell them myself. Fortunately, one of the Sunday school teachers, Tomasi, is a retired policeman. I handed over to him and he did a great job of controlling the church. He even took photographs. He asked Naca to go to the police post in his truck and bring the constable back here.'

'How are Vili's parents now?'

'They're grieving and still shocked. Either Tomasi or I were always with them in the church. I cancelled Sunday school. We still had Sunday service at half past ten, but we held it in the school shelter shed. Vili's parents attended. Afterwards, they and their younger children joined my family here for lunch, then they went home to rest.'

'*Vinaka*, Pastor Joni. You and Tomasi have shown great sense and done all that you could. What can you tell me about Vili?'

'Ah, Vili, he can't be replaced. A delightful boy. Great potential, I believed. He's with God now.' The pastor bowed his head for a few moments, then finished his cup of tea. Musudroka helped himself to another scone. Horseman frowned at him.

Pastor Joni started speaking again. 'You can see how it is here—we're at the end of the road, far from the bustle and crowds of the coast and the main valley. It seems too cut off for our children. They don't do particularly well at school, very few go away to high school. Even children who are bright enough are shy, a bit scared of boarding school. They'd rather stay here and farm, or get their drivers' licence and drive a truck or a bus. Some of them get jobs at resorts, both boys and girls. But because they haven't got much education, their jobs don't bring in much money, so little comes back to the village. No one here minds, but there's not much money here, never mind that everyone works hard.

'Vili was quite different. He went off to high school full of eagerness and he did well. He liked agriculture and started a spice project here. Vanilla and nutmeg. He was full of plans—high value, low weight, he said that's what we need in our remote spot, and that spices fit the bill. Oh, he was enthusiastic.' The pastor's eyes filled and he rubbed them.

'Did he continue with the spice project?' Horseman prompted.

'*Io*, he did, even though his own plans to go to agricultural college failed. His parents aren't well off, and with three younger children to bring up, they thought Vili should get a job. He was lucky to get a job as a trainee book-keeper with the Native Land Trust Board. Well, everyone says he was lucky, that's a respected institution. However, I think the NLTB was lucky. Vili radiated a keenness that would impress any employer and his school results were very good indeed. He's still at the NLTB after five years, and now a senior book-keeper. What am I saying? He's dead, isn't he? Who would want to kill Vili? It's inconceivable!' The pastor pulled a handkerchief from his pocket to wipe his tears.

'How did he manage to continue the spice project, sir?' Musudroka asked.

The pastor smiled. 'Oh, Vili wasn't afraid of hard work, Constable, and he was a born leader. He returned here most weekends and on all his holidays. He motivated people here to work some hours in their spare time, and the necessary work was done. And, although it's still small, it's making money. Vili kept accurate records of how many hours people worked, and proceeds from sales were divided among the participants fairly. Vili took nothing for himself, beyond the hours he put in. The records were public, so anyone could check and, naturally, each worker kept an eye on the others.'

Horseman smiled. 'Of course, I can easily imagine that. He must have been a very popular man.'

'He was indeed. He wanted to expand the area of the spice gardens, and he got the elders' permission to do that twice already. But there was some difficulty about his latest proposal.'

'What sort of difficulty?' Horseman asked.

Silence fell while Mere poured them a third cup of tea. The pastor stared at his cup, pondering. When he looked up, he said, 'It's to do with land allocation here. That's all I can say. You know I'm not from here myself, though I've been here twenty years now. I'm from Vanua Levu. I'm not privy to the deliberations of the chief and elders.'

Horseman shook his head slightly at Musudroka, just in case the inexperienced detective decided to probe the point further, and finished his cup of tea.

'*Vinaka vakalevu*, Pastor and Mrs Tora. Your hospitality has been wonderful. You've fortified us for the rest of the day. Now it's time we visited the church.'

'*Io*, you're most welcome, Inspector, please don't let us detain you.' The pastor escorted them down the steps and stayed there, watching as they walked next door to his church.

4

Two men waited at the ox-blood door of the church. The shorter, burlier one stepped forward and stood to attention. His *sulu* was wrapped beneath his paunch. The broad gap between the top of his *sulu* and his blue polo shirt looked like a hairy brown belt.

He shook hands with the detectives who presented their IDs. 'Constable Tomasi Kana, retired, sir,' he said in formal Fijian. 'Pleased to be of service and to meet you, Inspector Horseman. May I present Mr Ilai Takilai, our village headman.' Deep furrows curved from the headman's nose to the corners of his unsmiling mouth. His handshake was firm.

'I welcome you to Tanoa on behalf of Ratu Osea Matanitu, chief of Tanoa and associate villages. Ratu Osea is in Suva today. He grants you permission to conduct your investigations here without hindrance. When he is next here, he will be pleased to welcome you formally with a *sevusevu* ceremony.'

Horseman clapped his hands together in the traditional gesture of thanks. Musudroka followed.

'*Vinaka vakalevu*, sir,' Horseman replied. 'I'm grateful for your cooperation, and look forward to talking to you soon.'

'Of course, I am available to you, but I regret I cannot be of much help. I am deeply grieved by this tragedy. However, I have no light to shed on it. I'll say goodbye for now.' The tall, lean headman nodded formally and walked away.

By contrast, Tomasi Kana was eager, even ingratiating. 'You

know, sir, I myself played for Police many years ago.'

'Well, Mr Kana. Police have always been near the top of the ladder, eh.'

'Please call me Tomasi, sir. I never achieved your success. I was proud to play for the second grade team, however.'

'Nothing like it, is there, playing rugby in a team of fellow cops? *Vinaka* for the help and advice you've given us already, Tomasi. If it weren't for your knowledge and ability to take command, any evidence here could have been destroyed or compromised. I'm grateful.' Horseman clapped once.

Tomasi smiled his pleasure. 'I'm happy to help. This is a disgraceful crime. I'm on unofficial guard here, to stop curious people going in. A search officer and another constable arrived less than an hour ago.'

'Well done, Tomasi. We'll no doubt see you later.'

Musudroka pushed open the heavy door. Swollen with damp, it scraped against the floor. He lifted it on its hinges by tugging the door handle up. 'They should take this off and rehang it. Maybe even tightening the hinge screws would fix it.'

Horseman was surprised. 'Where have you been hiding your carpentry knowledge, Tani? I'm impressed.'

Musudroka blushed. 'Dad's a carpenter, sir. He's always going on about people not maintaining their houses and furniture properly.'

'I'll remember that. Let's see what we've got inside.'

The white-walled church was modest but had nice proportions and a simple dignity. The corrugated iron roof had quite a steep pitch and was painted light blue like the rafters, bringing the sky inside. The window shutters on both side walls were propped open by bamboo poles, letting in plenty of light. Rolled mats were piled against the walls, but several remained in the centre of the concrete floor. A cross was fixed above the communion table, and a lace-edged cloth hung on the front of the pulpit, embroidered with the text 'God is love' in Fijian.

Two constables in disposable white overalls, caps, and bootees were crawling on the floor, systematically sweeping with hand brushes into dustpans. The floor was taped in squares, each labelled with a code. One officer grinned at them as he tipped the dustpan into a plastic bag, sealed and labelled it. He alerted a third officer, who turned and walked over to Horseman and Musudroka. '*Bula, bula,* Detectives, I'm glad to see you.' He peeled off a glove and held out his hand. 'Ashwin Jayaraman, SOCO. Call me Ash, please.' They all shook hands.

'Inspector, you must get very tired of people telling you of their childhood hero worship, but it's so true in my case!'

Ash did look young, but Horseman was always disconcerted when adults told him he was their childhood hero. He preferred to ignore the fact that he wasn't getting any younger. He also hoped the SOCO wouldn't want him to get down on his knees.

'*Vinaka,* Ash. What have we got?'

'Tricky, boss. I only got here an hour ahead of you and had to train the constables. We're halfway through the floor. No power, so we can't vacuum. I'm taking samples from the mats where the body was placed. There's blood, some hairs, little else. The church was cleaned well on Saturday afternoon, so you'd think traces of the victim and the murderer, or murderers, should be clear. But there are no obvious drag marks, scuffing of the mats, blood traces from the door to where he was placed. My guess is the victim was already dead, well wrapped in cloth or plastic and dragged or carried into position.'

Horseman looked around and nodded his agreement.

'Grab a suit from the bag and come over to the site.'

The two detectives readily complied. Musudroka looked proud to be wearing search garb for the first time. The mats were surprisingly undamaged.

'The entire mat where his upper body lay will go to the lab. But I want you to smell it before I bag it. It's odd. Something familiar, but I can't place it.'

Just what Horseman feared. Musudroka was already on his knees, sniffing like a dog. Horseman lowered himself carefully, put most of his weight on his left knee, and followed suit. Straight away he pushed himself up, smiling. 'It's vanilla.'

'*Io*, of course!' Ash kneeled again and sniffed, then jumped back up. 'I wonder how?'

'Vili ran a spice project here. The pastor told us they grow vanilla. Perhaps that's where Viliame was killed.' Horseman said. Unjustified hope surged through him. Maybe he could wrap this case up by Friday!

***

Tomasi was only too ready to tell the detectives about the village spice project—Viliame's project really. And to show them the path, which started at the eastern end of the village. Ash left the two constables to finish the church floor and joined them. The four men spread out about a metre apart and slowly headed east from the church, scanning the ground for any disturbance, any discarded object.

Tomasi pointed to the last house, twice the size of the others.

'This is Ratu Osea's house. He built it when he retired from the army. He spends a lot of his time in Tanoa now.' It stood a little apart, elevated on sturdy posts, clad in weatherboards and roofed in iron overlaid by thatch.

The officers worked their way through an open area of washing lines and a few sheds. Chickens strolled about leisurely, pecking in the earth. Out of reach of the washing, a couple of goats tethered on long chains cropped the mix of grass, herbage, and would-be shrubs that had no chance.

'They're finding more than us.' Musudroka called out.

'They're closer to the ground,' Ash replied. 'But I won't ask you to get down on your knees yet. Just be alert for anything unexpected and focus on your own section.'

Beyond the goats' range, the vegetation sprang upwards: a dense mix of ubiquitous hibiscus, ginger, wild passionfruit, and kikuyu grass. Among these were the invasive young lantana and, trailing across all, that opportunist thief of sun and space, the morning glory vine. This was the site of a fallow garden. The heads of cassava plants rose here and there, sprouting from bits of tubers left in the ground after harvesting.

The path to the spice gardens was wide enough for an overladen wheelbarrow. Ash told them to walk two by two, one pair about five metres ahead of the other. Tomasi cut them sticks with his machete, so they could part the thick scrub and see through to the ground. They came across rotting bits of paper and cardboard, indestructible foil packets, plastic bottles, and fish cans in various stages of rusting decay.

'Time for a village working bee,' said Tomasi. 'I didn't know it was as bad as this.' He sounded embarrassed.

'It looks fine from on top,' Horseman reassured him. 'We're only seeing the litter because we're parting the surface. Really, I'm impressed. Tanoa is a clean and tidy village.'

'*Vinaka*, sir. You know how it is. Our chief likes everything in order around the place.'

After ten minutes, the track narrowed again as it climbed towards a ridge. Horseman paused at the crest, looking out on a new landscape. Here the forest was taller, the canopy free of morning glory. The straight trunks of Honduran mahogany reared among the jostling native species. Geometric emerald patches broke up the natural jumble. He tried to make sense of the patches, but failed. It looked as if triffids were strangling ancient Roman colonnades.

Tomasi pointed. 'See the vanilla? The deep green?'

'*Io*, but what sort of plant can it be?'

'It's a kind of orchid, but it's a vine that climbs up trees. Vili planted support trees that are only small, so the vanilla doesn't get beyond reach. The workers prune the trees and train the vines along lateral branches connecting the trees.' Tomasi spoke with pride.

'That sounds like a lot of work.'

'*Io*, it's complicated. Vili studied about vanilla and trained the workers well.'

Horseman fished his binoculars from his backpack. 'I can make sense of it now. How beautiful!'

He trained the binoculars on jade outcrops which resolved into straight lines of bananas interplanted with bushes. Horseman pointed. 'And those?' he asked Tomasi.

'Nutmeg—the young trees only need shade for the first few years. Vili decided to use bananas as temporary shade to provide a cash crop until the nutmegs produce. Clever, eh?'

'Very. Viliame will be a great loss, I can see.' The information was fascinating, but it was high time they searched the vanilla gardens.

'Tanielo, you help Ash check out the vanilla patches. He'll tell you exactly what to do and how to do it. Watch, listen, and learn, young man!' Musudroka grinned, jumped to attention, and saluted Ash. Horseman watched for a few moments as the two young men approached the nearest vanilla patch.

'He likes playing around, your young DC, doesn't he?' Tomasi said in a neutral tone. 'In my day, he would have been disciplined for making a joke of a salute.'

'Musudroka's young and likes to have a bit of fun. But he works hard and he's very keen to learn. He'll do well if he sticks with it.'

'Oh, he'll stick with it as long as you can stick with him, in my opinion. You're a hero to him.'

Horseman shrugged. Perhaps the older man was wiser than him. Perhaps he should be stricter with Musudroka, more formal. Still, he didn't want to stifle Musudroka's youthful enthusiasm.

'Tomasi, you're an enormous help to us here. Without your police experience, the investigation wouldn't have got off to such a good start. Have you known Viliame all his life? Tell me some more about him.'

'Io, I've known him all his life, but not so well as others. Until I retired, I served in different districts, from Vanuabalavu in the east, to Nadi in the west, even Kadavu, way to the south. But every year I came back here on leave with my wife and children so I kept up with village life. When I retired, he was already away at boarding school, but he was home for the holidays. Then he got a job at the NLTB in Suva, but he returned here frequently on weekends, as well as on his annual leave.'

'What was Viliame like?' Horseman asked.

Tomasi shook his head sadly. 'I think the best way to give you a sense of what he was like is to say that he was an individual. He didn't follow the crowd.'

'Did you like him?'

'I did. He was energetic and hard-working. Always positive. He did things, rather than watch the world go by. I admire all those qualities. I wish I shared them myself.'

'Popular, was he?'

'True, he was. With all the young people especially. But he was also the kind of boy all the mothers have a soft spot for—they looked forward to the weekends because Vili would come on Saturday. Strange, isn't it?'

'What about the village fathers?'

'I don't know, perhaps there were a few old noses out of joint.'

'Why?'

'I don't know. He was a credit to our village, that's what most of us thought. But you know how it is, some could have been jealous of his achievement, his popularity. Some might have resented him because he showed them up.'

'Wise words, Tomasi. Human nature doesn't change, does it? Who may have been jealous, or resented Vili's success?'

The older man shook his head slowly. 'That I do not know, sir.'

***

Horseman sensed that was all Tomasi wanted to give him now, but it was a pretty clear indication that at least some elders resented Vili. But would that be enough to deny the profitable spice project access to additional land? Horseman looked at the forested valley before him, the next ridge. There didn't seem to be competing enterprises nearby.

Shouts from below put an end to his conversation with Tomasi. Ash and Musudroka waved and beckoned. 'Wait here, if you don't mind please, Tomasi. The fewer people trampling about, the better.'

The path wasn't steep and he was able to join his smiling colleagues without embarrassing stumbles. He felt as if he were underwater, in a kelp forest bathed in green light. It was a lush, still world of fleshy vines hung with long green beans with an earthy, fecund scent. There was definitely no vanilla smell, not like the smell on the mat.

Ash said, 'Here, sir, between these two trees. No sign of violence, but there's this depression in the earth.'

The grass between two rows of vanilla was flattened. The soft earth had a shallow impression about the size of a human body.

'I agree, a body, living or dead, could have lain here. Or possibly two human bodies.' His colleagues raised their brows in agreement with this alternative idea.

'I never thought of that,' Musudroka mused.

'I can't smell vanilla, though.' He knelt carefully and sniffed the flattened grass. 'Not on the ground either. I'll ask Tomasi about that. You carry on here, then search the other gardens.'

'I'll take pictures and you measure, Tani,' said Ash. 'Length, width, and depth.' He pulled a tape from his backpack and handed it to Musudroka. Then, we'll take samples of the soil, plants, and any debris in the depression. I'll take them to the lab. You could be a professional SOCO before you know it!'

***

Tomasi hadn't moved from the crest of the ridge. Horseman remarked, 'I'm curious about why there's no vanilla smell in the groves.'

'That's right. You don't get that smell until the beans are cured.'

'Really? How is that done?'

'Oh, it's complicated, just like the cultivation. Many processes and it takes a hundred days, longer in wet weather. There's a curing shed just over there.' He pointed down the valley, away from Ash and the others.

With the aid of his binoculars, Horseman made out a thatched roof. 'I'd be grateful if you could guide me, Tomasi. I would hate to wreck such a valuable crop.'

Tomasi beamed. 'This way, sir.'

Horseman radioed Ash to meet him at the curing shed. The path led from one grove to another through patches of forest. Horseman scanned either side of the path with the aid of his stick, but found nothing worth closer inspection. In one grove he caught the scent he'd been expecting—seductive, dark, and sweet. The bush material shed loomed in a cleared patch beyond the rows of vines. As they approached the broad verandahs the rich smell intensified. Heaven.

'The verandahs have no roofs as the beans need direct sun every day. They are taken inside every night and before it rains. If they get wet, they lose flavour. Rain often comes without warning here, and it's a problem. So they're building a new shed in the village.'

Wooden trays, each with a single layer of neatly aligned pods, covered the sunny verandahs. Tomasi invited Horseman to go inside. The shed was filled with racks, slotted to hold the trays of curing pods. No wonder the vanilla price was high—the cultivation and processing were labour-intensive. His admiration and sorrow grew for the murdered young man who was responsible for all this.

Laid out on a wooden bench were a hurricane lamp, kerosene, two cauldrons, and hand tools. Long-handled tools were stacked in a corner. Under the bench was a pile of folded grey blankets. Horseman picked one up and held it to his nose. A worn vanilla-scented blanket!

'The beans need to be wrapped in blankets in the early stage of curing,' Tomasi volunteered.

But everything seemed in order, undisturbed. If Viliame had been working here on Saturday, his clothes had probably absorbed the vanilla smell. Simple as that.

When Ash arrived with one of the constables, Horseman handed over the search to the experts.

5

The three officers returned to the village at one o'clock, accompanied by Tomasi. At the church, they found the constable on guard tucking into a hearty lunch donated by a villager. Despite the substantial morning tea at the pastor's house, Horseman was hungry and knew the others would be too. He'd bought rotis and fruit when they stopped at Nausori on their way; they would make do with that.

'We'll take a break now and return to the village after lunch. I'm very grateful for your assistance both yesterday and this morning. I hope I can talk with you again this afternoon.'

Tomasi looked disappointed to be dismissed, but didn't argue the point. 'I'll do whatever I can to help, Inspector. My wife would like to offer you lunch…'

'*Vinaka*, we've brought our lunch with us, so we'd better not waste it!' Horseman smiled.

Back at the car park, they found the log barrier an ideal picnic seat. After two pumpkin and pea rotis, Horseman felt much better. Ash and Musudroka looked satisfied too. Horseman snapped a large hand of bananas in three. 'Have them now if you want, or save them for later. The villagers are generous, but they're not well off here and we mustn't deplete their supplies.'

They all started on the bananas right away. After enjoying one, Horseman said, 'The vanilla smell on the church mat must have come from Vili's clothes. We need to check that he went to the

curing shed on Saturday afternoon. Ash, make searching for the
murder weapon your priority this afternoon.'

'Yes, sir. I hoped we'd find some trace on the path to the spice
plantation. Wishful thinking.'

'Maybe there's another path. Let's ask about that. And, while I've
no reason to suspect him, I don't want to depend on Tomasi too
much. Probably he misses his life as a cop and that's why he's
attaching himself to us. But we can't automatically trust him just
because he was a cop.'

Musudroka nodded. 'I like him, sir.'

'Me too,' Horseman said. 'Our life would be a lot easier if all
criminals were rude, uncooperative, and hostile, but only some are
like that. Others are charming, polite, and friendly to us. They're the
ones that test our mettle.'

The other two laughed. Ash was the first to speak. 'I can hear a
vehicle, can't you? A diesel.' Horseman could hear it now, too. They
finished the bananas while the diesel chugging amplified. A police
vehicle rounded the bend. Two people were inside. The smiling
passenger got out first and waved. Horseman and Musudroka
jumped off the logs and rushed to greet her, hands outstretched.
Detective Sergeant Susila Singh, her black hair smoothed back into
a ponytail, shook their hands.

'*Bula, bula,*' she said, and held out her hand to Ash. 'I'm DS Singh,
and I've brought Constable Dau to help, too.'

Ash introduced himself. They all shook hands again. 'Have you
had lunch?' Musudroka asked. 'I'm sorry I've eaten the last of our
bananas.'

'Yes, we've shared the excellent lunch Constable Dau's wife
made for him,' Singh said.

Horseman hadn't seen her for a month. He hadn't missed her at
all, so he was surprised how happy he was to see her smiling face.
Not just because she was so capable and would make his job easier.
He was so glad to see *her.*

'Right. Our first priority this afternoon is to find the murder site and weapon. Ash, when will you finish in the church?' Horseman asked.

'Half an hour, tops. I can search any other routes to the spice gardens then.'

'How many helpers do you need?'

'Two will be enough. One of us to focus on the path, another for the left of the path, the third for the right.'

'Good. Take Musudroka and one of the local constables. I'd like the other to guard the church, even though it will be open again when you're through. I want to know who comes and goes.'

'Sure, sir.' Ash and Musudroka looked like two eager hunting dogs, tails wagging furiously, impatient to get to work.

'Next, I want to check on the possibility that there were two bodies, not one, lying in the vanilla patch. In other words, a love nest. We'll start with the project workers. They were probably a close-knit group involved with the business side as well as the agricultural work. I don't know how many there were yet, but Sergeant Singh and I will speak to as many as we can this afternoon. Sergeant, can you interview any women in the group? I know you'll get more information from them than I would.'

They crossed the bridge and headed for the church. The riverbank was now deserted except for pigs and chickens. A brown dog, a wretched animal without a nose and part of his top jaw, limped around the fish-cleaning area, ingesting gut remnants. Horseman's stomach contracted. He feared a machete had mutilated the dog, punishment for sticking his nose in a forbidden place. As a child he'd witnessed such impulsive anger, powerless to do anything about it. It wasn't just the hungry dog who learned a terrifying lesson, but all who witnessed it.

They walked among silent houses towards the church. A post-prandial somnolence enveloped the whole place.

'How was your leave?' he asked Singh.

'Okay. Nice to be with my parents for a bit. I tried to help Mum, take over the chores and so on while I was there. I'm trying to learn to cook. But Dad would ask every night who'd cooked, and when it was Mum, he'd smile and look so happy, I wonder why I bothered. I chilled out, sometimes went in to Nadi on the bus to shop. After two weeks, I was more than ready to come back to the job. I missed work. When Superintendent Navala sent me the message about this case, I was overjoyed. I caught the first bus to Suva this morning. This is a horrible crime, though.' Singh shook her head. 'How are you, sir?'

'Great. The Junior Shiners had their first third grade competition game yesterday and I'm feeling proud. Amazingly, they scored against Marists—two tries!'

'Wow! They won?'

'No, but I thought maybe they wouldn't score at all. When it sank in that they'd taken points from Marists, they were jumping and hooting like mad things. The Marist coach gave his team an earbashing. They hung their heads in shame.'

'Yet the losers were elated. Weird.'

'All a matter of expectations, Susie. Next game, the Shiners will expect to score, and they'll do even better.'

'The credit's due to you, sir.'

'No, no, no. I know what needs to be done, but the boys are the only ones who can do it. Tanielo and the other volunteers have been essential, and they're learning how to coach. It's no use if the Shiners can't continue without me. You need a big support pool, even for a third grade Suva district junior team.'

When they arrived at the church, Ash asked, 'Would you like to see what's left of the scene before we pack up, Sergeant Singh?'

'I would, thanks.' She looked questioningly at Horseman.

'Sure, I'm going to speak to the pastor again, then I'll meet you back here.'

6

Horseman paused outside the pastor's house to politely announce his name, then went up the steps to the door and knocked.

'Inspector Horseman here,' he called again. A sad-faced young woman opened the door. She looked very like Mere Tora.

'*Bula*, miss. You must be the daughter of Pastor Joni and Mere.'

She didn't smile. She looked weary, her eyes red and swollen. '*Bula vinaka*, Inspector Horseman. I'm Kelera. My parents told me you were here. They're out at the moment, doing what they can for Vili's family.' As her tears started to overflow, she pulled a handkerchief from her sleeve and dabbed at her cheeks.

'Kelera, I'm very sorry about Viliame. From what I hear about him, he'll be a terrible loss to Tanoa. I wanted to ask your parents who worked on the spice gardens with him. If you can tell me, then I won't need to disturb your parents.'

'I'm afraid I'm just off to school. I'm a teacher. The bell will go any minute for the afternoon lessons, so I can't stop now, much as I'd like to help.'

'May I walk with you? I promise I won't delay you.'

Kelera looked doubtful, but was regaining her composure. She went back inside, returned with a basket packed with school exercise books, and shut the door behind her. Horseman had trouble keeping up with her as she hurried away up the slope behind the church.

'Someone killed Viliame deliberately. It's my job to find out who murdered him and why. It would be good to talk to his friends on the spice project. I hear that those who worked on it shared the income according to the hours they put in. Is that correct?'

'*Io* Inspector, that's how it worked. There's not much income yet, the crops aren't in full production, early days yet. Vili was wonderful, he could see the future and knew how it could be achieved.' She sniffed. 'I worked with him, along with Vili's younger brother, Sevu, his sister Elisa, and two other boys who were at high school with Vili. Others helped at peak times, but not so consistently.'

'That's good of you, Kelera. You wouldn't have much free time as a teacher.'

'I have enough. The only reason I haven't transferred to another school before now is to help Vili.' She sniffed.

They were only fifty metres from the school now, which consisted of two double classroom buildings facing each other and a third smaller building, on a level terrace. An open-sided shelter shed was attached to one of the classroom blocks. Children ran about on the *rara*.

'What time does school finish?' Horseman asked.

'Half past three.'

'Detective Sergeant Susila Singh would like to talk further with you, Kelera. Would the school be the best place? She can be here at three thirty if that suits you.'

'*Io*, alright. It has to be done, doesn't it? I'll be in my classroom— the one on the end over there.' She lifted her chin towards the room closest to the *rara* as a boy ran up to the bell stand and tugged the bell rope. 'I must go now, Inspector.'

'*Vinaka vakalevu*, Kelera.' Horseman walked the full length of the school terrace, looking at the houses strung out below as noisy children in blue and white uniforms ran to line up outside their classrooms.

Horseman could see the two constables laden with the SOCO bags and equipment cross the bridge to the car park. He returned to the church, which Ash had now cleared for re-occupation. Singh and Musudroka emerged from the shade to meet him, grinning.

Musudroka said, 'Sir, there's another path to the spice plantations. It starts further up the hill, between the school and the *rara*. It's longer than the other one, but it's the better choice when the lower one gets too muddy.'

'Well done, who told you that?'

'First person we saw—Waisele came out of his house right in front of us. Meant to be, eh. He's just going to check a couple of fish traps and he's coming back to show us the way.'

'Where's Ash? Did he go back to the car park?'

Ash appeared, shutting the church door behind him. 'We've got everything we need from here now, Inspector. The constables will be back in a minute. Can Tani come with us to search the second path?'

'Sure, just keep him in line, please. *Vinaka*, Ash, and good luck.' If Musudroka had a tail, it would be wagging.

Horseman turned to Singh. 'We'll have to make a difficult visit to Viliame's parents. Can't put it off. The pastor is with them now, so it's as good a time as any. Or as bad.'

***

As is customary on the death of a family member, the floor of Vili's parents' house was covered wall-to-wall in palm mats to receive visitors making their condolence visits. Their soft, leafy smell pleasantly pervaded the house. Narrow foam mattresses wrapped in bula-style printed cotton edged the mats, allowing visitors to prop their backs on the wall behind.

Pastor Joni introduced the officers to Paula and Eci, Viliame's parents, then to their children, Sevu and Elisa. The three detectives offered their condolences, which the grieving family accepted graciously.

Horseman sat cross-legged on a mattress, as did the other men. Mere and Vili's mother, both in full skirts, also sat cross-legged. Sergeant Singh and Elisa, both in trousers, sat as custom dictated, with both legs tucked to one side. Mere jumped up with surprising agility, brought in a tray of plastic beakers, and served everyone orange cordial.

Pastor Joni said, 'Will you join me in prayer for Vili's family, officers.' It was not a question. Everyone present bowed their heads while the pastor prayed for God's comfort to embrace the family.

After a few moments, Horseman spoke up. 'I do apologise for intruding Mr and Mrs Bovoro, but our job is to catch your son's killer. Murder is a shocking crime, infrequent in Fiji and rare in small villages like yours. I must ask, did Vili have any enemies here in the village?'

Both mother and father shook their heads, uncomprehending. Paula Bovoro spoke first. 'No one in the village would kill Vili.'

Pastor Joni nodded agreement. 'Someone from outside must have come here and killed him. Definitely.'

Vili's mother wiped her face with her handkerchief. 'Vili was popular, a leader among the young people. Everyone in the village loved him.'

Vili's sister glanced at her mother sidelong, then looked down again.

'What about outside the village. Did Vili tell you of any problems or disputes in his life in Suva, for example?'

'No, he was getting on well there. He was promoted again not long ago. The NLTB thought highly of him,' Vili's father said.

'Did he tell you about his work at the NLTB?'

Again, Vili's parents shook their heads. 'Not in detail,' said Vili's father. 'He liked it though. He sometimes said how he got satisfaction in sorting out a discrepancy in the accounts. He once said he was a sort of detective.' He looked straight at Horseman with a wistful smile, remembering.

Vili's mother asked, 'Why have you taken my son to Suva?'

This was always a difficult question. 'We must do this whenever someone is killed, ma'am. I am sorry, but Vili deserves the top doctor to examine him and find out how he died. We know he suffered a head wound, but that may not have killed him. Dr

Matthew Young at Suva hospital will examine Vili very carefully, so we can all be sure exactly how he died. After Dr Young is satisfied, your son's body will be returned here to you.'

'That can't bring him back to us,' Vili's sister said. Her mother looked at her reprovingly, but put her arm round her shoulders.

'I agree,' Horseman said. 'But it will help us find out who killed your brother, you can be sure of that. Now Mr and Mrs Bovoro, my colleagues and I won't intrude on you any longer. We're keen to talk with Vili's partners in the spice project, who include his brother and sister here. Perhaps you could suggest a quiet place where we could do that without disturbing anyone, Pastor Joni?'

The pastor nodded immediately. 'There's the church office. I think that would be best. You're welcome to use it whenever you need, Inspector.'

'*Vinaka vakalevu*, Pastor.'

'But there are two of you, so do you need two rooms for interviews?'

'*Vinaka*, that's not necessary. Perhaps, when we need to conduct simultaneous interviews, you would permit us to use the back of the church?'

'By all means, Inspector.' Pastor Joni said.

'Sevu and Elisa, could you come with us now? Mr and Mrs Bovoro, again may I apologise for our necessary intrusion. *Vinaka* for the most welcome drink.'

7

Despite the enormity of this crime and her sympathy for Viliame's family, Singh was delighted to be back at work. Horseman had chivalrously let her use the small church office. Pastor Joni's desk was clear except for a large Bible and two rusty wire trays which held an assortment of papers. A tall bookcase was laden with books and folders, the drawers of the filing cabinet closed, the keys in the lock. She was glad everything was neat and clean. She didn't sit behind the desk, but arranged two plastic chairs so she and Elisa faced each other across a corner of the desk.

'Elisa, have you any idea who killed your brother?' she asked.

The girl straightened and met Singh's eyes. She was shocked. 'No, how could I?'

'I noticed the way you looked at your mother when she said how popular Viliame was in the village. I think you know more about that than your mother. Am I right?'

Elisa looked down at the desk again. Then she nodded. 'My brother was the best at everything. He was always grown up, ambitious, yes, but only for our community, not for himself. He was friendly and fun too. Kind.'

Singh smiled. 'Can anyone really be so perfect?'

'He was to me.' Elisa's voice caught.

'But not to everyone?' Singh asked.

'Some people are jealous of him. It's natural. But they would never murder him!'

'Well, someone did, Elisa. And because of the remote location of this village, at the end of the road, it would be much easier for someone living here to kill him than for anyone else.'

'No, I can't believe that it was one of us.' Elisa was indignant.

'When did you last see Vili?'

'Saturday evening, in our house. We had dinner, my parents, Vili, Sevu, and me. Then while Mum and me were washing up, he went out. He never came back.' Her lips trembled, then she wept.

Singh waited until Elisa composed herself. 'What did you do after the washing up?'

'The four of us had a cup of tea and said family prayers, then I went to bed.'

'Did you wake up during the night?'

'No, not at all, ma'am.'

'Do you work full-time on the spice project?'

Elisa smiled softly. 'Oh no, but there's always something to do. Especially when the vanilla's flowering, we have to be out every morning early, from sunup to eleven. Each of us aims to pollinate nine hundred flowers by hand each day.'

'My goodness, I had no idea. That's intense!'

Elisa grew more animated now. 'You only get one chance. If you skip a flower, it's too late the next day.'

'Is it flowering season now, Elisa?'

'Oh no. We've already harvested this year's beans and we're curing them. Curing work needs to be done every day too, but only for an hour or two.'

'You must be a real expert, Elisa. What other jobs do you do?'

'Well, we have to clear weeds, cut the grass, train the vines, prune the support trees, but I don't do much of that. Vili says it's worth it, you know, because the price of vanilla is very, very high.' Her tears flowed again. She wiped them with her handkerchief.

'Elisa, does anyone disapprove of the project?'

'Not until last year, when Vili applied to the clan elders for more land to plant more vanilla and nutmeg. Vili prepared a proper application, he typed it up in Suva. He spoke to the meeting, answered questions. Then we waited for months. Finally he asked Ilai Takilai, the headman, if there was a problem. Ilai told him to be patient. Then, a couple of months ago, Ilai told Vili his application was not approved.'

'Did he give any reasons?'

'No, young people can't question the elders, can they? Vili had no choice but to accept the decision.'

'Your brother was energetic and clever, Elisa. Did he have any other plans for the village?'

The girl brightened now. 'Yes, he was full of ideas. But the spice plantation is the only one that's earning money, so far.'

'Tell me about his other ideas.'

'He wanted to get a chicken shed—you know. The Australian company, Henny Penny, helps a village to build a big shed, just the way they do in Australia. They bring the baby chicks and supply the food, and take the chooks away when they're the right size. They pay good money, too. Henny Penny thought our village might be too remote, but the main problem was our lack of electricity. So Vili found out all about that, and was talking to Fiji Electricity in Suva. He said electricity wasn't only for lighting the chicken shed, but could be connected to our houses, the church, and the school. We could power radios without buying expensive batteries. We could use all sorts of machines, even computers.'

'What happened with that?'

'I'm not sure. Vili didn't like to talk about it. Again, the elders considered his plan for a long time, then told him they couldn't give their permission.'

'He must have been so disappointed.'

'He was. But he was always so positive, keeping the rest of us cheerful.'

'What of your own plans, Elisa. What do you want to do?'

'I don't know now. I was happy to help Mum and Vili.' Her voice trembled. She met Singh's eyes, and the tears rolled down her cheeks.

Singh waited a moment or two. She couldn't back off yet.

'Elisa, did Vili ever talk to you about his life in Suva? Any problems at work, for example?'

The girl shook her head sadly. 'No. He said he got used to Suva, but it was expensive. He tried to save most of his pay for the project, and to help me and my brother go to school. He wanted to save more, but it was impossible with Suva prices, he said.'

'Did you ever visit him there?'

'Yes, twice. He arranged for me to stay with a cousin of a cousin. She and her family were nice to me. I went to Suva on the bus with Vili on Sunday afternoon and came back here with him the next Saturday morning. It was very exciting. So crowded and noisy. But smelly! All the taxis and buses puffing out smoke. I met Vili after work every day and we'd walk around the shops. He took me for a pizza, and curry. Once he took me to a Chinese café. It was all amazing, but I was happy to come back home.'

Perhaps her brother had been trying to open Elisa's eyes to a wider world, but she was happy with the simpler, less comfortable life in Tanoa.

'Did Vili have a girlfriend?'

Elisa smiled now. 'A lot of girls liked Vili. All of them, really. He tried to treat everyone the same, but I knew he only liked Kelera, the pastor's daughter. Nothing open, but I knew.'

'Did Vili talk to you about Kelera?'

'No, he certainly would never share feelings like that. It could lead to gossip, even though I would never pass it on.' Elisa's answer was so heartfelt, Singh didn't doubt her for a moment.

'What about Kelera. How did she feel about Vili?'

'I think she really liked him, but she's never confided in me. I think that's why Kelera puts in so much time on the projects. When Vili was here on weekends, they worked together a lot. They discussed everything too. Kelera keeps records about the projects. Being a teacher, she's very organised like that.'

'Would you say they were boyfriend and girlfriend?'

'I don't know. If they were, they both kept it secret.'

'Elisa, we'll stop here for now, but if you do remember any arguments or even disagreements Vili told you about, it's very important that we know. Even if you think it wasn't much, please tell us. You won't be wasting our time. Here's my card. A constable will be here for the next few days, so you can get a message to me through him. Just give him this card, okay?' Singh wrote Elisa's name on the back of the card and gave it to her.

Elisa nodded dumbly and took Singh's card, murmured '*vinaka*', and left the office.

Singh did not have high hopes of Elisa as a potential source of information. The girl was devoted to her charismatic brother, happy to have been his follower.

School would finish for the day in half an hour. Time to write up her rough jottings in her official notebook. She would be outside the door of Kelera's classroom by the time the bell rang.

8

Horseman set up two plastic chairs in the shaded church porch. 'Sit down, sit down, Sevu,' Horseman said. 'I just want to have a chat to find out more about your brother.'

The boy hesitated, then slumped onto the chair.

'How old are you, Sevu?'

'Sixteen, sir.'

'Are you still at school?'

Sevu shook his head. 'I didn't like it so much. Vili said I had to go to high school and he paid my fees. But I left last year, when I was fifteen. I didn't want to waste his money.'

'Why do you think you were wasting his money?'

'Dunno. I'm not brainy like him. He wants everyone to be like him. But he's the one who's different. I wasn't too good at exams. I like working on the spice project, and with Dad in our plantations. I like building things. I wanted to come back home.'

'Sevu, I know what you learned in those three years at high school won't be wasted, ever. So hang on to that. Your education will help you work better here or anywhere. But you don't need a lecture from me. Were you working with Vili in the spice gardens last Saturday?'

'Not really. In the morning Dad and I went to weed the cassava and dalo gardens, then we brought back some vegetables for Mum. Bananas and pawpaw too, enough to last until today. After lunch, I waited for Vili to get here and we checked all the groves and the beans in the curing shed, turned them, and packed them away. He hadn't been home for two weeks.'

'What did he talk about when he got home?'

Sevu looked puzzled. 'Just about how we'd done a good job. Don't let the weeds get out of control. Don't let the beans get wet. Oh, and he was glad to get away from Suva.'

'Did he say why?'

'Not really. Just that his job was giving him problems.'

'Any more details than that?'

Sevu frowned and looked away. 'Not much, I can't quite remember. He was talking to himself, really. Something about putting two and two together and not liking the answer.'

'Hm. Did you walk back home together?'

'Yes, I took him to see the new pig sty I'm building. I'm working on the new vanilla curing shed too, bigger and better than the one in the plantation. We're already using it, even though I haven't built the racks yet. We drew a plan on the floor and he showed me what to do. Then we went home to dinner. He went out afterwards.'

'Do you know where?'

Sevu shook his head. 'No. We just thought he was visiting friends. He didn't come back before I went to bed. He didn't come back at all, did he?'

'No he didn't. And we've got to find out why not. Did anything, any sound, wake you in the night?'

'Just once. I woke, then I heard something bang, like a door or a shutter. I thought it was the wind.'

'It might have been, too. I'll certainly check if anyone else heard a bang. We'll find out what happened to Vili, I promise you.'

Horseman hoped this wasn't another impulsive promise he wouldn't be able to keep.

9

About twenty children in white shirts and royal blue skirts or shorts filed through the classroom door in orderly fashion. Then, released from obedience, they scattered, exploding into shrill talk and laughter. Singh knocked. A woman of medium height in a calf-length, floral cotton dress was tidying the classroom.

'Miss Tora? I'm Detective Sergeant Susila Singh. Is now a good time to talk with you?'

The woman came to meet her and shook hands. She was young and very pretty. 'Please call me Kelera. Thank you for coming to the school. I can talk freely here.' She glanced over Singh's shoulder and called '*Moce mada*, Sasa.'

Singh turned to see a young man in pocket *sulu* and striped shirt wave as he passed the door. '*Moce mada*, Kelera.' He headed down the slope.

'Come in, please,' Kelera said. She moved a chair in front of her teacher's desk and seated herself behind it.

The room was so dim, Singh's eyes struggled to adjust after the glare outside. 'Do you mind if I open a shutter? I'm having trouble seeing.'

'Sorry, of course.' Kelera opened the shutter opposite the door, propped it, and returned to the desk.

'I want to talk to you because you were closely involved in Viliame's spice project. We're determined to find Vili's killer as soon as possible, for everyone's sake. Anything you can tell us about him is helpful.'

Kelera nodded sadly. 'I don't know who killed him, I can't even think about such evil. But this village is a strange place, Sergeant Singh. People who live at the end of a highlands road think differently. They're mostly good people, content to live by tradition and by the Bible. They don't see any need for change, even a change demonstrably for the better, like electricity. They accept the school because they themselves went to school. They want the children to be literate so they can read their Bibles and hymn books, but that's about it. Vili was one among very few who thought about a better future, and the only one who persisted with a project, despite the lack of interest from the elders.'

'He inspired those who worked on the spice project—I've seen that already. He must have been a very special young man.'

'Yes, he was.' Kelera opened a drawer, took out a white handkerchief, and held it to her face. 'Sorry.'

'Not at all. Did Vili have a girlfriend here?'

'Yes, me. I love him so much. I would do anything for him.' Her eyes filled again.

Singh was taken aback by her candour. 'Was your relationship public knowledge?'

'I don't know. We kept it to ourselves. No one's asked me about it or even hinted, but that doesn't mean they don't know. It's very difficult to keep a secret here.'

'I can imagine. Why did you keep it to yourselves?'

'Vili didn't ask me to marry him. I hoped he would one day. But if we were open with the village, there would be trouble if he didn't go ahead and marry me at some stage. I don't think he wanted to get married. Not yet, at any rate.'

'When did you last see Vili, Kelera?'

'On Saturday night.' She hesitated. 'We each ate with our families, then when it was dark, made our way separately to the spice gardens.'

'Where, exactly?'

'One of the vanilla groves.' She smiled. 'It's so lovely there, another world, protected. We were there no more than an hour, perhaps less. I left first, and returned by the upper path. Vili said he'd wait a bit and walk back on the lower track. I didn't see him again.'

'Did you see or hear anything on your return—either on the path or in the village?'

'No, and I was alert, as I didn't want to be seen. That's why I chose that path, because it ends just over there.' Kelera pointed out the open window. 'I can wait in the dark until there's no one around and go down to the school. I leave a lamp burning in my classroom. People think I'm working up here.'

'Kelera, you've said Vili was different from the other villagers here. That usually causes some resentment in a small community. Who resented him most?'

'I really don't know. The clan elders refused his applications for land this last year, but does that mean they resented him? They were always slow to consider his plans, even those they eventually approved. I thought that was due to lack of energy and dislike of anything new. I didn't think the elders actively opposed him, much less hated him. Their authority is secure, how could he be a threat?'

Singh could think of several situations where conservative Fijian elders had reacted violently to lesser threats, or no threats at all. Her terrified uncle and aunt were confronted on their humble sugar cane farm by enraged landlords just before their lease was due for renewal. Fired up by traditionalist agitators, the landlords gave them two days to leave, accusing them of profiteering, plotting to take over the country, and other preposterous claims.

'It's about perception, Kelera, even if there's no real threat. What are the concerns of the elders?'

'To give them some credit, yes, they say they're concerned about the community's low level of educational achievement, low income, not so many people with jobs living in the towns and sending back cash. I suppose I'm a bit cynical—I think their concern was because of lack of cash for themselves.'

'Do they have any plans of their own for the village?'

'Well, perhaps. The mahogany trees are ready for harvesting after forty or fifty years. The elders have great hopes of that, but I don't know of any actual plans.'

'Anything else?' Singh asked.

'There is something big coming up, but it's rooted in the past. The chief has got it into his head that God has not forgiven the people of Tanoa for killing a missionary in 1875. Rev. Charles Weston. He believes the burden of this sin weighs upon the murderers' descendants and has denied them prosperity. The plan is to invite the descendants of the murdered missionary here for an elaborate ceremony of apology and reconciliation.'

Singh was astonished at this approach to village development. Wouldn't electric lighting, a school library, and scholarships be a better way? But then, she wasn't religious by nature and often found it hard to comprehend the devout of any faith, even her own Sikh family.

'Is this a definite plan?'

'Oh yes, it's been going on for two years. It took quite a while to locate Mr Weston's descendants. My father was able to help, but it still was time-consuming. A year all up. Then all the correspondence, the discussions, and so on. However, eventually they got it all in place. Five descendants have accepted the invitation to receive the village's hospitality and apology. It's next Sunday. Vili's death put it out of my mind.'

'Understandably. You're the first to mention it. I wonder if Vili's death will postpone the plan.'

'I don't think there's time to change it now, even if the chief wanted to. The descendants are coming from Canada, Australia, and New Zealand. The village has paid for their flights, the best hotel in Suva, and all expenses. Many thousands of dollars.' She shook her head. 'I don't know what will be done. Probably Ratu Osea will talk about it with my father.'

'What's the general opinion in the village about this apology project?'

Kelera shrugged. Now the focus had shifted from Vili's death, she seemed a stronger, more decisive person.

'I'm not sure if there is a general opinion. The villagers have held fundraisers, planted extra crops, raised piglets and calves for the feast. These people are excellent at detailed organisation of events. But whether it's a good thing or not? I mean, the chief and elders decide what's to be done, and to question their decisions would be like questioning their authority—almost a sin. What the villagers give their minds to is how to implement the decisions.'

Singh understood the attitude Kelera was describing.

'You're a great help, Kelera. We'll speak again soon. Please think carefully about anything you saw or heard as you returned home on Saturday night.'

Kelera nodded abstractedly and sat gazing out the window as Singh left the room to find Horseman. If he hadn't already found out about the big event in just a few days, she needed to tell him right away.

10

'It seems to me, Pastor Joni, that the village is quite divided,' Horseman said. 'The chief and elders want to right the wrongs of the past through tradition, whereas Viliame and his followers want to get cash-earning projects up and running. They focus on the future.'

Pastor Joni was behind his desk in the church office. Horseman and Singh sat on the other side. The pastor leaned forward slightly, folded his hands together on the desk.

'*Io*, but everyone wants the same thing—that's a thriving village. Just different ideas on how that should be done. There's no reason why both strategies can't work together. I don't see them as incompatible.'

Singh spoke up. 'I agree, they needn't be incompatible. But when funds are limited, which everyone tells me is the case here, the reconciliation ceremonies and the cash-crop projects must be competing for those funds. Do you agree?'

Pastor Joni nodded slowly. '*Io*, if you put it like that, *io*. It could be difficult to do all these projects at the same time.'

'In crimes of assault and especially murder, we look for conflict, Pastor. It seems there's serious conflict here, and it's been going on for some time, wouldn't you say?' Horseman asked.

'I wouldn't say serious conflict, no, Inspector. Young people are always impatient, want to do everything overnight. Viliame had knowledge and leadership and energy. The spice gardens are a great project, and he and the young ones have done well. Everyone thought so.' Horseman glanced at Singh.

She smiled encouragingly. 'Yet I hear the elders are relying on the future sale of mahogany for income.'

'Oh, that's none of my business, but I know people hold great hopes for the future logging.'

'Do you know why the council didn't approve additional land for the spice project, sir? Allocating unused land wouldn't cost the village anything, would it?' Singh asked.

'I imagine they would prefer to make less rapid progress, to ensure success in the long term. But I don't know. They're conservative, you know. I don't believe there was any ill will towards the youngsters.'

Did the pastor really always believe the best of everyone? His attitude was certainly Christian as one would expect, but surely he could not ignore evidence that pointed the other way? Possibly he felt it was his duty to support the chief.

'Kelera told me you've been a great help in tracing the descendants of the murdered missionary,' said Singh.

'Reverend Weston, *io*. I was happy to take that on. The Methodist church headquarters in Suva provided specialist help. They have computers there, you see. I went to Suva a few times and saw how it's done. Fascinating. They put me in touch with the international church archives, whose people were very helpful and did genealogical research for us. They traced a number of descendants to whom I wrote, at the chief's request. He was gratified that five of them agreed to come all the way from Canada, New Zealand, and Australia to receive an apology from our chief for the sin of his ancestors.'

'All expenses paid, I heard,' Singh commented.

'*Dina*, Sergeant. The villagers are the penitents, begging the forgiveness of the Weston descendants. It is our obligation to look after our guests well. After all, to take a worldly view, the chief and council have initiated the ceremony for the benefit of the village.

They trust God will look more favourably on our village when this burden of guilt is lifted.'

Horseman asked, 'What effect will Viliame's death have on your plans for the weekend? Will the ceremony still go ahead?'

Pastor Joni shook his head. 'I don't know. The murder itself is dreadful, tragic. The timing couldn't be worse. Too close to the date to easily postpone the event, but also too close for us to recover from our shock, so we can welcome our guests wholeheartedly.' He sighed and looked up. 'I can only pray for God's guidance should the chief consult me about this.'

'When is he likely to do that?' Singh asked.

'I'm not sure,' Pastor Joni answered. 'Possibly tomorrow afternoon, when he returns to Tanoa.'

'As you say, he'll need to make some difficult decisions. Have you got any telephone numbers for him in Suva?'

'*Io*, I've got a few of his cards here.' Pastor Joni handed a business card to Horseman.

***

Ash and his team were waiting in the shade. 'Any luck, boys?' Horseman asked.

Musudroka was champing at the bit but deferred to Ash. 'We found the murder site! Well, it's pretty definite. Less than half way to the gardens, there's a trampled area. Not big, I'd say there was only one attacker. It looks like he fell to the side of the track. Found some blood too. We searched a wide area all around, but couldn't find a weapon. The murderer could have taken it with him, or tossed it or concealed it beyond the immediate vicinity.' He shrugged.

'Let's see the pictures, then,' Horseman said. Ash plugged his camera into a tablet and handed it to Horseman, who sat beside Singh so they could look at the photos together. They were good-quality wide-angled shots and close-ups.

Musudroka said, 'We stripped some branches for posts and taped off the immediate area, sir. We've taken lots of samples for the lab, too. All bagged and tagged, sir.' He looked hopeful.

'Man, that's great work.'

'I'll get going then, sir, if there's nothing more. I can take the constables with me if you like,' Ash said.

Horseman shook his hand. 'Do that please, Ash. You've all worked hard. Leave me my DC, though.'

Ash grinned. 'You can have Tani! I'll be in touch soon as, sir.'

Mere emerged from the pastor's house carrying a tray with steaming mugs. '*Bula* officers. Would you like to have a wash at the bench next to the house? There's soap and basins, a towel, and a barrel of water. That'll cool you down. Then, come back to the porch and have some tea.' She put the tray down on the concrete floor of the porch. The search team trooped off obediently to wash while Horseman and Singh took mugs of tea from the tray.

'*Vinaka vakalevu*, Mere. We're grateful. Tea is just what we need.'

Mere popped into the church and Pastor Joni appeared with two plastic chairs from the office. 'Forgive us, Inspector, we don't have much furniture about the place.'

'Not at all, Pastor. You've been very good to us,' Horseman said. But he sat gladly, stretching out his right leg.

'What's next, sir?' Singh asked.

'We need to eyeball this site, even though we've seen Ash's excellent shots.'

Kelera approached. 'Sir, I found two of the spice project team for you. Epi and Waisele. Shall I ask them to come over?'

'*Vinaka*, Kelera, that's wonderful. We'll talk to them as soon as they can get here.'

'Shall we take one each?' Singh asked.

'Sure. We'll go to the murder site, if that's what it is, after we've interviewed them.'

Viliame was a hero to young Epi and Wais, who supported what Pastor Joni and everyone else said about him. They'd worked on Saturday, clearing vegetation around the nutmeg trees and managing the curing vanilla. They had spoken to Viliame at the curing shed that afternoon and never saw him again after that.

Musudroka proudly escorted them to the suspected murder site, but it didn't reveal anything that Ash's photos had not. Horseman agreed it was probably where Vili had been killed. He never liked to rely on photos if it was possible to visit the scene. Context was vital to his understanding of the crime, but this scene provided no flash of insight. Neither could he and Singh spot any evidence the search team had missed.

'We'll hit the road. It's frustrating to be out of reach here. Even the vehicle radio is dead. I'll call Ratu Osea from the Kumi police post down the hill. If we're in luck, I could talk to him this evening.' Seeing her disappointed face, he added, 'You're welcome to come too. That goes without saying. But won't you need time to get settled in after your holiday in the west?'

'It's okay, sir. I'd like to meet the chief, too.' Her eyes, the colour of sunlit sea, shone in anticipation.

Horseman failed to get an answer from his call to the chief from the police post. Both his landline and mobile numbers went unanswered. Horseman left messages. He wanted to talk to Ratu Osea this evening, at least on the phone. He would try again at Nausori.

Musudroka dozed off in the back seat while Singh didn't seem in the mood for talk. When her head lurched suddenly, he realised she was dozing too. It suited him; he needed to think this case through as he waited for the post mortem results tomorrow. A young man was killed by one or more blows to the head while walking home on a village path on Saturday night. He was the leader of a young village development group which was opposed by conservative village leaders who fought the activists by doing nothing.

This scenario was not unusual in Fiji. But was it possible the passive opposition had erupted into violence and murder? There would have to be another trigger. Could the bizarre ceremony planned for the very next weekend be connected, and how? He shook his head at the thought of two years' work and the resources used for what was promising to be a grand and unique occasion. He was a Christian himself, went without saying for a Fijian, but it seemed a twisted theology to him. How could a non-existent burden of guilt be lifted by the forgiveness of the descendants of Rev. Charles Weston? The idea that the prosperity of Tanoa would then be assured smacked of superstition and magic ritual to him, not Christianity as he understood it.

They were nearing Nausori. He pulled into the car park near the bridge, where some cafés were open. The other two stirred the moment he stopped the vehicle.

'*Oi lei*, dark already!' Musudroka said, yawning heavily.

'Did I nod off?' Singh asked, stretching her neck and shoulders.

'Yes, you did. I need a drink and something to eat or I'll be nodding at the wheel too.' He just said it to make them feel better; his thoughts had kept him wide awake. 'Indian or Chinese? Or maybe a hamburger?'

'I wouldn't recommend this Indian place, sir. I think we're safer with a hamburger,' Singh said.

'Great,' said Musudroka. 'That's just what I feel like.'

Horseman would have preferred a couple of rotis, but fell in with the others. They trooped into the hamburger joint. The salty, greasy atmosphere sparked their appetites. They ordered hamburgers all round with a family-sized chips to share. Singh chose the least chipped formica table.

They demolished their so-so hamburgers in silence. Singh thoughtfully nibbled at a giant chip. 'Tanielo, do you know anything about this kind of reconciliation ceremony that the village is doing?'

'Sorta, but nothing like Tanoa is organising. There are reconciliation ceremonies after disputes are resolved, or the chief might insist on one after someone has caused serious offence, or done some wrong, or for young people for persistent bad behaviour in the village. The offender has to offer a *sevusevu*, a gift of kava to the chief, listen to a lot of long speeches, and apologise very humbly. After that, all is forgiven. Supposed to be.'

Singh frowned, looking puzzled as she munched.

Horseman said, 'It's a strange notion Ratu Osea has got hold of. He's become obsessed with an ancient crime that for him is controlling the present. There's more than enough present crime for me without worrying about something that happened a hundred years ago, however horrific. I can't wait to meet the chief. Which reminds me, I must try calling him again.'

Horseman went outside, hoping for a stronger signal. The chief's mobile was again turned off. He turned and smiled at the sight of Singh and Musudroka eating chips comfortably together. Aside from cracking a case, nothing gave him more pleasure in his job than seeing his team get along together. This case promised to be as tough as they come. But Singh and Musudroka looked confident—in themselves and each other. Singh's authority over the almost-raw recruit to CID was both natural and official. Musudroka looked up to her as someone who could teach him as much as for her rank. But the heap of chips was reducing rapidly, so he'd better get back. Still, he hadn't called the landline number, so punched it in half-heartedly, sure that no one would answer. He turned into the grimy café doorway, ready to end the call, when it inevitably rang out. He took a few steps towards the chips, then a deep voice startled him.

'*Bula vinaka*, Osea Matanitu speaking.'

Horseman stopped, then stepped outside again. '*Bula vinaka*, Ratu. Detective Inspector Horseman. You will have been expecting my call, no doubt, in connection with Viliame's murder at Tanoa last Saturday night.'

'*Io*, Detective Inspector. What may I do for you?' the voice was sonorous, calm, remote. Horseman felt an extended telephone call would not serve his purpose.

'Ratu, I need to talk with you as soon as possible about this. When is the soonest you could meet me?'

There was a significant pause. Then a sigh, or perhaps just a heavy breath—he mustn't infer too much from one exhalation. 'Morning tea at the Regiment Club. Half past ten tomorrow. Just the two of us would be best. Would that be convenient, Detective Inspector?'

'*Io*, Ratu. I look forward to meeting you then. *Ni sa moce*, good night.'

This was no formal courtesy—he was truly looking forward to their meeting. He knew local chiefs in remote areas tended to be conservative, but one who sought prosperity for his people through the expiation of the sins of long ago intrigued Horseman. He wasn't looking forward to telling Singh she wasn't required, but she could attend the morgue instead. She faced the dead with more equanimity than he did.

When he returned to the table, he was dismayed by how few chips remained in the large bowl. 'We saved you some, sir,' Musudroka said cheerily. 'All these are for you.'

11

A wind chilled by May snow on Mt Hood whipped through Portland in the afternoon. Melissa had not argued when her father declined her proposed walk. She had to admit she wasn't too sorry. It was undeniably bleak, and summer seemed far away. Back home, she had to wait until one in the morning when Joe might be home. The latest issue of the *American Journal of Sports Physical Therapy* couldn't hold her attention, even a follow-up study of recurring injuries among footballers following knee reconstruction. Relevant to her work, relevant to Joe, but she couldn't take in what she was reading. Eventually she put the journal down and allowed herself to worry about her trip to Fiji.

Joe was the first Fijian she had ever encountered. When she met the new admission at the Oregon Rehabilitation Institute, she immediately liked his handsome, open face and his charming formal courtesy. As she got to know him, his fortitude and dedication attracted her, not to mention the warm smile that lit his eyes whenever he caught sight of her. Over the months, their mutual attraction blossomed into love. But they were both aware that such a relationship was unlikely to last, although neither wanted to mention this. Melissa hoped they could make it work, despite a distance between them of six thousand miles and nineteen hours. Her first visit to Fiji was not just a holiday with her boyfriend, but a crucial test that would determine their future. Although he didn't speak about it, she reckoned it was the same for Joe.

She couldn't wait until one o'clock. It was already midnight. She'd call now. It would be seven o'clock on Monday night in Suva; he might be home. She texted him to check.

Half an hour later and no reply. She logged on to Skype and called him. Oh no, the connection must be down. On the third try, the switch-through to Fiji worked. She waited until the ring tone cut out, drumming her fingers. She'd make decaf coffee to fill in a few minutes before trying again. Just as the kettle switched off, her phone buzzed. She snatched it from the bench. Yay, Joe!

'Melissa, sorry darling, got back late. I was in the shower, trying to think.'

'No, honey, I'm sorry, I just couldn't wait for you to call. Let's video?'

'I'm on my phone, but why not?' He tapped video. 'There you are. A welcome sight for my sore eyes.'

'You too. How'd it go today?'

'Definitely murder. A young man. Not killed where his body was found. We've got a probable murder site, but no weapon. No one's confessed. So not looking good for a quick wrap-up, I'm afraid.' His voice was flat, his face weary.

'Joe, I've been thinking, too. Maybe you're worried I'll be offended if you ask me to postpone my trip. Honest, I won't. Not at all. I get it. I reckon I'd better postpone for a month. I can come in June, for sure.'

'Melissa, you're wonderful. But I don't want you to put it off.' He sounded bereft. 'I've never had such a good incentive to break the record for stone turning and get a result!' His cheery tone was fake, she could tell.

'Joe, you've gotta be free to devote yourself to the case, not be distracted by me.'

'I'm always distracted by you, Melissa.' His eyes flirted, but she would not be deflected from her purpose.

'You tell me how few murders you have in Fiji, Joe. Once you solve this new one, how likely is it that there'll be another in a month? In your district?'

'It's unlikely, but…'

'Others can handle the routine crimes. You can take your leave in June and relax.'

'Honestly, Melissa, my main worry is that you'll never come if you postpone your trip now. Some emergency with one of us will just keep cropping up.' His despair shocked her. She couldn't think of anything to say, and they were both silent for moments.

Finally she broke the silence, her will crumbling. 'I just want to make it easy for you, honey.'

'I know, but you're not. Listen, today was the first day, Melissa. Who knows what we'll uncover tomorrow? You could cancel your flight, then we solve the case on Wednesday. By then that flight will be full and you won't be able to come anyway. Wouldn't that be silly?'

'Crazy,' she agreed. 'I get the feeling you're bulldozing me, but… Okay, let's see what tomorrow brings.'

She wasn't sure how that call didn't go as she had planned. She was just the faintest bit resentful of the way he wouldn't talk everything through. Former boyfriends had displayed this same reluctance, but she'd thought Joe was different. But he sounded so despondent, even fearful, that she ended up complying with what he wanted. She didn't think that was a good pattern to build a long-term relationship on.

As her mother often said, she could choose to make the best of the situation, or she could choose to make the worst of it. She couldn't control what happened. She knew she wanted to give her future with Joe a chance, so she committed to leave for Fiji on Thursday and make the best of whatever she found there.

TUESDAY

12

The Fiji Regiment Club stood near the top of the hill, which rose behind the Albert Oval and the Suva government buildings and courts. Some felt the Regiment Club overlooked these buildings metaphorically as well as literally, the military having toppled more than one government in Fiji's decades of independence from Britain. Horseman had been at the club before as a guest of a Fiji Rugby Union director. As he drove up the long curving drive from the gate, the fig trees seemed even larger, their foliage denser than he remembered. The graceful colonial building, deep verandahs shaded by sweeping eaves, was not at all military in character, but suggested an elite domesticity besieged by the forces of nature and ever so slowly succumbing.

His right leg was behaving today; he was relieved that he didn't limp up the steps. The doorman recognised him.

'*Ni sa bula*, Josefa Horseman. Welcome to the Regiment Club.' He grasped the polished brass handle and opened the door with a flourish. 'Ratu Osea has already arrived and is waiting for you on the back verandah.'

An elderly waiter, his hair pure white, escorted Horseman through the timber-panelled rooms to the back verandah. This side of the building was elevated above the slope, the surrounding trees not so oppressive. A slight breeze freshened the hot air. The light tracery of foliage filtered the light but did not obscure the sparkle of Suva Bay, dark blue this sunny morning. From this vantage point,

Suva looked a picture-perfect little South Pacific port. He was delighted that the city could look so beautiful despite its flaws.

'Here is Ratu Osea,' the waiter announced. The older man seated at the cane table rose and held out his hand. Like Horseman, he was middle height for a Fijian and strongly built. His lined face was serious, and he looked at Horseman intently as he greeted him. His hand was large, lean, and dry, his shake firm and prolonged.

'*Vinaka vakalevu* for making yourself available, Ratu Osea.'

The chief smiled slightly. 'Not at all. I'm pleased to meet you, Josefa Horseman, as any Fijian would be. We all wish we could play rugby like you. It's my civic duty to help the police, especially in such an unheard-of crime at Tanoa. Let's sit down.'

'*Vinaka*, Ratu. This is certainly a beautiful outlook.'

'*Io*, we see Suva at its best from here.' The chief did not appear to be in any hurry. Horseman would let him set the pace.

Horseman had done his homework. Ratu Osea Matanitu had entered the Fiji Infantry Regiment after the elite Queen Victoria School on the east coast of Viti Levu. He served on United Nations peace-keeping missions from Sinai to Kosovo, rising to the rank of major, and was then appointed military attaché to the Fiji Embassy in Washington D.C. His was a surprisingly cosmopolitan career for a man who then retired to live in a remote highlands village.

The waiter disturbed the chief's reverie, if that's what it was, by serving them morning tea. A Victorian-looking silver service, polished to its gleaming best, was laid on their table: teapot, hot water jug, sugar basin, milk jug. While the waiter poured tea, a young lad set out white china crockery emblazoned in faded gold with the regimental coat-of-arms. He reappeared with a tray of predictable hot savouries. Horseman didn't mind predictable at all; he nodded and the boy served him curry puffs and sausage rolls. Horseman waited for the chief to start. At first it seemed he wasn't going to eat anything. Horseman, his appetite assailed by the fragrant steam, fretted. Silently, he offered the chief the milk jug.

'*Vinaka*, I don't take milk. Please go ahead.' The chief sipped his tea, returned the cup to its saucer carefully. Then, to Horseman's relief, he picked up a sausage roll and bit into it appreciatively. 'The Regiment does a good job at these traditional British things. I hope you agree, Inspector.'

Horseman hastily scoffed a curry puff; light, soft and spicy. '*Io*, excellent, Ratu Osea. I am grateful for your hospitality.'

The chief waved his gratitude aside. Perhaps now was the right time to turn to business.

'I understand you were away from the village when Viliame was killed, Ratu?'

The chief raised his eyebrows in assent. '*Io*, I drove to Suva on Friday with my headman, Ilai. Perhaps you've already heard about the ceremonies we've got planned for our special overseas visitors next weekend. They're the descendants of Mr Weston, whom my people murdered over a hundred years ago. He was on a peace mission, you know. My people were engaged in punishing on-again off-again raids against a few villages to the west where Mr Weston was teaching the word of God. Both sides captured prisoners for meat and labour, fired houses, assaulted and killed. It's believed our side was the instigator, but who knows the truth now?

'After some years, Mr Weston was having an influence and some around him turned to Christ. His followers asked him to come and make peace with us, believing a missionary would be immune from attack. He arrived at our village, the chief received him courteously, heard his message, and talked with him for some hours before inviting him to feast with his family and stay the night. Mr Weston accepted, but was careful to eat no meat, fearing it might be human.

'From the details you're relating, I imagine that there is a written record?'

'*Io*, Inspector. Mr Weston wrote up his journal before he left the following day. There are district officer reports too. Mr Weston was cautiously hopeful his representations had been well received. But when he set out to walk back to his home near our enemy village, he was attacked on his way, clubbed to death by warriors on my

ancestor's orders. The missionary was roasted and eaten in the
normal way, but I think his flesh may have been reserved for the
chiefly, who believed in the superstition that they could ingest the
powerful qualities and virtues of the living person by eating his
flesh.'

The waiter now arranged scones, cream, and jam on the table and
poured both men another cup of tea. The boy added a plate of
fruitcake fingers and another of orange and pineapple slices.
Horseman was relieved the chief helped himself to a scone, and he
quickly followed suit.

'Interesting, Ratu. What virtues do you think nineteenth century
Fijians would have seen in Mr Weston? They overpowered him
easily enough, didn't they?'

The chief looked at Horseman intently while eating his scone, as
if assessing whether this policeman was worthy of an explanation.
'Many clans had accepted the missionaries' teachings by this time. It
was only the remote hinterland clans of the largest islands that had
not. The intertribal connections would ensure that the people of my
village knew this. However persistent they were in their superstitions
and yes, devilish practices, they knew the missionaries' teachings had
won over other Fijians, who had stopped warring, stopped being
cannibals, and were learning to read and write. And, as now, these
other Fijians were more prosperous than they were. The
missionaries had achieved all this without force or violence, but
through prayer, the Bible, and God's help. Don't you think my
ancestors would see this God, embodied by Mr Weston, as
powerful, virtuous, and well worth eating?'

Disconcerted, Horseman asked, 'Do you mean the murder was a
shortcut to becoming Christian, rather than a last-ditch stand to
preserve their own religion?'

'We can't know how they thought really, can we? However, it
seems a likely explanation to me. Whatever the case, it was a terrible
crime against God. I've given this a lot of thought since I retired,
and I feel our collective guilt has held us back ever since.'

'How did you view Viliame's proposals for village enterprises?'

The chief now smiled slightly. 'Ah, that young man. He was a bit of an upstart, you know, thought he knew everything. But he will be a huge loss to Tanoa. He was definitely going places and could take the other young people with him. He set up and managed the spice gardens project admirably, and it's bringing in money now.'

'And the chicken raising proposal?'

'Ah, I thought we should be cautious in entering into a contract with a foreign company like Henny Penny. I know other clans have gone in for this, but my villagers like to be their own masters. That was the view of the elders. We should wait and observe how it works out elsewhere.'

'Ratu, did Viliame have any enemies? Was there anyone he offended or angered?'

The chief shook his head. 'Not that I know of, no. Some of us thought his plans were too ambitious, too fast-moving, that he should be more patient. But he was well-liked. I think you would have liked him too, Inspector.'

Horseman privately agreed. 'Will you go ahead with your reconciliation ceremony next Sunday?'

The chief shook his head sadly. 'I can't see how it can possibly be postponed. And it is now more important than ever. Do you see, with Viliame gone, it will be even harder for our young people to succeed. Vili led and inspired them. It's even more important for us all to know that God has forgiven us that grievous sin of the past, through the public forgiveness of Mr Weston's descendants.'

'I see.' Although this didn't square with the Methodist doctrine Horseman knew, he could see the logic. It could even be of psychological benefit to the community, if managed well. Yet something wasn't right here.

'Will there be any conflict with your plans for Viliame's funeral?'

'Now, I was about to ask you about that, Inspector. Vili is in the morgue at the hospital here, is he not? Do you know when he will be released for burial?'

'Not yet, Ratu Osea. I'll be speaking to the pathologist later today. I'll be in touch as soon as I find out. Would you consider holding Viliame's funeral before your guests arrive on the weekend?'

'It's a sad conjunction of events, but Vili's parents might prefer that. I'll be going to Tanoa this afternoon and will discuss these matters with Vili's family and Pastor Joni before I make a final decision about our reconciliation ceremony.'

'How can I get in touch with you in the village, sir?'

'The only way is to send a message to the Kumi police post. They're very obliging and send a constable up with a message.'

Horseman thought such a service was not quite within the remit of the Kumi constables, but couldn't think of an alternative until Telecom provided a line to the village. He offered the plate of fruitcake to the chief. It looked moist and dense with raisins, sultanas, and almonds. The chief took two fingers, so Horseman followed suit again.

'I extend an invitation to you and any other officers who may wish to attend the reconciliation on Sunday. Our Sunday morning service and *lovo* feast will also be an intrinsic part of our ceremonies.'

'*Vinaka vakalevu*, Ratu Osea. I would like to accept. However, I myself have a guest arriving from overseas on Friday, and I won't be able to abandon her.'

Now the chief smiled. 'Bring her along, she will be most welcome, Inspector.'

'*Vinaka*, I'll certainly try to persuade her.'

The two men spent another five minutes paying their respects to the morning tea before parting. As Horseman shook hands, the chief's eyes drilled into his own once more.

13

'G'day, Joe, come in. What's kept you, mate?' Dr Matthew Young greeted Horseman cheerily as he entered the pathologist's domain at the back of the hospital. Singh was already there, perched on a stool at the lab bench, also looking cheerful.

'Curry puffs and scones with strawberry jam. A long morning tea with Ratu Osea Matanitu at the Regiment Club. Something a bit disturbing about the man. Don't quite know what—just something about how intense he is, especially about this reconciliation deal. He knows his stuff, researched the history of the murder, tracked down Mr Weston's diaries.'

'He sounds eccentric at least,' Dr Young remarked.

'What are you two looking so chirpy about, anyway? What have you found, Matt?'

'Cause of death's simple this time, mate, just as Dr Tavua thought. Two blows to the head with a blunt object. The murderer really wanted to make sure he was dead. But it was the first blow that killed him, pretty much instantaneously. A well-aimed blow, a lot of force and the victim taken by surprise. There are no indications of a fight or struggle. The attacker was probably hiding just off the path, waiting for the victim to come along.'

Horseman was suspicious. His friend, the Australian chief pathologist, would not be looking so pleased with himself after such an unchallenging post mortem. 'What's the catch, Matt? Come clean now.'

'Oh, you know me too well, Joe. It's the weapon that's rather interesting. It must have been very heavy, but there's something more. Come and have a look.' Horseman expected he would have to view Viliame's corpse, but Dr Young ignored the body covered by a green sheet. He swivelled an oversized computer screen in Horseman's direction. The image of the head wound was blown up, sharp and detailed.

'Man, is this the new toy you told me about?'

Dr Young patted the computer screen. 'Sure is. Just what the doctor ordered, too.'

'The police labs could do with these, sir.' Singh said.

'Absolutely, but how? Not within the power of a humble detective inspector, I'm afraid.'

'Don't get off the track! Take a look here, mate.'

Horseman obediently followed the red arrow the pathologist was moving around the screen, tracing the extent of the wound, where the hair had been clipped back close to the skin.

'What do you see?' Dr Young prompted. 'Don't look at Susie now, she's under instructions not to tell you.'

Horseman peered closely at the horrific wound. Then he saw past the discolouration, the fatal distortion of the skull, the bone fragments mashed into skin and flesh. He saw a pattern surrounding the pulp of the worst damage. First a broken zigzag, then some wavy scallops, and outside those, a row of small circles. The rows were broken, but it was definitely a pattern engraved, no, imprinted on skin and flesh.

'It looks like traditional Fijian decoration. Could be on pottery or *masi*, bark cloth, or…carving.'

'Getting warm, Joe.'

'I get it now! The weapon must be a Fijian object, carved in detail. Mightn't have been a weapon, just something heavy that could be used as one. Wood or stone? There must have been fragments, Matt. You've seen them, you'd better tell me.'

'Okay, you went as far as you could, mate. I'll buy you a beer tonight.'

Singh laughed. 'Put him out of his misery, doctor.'

'It's wood, hard and dense. My guess would be *dakua* or *vesi*. There was scarcely any splintering, just a few tiny fragments. We'll get it identified.'

'You know your Fijian native timbers, Matt! I'm impressed,' Horseman said.

'Google, mate. Get up to date!' Dr Young winked at Singh. 'Now, look at this.'

At the tap of a key, the image morphed to a display of several weapons. Horseman recognised them as nineteenth century Fijian war clubs. He'd seen this group in a glass case several times at the Fiji Museum.

'Susie and I think something like the top left could be a candidate. Do you agree?'

Horseman's interest became excitement. 'Yes, I do. You can see those three patterns, in the same order. The others don't have anything like the same detail. I remember now, the plain clubs are deadly weapons of war, but the more elaborate one is a chief's ceremonial club, isn't it?'

'Exactly. Before you get too excited now, let's go to the Fiji Museum and talk to the experts.'

Horseman grinned. 'I was lucky to score a police car this morning, guys. We can all go in that.'

***

The Fiji Museum, like the Regiment Club, looked threatened by encroaching vegetation. In front, the Thurston Gardens acres were haphazardly tended, the gravel paths now mostly grass. The verandah was twice the depth of that at the Regiment Club. Horseman recalled with a smile many rugby parties held here in the past: fundraisers, balls, and dinners, lit by candles and paper lanterns. It was a special spot. These days, the Board preferred the air-conditioned uniformity of hotel function rooms.

Dr Sailasi Erasito was waiting for them in the lofty room housing

Fijian artefacts from precolonial times. Horseman's favourites were the replicas of the war canoes and sailing craft that dominated the room. There were no originals left. These brilliant boats had vanished from Fiji waters, but survived as the emblem on the Fiji Police badge.

They crossed to the weapons display, one of the most popular with visitors in the entire collection. Horseman failed to understand the pull these grisly artefacts of cannibalism had for foreigners. He found them horrible; he could only too readily picture the casual brutality of their routine use by men, and women too, without any sense of wrongdoing. Was this the mindset of Viliame's killer, or had he simply chosen his weapon for its certain deadliness?

'Here's the display from our website,' Dr Sailasi said. He stood back a little while the others crowded in. There were lethal clubs of different sizes and designs, most plain, but a few with carved decoration something like they'd seen on both Viliame's head and on the weapon in the image. Something like, but not the same.

'The club we wanted to see isn't in this display,' Horseman commented. 'Have you changed it around?'

'Yes, but we haven't changed the website. Come into my office where we can talk in private.'

The investigators exchanged glances.

Only a tactful soul would call Dr Sailasi's office messy. Even chaotic would be an understatement. On every surface were piles of books, journals, unbound papers in rubber bands or bulldog clips, or loose. Some of the piles looked about to collapse. Intriguing lumps of stone stopped loose papers from blowing away under the ceiling fan, which was on the high setting. Leaning against walls and poking out of baskets were haphazard collections of spears, arrows, wooden and cane objects whose functions were mysterious to Horseman. Dr Sailasi removed piles of papers from two chairs and put them on the floor.

'You won't believe it, but I know where everything is in here,' he said. 'Please sit down. Dr Young, please take my chair.' They all complied while the curator perched himself on the edge of a low filing cabinet.

'I don't often meet visitors in here, as you can see. But this matter is rather confidential. Tell me, why are you interested in this particular club?'

Horseman looked at the others. The detail of the pattern imprinted on Viliame's head could not be revealed to anyone outside the team. He thought fast. 'I'm sorry, I can't tell you about the crime we're investigating yet. However, we've come across a fragment of carved wood and the pattern is very reminiscent of this club. Dr Young found the image on your website. We'd like to see the actual object to compare.'

Dr Sailasi frowned. 'Well, the design is typical. The one we had on display isn't unique.'

'It would still be good if we could see the club.'

'Well, now I'm the one in a difficult position, officers. What I'm telling you is also confidential. I'm sure you will respect that. Our star war club exhibit is missing, I'm afraid.'

'Missing? What do you mean?' Horseman asked.

'About three weeks ago, first thing in the morning, a cleaner brought me a key he found in the lock to the weapons cabinet. He told me the chiefly ceremonial club was missing. I checked and he was right.'

'Did you report this to the police, Dr Sailasi?' Singh asked.

'Yes, I did. But before I did that, I told the director, who didn't want the news to spread. With his agreement, some colleagues and I searched throughout the exhibit spaces, the museum workshops, and offices and around the outside. We checked our key records, questioned all the staff who had access to keys. I believed it would turn up in the conservation lab, for instance. But no. No trace anywhere. So the director rang the police, who searched professionally, took fingerprints, interviewed everyone—a full investigation.'

Singh frowned. 'Really? I've been on leave until yesterday, so I hadn't heard.'

Horseman was put out. 'Well, I've been on duty, and I didn't hear either.'

'Inspector Chatterjee and his officers told us to tell nobody. He said security here is difficult and if word gets out, more thieves would be attracted to the museum. We can't prevent staff talking to their families and friends, but Inspector Chatterjee took the time to explain his reasons carefully to all the staff. So far there's been nothing in the press. We're thankful for that.'

'Any news from the police since the club went missing?' Singh asked.

'Not news exactly, no. Regrettably, we're getting used to the idea that we might never see that club again. Inspector Chatterjee or his team have made numerous visits to ask questions, then more questions. The Cultural Treasures legislation is relevant, of course. It's illegal for the museum or anyone else to sell that club to a foreign individual or organisation. It's protected and must stay in Fiji. I realise now that we should never have put that club on public display at all.'

Horseman didn't get this. 'Why not? You just said the club wasn't unique.'

'The style of decoration is typical of chiefly war clubs, although no two examples would be identical, in decoration or in any other way. No, it's not the style or craftsmanship. This club is unique because of its provenance, its history. It would command a very high price from a certain type of private collector.'

'Oh?'

'Yes, we didn't include the provenance on the label. That would encourage salacious interest, and we don't want that. But whoever stole it must have known.'

'Known what, Dr Sailasi?' Singh asked patiently.

'The missing club came from Tanoa in the eastern Viti Levu highlands. It's the club that killed the Reverend Charles Weston there in 1875.'

14

Horseman and Singh found a table at the Republic of Cappuccino, ordered iced coffees and a roasted vegetable panini to share.

Horseman couldn't wait to swap ideas. 'Whatever this is, it can't be a coincidence, can it? Three weeks ago, that club was stolen for the purpose of murdering Viliame. Is any other explanation possible?'

Singh chewed thoughtfully. 'I agree, it's unlikely to be a coincidence. But I can think of other reasons for stealing the club.' She sucked on the straw and closed her eyes briefly. 'Mmm, this is so good. Well, it could have been stolen for illegal sale and export, as Dr Sailasi suggested. The murderer hears about it, robs the thief, and takes it to Tanoa. He doesn't plan to kill Viliame at that point, but when he does, he's got a lethal weapon to hand.'

Horseman had to concede the possibility. 'Okay, then why does the murderer take the club to Tanoa?'

Singh took another bite. Horseman smiled at her delaying tactic. 'Because it's his village and he believes it won't be discovered there. He stows it away secretly.'

'Why did he steal it from the museum thief?'

'Well, he could have known the provenance, wanted to save the club for Fiji.'

'Then why not return it to the museum?' Horseman persisted.

'Maybe because the museum demonstrated it couldn't safeguard it. So it should go back to Tanoa, where it came from in the first place.' Singh looked pleased with herself.

Horseman wasn't giving up his first theory. 'Fine, that's plausible. However, I think it's more likely the murderer and the thief are one and the same. Whether he stole the club in order to kill Viliame, I agree that's a question mark.'

He pushed the plate of panini slices towards her. 'Please finish these, Susie. I need a proper coffee now. I'm still sloshing with tea from this morning.' He waved a waiter over and ordered an espresso.

'I spoke with Ratu Osea at length this morning. He told me all about Mr Weston's murder back in 1875. He's very fervent about it. Seems a bit fanatical about this reconciliation ceremony he's planned. He's got to be a suspect. But it's hardly chiefly to sneak into the Fiji Museum at night and rob a display case, is it? I can see him delegating the theft and even the killing, though. He'd believe he was doing God's will.'

'That's a stretch, sir. He says he was in Suva last Saturday.'

'If he delegated the murder, he wouldn't need to be there. First, we need to acid test that alibi.'

Singh balanced her notebook on her knee. 'And?'

'Two, talk to Chatterjee, get his case files if we can. There's no need to investigate the museum theft from scratch. Three, gather all the information we can about the Tanoa elders—they seem to be the ones who opposed Vili.'

Singh nodded, jotting neatly. 'Now we know what we're looking for, let's go back to Tanoa, ask more questions, and extend the search.'

'Fine. I reckon that the killer would never toss that club in the bush, though. It's much too precious, in every way. And we can hardly turn out the contents of all the houses.'

'True. But if we had a CID officer there full-time, he could observe, get to know people better,' she suggested.

'Okay, I'll put that to the super. That would have to be Tanielo, if he could keep his mouth shut.'

Horseman waited while Singh finished the last panini triangle. 'Any luck this morning at Vili's digs?' he asked.

'So so. We've sealed his room at the NLTB single staff hostel. Tanielo and I had a quick look, but nothing jumped out at us. Tani will go back with the SOCOs this afternoon. I've got an appointment at three o'clock with Vili's superior at the NLTB.'

'Good. Let's go back to the station. I'd better put the super in the picture right away.'

***

Detective Superintendent Navala didn't say anything for quite a while. He sat back in his chair and stared at Horseman. The unflappable boss looked like he didn't know what to do. He ran his hands over his face. Horseman noticed a slight tremor.

'*Oi lei*, Joe! This changes everything. No doubt you and Singh have talked it over. What do you propose?'

'Three things to start with, sir. First, we need to liaise with Chatterjee and get access to his case files. That would be more successful coming from you. Second, we need a CID presence in the village, around the clock. Extend the search now we know what we're looking for. Get to suss out the political undercurrents. My suggestion is DC Musudroka—he's Fijian and young, Vili's helpers may confide in him. Third, we need to probe the lives of the Tanoa elders.'

'That makes sense. You left out something, though. Pray to God for some evidence. I'll go and see the deputy commissioner about Chatterjee's investigation. I've never heard any mention of it—how'd they keep that quiet?'

It unsettled Horseman to see his boss so disturbed. He realised for the first time how he relied on the unfailing calm of this big man.

The super rubbed his hands over his face again and got to his feet. 'And why did they want to—keep it quiet, I mean? And who are *they*?'

He wasn't really asking Horseman, who simply said, 'Good luck, sir.'

15

The General Manager of the Native Land Trust Board, Ratu Sirilo Qerewaqa, sat at an impressive mahogany desk at right angles to the spacious windows overlooking Victoria Parade. Singh hoped she masked her surprise at his wheelchair. That explained the lift, the first she'd ever seen in a three-storey building. It probably also explained Ratu Sirilo's unhealthy obesity.

'Forgive me for not standing, Detective Sergeant Singh, but as you see...' He reached across his desk to shake hands.

'How do you do, Ratu Sirilo. My condolences on the loss of Viliame Bovoro, your employee.'

Ratu Sirilo bowed his head sadly. '*Vinaka vakalevu*. Indeed, all of us at the Board are shocked by the news. His death is a loss to us. Please take a seat at the table.'

Ratu Sirilo picked up a buff government file and wheeled himself over to a glass-topped conference table. Singh sat and placed her notebook on the table. A tiny Indian assistant entered with a tray of tea and water. Tea was the last thing Singh felt like, but she accepted a cup with a smile, then poured herself some water.

'Sir, I know nothing of Viliame's work at the NLTB. What can you tell me?'

He opened the file. 'As I'm sure you know, one of our main roles is to centrally manage the leasing of the land owned by native Fijian people through our customary landowning groups, the tribes and clans. If a farmer, business, or developer expresses an interest in using a block of native land, then that lease is drawn up by the Board to the agreement of both parties. Then it is legally ratified and managed by us. All rents are paid to the Board and income distributed to the landowners after costs are deducted. So, you'll understand the Board's main work is surveying and accounting. Viliame was identified as a bright boy when he joined us after high school. He should have gone to university, but we were glad he chose the Board after topping the public service examinations. We trained him as an accounts clerk. He was quick to learn. The Board sponsored him to take the FIT book-keeping certificate, and then the Diploma in Accountancy. He was to finish the diploma at the end of this semester. His work has always been of a high standard.'

'Was he popular with his colleagues, Ratu?'

'I haven't heard otherwise, but I'm not the best person to tell you about that, Detective Sergeant.'

'Was he working on any controversial projects?'

Ratu Sirilo smiled. 'The Board's work is not often controversial, but it can happen—usually when we're involved in a court case. As far as I know there was nothing like that. Viliame was a skilled book-keeper, soon to qualify as an accountant. His job was technical. However, you are welcome to talk to Vili's supervisor and other colleagues if you think that may be of help.'

'Many thanks, sir. Yes, I'd like to do that.'

'Rajeshree will take you to Viliame's section, then. Any way I can help you further, please get in touch.'

'I will. Thanks again, Ratu Sirilo.'

Rajeshree appeared as if by magic and led Singh towards the stairs. The lift must be reserved for Ratu Sirilo's use. Fair enough.

'Rajeshree, did you know Viliame?' Singh asked.

'Oh, not so much, you know. Just by sight and to say hello. I met him a few years ago at a Diwali staff party—he looked great in Indian clothes! Since then we've just chatted when we run into each other. I can't believe someone murdered him!' Rajeshree sniffed and rubbed at her eyes, removing make-up intended to conceal an acne flare-up.

Singh wondered if she'd known him better than she admitted, or would like to have done. 'Did he talk about work at all?'

'Not really. He might just mention how busy he was, or he had exams coming up for FIT.'

'Did you ever see him outside the office?'

'You mean like a date? No. Occasionally I'd run into him in the street or a shop. By chance,' she added.

The accounts section occupied a very large, open office to the left of the stairs. Rajeshree led Singh through a central passage between desks to a separate office at the end partitioned with flimsy glazed panels about two metres high.

A middle-aged man looked over the top of his glasses at them as they stood in the doorway. 'Mr Ghosh, this is Detective Sergeant Singh. Is it alright to interrupt you now?'

'My goodness, I guess this is about poor Vili, isn't it. We can't believe what has happened. Come in, come in, ma'am.'

Rajeshree left and Singh took the empty chair opposite Mr Ghosh, whose warm brown eyes softened his tense and wary face. 'Were you Viliame's supervisor, Mr Ghosh?' she asked.

'Indeed I was. I can honestly claim to have taught him the ropes here. We've both been promoted in the five years since he started, but I'm still his line manager and he is still, or was, the most promising apprentice I've ever had, or likely to.' His face drooped.

'Can you tell me some more about him, and his job?'

'My goodness, Vili was different from the others. Usually, the young recruits are clock-watchers, not really interested in the Board and our purpose. They just want some routine tasks which they do unquestioningly, spend the minimum time, and get paid. Someone like that can learn bookkeeping and work alright under supervision but will never make an accountant, much less auditor. You know Miss Singh, an accountant is a detective, constantly on the lookout, asking questions of every single number that comes to his attention. You will understand that, being a detective yourself.'

Singh nodded. 'And Vili?' she prompted.

'Vili was a natural auditor, a natural detective. He still had to take his final exams, but already he was a gifted accountant. He was aware of the big picture, was never content with a routine task unless he understood where it fitted in. That was his strength.'

'Did his ability create resentment or jealousy among his colleagues?'

Mr Ghosh shook his head. 'I don't know. I suppose it's possible. I wasn't aware of it. Vili had an easy manner, I thought he was well-liked. Some of the other young boys teased him about his habit of working late, or always having his nose in a book, but he laughed it off. I think those who did that thought he was stupid for working harder than he needed to. That sort can't comprehend anyone being passionate about their work.'

This rang very true with Singh, for it was her experience exactly. Friends and family were astonished, and still were, that she strove to become a detective when just about any other job was easier.

'Was he ever promoted over the head of older colleagues, for example?'

'Well, yes he was, but you can't be suggesting someone would kill him for that? For being passed over?' Mr Ghosh sounded annoyed now.

'No normal person would kill another for such a reason, I agree. But murderers are not normal people, sir.'

Mr Ghosh shook his head in sorrow.

'Did he work on particular projects, or particular districts?' Singh asked.

'Both at different times. We rotate the young clerks to give them a broad experience—it's part of their training.'

'What was his most recent area?'

'He was managing disbursements to landowners in the Central Division.'

She was pretty sure Tanoa was in Central. She made a note to check. 'Who were Vili's particular friends at work, Mr Ghosh?'

'You know, he didn't have much free time. He was always

friendly, but I'm not sure he had close friends at work. He went back to his village most weekends, he went to evening classes at FIT and had to study, But maybe you could speak to Samuela, they both went to FIT and stayed in the staff hostel.'

'Thank you very much. Is Samuela here now?'

'Unfortunately, no. He left early this afternoon to go to his accountancy class.'

'If I could just note down his details, I'll be off then, Mr Ghosh. Thank you for your help. I'm sorry for your loss. Vili must have been a good person.'

'He was, Sergeant Singh, he was. My goodness, I will never see his like again.'

***

Singh climbed the stairs to the first floor of the NLTB staff hostel and ducked under the blue-and-white tape isolating the section of verandah outside Viliame's room. Ash was examining the contents of the wooden desk while his offsider dusted for fingerprints.

'Hi, Ash,' she said.

The SOCO was startled and turned. 'Hi, Sergeant,' he said, grinning. 'Sorry, I didn't hear you, nearly jumped out of my skin. What can I do for you?'

'I just thought I'd take a look at Vili's room while I'm here. I'm here to meet another NLTB book-keeper who was friendly with Vili. Find anything interesting yet?'

'Pretty much as we'd expect from a young man studying accountancy who's interested in agriculture. We're lucky he's orderly. There's a folder of correspondence and diaries for the years he's been in Suva. You'll want to take those away.'

'Yes, please. I'll just have a quick look here. My appointment with Vili's friend isn't until five o'clock.'

She scanned the tall bookcase beside the desk. As Ash said, most of the titles fitted in with Vili's interests. There were also some paperback thrillers and two nineteenth century classics of Fiji anthropology: *Fiji and the Fijians* by Thomas Williams and *Life in Feejee: Five Years Among the Cannibals* by Mary Wallis. Singh knew of them, but had never read them herself. She resolved to do so; maybe she'd understand places like Tanoa better.

Vili's clothes were neatly arranged in a battered chest of drawers. On top of the chest stood a framed family photo and a zippered sponge bag. No mirror. A few jackets and long-sleeved shirts hung from a rail attached to the wall. A steel-framed single bed jutted from under the louvred window into the middle of the room. It was a simple working room to accommodate a man who spent nearly all his weekends away.

'Okay, Ash, call me if you find anything.'

'Sure. Are you going to Tanoa tomorrow?'

'Not sure yet. Maybe.'

'We'll be there searching for the club, but I don't hold out much hope. This killer is a planner.'

'I agree. Maybe see you up there.'

Next, she went down to Samuela's room on the ground floor. A tired-looking twenty-something Fijian man answered her knock. He towered over her. He was overweight, already suffering from his sedentary occupation. His room was identical to Vili's, except it had no bookcase. All the wall space was covered in rugby posters featuring Fiji players and other teams as well: the All Blacks, England, Wales, and France. Horseman was there on the wall too, a few years younger.

Singh sat on the desk chair, leaving the bed for Samuela. 'You must be feeling sad, Samuela. I believe Viliame was a friend of yours.'

He nodded. 'You can call me Samu—everyone else does. Yeah, we get on pretty well. Vili keeps to himself pretty much, he's so busy with study and his weekends in the highlands.' He shook his head. 'That's such a long way to go every week, so he doesn't have much spare time. But we study the same course at FIT, so we see each other a bit.'

Samu's use of the present tense brought a lump to Singh's throat. She swallowed. 'What did you do together?'

'Sometimes we go to the rugby, and the cinema, especially action movies. He's cool.' His eyes filled and he looked away.

'Did you work closely together at NLTB?'

'The last two years we've been in the same section. He's a way better book-keeper than me. So smart. He has an eagle eye, you know. He's an assistant accountant, supervising four trainees.'

'Including you?'

'No, just the trainees. I'm a qualified book-keeper, but I suppose Mr Ghosh thinks I'm not ready for trainees yet.' He looked at her, smiling. 'I agree with him.'

Singh wondered if he just lacked confidence. 'Did you talk about what he was doing at work?'

'Not much. I guess we both knew what we were doing, so there wasn't any need.' He looked up hopefully, wanting this to be helpful.

'What did you two talk about, Samu?'

He shrugged. 'Sometimes our courses, assignments. Sometimes his village projects. He could be a successful business man. But he wants to help the people in his village too.'

'Did he mention any specific people in his village?'

Samu frowned, concentrating. 'Not much, but I remember him mentioning the pastor and the chief, his parents and the friends who worked on the spice gardens.'

'What did he say about them?'

'He once said the pastor's daughter liked him. He wanted his little brother to go to university, but the kid wasn't interested.'

'Did he talk about any opposition to his plans for the village?'

'Now you mention it, I do remember something now. Yes, he came back to work one Monday in a bad mood, which wasn't like him. He snapped at me a few times during the day. Vili was always polite. Then he came up to me at our FIT class that evening and apologised, said he was so upset that the clan elders had refused his request for more land.'

'Did he name anyone?'

This time Samu screwed up his eyes in the effort to remember. 'He might have, he might have, but I can't recall the names. I'm sorry.'

'Never mind. Names are hard when you've never met the people. You know, I bet that name or names will just pop into your head before too long. It'll help if you focus on that meeting with Vili at FIT from the beginning. Visualise how he looked, how he came up to you in class, what he said from the beginning. Your memory will return. And when it does, please call me. Here's my card. Any name could really help us.'

'Really? I'll do what you suggest. Try, anyhow.'

'I'm sure you'll remember, Samu.' When they said goodbye, the young man looked hopeful, even confident.

16

'Can I give anyone a lift back to the station?' Horseman asked the police volunteers who were yarning together after Shiners' training. Those points taken off Marists had spurred the team on, no doubt about it.

Only Musudroka accepted; the others were off-duty. As they crawled along in tedious traffic, Horseman asked, 'Well, Tani, what's the upshot of your enquiries today?'

'DS Taleca's been upgrading my computer search skills, sir. I'm shocked that Google can't find everything we need. I've searched media files for mentions of the Tanoa chief and elders, then we went out to the university library. Wow, what a heap of paper they've got there! We found extra references for the same list of people. Then a librarian looked up the Weston murder for us—they've got heaps on that. We borrowed some books, and the librarian's going to copy everything that wasn't for loan. That's service for you. She really did seem very pleased to help us.'

'Glad you're learning, Tani. What have you found out?'

'Sir, we're still compiling all the printouts. I haven't had time to actually read anything yet.' Musudroka sounded hurt.

'Well, if DS Taleca thinks you're to be trusted, take a couple of those books home with you tonight and start reading.'

'*Io*, sir.' Musudroka grinned; he enjoyed this banter. To him, as to most Fijians who grew up bombarded with affectionate teasing from their families, it signalled belonging.

It was half past six and almost dark when Horseman and Musudroka got back. They found the others catching up on paperwork under Singh's able supervision. The super had asked Horseman's team to stay in the station so he could brief them on what they all now called The Case of the Cannibal Club, or the Triple C. It was past seven when the super entered the room, his face grave. He was always rather serious and reserved, but Horseman had never seen him looking so down.

'Sir, take a seat, please.' Horseman jumped up and offered his chair and desk to his senior. 'Gather near my desk everyone. Tani, get Superintendent Navala a cup of tea, please.'

'*Vinaka*, I won't say no this time,' the super said.

The others waited in silence until Musudroka set a large white mug of tea before the super. '*Vinaka*,' he said. 'You will observe I'm not carrying a box of files. Not even one. That's because Chatterjee's super won't give them to us. Yet. But I'm not going to give up. This sort of competition for territory and, I hate to say it, downright jealousy and suspicion has no place in the Fiji Police I've served for thirty five years.' He shook his head in sorrow.

'It's clear there's a connection between the theft of the club and its use to murder Viliame. It's clear the thief of the club and that poor young man's murderer may be one and the same, or at least connected. However, Inspector Chatterjee's superintendent doesn't want to share the case files.'

'Did he give you a reason for that, sir?' Horseman asked.

'Oh, several! Let me think, now. One: the case is at a critical stage and may be jeopardised by widening the tight circulation list. Two: the case is politically sensitive, which makes me even keener to find out about what they've uncovered. Three: there are international repercussions, again sensitive. Four, and this is what I think, not what I was told: Chatterjee found out all this allegedly sensitive information and he reckons it's his personal property. It disgusts me, it really does.'

Horseman was again stunned to see his reserved boss express

such strong emotion, or indeed any emotion. 'Do you want us to interview the museum staff again and try to find the thief ourselves, sir?'

The super sighed. 'No, I was forbidden to run our own parallel investigation. And I don't want you distracted by competition either. Of course, you can interview anyone you feel you need to in connection with Viliame's murder. There's considerable overlap between both cases, the museum's stolen artefact being our murder weapon. That can't be helped.'

'So we could interview museum cleaners if we consider they may be able to help us to discover Viliame's murderer.' Singh said.

'Of course, and you don't need my specific approval. However, I will pursue this matter of the Chatterjee files further, mark my word. Vital principles of cooperation for the public good are at stake. If you want me, I'll be in my office drafting a letter to the deputy commissioner. I'll do my best to get us access to those files.'

With that, the super picked up his mug and left the room. Horseman followed. 'Sir, anything I can do to help?'

'*Vinaka*, Joe, but this one is up to me, for my sins.'

'Sir, I know it's not at the top of your list right now, but if you haven't had time to draft in extra officers…'

'Oh, I forgot to tell you. Sorry. I've managed to get two extra constables seconded to the case. But on reflection, I can't authorise Tanielo's deployment to Tanoa full-time. He still needs a lot of support. The place is too isolated, out of radio reach. And there's a murderer in that wretched village, I'm sure.'

'*Io*, sir. I realise I didn't think that through. I never intended to put Tani at risk.'

'We can ever only do our best with the resources we've got, Joe. There will always be hill villages at the end of roads going nowhere.'

***

Melissa woke around two o'clock in the morning, but couldn't go back to sleep. She made herself camomile tea, drank it in bed with her *American Journal of Sports Physical Therapy*, but sleep did not come. If only she knew how Joe's case had gone that day. Three o'clock Tuesday morning in Oregon meant it was ten o'clock Tuesday night in Fiji. He was probably still up. She gave in and called. He answered right away.

'Joe honey, sorry to disturb you. I can't go back to sleep until I know how things went with you today.'

'I'm glad you did, darling. I didn't want to wake you, it must be—what—3:00 a.m. there?'

'Yep. How did it go today?'

'Melissa, we made progress today. We discovered the murder weapon! You never know, with more luck, we could just wrap this one up by Friday.'

'Wow, Joe, way to go! I guess you'll get DNA off it and all that?'

'Not yet, we're still looking for the actual weapon. When I said *discovered*, I meant we've identified it, and it's one of a kind.'

'Intriguing. What is it?'

'A historic artefact, stolen from the Fiji Museum here in Suva. I can't go into details, but we're sure.'

It hurt that Joe wouldn't admit her to his trusted circle. But her feeling was unjustified, she knew; he was simply doing his job. She mustn't start getting resentful. 'I hope you get hold of it pronto, then!'

'Me too. We're going up to the village tomorrow. A few lines to pursue, as well as finding the weapon. What about you? Are you packed?'

'I've started. My last day at work will begin in five hours. So...' She stifled a yawn. Maybe the camomile was working now.

'You need sleep! Sweet dreams, Melissa. Wish I was with you.'

'Ditto. I'm guessing you'll make an early start?'

'Crack of dawn. Good night, darling!'

Melissa hoped she didn't come across as a worrier. Joe wouldn't like that, long term. Long term! She often caught herself making wishful assumptions, these days. Just chill, enjoy the holiday with Joe for what it is, whatever happens, long, short or medium term.

WEDNESDAY

17

The SOCO Subaru was in the Tanoa car park when Horseman, Singh, and Musudroka arrived, together with an extra constable to assist the search. They all hopped out. 'Like a cuppa before you go?' Horseman asked Musudroka.

'*Vinaka*, sir, but we'll find the SOCOs and get cracking. They're expecting us.' The constable looked disappointed but said nothing.

'Great, see you two later.'

Ash had certainly fired up Musudroka with the SOCO work, and that could only be good. Horseman retrieved a thermos of coffee and a couple of enamel mugs from his kit bag. He liked his coffee black, but found a sachet of Longlife milk for Singh. 'Yes, please,' she said. 'Any sugar?'

He kept a screw-top jar permanently in his bag. Ex peanut butter. Into it went the paper sachets of sugar served to him in cafés, which he saved for the jar. A vestige of the frugality absorbed in his boyhood, where 'waste not' was the eleventh commandment. He passed the jar to Singh, who extracted two sachets and passed it back. She fished a packet of Lal's coconut biscuits from her backpack and offered it to Horseman, who took three, then placed the packet in the well between their seats.

As she busied herself with constructing her substitute latte, which she stirred with the end of her pen, Horseman said, 'I'm not at all sure how to play this today. There are good reasons to withhold the information about the Weston war club, not least our orders to keep it quiet. But if we do, all that we can hope to do today is to talk to more villagers, try to find out more about Vili and his activities. So far, everyone's singing from the same songbook.'

'We could discover a contradiction any time,' Singh said.

'True. If we ask about old war weapons in the villagers' possession, they'll soon draw the obvious inference. But if we told the chief and the pastor about the theft from the museum, their reactions could be very interesting. I don't feel I owe Chatterjee anything while we're shut out. We could even have a public meeting and make a general announcement. Maybe that's going too far. What do you think, Susie?'

Singh sipped her coffee, non-committal. 'Could work, sir. I don't know. I think I'd rather go with your first option—ask around about war weapons and see where it takes us.'

'Okay, we'll do that. I guess it's wise to keep quiet about Triple C.'

As they crossed the bridge, the curtain of mist rose. A *bilibili*, a bamboo raft, burdened by great stacks of palm fronds, pulled into the beach below them. Men and women hurried to help unload. The two detectives paused to watch. The helpers cut the vines that lashed the cargo to the deck, carried the bundles of fronds up the bank, and dumped them on the ground. Underneath the palm fronds were bamboo poles, which the workers unlashed and carried away. Then a second *bilibili* rounded the bend upstream, the crew poling into the same beach.

'I guess this scene would have been much the same a hundred years ago,' Singh said.

'Probably just the clothes that would be different. Yes, a glimpse into the past,' Horseman said. 'Ratu Osea has obviously decided to go ahead with the grand ceremony. The place is like a beehive. Look, the mist is clearing. See the men putting up feasting shelters on the *rara*? That'll be what the loads of bamboo and palms are for.'

'People look more cheerful, too,' Singh observed.

'Perhaps the need to put on a good show will boost village

morale. But it's time for us to start work too. We'd better pay our respects to the chief, if he's here,' Horseman said.

'I bet the newish Land Rover in the car park belongs to him,' Singh said.

They hadn't gone far along the main village path when Tomasi came out of a house ahead and waited for them to catch up.

'*Yadra*, good morning, detectives. I saw you crossing the bridge.'

'*Yadra*, Tomasi. We stopped to watch the *bilibili* coming ashore. A real scene from yesteryear. Everyone's hard at work. I take it the ceremony is going ahead on Sunday?'

'*Io*, Ratu Osea thinks it must. We can't disturb our guests' arrangements and we should fulfil their expectations. Our reputation is at stake—they would think we are not to be trusted if we postponed the ceremony. Possibly they wouldn't agree to come if we set a new date. This is Ratu Osea's reasoning.'

'Fair enough. What a difficult decision he had to make.'

'*Io*, Inspector.'

'Tomasi, is Ratu Osea in the village now? Sergeant Singh and I would like to pay our respects before continuing our work here.'

'Ah, good to see you're a respecter of tradition, sir. Ratu is certainly here, but he may be in conference now. Let's go to his house and see. As you know, it's at the eastern end of the village.'

Singh chatted to Tomasi as they walked. Horseman was relieved Tomasi's manner with her was easy: it wouldn't be unusual for people in the remote hinterland to be tight-lipped with an Indian police officer.

The chief's spacious house looked recently painted; cream weatherboards with red window frames and doors. The windows were fitted with glass louvres instead of timber shutters, but the house was far from ostentatious. The chief's military career and diplomatic post must have enabled him to accumulate substantial funds. Was the chief a man of simple tastes, at heart a barracks soldier? By the end of today, Kelepi Taleca should have discovered more about Ratu Osea's assets.

They waited near the foot of the steps as Tomasi called out to announce their visit. In a few moments the village headman, Ilai Takilai, emerged, shutting the door gently behind him. He came down the steps and addressed Tomasi quietly. Then he turned to Horseman, hand outstretched. 'You are welcome, Josefa Horseman. And your sergeant, also—welcome Ms Singh. Ratu Osea apologises that he must attend to business this morning. He would be honoured if both of you could join him for a very simple lunch at one o'clock.'

Horseman glanced at Singh, surprised. He bowed his head, clapped his hands once, open-palmed. Singh clapped too. '*Vinaka vakalevu*, sir, we would be honoured to accept,' Horseman said.

The man nodded and clapped in return. 'Good. Ratu will be most grateful.' He returned to the house.

'Tomasi, could we speak to you further in private, please?' Horseman asked. Tomasi lifted his eyebrows in assent.

'Where would be a suitable place?' Horseman asked again.

'I can offer my house, with pleasure. Just back along the path, as you saw.'

Horseman thought this was hardly likely to be private. 'We don't want to disturb your family in any way at all. Perhaps I'll look in on Pastor Joni and ask him if his office is free. He's happy for us to use it.'

'It's only me in the house, Inspector. My youngest son will hang around the SOCOs as long as he can. He's the only child at home now. My wife's at the school making costumes for the *meke* dances on Sunday. So we can be private at my house.'

'*Vinaka*, Tomasi. We appreciate your offer,' Singh replied with a smile.

Tomasi's house was more modest than the chief's. The roof and walls were of reeds, mud plastered and whitewashed. Palm thatch covered the corrugated iron roof. Inside, the floor was laid with reeds and topped with palm mats. A blue-checked cotton curtain partitioned off the sleeping area. Cupboards were built into the side wall opposite the curtain with some open shelves above. There was no other furniture. A lean-to corrugated iron roof projecting from the back wall protected the open cooking fireplace.

The place was airy enough. Windows on the front and back walls, their wooden shutters propped open, provided good ventilation, but the place had a damp earthy smell, indicating the floor beneath the springy reeds was earth. This smell always evoked decay to Horseman and depressed him. He had grown up by the sea on the island of Ovalau, where any houses not elevated were built on sand. Their smell was dry and salty, which seemed healthier to him. He knew it was just what you were used to growing up. But this earthy smell added to the oppressive feel this picturesque village gave him.

Horseman sat with his right leg stretched in front of him: he couldn't risk straining his knee by sitting cross-legged. Tomasi propped his back against a wooden post. Singh was the only one of the three who seemed able to sit on the floor unsupported, her legs neatly tucked to one side.

Singh glanced at him questioningly and began. 'Constable Tomasi, I know you've been thinking carefully about Viliame's death since we spoke on Monday. Can you tell us anything more?'

'I still can't understand it, Sergeant. The more I think about it, the more I believe it must have been someone here, a fellow villager, who killed Viliame. It's possible outsiders slipped in to murder him and then left, but they would need to have come on foot, and go back to wherever they came from in the dark, or stay in the bush until morning. Possible, but difficult, dangerous for anyone who doesn't know our lands like the back of his hand. That could only be one of us. But it beats me who in the village would kill that boy.'

'We're thinking the same way,' Singh replied. 'You know everyone here. Someone hated Vili or someone was scared of him.'

Tomasi was shaking his head. 'I've already told you about the elders knocking back the proposals he worked so hard on. They probably thought he was big-headed, but he didn't scare them, I'm sure. They tolerated him. They wouldn't kill him!'

'As we know, someone did,' Horseman said. 'What if someone

was desperate for something Vili had in his possession. They killed him to get it. Or to get it back, maybe, if they believed Vili had stolen it from them. Does that ring a bell?'

Tomasi looked bewildered. 'I understand, but what could that be? What could Vili have? He had a good job, but he was young, he couldn't have saved much. And I bet he kept his money in the bank.'

'You'd be surprised how little money some people will murder for,' Singh said.

'Such people must be crazy!'

'Probably Vili's murderer is crazy in some way. But perhaps it wasn't money he was after. It might have been something only valuable to the killer,' Singh replied.

'A person, perhaps a woman. Did you say Vili had a girlfriend?' Horseman asked.

'I don't know. Maybe in Suva,' Tomasi suggested.

'We know this is a village which greatly values tradition—customs, ceremonies,' Singh said. 'We noticed when we arrived you've kept up skills like building *bilibili* for river transport. Is there any traditional wood carving or other crafts carried on here?'

'Some of the women make pots. The clay here is suitable. In the old days we traded pots with the coast—all went by *bilibili* down the river. Nowadays the women make smaller pottery for the shops in the tourist resorts and Suva, even Nadi.'

'How interesting,' Singh said. 'I'd like to see some while we're here, if I may.'

Tomasi smiled. 'The potters have been busy. They will present gifts to the Weston descendants on Sunday. There'll be a display at the school too.'

'Wonderful! I'm looking forward to seeing them,' Singh said.

'What about wood carving?' Horseman asked. 'Copies of old priest's dishes, weapons, and so on.'

'Not in recent years, no.'

'People must have traditional carvings from the old days stored away, though. Handed down through the generations?'

'Some may, but I don't. People don't talk about them, if they do have such things.' Tomasi looked a bit wary.

'Why would they keep such keepsakes quiet?'

'Oh, there's no reason for secrecy. Not at all. I meant that I haven't heard anyone mention any old carvings they own. That's all.'

'Who would be most likely to have such things?' Singh asked.

'I don't know. The chiefly families, I suppose. The clan elders.'

Horseman glanced at Singh. '*Vinaka vakalevu*, Tomasi. We'll leave you in peace.'

'Oh, not too much peace and quiet today, sir! We all have jobs to do to prepare for our big day on Sunday.' He sprang to his feet. 'Let me get you a drink of water before you go. I've neglected you.' He picked two cups from the shelf and poured water from a kettle.

'*Vinaka*,' they both said, drinking gratefully.

'We'll be just on time for lunch if we leave now,' Horseman said. He hoped this meal would provide them with something to chew on, other than food.

***

Ilai Takilai appeared on the porch as Horseman and Singh arrived at the chief's house. As usual, his face was serious. He greeted them in Fijian. 'Welcome, Detective Inspector Horseman.' He nodded at Singh and stood aside. 'Please enter, both of you.'

They took off their sneakers and placed them side by side next to several other pairs lined up by the door.

'*Vinaka vakalevu*, we are honoured,' Horseman said. The low doorway forced both men to duck. Singh bowed her head respectfully. A teenage boy offered to take their bags. Horseman retrieved a paper bag of ground *yaqona* root before handing his backpack over.

Ilai ushered them through to a large room taking up the full width of the house. A huge rectangle of decorated *masi* hung on the back wall. Fine pandanus mats covered the floor. A dark wooden *tanoa* stood in the centre. Ilai invited them to sit down. Horseman managed to sit cross-legged. He hoped the *sevusevu* ceremony would be brief.

Ratu Osea entered from the opposite door, smiled, sat down on the other side of the *tanoa*, and clapped once.

'Welcome, honoured guests, to our poor village…' He continued for a few minutes of ritual welcome, emphasising the poverty and unworthiness of the village and its people, and the greatness and generosity of the police officers.

Horseman then placed the one-kilo bag of *yaqona* before the wooden bowl, murmuring gratitude for their welcome.

'Please accept this paltry token of our thankfulness for your kind invitation. We impose on your hospitality in a time of grief, for which we are truly sorry.'

Ilai, crouching low, picked up the *yaqona* and sat beside the chief. 'Ratu Osea accepts your most generous offering with humble thanks, and grants you and your officers the status of villagers for the duration of your duties here.'

Horseman again expressed his thanks and apologies effusively.

Ratu Osea clapped three times. The boy appeared, added ground *yaqona* and water to the *tanoa*, and stirred the contents for some time. He kneeled to serve the chief *yaqona* in a coconut shell cup. The chief drained the cup, and the others clapped three times. '*Maca*, empty,' they responded. The boy then served Ilai and the guests, who clapped in thanks. After two rounds, the chief signalled his refusal to the boy, who retreated on his knees.

The chief stood up. 'Our resources are very poor, but let's see what we can offer you for lunch.' Ilai opened the door behind and they went through to another large room, the right side set up with a dining table and chairs, and homely sofas set in a square on the left. The table was covered in a blue cloth, with a terracotta bowl of frangipani in the centre. Four places were set.

A smiling woman carried in two platters and laid them on the table. She had the same square face and prominent nose as the chief.

'My daughter, Ana', the chief said with a hint of pride.

'Please sit down and tuck in,' Adi Ana said. 'No ceremony here, officers!' Was she being ironic?

When they were all seated, the chief said a brief grace and passed around the platters of chicken, *dalo*, and salad. After a few minutes, during which the others tackled the food with gusto, Ratu Osea spoke.

'Officers, I assume you have noticed we're going ahead with the preparations for our ceremonies next Sunday.'

'*Io*, Ratu,' Horseman said. 'I quite understand your decision. May I ask when you're planning to hold Viliame's funeral?'

'On Friday. Superintendent Navala assures me we can bring Vili back home tomorrow.'

Horseman bowed slightly. 'His murder has had a big impact, Ratu.'

'*Io*, my people's usual excitement before a big ceremony is muted. But they are rallying and we can rely on them. Under Ilai's able direction.'

Ilai nodded sombrely. 'All the preparations are in hand, Ratu.'

The chief continued, 'It always helps to have routine tasks to do in times of crisis. I believe this ceremony will relieve our distress, not add to it.' He looked at Horseman. 'May I ask about your plans, Inspector?'

'My officers are searching for the murder weapon. Sergeant Singh and I will talk to more people close to Vili.'

'What sort of weapon are you looking for?' the chief asked.

Now he was put on the spot, Horseman's strong instinct was to play down what they knew about the club. He decided to go with his instinct.

'We know Vili was killed by a blow to his head by a heavy wooden object. But the questions of who killed him and why are still very much open, I'm afraid.'

Both the chief and his headman looked grave, their faces giving away nothing.

'I would appreciate your own thoughts about the *who* and *why*, sirs,' Horseman said, glancing at both men.

'We're thinking about little else, Inspector,' the chief answered calmly. 'I can only imagine a dispute, probably with another young man, which escalated in the heat of the moment and Vili was struck. Probably his death was not intentional at all, therefore not murder.' He looked at Ilai.

Ilai lifted his eyebrows in agreement. 'Let us pray that is so.'

Adi Ana entered, took away the lunch things, and quickly returned bearing a tea tray. She set out cups, saucers, and plates, poured tea, deposited a plate of iced and sliced cake before her father, and departed with another cheerful 'Help yourselves!'

Ratu Osea smiled indulgently. '*Io*, please help yourselves to Mere Tora's banana cake. Ana's service is rather casual, but the cake is excellent.'

It was indeed. Singh took it upon herself to pass the milk and sugar around. The tense atmosphere lightened a little.

After only one piece of cake, Horseman glanced at Singh, who pointedly looked at her watch and rose. 'If you'll excuse me gentlemen, I must be going—I have an appointment. Thank you for the wonderful lunch.'

Horseman got to his feet too. '*Vinaka* for your hospitality, Ratu Osea. I no longer feel like I'm trespassing on your land.'

The chief nodded benignly. 'You're Tanoa villagers for the duration, Inspector. We're honoured to help the police. That goes without saying. May God bless your investigation.'

18

Rhythmic drumming came from the direction of the *rara* as they walked along the main path.

Horseman smiled. 'Sounds like *meke* dance practice. Vili's brother will probably be there, so I'll head over.'

'I'll be late for my two o'clock with Mere Tora if I stop off to watch. Let's compare notes later,' Singh said.

'Right, Susie. Although I've nothing to compare yet.'

As he approached, the chanting of vigorous male voices joined the drumming. A gap between houses revealed the *rara* further up the slope. The sight gladdened him, even though it didn't help one jot with Vili's murder. He hurried up to the terrace.

Four rows of uniformed schoolboys, older boys and young men behind them, danced and chanted an aggressive *meke* of welcome. Tomasi directed the squad with his police whistle, and teacher Sasa demonstrated the moves at the front. Horseman watched from the sideline. The demands of the *meke* would surely help lift the boys' confusion and grief for Vili.

As the front line advanced, five young men rushed forward, brandishing sticks at Tomasi. Sevu was one of them. But no, not sticks. They were clubs, similar in shape to the murder weapon. Here was something! Impatient as he was, he'd have to wait.

When the rehearsal ended, Horseman approached Sevu. 'That was a scary attack you launched! You lot put on a good show.'

'*Vinaka*, but our hearts aren't really in it.' Sevu looked down.

'You're a brave boy to carry on like this, Sevu. I've come to ask if you remembered anything more about Saturday.'

'No, sorry. I thought about it, like you asked, but I only remember what I told you.' Now he was away from the others, Sevu's face crumpled.

'How about the bang you heard in the night?'

Sevu shook his head, regretful.

Horseman persisted. 'Any odd behaviour since then? Anything you've noticed could be a real help.'

'All I've done is help Mum and Dad with the condolence visits, catch up with work in the plantation. Everyone's been kind.' Sevu wasn't the most alert of boys, but maybe he was right and there had been nothing to notice.

'Your clubs are realistic, pretty impressive!' Horseman said.

Sevu smiled a bit. 'Oh, they're just lightweight mock-ups.'

'Well, you scared me. Who looks after them?'

'Tomasi. But Sasa keeps them at the school. Kids would love to take them home, but he counts them in and out of the storeroom. Strict as.'

'*Vinaka*, Sevu. I mean it when I say we will do everything possible to track down your brother's killer. Everything.' Horseman offered his hand and the boy shook it firmly. Sevu's troubled brown eyes welled over. The tears rolled down his cheeks before he rubbed his face on the sleeve of his tee shirt.

'But you can't bring him back, sir. Not even you. Now I need to help my father. *Moce.*' Sevu headed off in the direction of his house.

***

After Tomasi had put the young schoolboys through their paces again, Horseman walked back to the school with Sasa. Horseman wondered why Tomasi had never made corporal in the force—he seemed to have a talent for drill. He would requisition his service record back at the station.

Sasa carried a sports bag with the props: the clubs and presentation whale's teeth, whittled out of balsa wood. A few boys had charge of the light dancing drums, packed in drawstring bags made from old towels. The rest of the pupils made straight for the school water taps, laughing and jostling a little. Then they moved off to their classrooms without being told.

'They're well-behaved children,' Horseman said.

'*Io*, good kids. They love performing and try very hard. I wish they loved reading and maths as much as singing and dancing. Oh, they love rugby too!'

'Goes without saying,' Horseman agreed.

'I'm from near Labasa myself. Now that's a crowded town, full of schools and children, mostly Indians. There's a lot of competition, parents are ambitious. Sometimes that's not fair on kids, I know, but it toughened me up academically. I saw how much some kids cared about their marks and it made me care too. For these kids, so cut off here and all more or less related, well… a bit of competition could stimulate them more.'

'How long have you been here?'

'Three years. I'm getting married at Christmas. My fiancée's not too keen on coming here to live, so I've applied for a transfer. If I get it, I'll miss Tanoa in a way. It's a different world.'

'Did you know Viliame?'

'Not well. He was only here at weekends, when I often go to see my fiancée in Suva. When we saw each other we would joke about our buses passing on the road on Sundays. He was a great guy. It's amazing how he's got the youth off their backsides and doing something worthwhile. What a loss!' Sasa fell silent.

'As an outside observer, did you notice opposition to Vili's plans for the village?'

'I didn't notice anything, no. I did hear that the clan elders were sitting on his land applications. My guess is that was only to score a point, because he wasn't humble or respectful enough. I can't see how they could oppose growing more cash crops, do you?'

'No. It would serve everyone's interest, you'd think. I hear that people have faith that the mahogany sale will bring them riches.'

'*Io*, but nothing's happened yet. No schedule for logging that I've heard about. I hope it comes to something for Tanoa.'

'Were you here last Saturday night?'

'No, I managed to get away to Suva on Friday afternoon. I came back by bus on Sunday afternoon. I couldn't believe what had happened. I mean, nothing happens here. No crime, let alone murder.'

The boys had deposited their drum bags outside a door in the middle of the classroom block. 'Is this the storeroom?' Horseman asked.

'*Io*, there's stuff in there that's pretty attractive to kids, so we keep a padlock on the door,' Sasa replied. He fished a key from his *sulu* pocket.

The room was narrow, with orderly racks of shelves on both sides and tin trunks underneath. Sturdy hooks were fixed to the end wall, suspending large drawstring bags and some Fiji Army duffel bags. Some of the shelves held folded mats.

Sasa waved his hand. 'Quite a bit of this has nothing to do with the school—it's the property of the clans. There's room to store it safely, so why not? Stacks of good *masi*, sinnet rolls, raffia, dried skeins of palm and grass fibre.' He gestured again. 'I'd better get back to my class.' He hung the drum bags on hooks, put the play clubs and fake whale's teeth inside one of the trunks on the floor, and shut the lid.

'There's plenty of scope for concealing things in here, isn't there? I'll get my SOCO to look over this. Can you leave the key with me please, Sasa?' Horseman held out his hand. Sasa looked surprised but handed it over.

'How many copies are there?' Horseman asked.

'I don't really know, sir. We three teachers each have one, because we don't want it hanging on a hook where a kid could take it. I don't know if anyone else in the village has one.'

'If a lady wants to use *masi* for a special occasion, does she ask one of the teachers to open the store for her?'

'*Io*, that's what usually happens. But I wouldn't know if a villager did have a copy of the key and let themselves in. How could I?'

'You couldn't, Sasa. Don't worry, I don't hold you responsible for the contents of the store.'

Sasa's brow cleared. 'That's a relief. I hadn't thought the key thing through until now. You're right. If we're going to have a key, we need a better system.'

Horseman smiled. 'Can I ask you to think about any time you may have noticed someone going into the storeroom? Apart from the teachers, that is. Here's my card.'

'Do you think it's important, sir?'

'At this stage we don't know. We'll catch this killer in the end, but sooner would be better.'

'*Dina*. I'll do my best, Inspector Horseman.'

19

'*Bula*, Mrs Tora,' Singh called out as she reached the pastor's house beside the church. The door remained shut.

'Ah, Sergeant Singh, *bula vinaka*.' A moment later Mere Tora hurried from behind the house, a laundry basket on her hip. 'Forgive me, I was at my washing line. It looks like rain.' She shook hands and smiled a tense smile. 'Please do come in and have a cup of tea with me.'

Perhaps Mrs Tora needed a cup of tea and a sit-down more than she did herself. 'That would be lovely. *Vinaka*.'

They went inside the cheerful home, which Singh found so much more pleasant than the formality of the chief's house.

'You look like you could use a rest, Mrs Tora. Let me put the kettle on for you.'

The pastor's wife recovered her energy at this challenge. 'Now, now, you mean well, Sergeant, but you are my guest and besides, you don't know where anything is! Please sit yourself down at the table and we'll talk while the kettle boils.'

Singh did as she was told. 'I've just enjoyed your iced banana cake at Ratu Osea's house. So please, I don't need anything more to eat.'

Mrs Tora beamed at her. 'Yes, I like to help Adi Ana when the chief is here. She's not so interested in cooking and entertaining. But you'll definitely need a bit more to get you through the afternoon.'

So, against her better judgement, Singh sipped at her piping hot tea and accepted a dainty coconut macaroon.

'Mrs Tora, I've not been able to talk to you alone before. You're observant, I can tell you've got a pretty good idea about what goes on in the village. Can you tell me about last Saturday night? Just start with what you were doing.'

'Oh my dear, last Saturday seems like a year ago, another age! How can it be just four days ago?' She looked bewildered.

'Maybe just start from what you were doing.'

'Well, Saturday's always busy for us, preparing for our Sunday, which is no day of rest for me, or any of our family!' She sipped her tea before continuing, looking out the window as if it opened on the past,

'In the morning, I was busy with housework. We had leftovers for lunch. You wouldn't understand how this kerosene refrigerator has transformed my life, dear. I hate wasted food, even if it does go to the pigs. But why should the pigs get it if it's still fit for humans, stored in the fridge? Pigs will eat absolutely anything—they don't need my good cooking! Oh, sorry my dear, I'm rambling.'

Singh hastened to reassure her. 'Not at all. I understand completely. I grew up without a fridge in the house.'

'After lunch I got ready for choir practice in the church, as usual.'

'Was anyone missing from choir practice?' Singh asked.

'Kelera didn't go. Vili arrived early, around lunch. The two of them went off to the gardens to meet the other spice workers. It didn't matter, Kelera knows all the hymns. But now I cast my mind back, Tomasi wasn't at practice either.'

Singh noted down everything. Although she had a good memory, the fear that she wouldn't remember a critical detail always nagged her. She wished she was like Horseman, who took few notes and seemed quite relaxed about it.

'And after choir practice?' Singh asked.

'A few other women and I cleaned the church and put fresh flowers in the vases. I replaced the communion table runner with a fresh one, starched and ironed. Then I spent quite some time on food for the Sunday *lovo*. The men like to think they do all the *lovo* work, but really, the women spend a lot of time preparing the vegetables. Sometimes the men expect us to pluck and dress the chickens they kill too. It takes no time to kill a chicken now, does it?'

Singh smiled sympathetically.

Mrs Tora continued. 'I'm always asking myself, "Where does the day God gives us go?" But then I remember He made the days just the right length so we don't get too burdened by our work and forget about Him. Anyway, when I got back here it was twilight. Kelera was already frying some fish so we got our meal early. I baked the soda bread for Sunday. Then our family Bible reading, prayers, and bed.'

'Your children, Mrs Tora? Were they with you all evening?'

'Yes, except for Kelera. She went off with the Tilley lamp to her classroom to prepare her Sunday school lesson. She says it's too noisy to concentrate here, and she's right! My husband says the same—he goes to the church office to read and write his sermons.'

'When did the pastor and Kelera return home?'

'I'm not sure of the time really. When Joni got back he began our Bible reading. Kelera wasn't back before we all went to bed. You'll have to ask her. Why?'

'Vili's killer brought his body to the church sometime during the night, Mrs Tora. The police need to talk to those villagers who were up late. Someone must have seen the killer.'

Mrs Tora shuddered. 'It can be very dark here, Sergeant. I was inside. Joni always notices the sky—when the moon rises and so on. You could ask him.'

'Mrs Tora—Mere, do you have any suspicions at all about who might have killed Vili?'

The pastor's wife, good woman that she was, shook her head sadly. 'I don't.'

'Everyone seems to be aware of conflict between Vili and the clan leaders about his plans for more plantations.'

'Oh sure, he rubbed them up the wrong way, but murder? Never!' Defiance crept into Mere's voice.

'What do you think Vili's death is about, Mrs Tora?'

'What all crimes are about, my dear. Good and evil. The police should think about that more. It's about good and evil. And in this case, evil has killed good. Vili was good. Evil has captured someone here. Satan has made him kill what was good.' Her voice quavered and she wept.

Mrs Tora's fervour impressed Singh. She'd been asking herself whether she should tell Kelera's mother about her daughter and Vili. Now, sitting opposite the quietly weeping woman, Singh didn't have the heart. Mrs Tora might well be right about Satan. But as a police officer, she must find the human being who had done evil. For that she needed hard evidence.

20

Horseman couldn't raise Ash on the radio. Maybe the search team was in the spice gardens over the ridge and out of range. Ridiculous! The rollout of the new, more powerful radios couldn't come too soon. He could either go back over the bridge to their vehicle and try the stronger radio, or walk over the ridge. He decided to walk.

'I'll follow you, sir,' Singh said when he radioed his plan to her. 'I've just left Mere Tora. Speak to you soon.'

As he walked along the lower path to the plantations, Horseman felt slightly cheered by his talk with Sasa. He was a bright young man, with a cooperative attitude. There was a good chance he'd retrieve from his memory any incident involving the storeroom. If there'd been one, that is.

He gave the radio another try. This time Ash responded. 'Ash, sir. Just about to call you. We've got something here. In the bracken, between the top path and the lower one. Over.'

'Right. On the lower path now. I'll wait for Sergeant Singh to catch up. Sing out when you see us.' He turned and looked back over the village. Distance made it picturesque: the scattering of steep thatched roofs, some smothered in bougainvillea and allamanda, the blue-and-white of the schoolchildren running, now released for the day, and the grass so green. Further off loomed the dark stone keep of the old fortress. He'd like to prowl around there one day when he had enough time.

By the time Singh caught up, ominous clouds were rolling in.

They left the track and headed diagonally up the slope through bracken, lantana, and grass. Horseman stopped, gave a piercing whistle, and waved. The searchers yelled back. They were higher up on the right. He glimpsed the scarlet of Musudroka's Tribal Surfer tee shirt, then all four searchers came into view.

'What've you got?' Horseman asked. 'The weapon?'

'No, but something, we think. What do you reckon?'

The searchers stepped back to reveal a trampled area two metres in diameter, screened from view by creeping lantana. Someone had removed the brittle old wood from the central space and carpeted it with bracken. Whoever had made this hideout wanted to be comfortable for longish periods and on repeated occasions.

Singh dropped to a crouch, rotating on her haunches. 'See, he's made spyholes. Let's check what he was spying on. Ash, can you see me when I look out?' She put her face to one of the small gaps in the thicket.

Ash checked from different angles. 'No, if I didn't know you were there, I certainly wouldn't suspect anything. It's a nice cave, isn't it?'

Musudroka spoke up, excited. 'See what's been going on in there?' He waved an evidence bag in front of Horseman.

'Ah yes, smoking. Looks like roll-your-own.' He opened the bag and sniffed. 'Imported tobacco, not home-grown leaves. But we'll leave that to Forensics to rule on. Anything else?'

Proud Musudroka passed over some more bags. There were fabric scraps, a button, and a black plastic lid.

Horseman said, 'My guess is a lens cap from a pair of binoculars. This is a regular birdwatcher's hide!' He smiled at Musudroka's obvious confusion. 'Just joking, Tani. What was he watching?' He turned to Singh. 'I think our watcher is a man, don't you?'

'I think so, sir,' Singh agreed. 'Village women wouldn't have time to spend hours on end spying. There's a view to both the upper and lower paths. You can't see the paths from the hideout unless you stand up, which would defeat the purpose. But you can certainly see any adult walking past, from the waist up, at least.'

Horseman dropped down beside Singh and checked. He didn't wince. His knee hadn't let him down all day. Maybe it was going to be okay. 'You've left nothing behind?' He examined the bracken and the tangled lantana hedge, just to be sure. Then he pushed himself up with his hands to be on the safe side of embarrassment.

'And our biggest prize—one bush knife.' Ash grinned and handed over a large brown paper bag. Horseman and Singh looked in. The first warning drops of rain fell.

'He must have needed to do some trimming from time to time. How long do you think this has been here?' Horseman asked.

'I really don't know, sir.'

'When can we expect results on these, Ash?'

'I'll do all I can, sir.'

'*Vinaka*, Ash, I know you will.' Horseman smiled. 'And I've got another search field for you. It's indoors, what's more! Could you please conduct a thorough search of the school's storeroom? The one where the *meke* props and paraphernalia are kept. Here's the key. I noticed the boys rehearsing this afternoon with model war clubs. They're kept in a tin trunk on the floor. I know it's only a slim chance Vili's murder weapon is there, but we have to check. Who knows what else you might turn up? Have a look around the classrooms and office too. Get the teachers to open up any cupboards big enough for the club. Anything else today, boys?'

'We've bagged bits of rubbish, sir. I can't see it'll be of any use, but it's going back to the lab. We could keep searching forever, you know how it is. But in the absence of more evidence, I wouldn't recommend continuing the search, sir. Not unless you want us to search all the village houses?' Ash sounded hopeful.

'No evidence justifying a warrant yet, Ash. Sorry. Keep going at the school until you're satisfied. Can you give your apprentice Tanielo here a lift back to Suva?' Musudroka looked pleased. Ah, the energy of the young!

'Sergeant Singh and I have a couple more interviews, then we'll head off. Well done, all of you! *Moce mada.*'

The searchers hurried off, cut leaves from the nearest banana trees, and strolled towards the school beneath their makeshift umbrellas.

***

Horseman and Singh were thoroughly wet when they got back to the Land Cruiser.

'Ash and the team are pushing things along better than we are, Susie. I got nothing from those last interviews. Do you reckon those kids really have no suspicions?'

'Can't tell. Probably they don't want to tell us about them if they're just speculation. I can understand that.'

'Yes, of course you're right.'

Horseman drove the vehicle out of the car park and around the bend of the rutted gravel road leading away from Tanoa. 'I'll be glad to get back to Suva in daylight for once. It's depressing leaving and returning in the dark,' he remarked for no particular reason.

'I got nothing from our lunch with the chief and his headman apart from *yaqona* and food. Ratu Osea is affable, but he doesn't give anything away, and Ilai's a man of few words, isn't he? The most taciturn headman I've ever met. He's supposed to be the chief's spokesman!'

Horseman chuckled, remembering the stilted conversation. 'Yes, but that's not a crime. I reckon one of them is behind Triple C, maybe both. We've got to hammer away to get evidence. Or get lucky.'

'Some luck, please,' Singh said fervently.

Horseman smiled. 'Vili's brother Sevu couldn't tell me anything more. I can't see that young man filling Vili's shoes. But he'll try and who knows? Once a leader goes, another emerges, often an unlikely one. How did you get on with Mrs Tora?'

'Her interpretation is that evil has killed good. She didn't tell me anything helpful. I wondered if she knew about Kelera and Vili, but didn't have the heart to ask. It seemed like breaking confidence with Kelera, even though I didn't promise not to tell. She thinks the world of Vili, as everyone else seems to.'

'Except at least one person, who hated him.' Horseman sighed. 'I really wish I could have been harder with Ratu Osea and Ilai. But I just couldn't, not in the chief's home, eating his food, being treated as an honoured guest! Our respectful behaviour to chiefs is so ingrained, so hard to overcome, even when our official duty demands that we suspect everyone equally. Now Tomasi is a retired police officer, but I'd be less shocked if he turned out to be a murderer than if it was Ratu Osea. Isn't that crazy?'

Horseman found he needed Singh's logic and practicality more and more. He trusted her enough to use her as a sounding board for his own speculations. He didn't know why he hadn't told her Melissa was arriving for a holiday on Friday. He should. He must. Apart from the super, he hadn't told anyone yet.

21

Melissa said her goodbyes to her colleagues and left the hospital. She smiled to herself, touched by their excitement for her. Tomorrow she'd spend in airports and in the air, arriving in Nadi, Fiji early on Friday morning, skipping almost a day in the process. Always jittery before a flight, she decided to walk home to settle her nerves.

The walk didn't really help. She fumbled the key in the lock. Her hand trembled as she poured her camomile tea and carried it through to her bedroom. The open suitcase, neatly packed, reassured her some. There was really nothing more to be done that would take more than five minutes. She kicked off her shoes and padded into the living room, sat on the sofa to drink her tea, and tried to relax.

She pulled the coffee table closer, put her tea down and her feet up, stuffed a cushion behind her head, and closed her eyes. When that didn't work, she couldn't resist picking up the wallet from the table and checking each item: passport, Fiji visa, vaccination record, air ticket and itinerary, printed in duplicate, US$500 emergency cash, the compact Fiji information brochure the embassy had sent her. All there. She had to talk to Joe one more time.

She made an omelette with her last two eggs and ate it with odd remnants of salad vegetables. It was now 8:00 p.m. on Tuesday in Oregon, so only 3:00 p.m. on Wednesday in Fiji. Far too early!

But she sent him a text anyway: 'Skype in 2 hrs?' She waited, tried to distract herself by cleaning out the fridge. She switched on the

CNN news, but nothing registered. It was eleven when her phone rang. She snatched it up. 'Ready now?' Good, Joe must be home early, she knew he'd never Skype at the station. She tapped in to video call, tried to relax her face.

'Hey Joe, how's it going? I can't see you yet.'

'Hang on, okay now?' His voice warmed her. Then his face came into focus. As usual, he looked tired out, but she could tell he was happy to see her.

'I'm all set, honey, checked everything a zillion times. I can't wait to be with you!'

He smiled, his eyes crinkling. 'Me too!'

'How's your case going, Joe?'

He sighed. 'No breakthrough today, Melissa. We've got our suspicions, but no evidence yet. We're waiting on forensic results, goes without saying. This killer is organised and careful. Communications are limited and we spend a lot of time travelling to and from the scene. It's the usual story here—everyone's cooperative, but they either know nothing or they're keeping it to themselves.'

'Joe, this isn't a good time for me to come. I can still change my tickets. I don't want to get in your way. That's the last thing I want.'

'I know, darling. You're a saint. My job's unpredictable. But we agreed last night, if you postpone, there's no guarantee I'll be free later. I want you to come. Please.'

'Whatever you want. I know you can't let your team down, honey.'

'We'll handle it somehow. I've got the super's support. Don't look so worried, Melissa.'

She didn't want to go on and on. He wouldn't like that. She put on what she hoped was an enthusiastic face. 'Okay, let's do it, Joe!'

He looked relieved. 'That's my gal!' he said in his hopeless attempt at an American accent. Melissa laughed.

'I promise I'll be at Suva airport to meet you. The super insists.'

'Right. I'll call you when I land in Nadi. While I wait for the plane to Suva.'

'Can't wait, darling. Good flight.'

'I will. I love planes,' she lied. 'Love you too, Joe.'

'Now I find out I have to compete with planes! I don't think I'll win. *Moce mada*, Melissa.' His handsome face vanished.

She went to bed but lay there, worrying about her competitors: his job, his family, colleagues, and possibly most of all, a clever murderer.

THURSDAY

22

It was nine o'clock in the morning. Singh and Ash had already given succinct reports on what Horseman already knew. He stared at the whiteboard. The incident timeline was distressingly sparse, and the connecting links between the names and attached photos were few indeed. Nevertheless, he valued case review meetings. Face-to-face was far more productive than phone conferencing and emails. More motivating too, just like half-time in a rugby game.

'Sergeant Taleca, time for you to tell us what you've been doing here in the back room while we've been tramping about the hills.'

Kelepi Taleca ducked his head to conceal his pleasure at being addressed as *Sergeant.* 'Boss! I've not been slacking in the back room, not at all. We still don't know exactly what Vili suspected was amiss at the NLTB. However, given he was murdered, there is no problem with us seizing any files and computers we decide are relevant under Fiji Commission Against Corruption legislation. That's FICAC to you!' He pulled out a sheaf of papers and waved them back and forth. 'So, these warrants will be executed today at NLTB. They're for Vili's own working files, and all those he signed out for his projects during the past year. We'll also seize all files related to Tanoa village and the district.'

Backs straightened, all the officers alerted by the prospect of action.

'I spoke to the Secretary of the Provincial Council, who has arranged our access to Council files related to Tanoa. We can pick them up later today.'

'Well done, Sergeant,' Horseman said, leading the clapping.

Taleca stood and bowed. 'It's a lot of reading, boss. Fortunately, two officers from the Financial Crimes Unit are going to be working on this full-time. At least one FICAC accountant, too. They'll get it moving along.'

'Even better,' Horseman said.

The super appeared in the doorway while Taleca was speaking. Everyone jumped to their feet.

'Superintendent Navala, please take the floor, sir,' Horseman said. They were all keen to hear where the super had got with Triple C.

Navala gestured for them to sit down. 'Unlike DS Taleca, I regret I have not been successful in my mission.' Shoulders slumped in disappointment; only Singh's posture remained alert.

'I met with the deputy commissioner, confident he would release the Cultural Properties Unit's files to us when I filled him in on the facts of our case and the certainty that the two cases are connected. I am disappointed that he refused us access. However, I won't give up. I firmly believe we have a right to that information. I would certainly give the IO of an overlapping case access to our files, if the boot was on the other foot. There you have it.'

'What can we do, sir?' Singh asked.

'I will pursue the matter, Sergeant. I have an appointment this evening with the commissioner. If that fails, I don't know. Does anyone know the president?'

'I don't, sir. But my wife might know his wife. Will that do?' Taleca looked serious.

The others laughed, and even the super smiled. 'I'm sure it will. Please ask Mrs Taleca on my behalf, Sergeant.'

'Okay troops, jobs for today and tomorrow,' Horseman said, rubbing his hands together.

The super interrupted. 'Excuse me, I think you have a general announcement to make, Detective Inspector. Now would be the best time, I think.'

Horseman looked at the curious faces. He had already decided to send the team an email. The coward's way out, especially as most would be out of the station all day and wouldn't get the message. The super was right, it was time to come clean.

'*Vinaka* for the reminder, sir. On Friday, a friend of mine from the States is arriving for a holiday in Fiji.' Could he avoid mentioning the sex of his friend? Not really. 'Melissa's visit was planned months ago, and Superintendent Navala approved my leave. However, as you know, serious crimes, although not frequent in Fiji, thank God, are completely unpredictable. Clearly, I can't take that leave now.'

He had their full attention. 'Our super has ordered me to take one day's leave tomorrow. Therefore I won't be able to go to Viliame's funeral at Tanoa. Sergeant Singh will attend with Musudroka and discreetly continue enquiries there.

'As for today, Sergeants Singh and Taleca will take charge of our social visit to the NLTB. As soon as we get the stuff back here, we'll start work on the files under the direction of the experts. Except for DS Singh, who plans to talk to Vili's NLTB colleagues again. What support have you arranged, Keli?'

'Boss, we've got a Finance Unit guy and an IT expert, and two uniforms to fetch, carry, and guard. Enough, do you reckon?'

'Good job, Keli. Let's hope our raid will be a surprise.'

They sprang to their feet. Everyone welcomed the excitement of an office raid. Dramatic action but little risk.

***

When the super forced him to tell the team about Melissa's visit, reality smacked Horseman in the face. In spite of Navala's support, any number of things could happen with the case to prevent him being at the airport on time. He'd been in denial. Of course he needed support and backup. Well, he knew who to call. And his mother had to find out sometime.

Come to think of it, she was staying in Lautoka right now with his elder sister Julia. As Lautoka was only half an hour's drive from Fiji's main airport at Nadi, she was ideally placed.

He tried his sister's home phone. No luck. The kids would be at school, so perhaps his mother and sister were out somewhere together. He called the mobile phone he'd given her as a present. For some time Mrs Sala Horseman had held this gift, so desirable to the rest of the world, in disdain. He didn't blame her, as she often paid extended visits to relatives in villages out of mobile service range. Not only that, but for years she had worked as a rural district nurse, where telephones did not exist. This independence had stayed with her all her life. But against the odds, she was now warming to the mobile phone, even starting to use the text function.

This time his mother did not reply to her mobile. So Horseman left a voice message and a text. He was confident she'd be in contact before the day was out.

23

Samu was late. Singh sat at a central table in the Sunshine Food Court nursing a paper cup of chai tea and waiting. She had a good view through the two open sides to the footpaths on Carnarvon and Loftus streets.

She'd been bowled over by the boss's announcement about his leave. A bit amused too. Navala clearly bulldozed him into telling the team. She respected Horseman's need for privacy, but—an American girlfriend!

Samu's tall bulk flopped onto the chair opposite her. He must have entered through the door to the office premises at the back.

Samu puffed. '*Bula*, Sergeant Singh. Sorry I'm late.'

'No worries, Samu. Would you like a cold drink maybe?'

'A Coke, please. But I haven't got much time, I've got to catch a bus. I mustn't miss my class at FIT at four o'clock. I'm allowed to leave work early for that, but there's not much spare time.'

'I'll get it now. You gather your thoughts,' Singh said hastily.

When she returned with the icy Coke, Samu held the bottle to his face and rolled it over his skin before unscrewing the cap and taking a long swig.

'*Vinaka*, I needed that.'

'You're welcome, Samu.' She gave him a moment to settle. He was clearly stressed.

'You may as well have thrown a bomb in the NLTB today,' Samu said resentfully. 'You really shook us all up. No one knew what was happening.'

Singh gloated inside, but she kept her face serious. The raid had indeed gone quite well. She still wasn't sure whether the calm response of Ratu Sirilo when she presented the warrants was due to his chiefly need to be calm in crisis or whether he'd been tipped off.

'How are things now? Settled back to work this afternoon?' Singh asked.

'Guess so. Sorta. But it's hard to focus. The files that were taken, for example—it seemed like tons of them when the police carted out the boxes. But only a couple of people were working on them actively. We've still got access to the central server. It's just the shock, I guess. Why didn't you tell us you needed those files? I'm sure Ratu Sirilo would have handed over whatever you needed.'

Now was not the time to teach Samu about police procedure. 'It does seem impolite, Samu, for sure. However, you'll understand that warning criminals that we're coming to search and seize their property could give them time to get rid of the very evidence we need. That would jeopardise justice, don't you think?'

'Sure, with criminals. But this is the NLTB!' He drained his Coke.

'Your loyalty does you proud, Samu.' No need to remind him of the number of NLTB officers or board members who'd been charged with theft or fraud in the last decade. Hardly any of them led to a conviction, so Samu probably felt they were victims of malice.

'The NLTB protects Fijian lands.' Samu sounded confident.

'Yes, it's a very important job.' Neither was it the time to remind him the board had failed to protect Indian lessees a few short years ago.

'Samu, when we met on Tuesday you recalled Vili was concerned about something he'd come across at work. Have you remembered more about that?'

Samu brightened. 'I followed your suggestion, and I was amazed that more of what he said did come back to me, little by little. But not in as much detail as I hoped.' He looked rueful and apologetic again. Singh waited until he was ready, suppressing her desire to give him a shake.

Samu began again. 'It's probably not enough for you, but I remember waiting at his desk one day when we were going to FIT together. He said something like, "You know, mahogany roots invade everything," sounding worried. We were running a bit late, so I didn't ask him what he meant. Do you think this has anything to do with his murder?'

'I don't know yet. It's a piece of the puzzle, and each piece helps. Before long we'll understand who killed Vili and why. Anything else you can tell me?'

'Another time, we were doing an assignment together in the canteen at FIT, sharing a Coke. Vili was looking like he was far away—he did that a lot recently. Then he said, "I just saw my great grandfather's name in a file. What a shock." I asked him what he found, and he just said, "I don't know if it's true, I can't believe it can be true." Something like that. He didn't want to say anything more, so we went back to our assignment. That's it. Sorry I'm not much use.'

'Samu, what you've told me may prove very useful indeed. It tells me quite a bit about what was troubling Vili these last months. *Vinaka vakalevu.*'

Samu looked down, blushing. 'I have to run now, Sergeant Singh. Sorry.'

'That's fine, Samu. I'm very grateful. Please, don't hesitate to phone me if you remember more.'

'*Vinaka. Moce*, Sergeant.' He hefted his backpack onto his shoulders and hurried off, knocking over a chair on his way.

The first bars of the Fiji national anthem interrupted her thoughts. She picked up her phone hastily.

'May I speak to Sergeant Singh, please?' The voice was soft, uncertain, but Singh recognised it straight away.

'Is that Kelera? This is Susie Singh. Where are you?'

'I'm ringing from the Kumi police post. I want to speak to you. I'll be able to come to Suva tomorrow, after the funeral. School has been cancelled for the day. Could I see you then?'

'Can you tell me what it's about now? If you think it might be important, the sooner I know the better.'

'Of course, I understand, but that's not possible. Not now.' Kelera was almost whispering.

'I will be at Tanoa tomorrow, Kelera. DC Musudroka and I will be attending Viliame's funeral as police representatives. I can talk with you either before or after the funeral, or both. Will that be okay?'

'I hope so, but I'm not sure. Let's see how it goes.' Her whisper dropped even lower so Singh could barely hear. 'I need to get away from here. Maybe I'll come to Suva anyway. For the weekend.'

'We'll speak tomorrow, Kelera. I understand it's difficult for you right now. See you then.'

'See you tomorrow,' Kelera whispered.

Singh was worried. It was natural Kelera was reluctant to speak at the police post, where she could be overheard. But Singh had detected a note of real fear in her soft whisper. What or who was she scared of?

24

Could he miss Junior Shiners' training this afternoon? No, he just had to make it. Sifting through the seized NLTB files under the direction of the forensic accountant was important, but he knew his skills in this area were average at best. He could contribute no more to this task than any other conscientious detective. Besides, he had to admit that worrying about Melissa's arrival was disturbing his focus. He managed to get two more officers from Financial Crimes seconded to his team starting from tomorrow. That was the most useful thing he could do.

He arrived at Albert Park on time, and managed a light jog across to the grandstand to the cheers and hoots of the ragtag assembly of Shiners.

'Eeeeh, Josefa Horseman. You come today!'

'Watch me, coach, watch me! I been training, coach!'

Tevita stood apart, quiet. Back in January, when Horseman returned from the US, Tevita had urged his hero to revive the fledgling team that had fallen apart the previous year. The boy felt responsible for getting the Shiners going again, and he was right.

'Tevita, are you okay? You're not getting sick, are you?'

He beamed at being singled out by his hero. 'No, Joe. I'm tough. You know. Where you been, Joe? I don't see you around the streets all week.'

'You don't miss much, do you, Tevita?' The boy looked even more pleased with himself. 'You're right. I've got a case in the hills.

I've been up there a lot. But I came back so I could come to training today.'

Another cheer went up. Musudroka walked in with another volunteer cop, looking surprised to see Horseman already there. 'Glad you could make it, sir.'

'Right, let's get these champions moving,' Horseman shouted. 'DC Musudroka will lead off round the oval. Who can overtake him?'

Musudroka grabbed a ball and set off at an easy lope, increasing his pace when any boy passed him. Horseman marked the finish line with the kit bags. Musudroka touched down, then leapt up, waving his arms in triumph. All the boys threw themselves over the imaginary line, each scoring a try in his imagination.

'Don't wind yourselves before you get started boys. Twenty push-ups now. Let's grow those shoulders! One...'

Not all the boys could make the twenty, but each tried his utmost. That's what Horseman found rewarding and yes, even touching about these street kids. They had rough lives, some kicked out of their homes, some beaten or neglected. Marginally criminal. Yet show them some positive discipline, admit them to the magic circle of a rugby team, and they would do anything for you, anything.

'Right, Shiners. Form your passing lines, four in a row. Up to the centre line, then back. Steady pace now. Stay in your lines!' The two volunteers jogged along beside the first and last lines, yelling instructions. The jagged lines started to straighten.

His phone rang. '*Bula*, Josefa. I got your messages.'

How happy he was to hear her low, firm voice. '*Bula vinaka*, Mum. How are you?'

'*Io*, I'm well, as always. More to the point, how are you Joe? Is anything the matter?'

'Fine too. I've got a demanding case up in the hills. The timing couldn't be worse. I hope you can help me, Mum.'

'Happy to help, son. Is there some information you're seeking?' Her voice betrayed her eagerness. She'd been delighted to supply a vital piece of information in his first murder case, on Paradise Island resort.

'Not yet.' He drew in a deep breath. 'I have a visitor arriving at Nadi tomorrow. A friend from the States. She's got three hours to wait until her flight to Suva. I hope you may be free to meet her and look after her a bit, put her on the next flight, and so on.'

He'd managed to get it out. He knew what was coming next.

'Of course I will, Joe. Nothing I'd like better. But son, why are you telling me this now? With a few days' notice, I could rally the family around, put on a proper welcome, maybe a *lovo* at your sister's here. She could stay overnight at least, we could give her a whirlwind tour of the west before sending her on to Suva!'

'Sir?' Musudroka enquired. All the boys were back, looking expectant.

'Excuse me a moment, Mum.'

He yelled at the boys. 'Twice more up and down, Shiners. There's nothing more important than coordinated passing. DC Musudroka will let you try it faster when you're more accurate. Off you go, now.'

'Sorry. I'm at training, as you probably heard.'

'*Io* son, I'm proud of you for helping those rascals, you know. But I do need to know all about your friend. For a start, what's her name?'

'Melissa Martini. She's a physical therapist at the rehab centre at Portland Hospital where I had my knee operation.'

'Oh good, a physio, a fellow health professional. We'll have a lot to talk about. I like her already. But I surmise she's more than your therapist if she's chasing you all the way to Fiji!'

'Mum, don't tease, please. She's not chasing me anywhere. And you wonder why I didn't tell you? To avoid this interrogation, naturally.'

'Now who's teasing? Never mind, Joe. I'm sure Melissa Martini will tell me all I want to know tomorrow morning.'

'She'll probably be very tired. Go easy on her, Mum.'

'My word, I hardly need instruction in how to look after guests, do I? Don't worry son, I'll give her the royal treatment.'

'I know you will. *Vinaka vakalevu*. I'll text you the flight numbers and times after training. I'm going back to the station for more desk work.'

'Don't worry about that. Nadi's not LA. As you know, there are only three flights a week from the States. Julia's friend works at the airport. I'll get an update from her tonight. She'll let me know about any delays, too.'

He couldn't argue with the sensible Fijian way.

'What I do need is a photo, however,' Mrs Horseman continued. 'I'll make a sign with her name and hold that. But it would be good to recognise her. Julia has a laptop, so you could email Melissa's photo to her. I suppose you've got your sister's email address?'

'*Io*, sounds like you've made a lot of progress with the digital revolution.'

Mrs Horseman snorted. 'Digital revolution! These computer people do big-note themselves! They're just machines aren't they? Handy ones, too. Julia's been showing me a few tricks.'

'Great stuff! I'll send her the photo when I get back to the office and I'll text Melissa to let her know you'll meet her. I'm really grateful and Melissa will be too. Sorry I didn't let you know sooner.'

'No surprise there! *Moce*, Joe.'

Horseman turned his attention back to the Shiners and the passing drill. Their improvement was undeniable.

He shouted encouragement. '*Bula, bula, bula*! That's more like it. We'll have ten minutes dodging practice before our break. If you improve, your reward will be a full-scale Sevens practice game. Any objections?'

Amid more hoots, the trainers sorted out the trios for dodging practice. Horseman felt content for the first time since he got the call about the murder at Tanoa village. Helping the boys? He hoped so, but most of all he was helping himself, so how could he take any credit?

***

When Horseman returned to the station, he sent the team home.

'Get some sleep, and come back bright in the morning. Sergeant Singh and Tani will leave early for Tanoa. However, two extra experienced DCs from Financial Crimes are joining us. They'll really speed our progress with these NLTB files. I'll push on for a while here. Early as you like in the morning.'

He set himself up with his tray of files on his left, his meal of leftovers from the Shiners' dinner parcels provided unfailingly by Dr Pillai. Horseman smiled when he thought how proud the boys were to belong to a team with their own doctor. The food was simple, but good. This evening it was boiled dalo and yams, a few little tomatoes, and some snake beans. A small handful of roughly chopped chicken, a real treat for the boys, completed the meal.

Horseman ate slowly, checking methodically through the file as the forensic accountant had instructed. Nothing to note so far. He suspected the accountant had reserved for his own team the files he thought were most likely to show irregularities. Nevertheless, they had been selected because they had passed through Vili's hands or related to Tanoa and district lands, so each one had to be combed through. It was the thought that in these files may lie a clue to the motive for Vili's murder that kept Horseman pushing through the tedium of the repetitive task.

He took a few minutes to make a mug of tea to drink with the bananas that Dr Pillai always supplied. He thought about Kelera's whispered phone call to Singh. Kelera had sounded worried, maybe frightened. Did she know who the killer was, and did the killer suspect that she knew? It seemed the most likely reason for her fear.

Singh said Kelera might simply have been concerned about her lack of privacy in telephoning from the police post. He agreed, but had niggling doubts. He felt like rushing off to Tanoa this evening, but knew that would be foolish and almost impossible. Singh had acted correctly. He was glad she'd confided in him about the hint of fear in Kelera's voice, but he mustn't overreact.

He'd just started on the file again, banana in hand and tea by his elbow, when in walked Superintendent Navala. He greeted Horseman with a nod and a tired smile. '*Bula*, Joe. Still at it?'

Horseman stood up and shrugged. 'I won't be able to put in a full day tomorrow, sir, so…'

'Joe, you have leave tomorrow. We will carry on without you. We might even make progress, you never know.'

'*Io*, sir.' He smiled. 'No one's indispensable, least of all me.'

'I've just come from the commissioner. He gave me a good dinner in his office suite too. Served by a constable at his conference table. A first for me. Do you want the good news or the bad news first?'

'The good, please.'

'We've got access to the Chatterjee files, at last.'

'Fantastic, sir. I just about gave up on that one.'

'Never give up, Joe, that's the lesson from this. I was so mad I took it all the way to the top. I probably should have done that more often in my career. Would have been more successful.'

'I'd say any police superintendent is by definition successful,' Horseman said awkwardly.

'*Vinaka*, but I realise that it's only now, when I'm about to retire and have nothing to lose, that I have the courage of my convictions. That's far from ideal, don't you think?'

Horseman simply didn't know how to respond to the super's confiding in him like this.

'But I'm embarrassing you, Joe.'

'Not at all sir. I'm privileged to hear your thoughts. What about the bad news?'

'Ah yes. When I said *we* have access, that's literally it. You and me only. No digital files, just the paper. The files don't leave my office. They're the original files, no photocopies or scans to be made.'

'Inconvenient, but I can live with that. I can't wait. When do we get them?'

'Eight o'clock tomorrow morning. I was promised that. If they're not here then, I'll give it half an hour, then go in person to collect them. I'd like that.'

What a boost to Horseman's spirits! 'I feel better already. I'll finish the file I'm on now, then call it a night, sir. I'll happily hand over the rest to the DCs from the Finance Unit tomorrow. I'll be here before eight o'clock, just in case the top-secret Chatterjee files arrive early.'

He meant what he'd just said. He was honoured to have such a rare glimpse into the super's personal thoughts on the eve of his retirement. He would help his boss all he could.

FRIDAY

25

They hadn't expected Detective Inspector Chatterjee to deliver the files himself. But at twenty past eight, Reception called Horseman to announce DI Chatterjee's arrival. Horseman met him at the top of the stairs.

He was equally surprised by Chatterjee's appearance. The head of the Cultural Properties Unit was a slender man of Horseman's own height, who seemed both too young and far too well-dressed to be a policeman. He couldn't imagine Chatterjee in uniform. His long, straight hair was brushed back and tucked behind his ears. Some sort of gel must keep it in place. His neat moustache and goatee lengthened his face, while small, gold-rimmed spectacles added a scholarly quality. The linen suit and emerald shirt fitted him like a glove. A constable followed him, carrying just one archive box.

They introduced themselves. Chatterjee offered his hand but did not return Horseman's firm grip.

'Thank you for bringing the files yourself, Inspector Chatterjee. Superintendent Navala's office is just along the hallway.'

'As you know, I didn't want them out of my safekeeping. I certainly won't trust anyone else to deliver them. I may not ever see them again, the number of idiots about.'

Horseman knocked on the super's door and made the introductions. A constable brought tea.

Navala began. 'We do appreciate this opportunity for a briefing, Inspector. This is a bonus. What do you make of this rare kind of theft?'

'It is unusual in Fiji, sir, I agree. But not so if we take the global view. I'm fortunate enough to have experience both in my unit's counterpart in India, and in UNESCO in Paris. The scale of illicit trafficking of cultural property is mind-boggling, absolutely mind-boggling. How does US\$ 6 billion a year sound to you?'

'I agree, that's mind-boggling, Inspector. How does our little Fiji Museum's missing war club fit into this global scene?' Navala asked.

'Sir, because the club is the only item taken, indications are that it was stolen to order. The source of the order would be either a private collector in America, Europe, or even China, with a specific interest in pre-colonial Fijian weapons, or a crooked dealer who would sell the item on to legitimate museums keen to extend their collections in this area.'

'What would the price of our club be, d'you know?'

Chatterjee inhaled audibly through his teeth. 'Substantial, substantial, not only because of its quality, but its provenance. Cannibal weapons proven to have killed Christian missionaries carry a prurient attraction, inflating an already-high price due to rarity. It could be limited only by the collector's degree of obsession.'

Horseman seriously doubted this, but knew nothing to contradict Chatterjee's claims. This was a new world to him.

Navala continued. 'Have you identified any dealers involved in smuggling Fijian artefacts?'

'Not as such. That is why this case is so vital. It's the first instance of theft of a cultural treasure since my unit was set up, that we're aware of, that is. Who knows, it could be just the tip of the iceberg, so to speak.' He shook his head dolefully.

'What has been the focus of your unit, generally speaking?' Horseman asked.

Chatterjee leaned forward, eager. 'I've set up a specific database to register stolen objects, on the model of the Italian Carabinieri. Theirs has two million entries. Two million! I'm liaising with the Fiji Museum, the university, and overseas institutions to develop a complete catalogue of Fiji cultural items held in their collections.

This will take some time, but I've made a start.' It was easy to see this last project was his true passion.

'It's exciting to take up a new challenge, isn't it?' Navala commented diplomatically. Chatterjee nodded.

Horseman indicated the archive box on the super's cupboard. 'Did you get any leads on the club from the museum staff?'

'Sadly, no. Short of a confession, what can you do? No one saw anything amiss until the morning cleaner found the display case key in the lock.'

'Did the SOCOs find anything—fingerprints?'

'Negative again. I concluded it was a professional job. It all points to transborder trafficking.'

'Did you explore possible local motives for the theft?' Navala asked.

'The only one is the greed motive. It's galling that 98 percent of the final purchase price of stolen cultural property is retained by middlemen. Our petty thieves or corrupt museum staff are accepting small change in return for risking their liberty. That's if locals did carry out the burglary.'

'So, what did you concentrate on, Inspector?' Navala persisted.

'In line with my training, sir, I've approached the problem from the receiving end. I've set up alerts through Interpol and UNESCO databases. I scan acquisitions of overseas museums, particularly those with noted Oceania collections. I also scrutinise auction and sale catalogues of the major art dealers. If the club's offered for sale, I'm confident I'll learn about it quick smart.' Chatterjee leaned back again and re-crossed his legs.

'And if it was stolen to order by a private collector? The other possibility you told us about?' Horseman continued.

Chatterjee frowned. 'Yes, in that case, we'll probably never see nor hear of it again.' He paused. 'Although strange recoveries have occurred. Did you know 265 items from the museum in Corinth, Greece were seized from a fish warehouse in Miami last year? So, there is hope.'

He withdrew an A4 buff envelope from his briefcase and handed it to Navala. 'This is a receipt for my files and an agreement about the conditions of their release. I understand you've already agreed to them verbally with the commissioner. Sir, could you please sign both copies and return one to me?'

'Of course. I don't fully understand the need for these conditions, but I will certainly comply with them as I have already agreed. I do understand the importance of your work, however.'

'I'm grateful, Detective Superintendent. I hope the files help your own case. Please get in contact when you no longer need them, and I'll come to pick them up.' He offered his hand to both men, straightened his jacket, and departed.

The super shook his head. 'Back to work on his database with one entry, I suppose. Do you think he brought them himself because he's got so little to do, Joe?'

'Oh, I don't know, sir. Every database begins with a single entry, doesn't it? Don't forget there's all that liaising with international stakeholders. He'd be burning the midnight oil with that.' They both laughed, Horseman's first good laugh of the week. Come to think of it, he'd never before witnessed the super laughing. Ever. It took a while for their tension-busting chuckle to subside.

'I shouldn't laugh, Joe. These days, I spend at least half my time in what's called liaising. Glad I didn't get any higher, or it'd be all my time, eh?'

'Did you get Chatterjee's story from the commissioner?'

'I did. Father has a garage in Lautoka which does well. Seems he's a graduate in fine arts and archaeology from New Zealand, and it's true, he did an internship with UNESCO in Paris. He worked in India too, but not with the police. It was with the Delhi Museum. He was sussing out a job at our museum when he returned to visit his family. The South Pacific Forum has been talking about doing something about protecting cultural property in the region, so our commissioner thought he'd beat the forum to it, rather than follow some future policy they dictated. So he created the Cultural

Properties Unit. Bright boy presents himself and gets taken on, reporting directly to the DC. Does his basic police training, then CID, and within the year he's a DI and head of the unit. Which consists, by the way, of himself and two constables.'

'He's convinced of his own importance, that's for sure. As you say, he's bright enough. I hope we can unearth some treasure from his files. But I liked him, you know. He's one of the very few people I've met since I came home who hasn't pumped my hand for a minute and told me how sorry he was I couldn't play rugby anymore.'

The super gave him a shrewd look. What did that mean? Maybe that he was being egotistical. He shouldn't have shared that.

Superintendent Navala weighed the box in his arms before handing it to Horseman. 'I reckon there's not more than a day's work in here, but let's see.'

They cleared the super's desk, divided the files between them, and started work in companionable silence.

26

Horseman arrived at the shabby little terminal at Nausori, which bore the misleading sign, Suva International Airport. He wondered what Melissa would make of it. He'd warned her that there were only six international flights arriving at Suva each week from Australia and New Zealand, serving mainly business visitors. But the airport linked many Fiji islands with the capital, and in daylight hours it buzzed with small aircraft traffic.

This was how he felt before a rugby game: hyped up, expectant, happy, but anxious too. He hadn't realised how desperate he was that she would love Fiji. The terminal was clean enough, but needed a spruce up, and Melissa would hate to see that thin dog gnawing at its mangy hide, and the dull-eyed toddler wracked by bouts of coughing. He wanted everything to be travel-brochure perfect for her, but that was crazy.

Here was the Twin Otter from Nadi now, taxiing to a stop about 100 metres from the terminal. He was at the glass, ready to catch his first glimpse as she emerged onto the steps. Thirteen passengers disembarked. A couple of minutes later, the pilot and co-pilot descended and the baggage was unloaded.

Hours ago, his mother had phoned to say Melissa had arrived and he'd spoken to both of them. Melissa was about to buy a Fiji SIM card so she could use her own phone, then Mrs Horseman was going to take her out for a proper breakfast. What had gone wrong? He hurried to the Fiji Airlines counter. Yes, Melissa Martini was booked on the flight, but the clerk needed the passenger manifest from the pilot before he could say whether she had boarded the plane. The pilot turned up two minutes later, told him Ms Martini had not turned up for the flight, despite repeated calls broadcast from the Nadi check-in desk.

No need to worry. Due to his mother's enthusiasm for her role as hostess and tour guide, they'd probably just got back late. No other explanation was possible. Then why was he gripped by terror, his chest in a vise?

He pulled his own phone from his pocket when it startled him by ringing. He fumbled at the screen but managed to answer on the third ring. 'Mum? Melissa?'

'Sir, it's Singh. I'm at Kumi Police Post. Thought I should call you. I've already radioed CID and reported to the super, so no need to do that.' She sounded very worried.

A new fear slammed him. 'What's happened, Susie?'

'It's Kelera. Maybe nothing, but I'm concerned after her call to me yesterday. She didn't turn up to Vili's funeral this morning. Well, that's understandable, she could have been too distressed. But now, the feast's getting underway and no one can find her. Her family is alarmed.'

'What did the super say?'

'He thinks it's too early to report her as missing, says to wait until tomorrow for her to show up.'

'Probably she's taken herself off to be alone, as you say, can't face the ceremonies and people. But I would act as if she's missing, even so early. After the feast, organise a search. Are the Kumi Police Post cops at the funeral?'

'Two of them. Neither of them were on duty when Kelera visited their post to phone me yesterday.'

'You're the senior officer on the spot. I want you to order all the Kumi officers to Tanoa. One officer only to remain at the post to relay communications. Question them about Kelera's call. I only wish I could go up there too. But Melissa missed her plane to Suva.'

She was with my mother, but I've got to track her down. My God, two missing women in one day!'

'Don't worry, sir. You're on leave. The super and I agreed to leave you out of this. But I knew you'd want to know.'

'I appreciate that, Susie. Very much. You can handle this, no problems. I hope to hear from you with good news before too long.'

'I'd better get on with it then.' She sounded uncertain, most unusual for her.

'Remember you're in charge there, Detective Sergeant. Be clear and firm, as you always are. You will need to ask the local cops for information, but do not ask their permission or apologise for any of your orders.'

'*Vinaka*, sir. I'll do that.' Her voice was firmer already.

'Susie, no one could do this job more effectively than you. Good luck!'

'Be in touch, sir.'

As he ended the call, he noticed a missed call alert. Damn! His mum had tried to get in touch while he was talking to Singh. He called back. Please let her answer!

'Josefa?' Mrs Horseman asked uncertainly.

'Mum, what's happened? I'm waiting here at Nausori. Is Melissa with you?'

'*Io*, she's right here, safe and sound. I'm afraid this is my fault, Joe. I wanted to take her somewhere really nice, like what she's used to in the States, so we got a cab to Denarau Island and had a beautiful breakfast, brunch really. At the Hilton Resort. We walked along the beach. Melissa—I do so like her, Joe—noticed the time was getting on, so we came back. But the cab was held up by an accident, there was no way the driver could get around it, the police were directing traffic...'

'Mum!' Horseman sighed. 'I really wish she'd been on that plane! But it's done now. What's happening?'

'She'll be on a flight in another two hours. Here she is.'

'Joe, I'm so sorry.'

'*Bula,* Melissa. Welcome to Fiji. It's so good to know you're almost with me.'

'I've had a lovely time, Joe. Your mother is so kind and welcoming—I've really had a great time, until I missed the plane. I knew you'd worry.'

'Have you got your phone up and running now?'

'Sure, honey. Got the SIM card, I'll just set it up while we wait. Oh, I saw your face on a road safety billboard! Your mom tells me they're everywhere. I didn't know you were a celebrity, Joe! Anyway, I'll speak to you before I get on the plane and I'll be with you soon. Ciao!'

He was relieved and wrung out. He rubbed his hands over his head. It was really time to renovate this airport. It hadn't occurred to him before what a bad impression it must give visitors. The truth was, in less than an hour he'd become annoyed and exasperated with everyone: his mother, for Melissa missing her plane; this tinpot airport, for not being fit to welcome Melissa; the super, for not supporting Singh more actively; the Nadi cops who'd held up Melissa's taxi; the useless cops at Kumi post; and even Melissa, for arriving at a very bad time indeed. He was so guilty at this last thought that he groaned aloud. Most of all, he was furious with himself for not being able to put everything right.

He went into the men's, which stank of urine and worse, despite a superficially clean appearance. He splashed his face with water and washed his hands, considering what was best to do. He'd have time to spend an hour back at the office with the super before returning here. He wanted to support Susie. But Melissa was here in Fiji and he could not abandon her.

***

'Joe, what are you doing back here?' The super was irritated.

After he'd explained, Navala seemed amused. 'You've come all the way back here for an hour? Now that's taking duty much too far, Detective Inspector. You are on leave!'

Horseman felt a bit foolish, now. Of course, the super was right.

He held up his brown paper bag. 'I have to eat, sir. I can't eat anything at what passes for a canteen at the airport.'

'Fair enough. What do you want to do? Read more Chatterjee files?'

'If you want me to, yes. But first, can I get up to speed on the Tanoa situation?'

'Singh will organise the search for the pastor's daughter, who has most likely simply escaped Tanoa for a bit. She'll do that most competently.'

'I agree, sir. But I feel I should be there, too. Kelera wanted to come here today to give us information. If Vili's killer knows...'

'I understand how you feel. I also know you need to be back at the airport before too long.'

'Sir, can we just organise more support for Susie? It's intolerable that she has to drive to the Kumi post to radio or telephone. Tanoa is cut off and the situation there could now be dangerous.'

The super raised his eyebrows in agreement. 'Nothing we can do to change that, Joe.'

'Sir, I know the new Motorola radio equipment is due. Have any shipments arrived yet? If so, the situation surely warrants using one of the pilot vehicles. From the specs I've seen, the vehicle-mounted radios have the reach to communicate with Tanoa.'

His boss shrugged. 'I know some equipment has arrived and the techs are checking it out.'

'Susie will return tonight, sir. Before then, why not get the techs to test it with her? I don't know if the new stuff is compatible with the field radio she's using now, but they could test that today. If not, we'll need to requisition one of the new vehicles and a number of field sets and test them out tomorrow. I can't think of a better field test, myself.'

'True. Leave that to me. Whatever is possible, I'll organise it.'

'*Vinaka*, sir. Next Singh needs more support than Musudroka and the local uniforms. I propose you deploy at least one more detective, perhaps DS Taleca? Plus as many experienced constables as possible to go to Tanoa in the morning.'

'I don't know where I'll get them from, but I'll try.' Navala sounded more positive.

Kelera's safety was at stake. Even Singh could be at risk. Horseman persisted. 'A second vehicle would provide more flexibility, too. I assume that could be the current Land Cruiser we've been using?'

'That should be okay— the vehicle is signed out to this case. Look Joe, I can organise what's possible on one condition.'

'*Io*, sir?'

The super looked stern. 'You eat your lunch and get back out to Nausori airport in time to meet your guest. Your job is to look after her.'

'*Io*, sir. Please keep me in touch.'

Horseman surprised himself by pushing the super so hard. But it was the super who had told him only yesterday, 'Never give up!'

27

It was only after the funeral service for Viliame that anyone seemed to notice Kelera's absence. Kelera hoped that the villagers were ignorant of her relationship with Vili, and maybe they were. It hardly seemed likely to Singh, however. Only one person needed to glimpse each of them heading off to the spice gardens on Saturday nights, no matter they took different paths, and the secret would be out. Unless it was their own family members who found out about them. They would certainly guard their secret, for who would want to smart from gossip about their own daughter or sister? No one. Vili's younger sister had guessed correctly about her brother and Kelera, but Singh was sure Elisa would never confide this to anyone else, even her parents.

Singh stood near the church, watching the village women, and some men too, carrying large pots and platters of food over to the thatched feasting shelters erected for Sunday's ceremonies, now co-opted for Viliame Bovoro's funeral feast. Pandanus mats carpeted the ground beneath the thatch, bolts of floral-print cloth were unrolled along the centre of the mats as tablecloths and the food was arranged. The drifts of smoky vapour from the *lovo* set Singh's tastebuds tingling.

Mere Tora came up to Singh, smiling. 'My dear, come and sit with my family, over here. We do appreciate your presence, you know. Come, you're most welcome.'

The kindly pastor's wife sat next to Singh. On her other side was a son, a boy about twelve who would look exactly like the pastor in ten years. He might also grow up to be an eloquent speaker, but for now he was tongue-tied, staring determinedly at the food. Singh couldn't elicit more than one soft syllable from him in response to her friendly questions.

The pastor prayed in Fijian. The whole community sang a hymn that Singh did not know but which moved her. Then they passed dishes and tucked in heartily to the mounds of baked pork, river fish, and heaped vegetables. Gradually, the feasting lifted their sadness, earnest conversations became bright chatter, and laughter broke the gloom. The half-full platters disappeared, replaced by trays of small puddings. Singh adored Fijian puddings, a special treat of her childhood in the backblocks of the west. They were a sweet mash of cassava, banana, and coconut, intricately tied in a leaf and steamed in the *lovo*. So filling, they induced contentment and sleep.

However, she had a job to do, which could wait no longer.

'Mrs Tora, where do you think Kelera could be?'

'I don't know, dear. This is not like her. I know she is most distressed by Vili's death, but she has a strong sense of duty. I'm disappointed she has missed the funeral. She's not in our house, that's all I know.'

'Pastor?'

Pastor Joni shook his head. 'I feel just the same as Mere. Kelera's absence is inexplicable.'

'Yesterday, Kelera telephoned me from the police post at Kumi. She told me she would come to Suva after the funeral today to talk to me. She may have wanted to give me information about Vili's murder.'

Kelera's parents looked stunned. 'I knew nothing about this, did you, Joni?'

'Not at all. She didn't come home until just before dinner, but I thought she'd been working at school or the spice gardens. I was busy preparing the funeral service.'

'Would she walk to the police post? Could someone have driven her there?'

'She could have walked. The vehicles here each made trips yesterday, bringing in extra supplies for today and Sunday.'

'Waisele or Isi might have picked her up along the way. They were both carting yesterday. I hear Ali brought a load of vegetables up from his farm down at the road junction. So kind of him. His farm's about forty minutes' drive from here. If he passed her on the road, he would have offered her a lift. He's here today.'

'I'll ask all of them,' Singh said. 'Most likely Kelera will return when she's ready. But I'm going to start a precautionary search as soon as possible this afternoon. Could you spread the word that any volunteers should meet DC Musudroka and me at the school in half an hour?'

'*Io*, anything to help. Are you sure it's necessary?' Mrs Tora's eyes widened in fear. Her husband put his hand on her shoulder. 'Let's follow Sergeant Singh's advice, my dear.'

Singh had turned Kelera's parents' puzzlement about their daughter into alarm. She regretted that, but she had no choice. She spotted Musudroka talking to some young men and caught his eye. When he joined her, she filled him in.

'Circulate and sound people out about when they last saw Kelera. Take notes—we need an accurate timeline. Invite them all to join the search, but no pressure. Many will have jobs they must do winding up the funeral feast. Some may have ideas about likely places to search. I'll need to stay around the village to coordinate. I want you to lead a small party to the spice gardens. That's got to be one of the most likely places she would go if she simply wanted to avoid people. Divide up and search along both paths. You know the drill.'

'Yes, Sergeant, starting now!' Singh was pleased to see him perk up at the prospect of action. She felt the same.

'Get all the volunteers to gather near the church for a briefing first. We don't want any lone rangers going off half-cocked. Half an hour to round them up, Tani.'

Pastor Joni was as good as his word, even setting up the church porch with trestle tables and chairs. He produced an official Lands Department survey map of the area and interpreted the main features around Tanoa for her. Mere Tora rustled up a huge pot of tea and plenty of cups from the church's store. Their fear had become purposeful action.

As each volunteer showed up, Singh wrote their names in one of the spare exercise books that lived in her backpack. She recorded when and where they had last seen Kelera and where they thought she might have gone. Eventually, twenty-three adults and thirty children turned up. It was touching that Kelera's pupils wanted to help, but Singh sent them home. Musudroka led nine searchers to the spice groves over the ridge. Both Tomasi and Ilai volunteered to lead parties, so Singh directed Tomasi and six others to search the village and the adjacent plantations. She asked Ilai to supervise the remaining six in a search along the river banks and cliffs. Pastor Joni joined Ilai's party.

Within five minutes all had disappeared from her view. Loud calls of 'Bula! Kelera!' from different directions reassured Singh. She read through her notes on the searchers, annotating each entry with a number. This ranked each sighting of Kelera from earliest to most recent. From this data she would construct a timeline. She fished a ruler out of her backpack, turned to the double page in the centre of the book, and began. All the searchers had last seen Kelera either yesterday or the day before. None had seen her today. She ruled three lines representing those days across both pages. She crossed each line with vertical bars representing hours, labelled them, and began to add red crosses for each 'last sighting'.

Mere placed a sweet-smelling cup of tea at Singh's elbow. 'Milk, dear?'

'Yes, please. I'm very grateful for your support, Mrs Tora.'

'It's my Kelera who's missing, my dear. Bless you, what's this you're doing?'

Singh explained. 'When I've finished, I'll visit every house in the village and ask when each person last saw Kelera. When the timeline

is complete, we'll have a full record of these last days. I just hope
there's someone who saw her this morning. We can ask those who
saw her most recently to try to remember more about that time.'

'You're a real scholar, my dear, like Pastor Joni. He did something
very similar, a timeline of Jesus' life, combining all the incidents
related in all four gospels.'

'I'm impressed! He'd make a good detective,' Singh said sincerely.

'Little Kelera helped him. He explained it all to her. No wonder
she became a teacher. Don't forget to drink your tea, dear.'

Singh added milk and obeyed. Mere poured her another cup. 'It's
likely Kelera will come back home of her own accord long before I'm
finished with this. But I hope you understand it's better to do as much
as we can to find her now, in case she's lying injured somewhere.'

'You're very sensible. I'm going into the church to pray in
quietness. When I come back, we'll go together to visit people's
homes. I can introduce you and I think that will help.'

'It will help immensely. Thank you.' Singh fought back tears.

'God can help much more than me. I'm going to ask Him now.'

The search parties returned one by one, having found no trace of
Kelera. Singh allocated new areas to each party, but they returned empty-
handed again. By this time, the sun had set behind the western range and
the light was fading. The searchers were tired. Time to call it a day.

Her timeline aroused interest among the villagers Singh and Mere
visited. Everyone seemed happy to talk about Kelera. But no one
had seen her today. The last people to see her were still her parents,
because she was at home when they had gone to bed.

Singh raised her voice, a bit hoarse after speaking all afternoon.
'*Vinaka vakalevu*, people of Tanoa. You have worked hard to find
Kelera. I am so grateful for your cooperation. I'll be back in the
morning, with more police support. I hope that by then Kelera will
have returned. But if she hasn't, we will continue the search. In the
meantime, please ask yourselves where she might have gone.'

Singh would do her utmost to find Kelera. She believed they
would succeed. But she feared Kelera would not be alive.

28

Horseman lay beside Melissa, watching her breathe. Her elfin face and fair skin, her nose sprinkled with light freckles, made her look young and vulnerable. They'd tumbled into bed as soon as they got inside Dr Matthew Young's colonial cottage. She'd been alarmed when he enfolded her in his arms in the living room.

'No need to look over your shoulder, now. Matt Young's discreetly taken himself off for a long weekend.'

'I'm looking forward to meeting such a thoughtful man, but I'm glad it's not right now.' She returned his embrace, kissing his mouth tenderly. His doubts vanished and he guided her to his bedroom.

He'd let her sleep now. She must be tired after the long journey, the time zone shift, not to mention coping with his mother and missing her final flight. He felt tired himself, but was much too keyed up to sleep. Also too happy. He propped himself on one elbow and gazed at her some more. Strands of light brown hair were stuck to her face. She wasn't used to Suva's sticky air. He got up and switched on the overhead fan and turned it to low. That should help. He padded back to the bed and covered her with the thin cotton sheet. He didn't want her to catch a chill. She smiled in her sleep.

Horseman decided not to think about a future for him and Melissa. Just enjoy this time together and see where it led. In the taxi home from the airport, she'd readily agreed to his proposal to go to a café for lunch, then a walk around Suva. It looked like it would be an extremely late lunch now.

He showered, dressed in fresh clothes, and was stretched on the sofa perusing a rugby magazine when Melissa appeared in the doorway. She was wrapped in the new fluffy towel he'd bought for her. She flopped on the sofa next to him and kissed him. 'Wow, I feel bleary, how long was I asleep, Joe?'

'Two hours. Have a shower, darling. Then we'll go out for lunch.'

'Sorry, honey. You must be starving.' She picked up her suitcase from the middle of the floor. 'Be right back.'

She came back looking fresh, her short hair feathered around her face. How could he tell her? 'You look irresistible in those short shorts, darling. But—I hate to say this—they're not the thing for the Suva streets.'

'Are you telling me what to wear, Joe Horseman?' Her blue eyes challenged him.

'No, I'm just giving you the heads-up on local custom, honey. You want to learn about Fiji, don't you? Well, you'll attract disapproving glares from some and salacious stares from others in your very cute shorts, which are fine in a resort, but not on the streets. It's just the way it is here.'

She sighed her resistance. 'What should I wear then?'

He tried to sound light and jokey. 'Knee-length pants or skirt. None of that terrific taut midriff showing, I'm afraid. Sorry.'

She was offended, he could tell. She left the room without a word. He should have told her about that before she'd got dressed. No woman would easily accept being told she'd worn the wrong thing.

But when Melissa reappeared, she'd clearly decided to forget it. She wore white capri pants and a loose cotton shirt. 'You look gorgeous,' he said. 'Of course, you looked gorgeous in your tight shorts, but now you'll fit right in.'

'Joe, you're right, you gotta tell me what I should do here. I don't want to offend people.'

Melissa put on sunglasses and a floppy hat. They started walking down the hill towards the centre of town when a cab slowed beside them. Horseman waved. 'Let's take this, you must be starving.' He certainly was.

The taxi laboured to a stop outside the café. 'Republic of Cappuccino? Cool name!' Melissa was delighted, so Horseman was happy.

'The ROC started not long after a military coup, when the new leader declared the Republic of Fiji, severing ties with the British monarch, Queen Elizabeth, until then Fiji's head of state. It was a very cheeky name then, but the owners got away with it.'

'I love it! I really should have done more reading for this trip, Joe, but I've been so busy at work, and with my Masters… I'm quite ignorant about your lovely country.'

'No worries, I'll fill you in. I've got to be good for something, I suppose.' She elbowed him in the ribs, smiling. 'It's always full. Simple food, great coffee, and most important of all, air conditioning.'

'And a very cool name,' added Melissa.

The staff greeted Horseman enthusiastically, not hiding their interest in Melissa. They shared a salad and iced coffee. Horseman pulled out a tourist map he'd picked up and spread it on their table.

'We're here on Victoria Parade, the main city street. Definitely the best end of town. The top two hotels are opposite, on the waterfront. The gardens, Albert Park, the museum, and government buildings are on this side, further along. As we head west, the city centre widens out. Socially too. The city market's near the western fringe of town. And so is the Suva Central police station, where I work.'

'Let's hit Victoria Parade then, babe.'

As they ambled along, Melissa exclaiming with surprise and delight at the run-down shops, mean hole-in-the-wall eateries and shadowy interiors glimpsed through dirty glass, Horseman tried to look at Suva from Melissa's viewpoint. He saw too much peeling paint, too few attempts at improvements, too many beggars (well, one was too many for him).

They soon came to the emerald of Ratu Sukuna Park, which

interrupted the buildings on the southern side of Victoria Parade.

'Oh honey, that park's right on the bay. Can we cross over? It looks like there's a wall we can sit on for a bit.'

'Sure, the main street's roughly parallel with the shore. It's just that you'd never know. It's flat here and you can't see over the buildings.'

The park was bright with clipped hibiscus and crotons. People rested on benches or ate snacks on the grass. A hopeful emaciated dog limped to meet them. Melissa reached out.

'Don't touch it, Melissa,' Horseman said sharply.

Stunned at his tone, she retracted her hand. 'Why, Joe? The poor dog's limping and so thin. Look at her swollen teats. She's got pups.'

'I know. I feel sorry for her too. But she's probably diseased, and she might bite you.'

'But I can't just pass her by. Is there an animal shelter here that would look after her?'

'There's the RSPCA, but they focus on education and rescuing animals from cruel treatment. This dog's just a stray. There are hundreds more like her. Fijians accept stray dogs as a natural part of life. They believe dogs can fend for themselves.'

'I can't ignore her. She needs help. Where can I buy meat, Joe? I can at least give her a good meal so she can feed her pups.'

'Melissa, if you help the pups survive, there'll be another twenty diseased strays on the street before the year's out. Just from this one mother. You know that.'

'I do know. And you're right. But she's suffering, she's sick. I'm just a visitor, I can't take responsibility for her. But I can ease her hunger for a while. I intend to do that, Joe.'

Horseman had seen this stubborn side of Melissa before. Perhaps it was just as well she'd forgotten about relaxing on the stone harbour wall. Although the city council had improved the promenade and planted shrubs, an oily line of litter lapped against the wall on the bay side. A bloated dead dog could even be caught up in the revolting debris. He should spare her that.

He took her hand and smiled. 'I give in. There's nothing near here, though. We need to go a few more blocks to a supermarket, further to the butcher's. Or there's KFC here beside the park. Your choice.'

'KFC—much as I hate patronising them. She mightn't be here by the time we get back.' The dog, alert with hunger, trailed them cautiously to the chicken outlet. Melissa went in and returned triumphant. 'They're very obliging. A box of chicken pieces with no bones. Now come with me, little mother.' She led the dog to a quiet spot between two hibiscus shrubs and gave her the food piece by piece. They stood guard while she wolfed it down.

'Now we've got to give her the slip. I know you don't want her.' Melissa threw the last piece of chicken about five metres away, and they dashed in the opposite direction back into Victoria Parade. They strolled a little further into the beating heart of colonial Suva. Timber-balconied buildings lined narrow, crooked streets, holding their own against the invasion of concrete and glass. They came to the little triangle in front of the Tourist Bureau, where five streets almost met, in a jagged sort of way.

'Oh Joe, I meant to say, I saw one of these traffic cops in Nadi! Look, here's another one.'

Horseman glanced at the officer directing the traffic at this tricky not-quite intersection. 'What's wrong, Melissa?'

'Oh, nothing Joe. I'm just blown away by their bizarre outfits. The navy tunic is regular. But the white starched skirt, with the hem all jagged like shark's teeth? And sandals!'

Horseman pretended to be offended. 'That's the dress uniform of our Fiji Police, I'll have you know. And it's a *sulu*, not a skirt. You'll change your mind if you ever see me in it, young lady. Or better still, if you see a formal parade. I'll see if I can organise that, just for you. Name me a more smartly turned-out police force and I'll buy you dinner.'

'Joe, do you really dress up like that? I thought it was just put on as a tourist show.'

'Melissa! I'm a plain-clothes detective now, but for formal occasions I wear the dress uniform with pride. We cops love our uniforms, you know. For everyday duties, it's the light blue shirts and navy shorts, navy berets. Navy skirts for women. But we consider the traffic cops lucky to wear the *sulu* every day.'

'Please, dress up in it for me.' He loved the cheeky glint in her eyes.

'Only if you're good. Of course, traffic cops all marry young. They have to. Only a wife can handle all that laundering, starching, and ironing.'

'Joe Horseman. How dare you?'

'That's for mocking our police *sulu*.' They laughed together. 'But you must have noticed a lot of men wearing *sulu*, both in Nadi and here?'

'Yep. Odd at first, but hey, I'm already used to it.' They crossed the road at the officer's direction, Melissa giving him a surreptitious once-over as she passed. 'You're right, honey. That *sulu* is starched! And the poor guy's face is dripping with sweat.'

Horseman recognised the rhythmic rapping as they walked on towards the western creek, the cinema, and the vast verandahs of the Steamships Trading Company department store buildings.

'You're about to meet another stray, Melissa. I was hoping he'd be here.'

The rapping increased in volume, accompanied by a sing-song chant. 'Shoe-sine, Uncle, shoe-sine, Aunty. Like a mirror, like a mirror, eh-eh-eh! Shoe-siiiiine!' Tevita was in one of his regular spots, at the entrance of the Jubilee Arcade. He was looking in the opposite direction. Horseman planted one foot on his wooden box.

'*Bula*, Tevita, my sandals need your best service today, please.'

'Hey, Joe. *Bula, bula!*' The boy's face lit up. Then he noticed Melissa and became wary.

'Tevita, this is my friend, Melissa. She's come all the way from America to have a holiday in Fiji. Melissa, Tevita is a member of the Junior Shiners Rugby team. I'm their coach.'

'Oh yes, your mother told me all about the Shiners. I'm so pleased to meet you Tevita.' She held out her hand, which Tevita shook solemnly, while staring at her feet.

'Sorry, Miss Melissa, you got canvas sneakers. Today I no have canvas cleaner.'

'That's quite okay, Tevita. They're still clean. You better fix Joe, though.'

Tevita dusted off Joe's sandal, then wiped on a meagre amount of Kiwi polish with another cloth. A vigorous brushing restored the wide brown straps to newish condition, while a final light polish with a knitted cloth cut from an old singlet perfected the shine. 'Like a mirror, eh, Joe?'

'Like a mirror, Tevita. Good job.' Tevita rapped on the box peremptorily and Horseman obediently swapped feet. As Tevita repeated his process on the left sandal, Horseman casually asked, 'Did you hear about the break in at the Fiji Museum a few weeks ago?'

'Not me! No way!'

'I know it wasn't you. But some of those rascals talk to you, Tevita. If you do hear anything about it, please tell me. That will help me a lot.'

'I always wanna help. I not know about this one. But I will ask bad boys. For you, Joe!'

'The boys who hang around Thurston Gardens might have heard about it. They must know some of the museum staff, don't you reckon?'

Tevita nodded as he polished off Horseman's sandal.

'*Vinaka vakalevu*, Tevita.' The boy rapped his box and Horseman assessed his left foot. 'Great job, just like a mirror.' He handed Tevita ten dollars, far too much for a shoe-shine. Tevita would understand this was compensation for time away from his job, on mission for Horseman.

'Remember, Tevita, it's no help to me if you just make up a story. If you can't find out any news, please say you can't find out any news.'

'*Io*, Joe. You know!' They shook hands on their deal.

He explained the situation to Melissa as they passed the cinema, crossed the smelly creek flowing in to the working port, and reached the market. 'Now, Melissa, Suva market on a Friday is the jewel in Suva's crown. Just stick by my side. The only way to tackle it is to plunge right in.'

***

They decided to stay home. Horseman grilled some coral trout from the market and fried chipped cassava in coconut oil. Melissa, delighted with both the look and range of market vegetables, had also bought two large woven baskets to carry them back. She included as many as she could in her salad: four kinds of leaves, chilis, tomatoes, nuts, endive, coriander, and basil.

Horseman was contented. They cleared the dishes together. He resented the phone ring, and snatched it up. It was his mother. '*Bula*, Mum.'

'*Bula*, Josefa. How is Melissa?'

'She's fine. We cooked at my place, we're just clearing up now.'

'I won't keep you, Joe. You look after that young lady, now.' Her tone was playful.

'*Io*, Mum, I will.'

'I've been talking to your sister Eva. She's looking forward to taking Melissa for a picnic at Colo-i-Suva tomorrow. She'll get to your place around ten o'clock.'

'*Vinaka*, Mum. I'm sorry I can't go with them.'

'We understand, Josefa. Your job isn't a convenient one, but it's important, so we excuse you. I hope you crack the case soon, so Melissa can see something of you.'

'*Io*, but it's probably someone else who'll crack it. The super banned me from going up to Tanoa today.'

'That's good. What does it matter who does the cracking? *Moce*, son.'

'*Moce*, Mum.' Horseman realised it did matter to him. Quite a bit.

Melissa smiled. 'I love the sound of Fijian. It rolls along so rhythmically.'

Horseman didn't realise he'd automatically spoken Fijian to his mother.

'Oh, sorry. Mum was just reminding me that Eva's picking you up at ten in the morning for the picnic.'

'Your mother was just wonderful to me, Joe.'

'Apart from making you miss your flight?'

She chuckled. 'It all worked out.'

'I could have done without it,' Horseman grumbled.

His phone rang again, just as he was hanging up the tea towel. It was the super.

'Navala, Joe. Sorry to intrude. I know you want to be updated.'

'*Io*, appreciate that, sir.'

'Susie set up a methodical search, but no trace of Kelera by nightfall. The Kumi officers who were on post when she called said she set off walking back to Tanoa when she left. One of them handed her the phone and claims not to know anything more.'

'I doubt that, don't you, sir?'

'*Io*, but you can't expect them to admit to listening in.' The super shrugged. 'They'll resume the search in the morning with the reinforcements I organised. Only two extra constables, I'm afraid, but they're experienced.'

'*Vinaka*, sir.'

'You'll be pleased the techs tested the new equipment with Singh today. She received okay, even with her own radio. So it's looking better than I hoped was possible. Singh and Musudroka will take the pilot vehicle with the new Motorola gear installed. They should be in direct communication with us here in Suva. Even if not, they can certainly reach Korovou and Nausori stations, who can relay.'

'Sir, I want to be there. It's my responsibility. Melissa understands this. My sister is collecting her tomorrow and taking her out for the day. So I'm quite free.'

'No. I know how you feel but you're best placed here,

coordinating. There's plenty for you and me to do. I don't want to make that an order.'

The super hardly ever pulled rank, so Horseman did not argue further.

'When the pastor's daughter turns up, we'll revise our plan. Susie's looking up a couple of Kelera's friends in Nausori this evening. Let's hope she gets a lead from them. *Moce mada*, Joe.'

'*Moce mada*, sir.'

'Bad news?' Melissa asked.

'Not really, I guess. The super won't let me go to Tanoa tomorrow. I feel bad that Susie's got to shoulder the fieldwork up there.'

'Will that worry her?'

'No, she's capable and she'll probably enjoy it. She's got a strong hunting instinct.'

'Well, that's fine, then. Isn't it?' Was that a note of impatience in her voice?

'Yes. You make me sound like some sort of control freak. I'm not. I need to do all I can to make progress and the super's getting in my way.'

She got up from the table and took his hands in hers, looking him straight in the eyes. 'I think I'm the one getting in your way, Joe.'

Horseman was shocked. He wrapped her in his arms. 'No, Melissa! I'm so glad you're here!'

'Would it help if we sat down and you told me all about this case? You never know, I just might turn out to be a born detective.'

He kissed her. 'In the morning. Let's go to bed.'

29

Singh and the super had agreed that Horseman was not to be disturbed, at least for today, when the mysterious Melissa would land in Fiji. Singh shouldn't have been so surprised when he'd announced her arrival, no reason to be when she thought about it. After all, it would be more surprising if he hadn't met someone that year he was in the States—no CID and no rugby! Presumably it was the combination of the job and the game that had kept him single all this time. And what about herself? She only had the job—her family was only on the margins of her life now. The two weeks she'd spent with her beloved parents recently would last her for quite some time. And while she adored her nieces and nephews, she avoided her sisters and brothers, who were obsessed with finding her a suitable match.

She had to admit that apart from the job, another thing that kept her single was a lack of suitors. Oh, her parents had been approached by matchmakers offering suitable boys, and others had preferred the direct route, asking her for dates. She'd liked one or two of the latter, and wanted to get to know them better. However, when these guys found out that she would not give up her job on marriage, or even on having children, they disappeared, with sincere regrets.

What surprised her about her boss was how secretive he'd been about Melissa. Maybe secretive was not exactly it. He was a very private person when she analysed his behaviour. He was quite open about anything except himself. Perhaps this was why she felt such confidence and trust in him. She was sure he would guard his team's privacy with the same care he did his own.

How could she not respect his one day alone with his girlfriend—because Melissa couldn't be anything else, could she? If she could find Kelera and solve the murder without Horseman, then he could take the leave the super told her he had approved a month before, and enjoy a holiday with his girlfriend.

Mrs Tora had given Singh the names of Kelera's friends in Nausori and Suva—all of them from her Teachers College days. She had phoned them from the Kumi police post and, although they hadn't seen or heard from Kelera for a while, they willingly agreed to speak to Singh.

She pulled up in a Nausori back street, where modest timber houses raised on posts were close to the road. Behind them, half-acre strips of fertile silt ran down to the river. The yards were intensively cropped and productive, although regularly destroyed by floods. Here was the house she wanted; bright blue with yellow trim and shaded by a rain tree.

A work-worn woman, hair scraped back into a long plait, opened the door. Singh addressed her in Hindi. 'Mrs Bhagwan? I'm Detective Sergeant Susila Singh. Is Indira at home, please?'

'Yes, yes, she said you may come,' Mrs Bhagwan said. Singh removed her shoes and followed Mrs Bhagwan into a crowded living room. Three children were sprawled out watching television while a teenage boy was busy with schoolwork at a table.

'Please sit down, Ms Singh. I'll fetch Indira. She's in the plantation.'

'No need, I won't interrupt her for long. I'll find her.'

'Come through and go down the back steps, then.'

Singh salivated at the spicy aromas wafting from the kitchen. She put on her shoes and went down to the verdant garden.

'Indira, Indira, come!' Mrs Bhagwan yelled from the verandah.

Indira was a young version of her mother. She came to the steps carrying two plastic buckets. She put them down and shook hands with Singh.

'What beautiful tomatoes!' Singh said.

'Thanks, they do well here. I'm picking stock for the Saturday market.'

'Indira, as I told you on the phone, Kelera's friend was murdered a week ago, and she's not been seen today at all. Her friend's funeral was this morning, which makes her absence most out of character. The police are helping her family and friends search for her, with no success so far. When did you last hear from Kelera?'

Indira frowned. 'About three weeks ago. She came to do some work in the library in town. We met for a cup of tea and had a good chit-chat.'

'Did she tell you about the work she was doing in the library that day?'

'No. I guess it was connected with her school class. She's very conscientious. That little village school is lucky to have her.'

'Is the library open on Saturdays?'

'Yes, from ten o'clock. I think it shuts around four.'

'Did you make plans to see her again?'

'No, she doesn't come down so often these days. You see, her boyfriend works in Suva and goes to Tanoa most weekends, so that keeps her there. She's like me, helping in the plantation in her spare time. Who would have guessed it? She's always been more into books than farm work. That's love for you!'

'How long has she been seeing this boyfriend?'

Indira smiled. 'I don't know, Kelera guards her secrets. It must be more than a year ago she told me about him. She's really serious about him, but she's not sure he feels the same way. He'd be mad not to!'

Singh saw no reason to fill Indira in on all the details of Vili's murder.

'Did Kelera want to make a move away from Tanoa?'

'She was thinking about it, I know. But last year she decided to stay so she could help her boyfriend with his spice projects. I urged her to try for a transfer to Nausori, but she'd say "One day perhaps, not now".'

'Is there anyone else who might know her whereabouts?'

'Not many, I think. She did get a bit cut off up in the hills.'

Singh handed Indira the list of names suggested by Kelera's family. Indira looked at it. 'I know some of them, but not all. There's no one else I can think of. I'm sorry.' Indira frowned and shook her head.

Singh gave her a card. 'Please ring me if you think of anything else, and of course, if Kelera does get in touch with you. Thank you very much, Indira. Please give my thanks to your mother, too.'

The second address was a small concrete block house past the airport. A middle-aged woman, tall and thin, sat on a stool under an orange tree, scraping coconuts. Singh always liked to hear rhythmic coconut scraping at the end of the day. Comforting, like a slow heartbeat.

'*Bula vinaka.* I'm Sergeant Singh. Are you Mrs Kiti Waqa?'

'*Bula vinaka. Io*, I am Kiti.' She rose to greet her guest. Mrs Waqa was tall and thin, quite unlike her sister Mere Tora.

'I'm here about your niece, Kelera.' Singh explained the situation.

'My, my, how worried they all must be up there. May God have mercy! But I am so sorry, Kelera isn't here. We haven't seen her for a few months, in fact. She's a hard-working primary school teacher and she's occupied on weekends with agricultural projects in Tanoa. I think sometimes that she's too dutiful, too serious. You know?'

Singh did know, being a bit that way herself. She showed the list to Mrs Waqa, who took her time reading it, then shook her head.

'No, I'm very sorry, but I can't think of anyone else to add to your list, Sergeant. All I can do is pray that Kelera will return to us safe and well. God bless you.'

Singh thanked Mrs Waqa and departed for Suva. She made a brief stop at the Nausori police station to phone Superintendent Navala and fax him her list of Kelera's contacts. He would get officers working through the list right away.

When she returned to Suva station it was completely dark. Tanielo Musudroka was on the telephone. When he ended the call, she asked, 'How's it going?'

Musudroka shook his head. 'Nothing so far. Only half this list have phones, or phones that we can find numbers for, anyhow. The super roped Keli in and he's tracking them down. If anyone can find these people, Keli can. He's a bloodhound, the super says. By the way, he wants to see you, Sarge.'

***

'Detective Sergeant Singh, you've met our forensic accountant, Sai Balolo, I believe?' Superintendent Navala asked.

Singh nodded and held out her hand. 'Yes, yesterday, sir. Good to see you again, Mr Balolo.'

'Just Sai, please Sergeant. I'm not a serving officer, just a civilian employed by the Financial Crimes Unit.'

Navala eased her awkwardness. 'Sit down here, Susie, and listen to what Sai has to say.' Singh had started a separate notebook for the NLTB and financial side of the investigation. A green one. She retrieved it from her backpack and sat at the table, pen poised.

'You have something for us already, Sai?'

'Yes and no, yes and no. So far, there's nothing of interest in the files your victim Viliame was working on currently. So far. We're not through them yet, even though I've got a team on it.'

Singh tried not to look disappointed.

'However, we have come across something in the files on leases for the Tanoa lands.'

'We believed Tanoa was too far off the beaten track to have any leased land,' Singh said.

'That's so, and that's why none of the land is leased for agriculture or business operations. Were you aware there were mahogany leases, though?'

'Well yes, we saw mahogany trees in the forest and the leases were mentioned. Apparently there's a belief the mahogany harvest will solve all Tanoa's problems. Vili called it their magic bullet. He believed that was one reason the elders thought his cash crop projects didn't matter.'

Sai listened with great attention. 'Aha, I see. Your victim

requested these files a couple of months ago, even though they weren't assigned by his supervisor. His private research project, you might say. What I've found, and presumably he also found, is that back in the early 1970s, the area of the mahogany leases for the chiefly clan was doubled. This was due to the extinction of the clan that held the leases until that point.'

'I've never quite understood this clan extinction process,' Singh said.

'It happens naturally sometimes, when there are no male heirs to carry on in this patrilineal setup we have here. It was particularly common following the measles and influenza epidemics, when whole families were wiped out in a matter of weeks. That's the real reason this provision in law was made, I believe. The upshot is that the lands of the extinct clan revert to the State. But in reality, this was unacceptable, so in practice they reverted to the chief. This is what happened in Tanoa. And Viliame had flagged that in the file, so he must have thought it was relevant to what he was seeking.'

'Could it be that Vili was connected to this extinct clan through the female line? Is that why he was looking this up?' Singh asked.

Sai spread his hands wide. 'It's possible. Is there any other evidence pointing this way?'

Singh felt excitement mounting. 'Vili's NLTB colleague told me yesterday that he heard Vili muttering to himself something about mahogany roots spreading into everything.'

'It's a bit vague for a simple accountant like me, but it does fit. Some genealogical research could give you the information to support your hypothesis. The Registry office won't be open until Monday, though.'

Navala's face darkened as he stood up. 'If you ask me, it would be quicker to pay a visit to Ratu Osea's house here in Suva and ask him. Coming with me, Susie?'

'Now, sir?'

'No better time, is there?' Navala almost growled. This was not the calm voice of reason she expected from the super. Singh glanced at Sai, who was pointedly studying his file.

'No, sir. I'll just ring to let him know we're coming, shall I? I've got his card right here.' She flipped through her notebook for the card she knew she'd tucked away in it.

'That won't be necessary, Sergeant. Sai, if you can grab a photocopy of the relevant file entry for me, we'll be on our way.'

Sai handed the super a copy he'd made in advance of their meeting.

'*Vinaka vakalevu*, Sai. Where would we be without you accountants, eh? Let's go, Sergeant Singh.'

She had grave doubts they were adequately prepared to question, much less confront, Ratu Osea. But she couldn't possibly challenge a senior officer's order. She hastily shook hands with Sai and rushed to catch up with the super.

30

Superintendent Navala was silent during the fifteen-minute drive to Suva Point. As they turned left from Queen Elizabeth Drive into the leafy enclave of colleges and quiet residential streets, Singh felt less and less sure of herself. Not only because their mission was ill-defined and ill-prepared, but she always felt like a fish out of water in these elite suburbs, once the preserve of British colonial administrators.

Navala parked in the street, and they approached the front door along a path bordered by small clipped shrubs. The brass door knocker delivered a loud rap. Singh hoped no one was at home. But the knock was quickly answered by a Fijian woman, probably staff. The two officers introduced themselves and asked to speak with Ratu Osea.

'I regret Ratu Osea is not at home this evening, officers,' the woman told them respectfully.

'Ah, I'm sorry to hear that,' the super replied. 'I know he is expecting special guests. Have they arrived, by chance?'

The woman brightened. She took in Navala's age, bearing, and formal grey *sulu*.

'*Io*, sir, Ratu Osea is with them now. They are having dinner at the Grand Pacific Hotel. That is where Ratu's guests are staying, you know.' She was clearly impressed by this fact.

The super smiled and offered his card. '*Vinaka*, madam. Will you tell Ratu Osea that I called? I'd be grateful if he gets in touch.'

'*Io*, I will indeed. *Moce mada*, sir.'

As they walked back to the car, Singh waited for the super to say something.

'I'm not in the mood to let this go, Susie. It's off to the Grand Pacific for us.'

'Do you agree with Sai, sir? I mean, when he said that the reversion of extinct-clan lands to the chief was standard practice?'

'I don't know, Sergeant. I've heard it spoken of, but only with disapproval and suspicion. Whatever the legal position, it's simply wrong. What's more, I've a feeling Viliame would have thought so too.'

'Sir, with respect, we don't know if Viliame is related to the extinct clan, do we?'

'No, that's why I want to ask the chief about it, instead of waiting until Monday to start some time-consuming research project at the Registry Office. I was shocked by that theft—the Triple C. Ratu Osea has got to be somewhere behind that. What are our chiefs coming to? Their role is to protect us, speak truly, keep faith with us. Corruption is creeping through our society, Sergeant. Can it be that a chief can steal, even steal land from his people?' He shook his head.

Singh was surprised by the super's passion. Did Horseman share this reverence for chiefs? Maybe, but she doubted it. Her own parents and relatives certainly respected the Fijian feudal hierarchy, but readily discussed and criticised chiefs' behaviour, particularly in relation to Indian leaseholders.

The super pulled into the hotel car park. A smart attendant opened Singh's door. Nice, but embarrassing. Doormen in the same uniform ushered them in to the swish foyer. At least the long skirt she'd chosen for the funeral was appropriate, but she'd been wearing her clothes all day in the heat. She must at least wash her face and comb her hair.

'Sir, excuse me a moment, please.' She headed to a narrow passage she guessed would lead to toilets. She was right. She returned feeling a little better. If only she could stop Navala from going ahead with this misguided encounter.

A smooth waiter escorted them through a noisy bar, where drinkers competed for volume with a lively Pacific reggae band and a handful of jigging dancers. Then across a broad verandah to a dining room, with quaint timber panelling on three walls, the fourth entirely glass. The waiter spoke almost in a whisper. 'This is the mahogany room, sir. Panelled with the first harvest of Fijian mahogany.'

They stepped inside. The super gave a card to the waiter. 'We won't disturb Ratu Osea's guests. We'll wait here while you deliver my card and my request to speak with him.'

The room overlooked subtly lit gardens extending to the inky sea. Lights far off revealed the deep curve of Suva Bay.

Ratu Osea, his five foreign guests, Adi Ana, and another Fijian woman were dining at a window table. When the waiter delivered the super's card, the chief looked around. The two officers nodded to him.

The waiter returned, looking apologetic. 'Superintendent, Ratu Osea will speak to you soon. He requests that you be seated.' The waiter placed them at a small table near the door, then reappeared a minute later with coffee and dainty hors d'oevres. Singh, who was very hungry, thanked him and tried not to scoff the hors d'oevres too fast. The super didn't take his eyes off the chief's table.

After fifteen minutes, by which time the chief probably felt he had made his point, Ratu Osea rose, bowed to his guests, and made his dignified way across the room to the officers. Navala and Singh rose. The chief did not offer his hand. He nodded, sat, and gestured to them to sit down again.

'Good evening, Superintendent, I've not had the pleasure of meeting you before. Detective Sergeant Singh, I trust you are well. What brings you here? Progress on your investigation, I hope.'

Singh willed the super not to incur the chief's anger and, above all, not to make them look like bumbling fools. She smiled politely.

'Ratu Osea, I'm sorry to tell you that Kelera is still missing. After you left Tanoa this afternoon, we continued a systematic search with no result. I visited two of her friends in Nausori on my way here, and two officers are now following up with her friends and relatives around Suva. We have no results yet. Tomorrow I will widen the search at Tanoa.'

'I'm sorry to hear that, Sergeant. Kelera's disappearance on the day of Vili's funeral is disturbing to all our community. I believe this week has all been too much for her and she felt the need to escape. A failure to cope, perhaps. I trust God will restore her to us very soon.'

Singh bridled at his implication that Kelera's behaviour was somehow below standard.

The super simply said, 'I do too, sir. We will do everything we can.'

Singh looked at Navala, willing him to make his farewells and not charge into the dangerous territory of the NLTB files.

Navala sat awkwardly in his chair, slumping his back and hunching his shoulders so that his head would not be higher than the chief's. 'Ratu Osea, our investigation of Viliame's murder has uncovered irregularities in Tanoa district land registrations. As it is Friday evening and we cannot follow through on this until Monday, I thought it best to ask you to cut through the red tape and clear up a few questions we have.'

'It seems an unusual course of action, but why not? I always wish to help the police in any way I can.'

'In 1971, the area of mahogany leases registered to your family doubled. This seems to be because a clan was declared extinct, and the leases attached to the lands of that clan reverted to your chiefly family. Is this correct?'

The chief frowned and appeared to be thinking. 'I don't know, this was in my father's tenure. It might just be possible, Superintendent, but how is this relevant to your investigation?'

'I can't be certain yet, Ratu. Viliame was working on this file, among others. Did he ever ask you about these leases?'

'No, he did not. He had a bee in his bonnet about mahogany. He felt the prospect of the mahogany harvest after fifty years of growth had become a cult for some people. That's a valid point of view. Once the saplings were established, there was not much work for the holders of mahogany leases to do. If the processing and marketing of the timber is handled well, we should all do very nicely. However, a lot of landholders may well blow it, at the mercy of greedy foreigners and of their own ignorance. Whereas my approach, which you see coming to fruition this evening, is to put ourselves right with God, as a community. It's hard to look at those good people, my guests, and realise they are Mr Weston's flesh and blood. Don't you agree? But I run on.' He glanced at his watch. 'Will that be all, officers?'

'Almost, Ratu. I believe it would help us to examine your own records relating to the Tanoa lands and associated transactions. I have no desire to seize them under warrant, but I would be grateful if you would allow my officers to examine them. This could be done at your premises—there would be no need to take them away.'

Singh looked down at her notebook. No way was this going to work.

The chief was still for some moments, then smiled slightly at Navala. 'Superintendent, I can assure you I have no papers or records that have the slightest bearing on Viliame's death. Therefore there is no need for your officers to waste their time examining them. Now, if you will excuse me, I have neglected my VIPs for too long. Good night and God bless you.'

Ratu Osea rose and returned to his table as dessert was being served. The detectives left without speaking. Singh wondered what Horseman would have done if he'd been with Navala this evening. She could see no point in flagging their line of enquiry to the chief when he had no obligation to cooperate. Yes, she wanted to discuss this evening with Horseman, but even more, she was determined not to intrude on his privacy. She only hoped Melissa was good enough for him.

SATURDAY

31

Horseman woke beside Melissa as morning dawned. For a few moments he basked in happiness. Then the crisis of the case knotted his guts. He'd abandoned Singh in a dangerous situation in Tanoa. Everyone had assured him otherwise, but this was how he felt. He knew she was more than capable of shouldering field responsibility. Navala agreed, and managed to acquire the additional resources. So what was he worried about? Did he really think his presence would make the difference and crack the case? That would be ridiculous, egotistical, and he kicked that idea right out of field.

He got up and stood under the shower, enjoying the hot water washing over him as he stretched.

So as not to disturb Melissa, he did his floor exercises in the living room. The knee was pretty good this morning. He was grateful for that. Melissa had threatened to test it out today, and she'd be tough.

He cut up one of the small, sweet pineapples they'd bought at the market the day before, diced a red pawpaw, and stirred in passionfruit pulp and lime juice. Just as he put the bowl on the kitchen table, he heard the shower going again. By the time Melissa walked in, the coffee was ready too. They kissed and embraced contentedly.

She yawned. 'I lay awake for hours listening to barking dogs, honey. What's that about? It was like a barking competition. Howling, too. I never heard anything like it. Are they strays?'

'Some, maybe. I think most of the barkers are owned. They're on guard duty.'

'How can people let them bark like that at home? Nobody could get a wink of sleep!' She yawned again.

'I think one dog starts barking and they set each other off. As you say, it's a competition. It bothered me when I first came to Suva, but now I just don't register the din.'

'No, you slept right through it!'

'Here, what you need is coffee.'

After they both settled with seconds of coffee and toast, Melissa said, 'What's bothering you, honey? Is it your case?'

Horseman thought he'd successfully hidden his anxiety. He shrugged. 'I can't shake the feeling I could be doing more. But the super insists I coordinate from the station today.'

'Tell me about it, Joe. From the beginning. You never know, it might help.'

'Okay, you're in for a very strange story...'

Horseman was explaining their ideas about the Triple C when Melissa interrupted.

'I just don't get that, Joe. I understand the chief may feel that club is really his, or his clan's. But why would he need to steal the club from the museum? Couldn't he talk to them and come to some arrangement? Given the history, couldn't they make a loan to him, for ceremonies? Or, they could agree to restore legal ownership to the clan, who would then appoint the museum as caretakers? Happens in the States all the time.'

Horseman shrugged. 'Possibly, he might do that if he just wanted to use it for special ceremonies. But not if his purpose was murder.'

The puzzled frown made her face even cuter. 'I guess not. How sure can you be that the chief stole it?'

'Not sure at all. A chief probably wouldn't steal in person. He'd ask someone to do it for him, or maybe just express his wish for the object in others' hearing.'

'Wow. You don't give credence to the international theft-to-order theory?'

'Not much. It is a theft-to-order, but I think the motive's

personal, and that means someone in Tanoa. My boss thinks the chief's involved, but I'm not so sure. We've got to find who actually lifted the club to get any evidence.'

Melissa looked thoughtful. 'Have you got a short list, Joe?'

'If I consider means and opportunity, there are only two villagers who could qualify, that I know about anyway. There's Ilai, the chief's headman, also chiefly and ex-army. If the chief's pulling the strings, Ilai would be the first in Tanoa he'd turn to. But the chief spends a lot of time in Suva, there'd be people here he could ask.'

'And the second village suspect?'

'Tomasi, the retired constable who's always so keen to help us when we've been there. Good cop or bad cop, any cop knows robbers. He could easily arrange the theft. Knowing this, the chief might well have delegated to him. As a retired policeman, he's a respected elder. He could be relied on to be loyal, keep his mouth shut.'

'Honey, have I been invited into a lion's den tomorrow! I felt so privileged to witness authentic Fiji customs, but you got me having second thoughts now.' She laughed merrily.

'Melissa, don't worry. The ceremony will be very public, and you'll be among the VIP guests, the descendants of Mr Weston. But you're under no obligation to go to Tanoa. I'm afraid I must go, my team too. Stay home and rest, go downtown, watch rugby at Albert Park.' He leant over and kissed her. 'I want you to do whatever you please.'

'I want my first rugby match to be with you, honey. And sure, I'll go to the ceremony at Tanoa tomorrow. I couldn't miss that chance. What about your day at the station?'

'First, I'll be renewing my acquaintances among the thieves of Suva. I've got to track down whoever stole that club before the day is out.'

'Great, go for it, honey!'

'As for your program today, you have absolutely no choice. You cannot wriggle out of a picnic with my sister Eva today!'

'Joe, I'm keen to go. It's lovely of Eva to take me.'

'You'll like her and her husband. The kids are fun, too. Colo-i-Suva's beautiful—it's the only nature reserve near Suva. Wear your swimming costume under your clothes. There aren't many places to change, but you don't want to miss a dip in the forest pools.'

Melissa smiled happily. 'It sounds wonderful. I'll go get ready now.'

Horseman quickly cleared up the breakfast things. He woke up a mess, but now he accepted what he couldn't change, and he had a plan quite likely to succeed. Most important, he was in an optimistic mood that he knew would transfer to his team. How had that happened? Melissa. Talking things through with Melissa.

32

While the super sifted through the remaining NLTB files, Horseman met with the constables following up Kelera's family and friends. So far, nothing.

The radio technician transmitted at regular intervals to Singh in the upgraded vehicle. 'It's the ideal test run for us,' he said when Horseman thanked him for his efforts. 'This part of the eastern highlands has always been out of range.'

Now the tech ran into the CID room. 'It works, sir. They've arrived at Tanoa and Singh's come through clear as a bell!'

'*Oi lei*! Thank God, what a relief. You've solved a major problem for us, Constable. Can I talk to her from the set here?'

'Not quite yet, sir. We've only got the test receivers to work with now. Come to the radio room and you can call her. She'll have left the vehicle now, but her personal set relays through the vehicle transmitter. Should reach us fine.'

Horseman followed the technician, who took him through the operating procedures for the new digital equipment.

'Sergeant Singh, this is HQ. Over.'

'HQ, this is Singh. Sir, great to hear from you. Over.'

'*Bula*, Susie! I'm so relieved this works. Any news?'

'Afraid not, sir. Kelera hasn't turned up. Everyone here is worried now. Yesterday they thought I was overreacting. Some did, anyway.'

'The more time that passes, the worse her prospects look.'

'Yes, sir. I'll contact you as soon as there's anything to report.'

'Please do. Anything we can do at this end, just ask. If I can, I will. I need a reason to play with this new toy. Over.'

'Great toy, isn't it? Talk later. Out.'

Horseman returned to the super's office elated. Even though the case had not advanced, he no longer felt he'd abandoned Singh. He'd just taken up the Chatterjee files again when a constable knocked on the open door.

'Sir, you're wanted downstairs. A visitor insists on seeing you. Reckons he's on your team.' The constable smirked. 'Want me to get rid of him, sir?'

'No, I'll come.' He shrugged at Navala, and replaced the file in the box. 'These top secret files of Chatterjee's may be worthless so far, but if I don't read every page I just might miss the clue we need.'

The super smiled. '*Dina*. I'll help you when we're through with this lot from the NLTB.'

Horseman spotted Tevita immediately. The boy was trying to make himself inconspicuous by squeezing the left half of his body into the gap between the open door and the wall. Horseman grinned, and Tevita rushed to the public counter.

'*Bula, bula*, Joe! I need to see you. But *ovisa*, he not let me.'

Horseman extended his hand politely. Disapproving uniforms indulged in head shakes and smirks. '*Bula*, Tevita. It's okay. Visitors must stop here at the counter. What can I do for you?'

'Nothing Joe. I can do for you!' A wide smile cracked his face. 'You gonna be happy, Joe. You know!'

'True, Tevita? So soon? Come in and tell me all about it. Through here.' He raised the flap at the end of the counter and waved Tevita in.

The boy recoiled, backing away. 'No. Outside, Joe, please.'

Horseman followed Tevita down the front steps and through the gate. 'What's going on, Tevita?' Then he saw another teenager hunkered down beside the fence. He bounced up as Horseman approached. It was Pita, another Junior Shiner.

Pita took Horseman's hand, pumping it up and down. '*Bula*, Pita, have you got some news for me?'

Pita looked at his feet and nodded. '*Io*, Josefa Horseman.'

Tevita butted in. 'Pita, he no like police station. We talk some other place, Joe.'

'Pita, no one else can hear you here. I can't leave the station for long today.'

'I made a big mistake, sir. Maybe you don't want me to play for Shiners no more.'

'Man, I can't decide that until I hear what you've got to say.'

Pita drew in a long breath, still staring at his feet. 'I went with the boys to rob the Fiji Museum, sir.'

Horseman tingled. A breakthrough or bullshit? 'You'd better tell me all about it. Remember, this is no good to me if you don't tell me the truth, Pita.'

'*Io*, sir. I go with two boys. They had a key to the side door. I keep watch. I don't go in, sir.'

'Okay, did the boys come out the same door?'

'*Io*, sir. They had a big club. He stretched his arms wide. 'Even longer! They say a man was waiting for it. They want me to come with them to be lookout again.'

'Did you see the club up close? Can you describe it to me?'

Pita seemed to weigh his options on this one. 'It had carvings, patterns. Because it was dark, I didn't see all the details.

'Did you handle it?'

The boy shifted his weight from foot to foot. Then he shook his head slowly.

'Think carefully about this, Pita. You know we check all stolen items for fingerprints, don't you? When I get this club back for our Fiji Museum, I will soon know who has touched it.' If he was lucky. He hoped Pita was not acquainted with the iffy nature of fingerprints.

Pita stared at his feet some more, then said, 'I did touch the club, sir. But the boys don't let me hold it by myself. They said they must take it to the true owner right away.'

'Stay here, boys. I have to go back to my office now. I'll return in five minutes and take you for lunch in Hari Krishna's. We need to talk some more. Pita, if you tell me everything you know, I'll consider letting you stay on the team. No promises, mind you.' He put on a stern face.

He grabbed what he needed from the Triple C files. The boys were still waiting when he returned. That was a start.

Horseman let Tevita and Pita fill up on naan bread, curries, and rice at the Hare Krishna before getting down to business.

'Pita, did you go with the boys to deliver the club?'

Again, the boy considered his reply. 'One of the thieves went off somewhere, so I go with the other boy to deliver it. Just the two of us.'

'Where?'

'Behind the post office, sir. That's where we meet the owner. He was grateful.'

'Who is this owner?'

'I don't know his name, sir. I never see him before.'

'Did he pay you?'

Pita smiled. '*Io*, sir. He paid my friend forty dollars and me ten dollars, because I was just the lookout.'

Horseman guessed Pita was minimising his own role in the operation. He may have been a key player. Unless Pita identified his partners in crime, Horseman couldn't know.

'Here's how you can help me, Pita.' He extracted papers from the wallet file. 'Look at these photos. Please tell me which man paid you for the club.' Horseman laid down the A4 photos one by one. Pita's eyes fixed on one of them straight away. He squirmed in his chair. Horseman waited patiently, wondering how badly Pita wanted to play for the Junior Shiners.

Pita's eyes flicked around the café and then out the window, his gaze settling on the police station.

'Think back to that night, and picture the man again in your mind. Have another look.' Horseman placed each picture on the table again, one at a time.

'*Io*, sir. This is the man.' Pita pointed to the photo of Tomasi.

'Are you sure?' Horseman asked.

'*Io*, that's him.'

'Have you seen him before or since, Pita?' The boy shook his head.

'Do you know his name?'

'No, sir.'

Horseman knew much of what Pita said could not be relied on, but he had seen the boy's eyes fix on Tomasi's photo the instant he saw it, and now the boy had identified the same picture. Horseman was convinced.

'*Vinaka*, Pita, I need to write down what you've just told me.' He waved to the servery, making a T with his two index fingers. A pot of tea arrived in a few moments. Tevita enjoyed setting out the cups and pouring while Horseman started filling in an official statement form. The writing seemed to spook Pita. He fidgeted, his eyes roved about as if looking for an escape. Horseman didn't want to embarrass him if he was illiterate, so he said, 'I'll read this out to you, Pita. I want you to listen carefully, and stop me if I've got anything wrong, please. It's very important that every word is true. Tell me what's wrong and I'll change what I've written. No problems. Will you do that for me?'

The boy nodded. '*Io*, sir.'

Horseman read clearly, pausing after every sentence for Pita to confirm or correct. There were no corrections. Horseman placed the statement on the table in front of Pita. 'Would you like to read it through yourself, for a final check?'

Pita took the paper and appeared to read it. He looked up. 'That's right, sir'.

'*Vinaka*, Pita. Now you and I both have to sign, to promise this is a true statement.' They both signed. 'You've made a start to correct your very big mistake. If you continue to commit crimes, like stealing, there's only one future for you—Korovou prison. That's a bad place to be, Pita.'

The boy looked scared.

'I'm going to find this man now. If it turns out you didn't tell me the truth, you'll be charged for your part in stealing the club from the museum. You'll go to court and probably to prison. If you've told me the truth, I'll do whatever I can to save you from this fate. But if you do crime, Pita, you have to face the consequences. Do you understand?'

Pita nodded and rubbed his eyes hard with his forearm. 'Pita, where can I find you if I need you?' Pita looked at Tevita, who said, 'Try Jubilee Arcade, Hibiscus Court, or Government Buildings, Joe. I can help.'

'*Vinaka*, boys. Like an ice cream?' No need to ask. Horseman paid for the lot and returned to the station, licking his own ice cream, coconut ginger.

He really needed the new radio equipment to prove itself, and now.

'Sergeant Singh, this is HQ. Over.'

Nothing but dead air.

'Sergeant Singh, this is HQ. Over.'

He went to check on progress with the constables and the super. No one had anything positive to report. He rang the lab. By now there must be a clue from Vili's clothes, the bits and pieces the team had found at the church and at the lantana hideout at Tanoa. Nothing yet. Back to the radio room to try again.

'Sergeant Singh, this is HQ. Over.'

Nothing, then— 'HQ, this is Singh. Over.'

'Susie, thank goodness. What have you got?'

'Nothing yet, sir. Three search parties are in radio contact, so there'll be no delay if any trace of Kelera turns up.' She sounded despondent. Understandably.

'Can you speak in private?'

'Just a moment, sir. I'll go outside. Over.'

A little later, her voice came over the airwaves again, miraculously clear. 'Okay, no one can overhear me now. What's new?'

'A boy's identified Tomasi as the man who took delivery of the club from the museum theft. Where is he?'

'Leading a party in the outer plantations. Shall I call him in?'

'Yes. Treat him as dangerous. Don't reveal he's under suspicion yet. Tell him we need his help and bring him to Nausori station as soon as possible. I'll arrange to interview him there to save time. Bring the best constable with you, please. Kelepi can take charge of the search. Got that? Over.'

'Romeo that, sir. See you in around an hour. Over.'

'Susie, please be careful. Radio silence while Tomasi is with you. Stay safe. Out.'

33

Horseman waited on the Nausori police station verandah. He tried to plan his interview strategy with Tomasi, but he had no idea how the retired cop would react to his accusation. He'd just hang on to the ball until he reached the line.

It was noon when the new vehicle pulled up. Tomasi looked unconcerned, which was good.

'Let's go inside,' Horseman said, and led Tomasi and Singh into the interview room. A constable brought enamel mugs of sweet milky tea, then left.

Tomasi sipped his tea, then said, '*Vinaka* for inviting me, Inspector Horseman. I'm happy to help you in any way.'

'I'm pleased to hear that, Tomasi. You can help a lot. We have evidence that you employed some boys to steal a nineteenth century war club from the Fiji Museum on the night of 15th April. It was the club used to murder the Rev. Weston near Tanoa in 1875. They delivered the club to you that same night and you paid them fifty dollars for their services. Why did you do that?'

The blood drained from Tomasi's face, leaving it sallow. He looked from Horseman to Singh as if they were mad. 'What?' he asked. 'Some kind of joke?'

Faced with the detectives' silence and serious faces, Tomasi slowly shook his head from side to side. He noticed his tea and took a gulp.

'Tomasi, how did you get the key to the museum?' Horseman

asked. Tomasi continued to shake his head.

'Did you get the key from one of the staff?'

'Sir, I don't know what you are talking about! Believe me!'

Horseman did not believe him. 'What did you do with the club, Tomasi?'

'I repeat, I don't know anything about a war club in the museum. Where did all this come from? You said *boys*. Did some juvenile thieves tell you this? Nothing but lies. Maybe they're rascals I've come up against during my service. Probably they got a kick out of accusing me falsely. What on earth would I want with a war club?'

'You tell me, Tomasi. I'm still waiting.' Horseman nodded to Singh.

'Tomasi, shall I tell you why you may have wanted the war club?' Singh asked.

'Yes, go on. But this is the first I've heard of this theft!'

'The stolen war club was the weapon that smashed in Viliame's head last Saturday night, Tomasi. It's the murder weapon.'

Tomasi's jaw dropped. He stared at them, open-mouthed.

Singh continued. 'This isn't a theory, Tomasi. We have proof. Why did you choose this weapon to kill Vili? It was a lot of trouble to go to. Such a lot could have gone wrong at the Fiji Museum. I find it hard to understand.'

Tomasi shook his head. 'I know nothing of this! I've been framed!'

Singh turned to Horseman. 'Sir, I think it's more likely Tomasi stole the club for another reason. Then, when he decided to kill Vili, the club was simply the most convenient weapon to hand. Isn't that right, Tomasi?'

'No!'

'That's a possibility, Sergeant Singh. Which one of us is right, Tomasi?' Horseman asked.

Tomasi still stared.

'Have you had anything to eat today, Sergeant?' Horseman asked.

'Not since breakfast before six, sir. How about you?'

'Me, too. We'll get ourselves some lunch while you decide to tell us the truth, Tomasi. With your long police service, you know that's your only option. A constable will bring you something to eat. You can chew things over.'

Singh rolled her eyes at Horseman. They left Tomasi and walked out onto the verandah.

'I think he's genuinely shocked, Susie, don't you? Whether because he thought his crime wouldn't be detected or whether…'

'Do you think he might be innocent, sir?'

'There's that possibility. But you know, I watched Pita closely when I laid out the pictures. He immediately recognised Tomasi, even though he said nothing until I pushed him to look a second time. Sure, Pita may be fudging the truth, minimising his own role in the theft. But I've no doubt Pita recognised Tomasi.'

'Good enough for me, sir. Maybe he organised the club theft at the request of the chief, but had nothing to do with Vili's murder.'

'Could be. If that's so, we've just got to keep pushing him hard on the murder and he'll eventually cave in on the war club. When we go back, we'll record the interview. Now, just around the corner is the main street. There's got to be a good roti seller there.'

'I want to check at the library first. Kelera occasionally visited it on Saturday. Her friend told me they'd met there three weeks ago. One of the staff should be able to tell me if she's been in since then. Wouldn't it be wonderful if she was studying there, right now?'

'You never know. We'll do that before we eat.'

***

The librarian knew Kelera, but she hadn't visited in the last three weeks. Horseman guessed Singh had let hope get the better of her. She said nothing but looked close to tears as they emerged from the busy library. Then she sighed and straightened her shoulders.

'I know a curry shop near the bus station. The goat's pretty good. It's only five minutes' walk. If you feel like it, that is. You won't find any decent coffee or posh panini in Nausori, sir.'

'Lead on, Sergeant Singh.' However, before they got to the bus station, a seductive scent broke through the dust-diesel mix. They followed their noses, lured by salty, yeasty baking.

'I've never seen this pizza place before. Must be new,' Singh remarked.

They went into a basic room furnished with trestle tables and benches. They ordered at the counter and sat near the window.

'Tell me how it's going in Tanoa,' said Horseman.

'Depressing. Half the villagers have joined the search, the other half are flat out getting everything ready for tomorrow. I think each group is starting to resent the other, too. People are bringing supplies in from other villages, Tanoans from all over Fiji are returning for the big day. Looks like the population has doubled already, lots of unfamiliar faces. It doesn't help the search.'

'No, it wouldn't. How are you managing?'

Singh flashed him a challenging look. What had he said? 'Fine, sir. As well as any other detective, if I may say so.'

Horseman was puzzled. 'Goes without saying.' He smiled.

'It's not a question of managing. The problem is we haven't found Kelera, or any trace of her. The searchers are more and more alarmed, even feeling defeated already.' She sounded irritated. He understood her frustration.

Horseman nodded. 'Yes, it's the same at the station. None of Kelera's friends and relatives have heard from her, all they can do is suggest others who might have done, so the list grows. With no useful feedback, the checking becomes just a mechanical exercise for the constables. They don't really expect to discover anything. The danger there is that they're no longer alert and can miss a clue, or not recognise it. That's what needs to be managed.'

Their pizza arrived. They tucked in while Horseman pondered. Had Singh resented his question about how she was managing? He certainly had not implied any criticism, but she seemed to have taken it that way. He wanted to correct her mistaken impression.

'Did you know that false blips are inserted every so often for radar spotters, to keep up their alertness levels?' he asked.

Singh took another slice of pizza. 'Come on, sir, I can hardly race ahead of the searchers planting false clues for them to discover.' She gave him a severe look.

Horseman laughed. 'I hadn't thought of that. Good idea, though. Pass it on to Kelepi, now he's in Training Division.'

He was relieved when she laughed too. 'It's great to have him at Tanoa today. He's in charge, maybe he'll *manage* better than me.' She smiled, so he hoped her resentment was over. He took another slice of what was a very tasty pizza.

'Speaking of clues, false or otherwise, there must be something from Ash, surely?'

Horseman shook his head. 'I checked before I left. Nothing from Forensics either. I'll call again before we go back to Tomasi.'

'Do you think Kelera's alive, sir?' Her green eyes were desperate.

'I don't know, Susie. She may be, the second day's not over yet. All the more reason to push Tomasi. If he didn't murder Vili, Kelera's disappearance might just give him the strength he needs to tell us who did. Let's nudge him to prevent another death.'

'How, sir?' Singh asked.

'Appeal to his conscience, appeal to his fear of the murderer. For a start.'

'What if Ratu Osea is the murderer?'

'As our super said, God help us. Tomasi won't give up the chief. He'd probably die first. But there's one thing—what a cop convicted of murder would suffer in prison could be even more terrifying. We can remind him of that.'

34

Tomasi straightened when Horseman and Singh entered the interview room. His colour had returned, his bafflement had worn off. He now looked both frightened and wary.

Horseman's follow-up call to the labs yielded nothing, so all they had was Pita's identification. And bluff, which often did work. Even the formalities helped: setting up the sound recording equipment, the bland statement of the time, date, place, and names.

'Tomasi, did you plan Viliame's murder?' Horseman asked.

'No, I didn't murder him!'

'Maybe you argued, he made you angry, and you struck him with the war club. Where were you? At your house?'

'No!'

'Where did you keep the war club you stole, Tomasi?'

'Nowhere. I didn't kill Vili. I liked him. I had no argument with him.' Tomasi was vehement now.

'Two boys stole the war club from the Fiji Museum and delivered it to you on 15th April, behind the Suva post office. The same club killed Viliame Bovoro, at or near Tanoa village, on Saturday 12th May. These are the facts. The upshot is that you arranged the theft of the club to kill Viliame.'

'No, this is not true!'

'How long have you known about the identity of the stolen club, Tomasi? I mean, how long have you known that it was the club used to murder the missionary Mr Weston in 1875?'

Tomasi opened his mouth, then shut it again.

'Who do you know on the staff of the museum?'

Tomasi shook his head. Horseman glanced at Singh.

'It will all come out. You know that. Better to tell us now.' Singh's voice was pure sympathy.

Horseman lowered his voice too. 'Why, man? You served in the police force most of your life. We know you organised the theft of the club. What I want to know is why.'

Tomasi leaned forward. 'Sir, I did it because I was ashamed. The presence of that club in the museum was deeply shameful to me.'

This was not what Horseman expected. 'Tell us the story from the beginning,' Singh urged softly.

'One of my colleagues retired and was lucky enough to get a security job at the museum. I ran into him on a visit to Suva and we had a good yarn. He took me back to the museum. I'd never been inside before. He showed me the war weapons display. He told me about the club from Tanoa, how it killed the missionary Mr Weston. He was joking, but I was ashamed. To think the people of Tanoa are notorious everywhere for the good missionary's murder! Everyone knows this, my friend said. I couldn't bear to hear that. I decided to take our club away so Tanoa's sin would no longer be on show in a glass case.'

'Did you ask permission from Ratu Osea to steal the club? I believe his ancestor sanctioned Mr Weston's murder.'

'Of course not, how could I implicate my chief in what I knew to be a crime, technically? But I knew he felt the same. Ratu Osea has spoken to us of this shame and how the sins of our forefathers have passed down to our present generation. Tanoa is not prosperous, we work hard just to feed ourselves and have a little to sell to pay school fees. We pray our reconciliation with the Weston descendants will lift this sin from us. God will bless us again.'

Horseman felt an urge to argue against Ratu Osea's proposition. He managed to stop himself, knowing it would do no good. His job now was to keep Tomasi talking, to drive in the wedge until the wall of lies split open.

'Perhaps the Director of the Fiji Museum would have removed the club from public display if Ratu Osea had simply asked. What do you think, Sergeant?'

Singh shrugged. 'Very possibly. I hear Ratu Osea has influence, he's respected.'

Tomasi butted in, impatient. 'Of course he's respected.'

Singh continued. 'The museum may even have restored the club to Ratu Osea's custody if he had only asked. I've heard of many such cases overseas. Why didn't you discuss this with your chief if you felt so strongly?'

Tomasi didn't reply at once. 'But I believe that the club was not the property of the Fiji Museum. It was not up to them to grant permission for this or that. Taking it away was not theft, it was restoring the club to Tanoa village.'

Horseman shook his head and forced a laugh. 'Man, you were a cop! You've heard this line from thieves so many times, I'm amazed you can say that with a straight face. That's what they all say, isn't it? Except an honest few who admit they steal to get money.'

'No, I am not a common thief!' Tomasi protested.

Singh turned to Horseman. 'You know, Inspector, there's a good reason why Tomasi didn't discuss this with Ratu Osea.'

'What's that?' Horseman asked.

'Because he stole the war club in order to murder Viliame. He planned Vili's death. Otherwise, he would have discussed his shame about the club openly with Ratu Osea. Isn't that right, Tomasi?'

'No!' Tomasi shouted.

Singh leaned forward. 'It's the only reason that makes sense. If you stole the club to kill Viliame, you couldn't discuss it with Ratu Osea, obviously. He would never sanction murder, would he?'

'Of course not! Our chief is upright.' His voice dripped with scorn for the outsider who could never understand.

'Well, then, I've made my case.' Singh said, smiling.

'Hang on a minute, Sergeant. I've just thought of another explanation,' Horseman said. 'How about this? Let's turn your story upside down. Let's say Ratu Osea requested Tomasi to lift the club from the museum. The reason he didn't ask the museum directly was that he, the chief, wanted it to kill Viliame.'

'No, what rubbish!' Tomasi shouted again.

'But why would Ratu Osea murder Viliame?' Singh asked Horseman.

'That's for Ratu Osea to say, not me, don't you think?' Horseman looked straight at Tomasi. 'Who's right: Sergeant Singh or me?'

Tomasi flung up his hands, beyond exasperated.

'Neither of you are right! As you very well know! I've admitted getting the boys to bring me the club. As you suspect, my security guard mate lent me a key and left the cabinet unlocked. No damage was done. I've already told you my reasons. I'm prepared to make my statement about that. Ratu Osea had nothing to do with it.'

Singh smiled. 'One more question first, Tomasi. If neither you nor Ratu Osea murdered Viliame with the club, who did?'

Tomasi dropped his eyes. The question seemed to sap his anger. Was he frightened again? 'I don't know,' he answered after a few moments.

'Come on, man! When did you take it back to Tanoa?' Horseman asked.

Tomasi's eyes glided about. Clearly, he hadn't thought about this part of his story. 'The next day, 16th April.' He sounded a bit uncertain.

'Took it on the bus, did you?' Horseman asked in a good-humoured tone. 'I bet that aroused interest from the other passengers.'

'Do you think I'm crazy?' Tomasi was derisive. 'I wrapped it in a blanket and put it in a sports bag. One of those long ones, for hockey sticks and cricket bats. Naca, my cousin, brought a load of dalo to Suva market that day. I returned with him in his truck.'

'That club's longer than a hockey stick,' Horseman observed.

Singh wrote in her notebook. 'And when you got back to Tanoa, where did you put the club?'

'In my house,' Tomasi replied promptly.

'I don't think you could have left it there for long, Tomasi. Not with your tidy wife and your curious young son. You were kind enough to invite us to your house last Wednesday. Forgive me, but there's not a lot of storage space, is there? Is the club still there now?'

'*Io.*'

'Good, what a relief. I'll radio Sergeant Taleca to pick it up right away. The new radio gear is wonderful, isn't it? Excuse me a minute, please, Inspector.'

'Certainly. Ask them to send in some tea, will you, please?' Horseman asked.

As Singh opened the door, Tomasi said, 'Wait. I've remembered it's no longer at home.'

Horseman was relieved. Tomasi may have become a thief and a liar, but something remained of the cop he had once been. He was still reluctant to waste police time by sending them on a wild goose chase.

Singh said, 'I'll order tea anyway.'

'So, where is the club now?' Horseman asked.

The man's eyes wavered again. He would've had time to concoct these details and get them straight. No wonder he'd never been promoted.

'I—I'm not sure,' Tomasi answered after a prolonged pause, just as Singh returned.

'Why not, did you pass it on to someone?'

'*Io*, I was worried about my son, like you said, so I put it in the storeroom at the school. The one they use for all the *meke* costumes. I hid it well.'

'My officers searched that room thoroughly on Wednesday. They didn't find it.'

'Um, I didn't put it there until Thursday, after the search.'

'*Oi lei!* Did Vili's murderer take the bag from your house before last Saturday and return it sometime before Thursday, then? And you didn't notice?'

'No, sir,' Tomasi muttered. Even he could see that rag of a lie wouldn't wash.

Horseman sighed. 'Okay, then. When Sergeant Singh radios Sergeant Taleca to seize that bag from the store room, and he can't find it, I'll add obstructing the police to your list of charges. Understood?'

Tomasi said nothing. A constable brought in tea.

Tomasi mumbled, 'I'm confused with the dates. I put the bag with the club in the storeroom on Friday when I returned with Naca.'

'Oh, you did, did you? Have you been to check it since?'

'No sir.'

'Why not?'

'I knew it was safe there, sir."

'Man, how wrong you were!'

'*Io*, sir.'

'Let me put a different story to you, Tomasi. You returned to the village that Friday 16th April, gave the war club to whoever asked you to bring it to him, and that was that. You weren't aware it was that man's chosen murder weapon.'

'No sir. I didn't give it to anyone.'

He might be telling the truth. Just. It was possible that Ratu Osea, or Ilai, told Tomasi to leave the club in the school storeroom. If so, that was clever. Tomasi could deny handing it over to anyone, without perjuring himself.

'Do you know who killed Vili? Singh asked.

'No, ma'am, I do not.'

'Tomasi, you've been with me since yesterday, searching for Kelera. I've been grateful for your hard work.'

Tomasi looked up, surprised.

Singh looked directly into his eyes. 'Do you know where Kelera is, Tomasi?'

Tomasi held her gaze, shaking his head slowly. 'I do not, Sergeant.' His voice was firm now.

'Do you know if Kelera is alive?'

'I do not. I pray she is.'

'Was Kelera at school when you took the sports bag containing the war club to the store room there?'

'No, school had finished. It was about six o'clock.'

'Kelera often did her marking and preparation in her classroom after the children left. Did you notice if she was there when you went to the storeroom?'

'I didn't notice.' But he frowned and broke eye contact.

'*Vinaka*, Tomasi. After I take your statement, I'm going back to Tanoa to carry on the search. If you remember anything that might help me find her, please ask the duty sergeant here to get in radio contact with me. The new equipment means I can act immediately on any information HQ in Suva receives.'

'Yes, ma'am.'

Horseman realised in focusing on the club theft and Vili's murder, he'd omitted an important question. 'Kelera's a pretty young woman. She must have had a few admirers, Tomasi.'

Tomasi shrugged. 'I suppose so, but I don't know who. The young men don't confide in me.'

'Well, I don't think they would only be young men. She's studious, quite serious, isn't she? Mature men are often attracted to young women like that.'

'Maybe, I don't know.'

'You were a cop most of your life. You're observant. Did you notice any man, young or not, paying her particular attention?'

'No.'

'Think, Tomasi. You owe Kelera, after holding up this investigation with your lies and deception. Picture her going about her work at the church, the school, the spice gardens. Do you see any man looking at her a lot, watching her? Hanging around her house or the school? Looking at her in church?'

Tomasi shook his head. 'No, sir.'

'Very well. Sergeant Singh will take your statement, then I'll be back to charge you as I told you before. You will be detained in the lock-up here at Nausori until transport can be arranged to Suva.' He picked up his enamel mug of tea and walked out, badly in need of fresh air.

He called the super and told him the news. Navala sighed. 'I agree with you, Joe. Tomasi may have been carrying out the chief's wishes, but he won't betray him. His confession to stealing the murder weapon isn't enough to charge him with Vili's murder.'

'No, we need just one piece of hard evidence. I've been nagging at the labs, but nothing so far.'

'Keep nagging, Joe. I've found it helps. And after you've charged our retired cop, you'd better get back here as soon as you can or I'll be finished with these files.'

35

By the time Horseman got back to Suva at three o'clock, the constables had completed contacting every person on Kelera's parents' list, plus others suggested by relatives and friends. They'd discovered nothing, so the super sent them back to their own units.

Horseman sat in Navala's office, the box of Chatterjee's files between them. 'I'll let Chatterjee know he can come and get these,' the super said. 'I finished reading them just now. Quite an education about the methods of our art crime expert. What did you make of them?'

'To be fair, I only got through about a quarter of them, and those focussed exclusively on finding the club. Chatterjee seems to have the world of art dealing at his fingertips, I'll give him that. But his assumption that the club was stolen to order for immediate export was dangerous. It limited his investigation, as we've seen.'

'*Io*, it raised questions in my mind. The reports of interviews with museum staff are so sketchy, I wondered if Chatterjee just wasn't very interested in that line. Or wasn't very capable. So, Joe, always remember our key question—who benefits? In Triple C, who benefits from a rushed investigation?'

'The thieves, who in this case are the young rascals and Tomasi. But I can't believe Chatterjee was in on this too.' What was the super getting at?

'No, no. However, if the Tanoa chief is pulling Tomasi's strings, he becomes the main beneficiary of a poorly focused investigation.

The closed circuit of the chiefs' network takes in the top echelon of the force, and we're proud of that. The choice of Chatterjee as IO suggests to me that someone at the top did a favour for Ratu Osea and ensured the museum case would never be cracked by giving it to an inexperienced officer. Classic, isn't it?'

This suggestion shocked Horseman. 'I'm not sure, sir. You mean a senior officer is complicit in the theft of the club?'

'No, that's not how it works. Top brass wouldn't want to know the details, Joe. Ratu Osea might just hint that the thieves may possibly never be discovered. If so, there's not a thing we can do about it. Just be aware of the possibility lurking in the background.'

Horseman couldn't go along with this. When did his upright, dedicated super become so cynical?

Navala sighed and continued. 'The second question this case raises is training. CID recruits specialists, like Chatterjee, who may have skills we need, but then neglects to train them properly as police detectives. All this fast tracking doesn't lead to fast results, or any results at all, as in this case. We can't blame Chattterjee, who's done as well as his limited training allows. I should write a submission, but is there any point when I'm retiring at the end of the year?'

'Absolutely, sir. I think you should. Your experience mustn't be lost to CID. That would be a disaster.' Horseman heard his voice shaking, to his surprise.

'*Vinaka*, Joe. I'll see. But as far as Chatterjee's concerned, I doubt he sees his future with us. He's not a cop by nature, and he hasn't had the training to make up for that. If he can wangle it, he'll be back in Paris in UNESCO with a tax-free obese salary and all the perks. Failing that, some sort of cultural advisory sinecure in the South Pacific Commission.'

Horseman's dismay deepened, but he smiled. 'Maybe, we'll see. How's the work with the NLTB files going?'

'Methodical, if not productive. As we haven't got any support available here since the search for Kelera began, the Financial

Crimes Unit has taken the files back to their own offices. Sai reckons they should be finished tomorrow.'

'Sorry I wasn't much help with that, sir.'

'Nonsense, you were called away by urgent developments. And you've had half a day off. Terrible! How is your guest, Joe?'

'Fine, thank you, sir. I'm sure she'll be enjoying herself at Colo-i-Suva with my sister and her family.'

'Good, good. Now we've got Tomasi, I trust you'll close this case quickly. As soon as you do, disappear with your guest immediately on that leave you've got due.'

Horseman felt aeons away from closing the case. He needed some space to be still and imagine. Perhaps while he was driving—that often worked. And there was someone he needed to visit without delay.

'Sir, before any paperwork attacks me, I intend to break the news about Tomasi's arrest to Ratu Osea in person. I know he's taking the Weston descendants on a tour today, so he may not have heard.'

But the super was in a rare talkative mood. 'Did Singh fill you in on our gate-crashing call on Ratu Osea?'

'A bit. We caught up when we grabbed a pizza for lunch.'

'You'll understand that I'll be *persona non grata* with him then. I was annoyed and let my emotions get the better of me.'

'No worries at all. I'll be as nice as I can be and hope he'll agree to meet me.'

'Good luck, Joe.'

'*Vinaka*. Why don't you call it a day? I'll let you know if anything important comes up.'

'You're right. There's nothing more I can do here. I can't get at the genealogy records until Monday. Everything set for the big day at Tanoa tomorrow?'

'*Io* sir. It's a different story with the new Motorola transmitters. Brilliant! *Vinaka* for collaring those for us. *Moce mada*.'

The super's eyes twinkled, but he looked bone-tired as he pushed himself to his feet, left his office, and started down the stairs.

***

To Horseman's surprise, Ratu Osea picked up his call immediately. 'It's always a pleasure to speak to you, Detective Inspector Horseman. However, now is not the best time. I am with my overseas guests for our reconciliation ceremonies.'

'I beg your pardon for interrupting, Ratu. I'd like to meet you as soon as possible. I have news of our investigation that I think you should be the first civilian to hear.'

'*Vinaka*, you may tell me now. Has Kelera been found?'

'Not yet. Ratu, I would prefer not to convey this news by telephone. I would appreciate it if you could agree to meet this afternoon.'

There was silence. Horseman forced himself to wait it out. Then the chief spoke again. 'We're having afternoon tea at the Fiji Regiment Club. You can meet me there in half an hour. On one condition.'

'I'll meet your condition if I can, Ratu. What is it?'

'Permit me to introduce you to my guests, Inspector. I've found some keen rugby devotees among them. They'll be impressed that you're my acquaintance.'

Was the chief being sarcastic? 'I would be honoured, Ratu. I'll be there in thirty minutes.'

Thank God he kept a decent outfit in his locker for such occasions, rare though they were. He grabbed his clothes and towel. With the help of the stair banister, he dashed downstairs to the shower room, emerging ten minutes later in tailored grey *sulu* and white business shirt. He flagged a passing taxi and arrived at the steps of the Fiji Regiment Club with three minutes to spare.

Ratu Osea sat with his guests at a round table set with the regimental silver service. A waiter was serving each guest with hot savouries, while another poured tea and coffee. Yet another waiter placed baskets of hot scones, trays of sandwiches, and cakes in the centre of the table for guests to help themselves.

The chief glanced up and beckoned with a tilt of his head. 'Friends, allow me to introduce our most distinguished rugby exponent, Josefa Horseman. Joe has successfully captained our Sevens national team several times, not to mention being indispensable in the Tri-Nations, World Cup, Commonwealth Games—you name it!'

Horseman really wished the chief hadn't said that. Was he deliberately needling him? He had no idea, but if that was the price he had to pay for the chief's cooperation, so be it. He went around the table, shaking hands and exchanging pleasantries. A guest pulled up a chair and so Horseman sat, feeling like a fly lured into the spider's parlour. His tea was poured, curry puffs placed on his plate. What could he do?

So he enjoyed his tea, curry puffs, and scones. He certainly enjoyed the knowledgeable rugby talk of two Weston descendants. However, after twenty minutes, he decided he had paid his dues and must extricate himself from the sticky web. He stood up and bowed slightly.

'This has been delightful, ladies and gentlemen, but please excuse me now. I'm a police officer in my other life, and I must return to duty.'

This revelation led to yet more friendly questions from the guests. They did seem nice people, and in another context he would have been happy to talk to them longer. He looked at the chief. 'Ratu Osea, can I speak to you for a moment, please?'

'Certainly, Inspector, if my friends will excuse me.' He led Horseman to a small table at the opposite end of the verandah, waving away the attentions of waiters.

'I can't tell you what a true pleasure it is for me to entertain these descendants of the Rev. Weston. They are such nice, simple people, so ready to forgive our terrible wrong.' He gazed at Horseman with his characteristic intensity.

'They sincerely feel that you have honoured them by your invitation to Fiji, Ratu Osea. One lady told me visiting Tanoa will forge a real connection with an ancestor she has only heard about.'

The chief lifted his brows in assent.

'Ratu, Tomasi Kana has been charged with procuring the theft of the very war club that killed Rev. Weston from the Fiji Museum and for receiving it, knowing it to be stolen. He is currently in custody at Nausori lock-up.'

The chief's face became blank, immobile as he continued to stare at Horseman. Shock, or was he just deciding how to play his hand?

'Ratu, I must ask you if you had any inkling of this?'

The bonhomie vanished. 'Not at all. How could I? Tomasi is a stalwart of the village now that he's retired. He takes part in elders' meetings, but he and I don't chat much.' The chief didn't sound the least bit rattled. 'How did he explain this crime?'

'He says he was so ashamed that this club was displayed in the museum that he felt he must remove it from public view. He also claims that the club rightfully belongs to the people of Tanoa, not to the Fiji Museum. He says he simply restored it to its rightful owners.'

'That's rather strange, don't you think, Inspector?'

'That's not for me to say, Ratu. However, with respect, you have expressed a similar idea of shame. You told me how the sin of murdering Rev. Weston has passed through the generations of Tanoa. It's possible that your speeches over the last years have encouraged Tomasi in this idea. Do you agree?'

'Anything is possible. Listeners often misunderstand the speaker's message. It was ever thus.' The chief appeared completely relaxed.

'*Dina*, that's true.'

'Is the club in your possession now, Inspector?'

'No, Ratu. Do you have any idea where it is?'

'None at all. Hasn't Tomasi given you this information?'

'No, he claims it is no longer where he hid it.'

'This is most concerning. However, I have no knowledge about this. I wish I could help you.'

'I'm afraid the search for Kelera has not found any trace of her yet. Officers have finished contacting her relatives and friends in Nausori and Suva. None of them know her whereabouts.'

Ratu Osea shook his head sadly, some mobility returning to his face. A moment later he looked into Horseman's eyes and smiled. 'On a happier note, I trust your American guest has accepted my invitation to visit Tanoa tomorrow?'

'*Io*, she's looking forward to it. *Vinaka vakalevu*. My colleagues will take Melissa up in good time for the ceremony. I'm afraid I can't leave Suva until noon.'

'Oh, she can come with my guests in the comfortable vehicle I've hired for the weekend. If she can be at the Grand Pacific at half past ten, they'll be glad of her company. They'll bring her back too, of course. It would be much better if she could arrive with the Westons for the official welcome.'

What could he do but accept this convenient arrangement? Yet he felt even more like the fly in the spider's web.

'*Vinaka*, Ratu. I'm sure Melissa would like that.'

'Melissa, what a pretty name,' said the chief as they stood and shook hands.

Horseman waited for a taxi on the steps of the club. When he switched on his phone, he found he had missed a call from Forensics fifteen minutes earlier. He called back immediately, relieved when Ash answered.

'Thought you might have knocked off for the day, sir,' Ash said.

Horseman ignored the jibe, aware he sometimes vented his frustration on the SOCOs by similar remarks.

'No way, afternoon tea at the Regiment Club, strictly in the line of duty, Ash. What have you got for me?' He tried to sound casual.

'Partial prints of a thumb and index from some of the hideout cigarette butts. They all belong to the same individual. We managed to dig up Constable Tomasi Kana's prints from the archived staff files. No match.'

'Can you be certain of that?'

'Yes. It was not Tomasi smoking in the hideout. Sorry sir, I know you'll be disappointed.'

36

The first drops fell as Horseman paid the taxi driver. By the time he got to the verandah, the rain was torrential. He kicked off his sandals at the door and dripped his way to the bathroom.

Disappointed was an understatement. He had reasoned that if Tomasi stole the murder weapon, he must be the murderer. He knew there wasn't enough evidence for a charge, but he was confident they'd get it very soon. Now the news from the lab showed his confidence to be mere wishful thinking. He must think it through again from the beginning.

But Tomasi had confessed to procuring the club— that would stand. Tomorrow they'd question his security guard mate at the museum and wrap that part up.

He hung his wet clothes on the line stretched across the back verandah. Could he be sure it was the watcher in the lantana hideout who killed Vili? Maybe that conclusion had also been too hasty. Whoever he was, he spent hours in there watching the paths. Could there be two watchers taking turns, one who smoked and one who didn't? Possible, but far more likely this was the secret activity of one individual, a smoker like Tomasi. But not Tomasi.

As he put the kettle on, he heard a toot and saw his sister Eva's van pull up. He took golf umbrellas from the front verandah and went out to meet them.

'We can't come in, Joe!' Eva called. 'We promised to take the kids to the new Disney movie at six. Another time!'

Melissa slid back the door and hopped out amid loud farewells. He high fived the kids through the windows, then went around to the driver's side.

His brother-in-law leaned out the window and whispered, 'She's a keeper, Joe. Mind you don't let her go!'

Horseman was sorry his family wasn't coming in. He saw them far too seldom. They'd lifted his mood just with a few words. But he had Melissa back, and that was heaven. They made tea and toast while she bubbled with delight about her new experiences.

'Honey, all the little indoor plants we buy at nurseries in Oregon—they're growing up there like weeds! Outdoors, beside the paths, clinging onto the rocks, looking perfect! It's so beautiful up there. And the swimming pools, the palm forest in the gullies...and all natural.'

'The pools aren't natural, you know. They dammed the creek in three places to make the pools.' He stopped. Why this urge to qualify her amazement?

'Honey, don't spoil it. It's natural enough for me. The falls, cascades, the pebbly stream—perfect! The bottom pool is so deep. The older boys jumping off the rope swing concerned me a bit, I guess. There must be injuries from that?'

'I haven't heard of any, but I wouldn't unless someone died and it made the news. I suppose it's risky. Fiji isn't the States.'

'Wow, those kids sure had a ball. Not a bored kid in sight!'

His ring tone jolted him back from lovely waterfalls. It was Singh.

'Got anything, Susie?'

'No. We called off the search because of rain. I stopped at Nausori on my way back to check on Tomasi. Looks like he'll be there for the night.'

'I just found out Ash got good partials on the cigarette butts. Only one smoker, but it's not Tomasi. They got his prints from staff archives.'

'Pretty disappointing, sir.'

He couldn't stop a sigh. 'Yeah, knocked me for six. But Melissa's back now. She's taken my mind off it for a bit.'

'Good.'

'We've got to revise our plan for tomorrow. Why don't you come here and we'll work it out?'

'Oh no, I won't disturb you, sir.'

'Not a bit of it. We need a new plan, and that's much better done face to face than over the phone, don't you think? Melissa may see connections that we don't. I know she'd love to try. Come over and we'll nut it out together.'

'Okay, if you insist. But I need to go home first to change. It's been a long hot day and now I'm muddy as well. Could be more than an hour if the traffic's bad.'

'Sure, we can show Melissa a real curry shop afterwards.'

When he told her that Singh was coming for a meeting, Melissa didn't seem particularly eager. Odd, but he remembered she'd be tired after such an active day, and still jetlagged.

'You don't have to sit in on our meeting if you don't want to, darling. Take a nap, if you like, you must be tired. I just thought it would be good to have your ideas.'

She put her arms around him, her lips brushing his ear. 'You're a funny guy, Joe Horseman,' she whispered. 'Why don't we both take a nap first?'

***

It was a good thing that an hour and a half passed before Singh turned up, although neither had a nap. They were up and ready to welcome her when the cab dropped her at the kerb. Horseman had brewed coffee while Melissa rustled through the things she had impulsively bought at the Friday market. She tipped banana chips and a bhuja mix into bowls and joined him on the verandah to greet his colleague.

Singh shook hands with Melissa and placed her shoes tidily at the door. Horseman wondered why she seemed shy and awkward. But after he served the coffee, the three of them sat round the table and settled to work, nibbling the snacks.

'Anything else from the SOCOs apart from the cigarette butts?' Singh asked.

'Not yet. Ash insists they can't rush processing the material. Viliame's murder isn't their only serious case. There's still a chance. We go back to our short list in Tanoa. We cross off Tomasi. That leaves us with Ilai and the chief.'

'Why would they want to kill him?' Melissa asked, wide-eyed.

Singh came in quickly. 'Both could be annoyed, maybe seriously incensed by a young commoner starting up new agriculture projects no one had ever thought of before. Successfully, what's more. Chiefly older men are the ones to initiate projects, then the others hop to it and carry out their plans.' There was a hint of impatience in Singh's voice, which was a bit unfair. How could Melissa have known that?

'I can understand them being annoyed, but murder?' Melissa was incredulous.

'A man beat his six-year-old child to death last year for continuing to sharpen her pencil after he told her to stop.' Singh clearly wanted to speed up their discussion. Did she have somewhere else to get to? Melissa fell silent.

Horseman filled the gap. 'Another possible motive has come out of the FCU analysis of the files Vili was working on before he died. He signed out some files that don't have anything to do with his official projects. It's possible Vili thought his family had a right to some land that reverted to the present chief's father decades ago. It's complicated. However, if Viliame had approached Ilai or the chief about the land... both might take his challenge as a threat.'

'Oh no, Joe. That sounds feudal.'

Horseman admired her perception. 'You're so right, Melissa. Traditional Fiji society *is* feudal. So the chief and his headman are the only two in the frame now.'

'But there could be others you just don't know about?' Melissa asked.

Singh answered, too quickly. 'Yes, of course, but we can only follow what we know now.'

'Kelera, this poor girl that you're searching for. Have you found nothing more?' Melissa asked.

'Nothing at all.' Singh looked down.

What was wrong with Singh? 'Help yourselves to more coffee,' Horseman said, passing the pot.

'Try this bhuja, Susie. I got it at the market. It's real good.' Melissa passed the bowl to Singh.

Horseman went on. 'No more needs to be said about what we don't know or haven't done. Let's plan tomorrow.'

'I must go back to Tanoa early. We can't give up on Kelera,' Singh said firmly.

'I agree. We have Tomasi's confession to Triple C and that's solid. Tomorrow I'm going to get him up early and ask my questions again and again until he starts singing. Susie and I don't believe his story that stealing the club was his own idea and no one else knew about it.'

Melissa frowned. 'Why don't you question the chief and his deputy—what's his name, Ilai? As they're the only guys you suspect?'

'We don't have anything on them, Melissa. Only logic and probability,' Singh answered.

Horseman hastened to explain Singh's rather abrupt reply. 'We have questioned Ratu Osea and Ilai, as far as we can go politely. They both claim they were in Suva last Saturday night when Viliame was killed. That alibi is confirmed by domestic staff, so it's still not really confirmed.'

'What do you mean, Joe?'

'His loyal domestic staff would happily lie in the chief's interest. Both Ratu Osea and Ilai deny knowing anything about anything. With no evidence, we can't go further with them.'

Singh chimed in. 'A major obstacle is this huge ceremony tomorrow. Melissa, you probably don't understand that two years of planning have gone into this. This is a one-off, or at least, a first for Fiji, so expect media to be there. The super talked about it last night. He's firm that if the chief wants it to go ahead, it goes ahead. We've no reason to stop it.'

Horseman said, 'My official role is to supervise security, but my own priority is to support Susie and the others still searching. There'll be government and church officials, related clans from near and far. Tanoa may be a small mountain village, but Ratu Osea is certainly not in the lower ranks of the chiefly pecking order.'

Melissa looked troubled. 'I had no idea Fiji was so different.'

'Cheer up, I'll take you to the Grand Pacific in the morning to meet the Weston descendants. You'll be part of the VIP party and be looked after like royalty. It'll be a day to remember, for sure. We Fijians know how to put on a good show, even in bad times.'

'I can vouch for that, Melissa.' Singh said.

Horseman and Singh exchanged a smile. 'And now, Susie and I will show you a proper curry shop. Ready?'

SUNDAY

37

'*Yadra* Tomasi, did you sleep well?'

Tomasi seemed tired, subdued. 'No, Inspector. They woke me at five and brought me here to Suva.'

'I hope you've been thinking about your situation.'

'*Io*, I regret getting the boys to steal the war club from the museum. It was wrong. I got carried away by my shame.'

'Good, the magistrate always favours a criminal who is sincerely remorseful. But you know that.' Tomasi winced at the word 'criminal'.

'Your old colleague, the museum security guard, is coming in at nine o'clock to tell his version of events. He won't have a job tomorrow, will he? Is there anything you forgot to tell us yesterday?'

Tomasi shook his head. 'No.'

'You see, I don't believe you were acting alone. It makes no sense. You say you got the club from the museum, took it back to Tanoa, and hid it. No one else knew anything about it.'

'*Io*, that's right.'

'And now it's no longer where you put it.'

'Correct.'

'Someone who knew nothing about the existence of the club found it hidden away in the school storeroom, took it, and murdered Viliame with it. Is that your claim?

'*Io*, sir.'

'Nonsense. At least one person knew about it. That's whoever took it from its hiding place, I suggest by previous arrangement with you.'

'No.' Tomasi was digging his heels in.

'Who could that be? The most likely people to know about the club are Ratu Osea and Ilai, the chiefly leaders. It's more than a century since the murder of Mr Weston. No one remembers. The museum has no information on display about the history of the club. It's only the insiders who know. And who has made reviving the Weston story his mission? None other than Ratu Osea.'

Defiant, Tomasi shook his head.

'I spoke to your chief yesterday afternoon to tell him of your arrest. He told me, like you did at first, that he knew nothing about the theft of the club. He's quite relaxed about you copping the blame. Pardon the pun. Ratu Osea asked you to get the club for him, didn't he?'

'No,'

'When you returned with the club, you gave it to Ratu Osea, didn't you?'

'No.'

'Oh, you gave it to Ilai?'

'No'

'Did Ilai instruct you to hide it in the school storeroom, for him to collect later?'

'No.'

'Really? Then you must have delivered it directly to Ratu Osea's Suva house?'

'No.'

'Tomasi, what did you do with the club after the boys handed it over?'

'Like I said, I took it to the school storeroom."

'You said you hid it in your house.'

'*Io*, um, wait a minute. You're confusing me!'

'It's too hard to remember lies, Tomasi. Make up your mind to tell the truth. Do the right thing. Be truthful, as your parents and pastor taught you. You should be ashamed of these lies, not of a century-old sin you did not commit.'

Tomasi's anguish was obvious—his face crumpled, his shoulders slumped.

'How many more hours do you want of this conversation, Tomasi? It's tedious for us both. A fine young man was killed by this club. A wonderful young teacher has disappeared. Did Kelera see you sneaking into the school storeroom?'

'No, I don't know anything about Kelera!'

'Ah, but you do know who killed Viliame, don't you?'

'No!'

Horseman thumped the table. 'What did you do with the club, Tomasi?'

Tomasi was silent.

'I'll have to charge you with Viliame's murder. I did not do so yesterday, because I was certain a police officer would see sense and tell me all that he knows today. However, you are the only person with a direct connection to Vili's death. You received the murder weapon. If you didn't give it to anyone, you fit the frame for his murder. Don't you agree?'

Tomasi covered his face with both hands, sat in silence for a full minute. His shoulders trembled.

Horseman missed Singh's velvet fist. Thinking of her, he softened his voice. 'Constable Tomasi Kana, tell me what you did with the club.'

Tomasi lifted his face and exhaled a shuddering breath. 'I brought it back in the sports bag as I said before. I took it to the chief's house. Ilai came out and received the bag from me. I did not see Ratu Osea at that time.'

'Well done. Don't you feel better already now you're starting to tell the truth?'

'No, I feel ashamed. You forced me to betray my chief!'

'Tell me why you delivered the bag to the chief's house.'

Tomasi dropped his head into his hands again. 'Because he asked me to.' His spoke in a hoarse whisper.

'When was this?'

'About ten days before the theft.'

'Did Ratu Osea tell you when and how to steal the club?'

'No, he left it to me. He asked me to help him and gave me a picture of the club and a brochure with a plan of the museum, marked with the position of the club. I was very surprised, but I also felt honoured to be entrusted with a challenging task by my chief.'

'Did he trust you with his reasons for taking the club?'

'He told me it was crucial to his mission to atone for the sin of our ancestors who killed Rev. Weston.'

'That's rather vague, Tomasi. Anything specific about how he was going to atone—like murdering Viliame?'

'No, sir! That is outrageous! Ratu Osea didn't tell me more, and I could hardly be so disrespectful as to question him. Imagine! Perhaps you can't imagine, as you are a part European and have no chief.'

A low blow. Good. Horseman shrugged and smiled. 'Maybe. Did the chief ask you to kill Viliame for him?'

'Never!'

'Did Ilai know about your mission for the chief? After all, it's Ilai's role to execute his wishes, isn't it?'

'*Io*, but all have different expertise, which Ratu Osea knows well. I assumed he chose me because as a police officer, I would know how it could be done and who could do it. Whether the chief confided in Ilai, I have no idea. Ilai has never spoken to me about the matter.'

'Did the chief kill Viliame, or did he ask someone else to do that job for him too?'

'I don't know who killed Viliame!'

'Were you disappointed Ratu Osea did not choose you to kill Vili?'

'No! He didn't! Kill Vili, I mean.'

'What has happened to Kelera?'

'Kelera? I know nothing about her. I respect her. She's the pastor's daughter and a teacher.'

'She's also very pretty. A sight for sore eyes. There must be a few men who enjoyed watching her going about her business.'

Tomasi shrugged.

'Be honest, man. You notice things in the village. You observed a man keeping a close eye on Kelera, didn't you? Gazing at her in church. Always chancing to cross her path.'

Tomasi seemed to consider this for a while.

'Is Kelera alive?' Horseman asked.

'I don't know. I pray she is.'

'As I do, Tomasi. But as time passes, it's looking less likely.'

'I did all I could. I was searching until Sergeant Singh tricked me! She said you wanted my help.' He looked wounded.

'I did and I still do. I need your help badly. And I know you can help me more than you have so far. Time is running out for Kelera. We must save her.'

The anger drained from Tomasi's face. 'All I can do is pray.'

Did he know it was already too late? 'No, you can do more, Tomasi. You can tell me two things: what you know and what you suspect!'

***

Horseman joined Navala for a late breakfast at Ollie's Oven, half a block up the hill. The super's breakfast preference ran to tea and fresh warm buns, so Ollie's was his favourite retreat. They sat with mugs of tea and cinnamon fruit buns at the front, where the old-fashioned louvres wafted cool air into the bakery.

'I got annoyed yesterday, Joe. I had to do something about that. So I called a clerk in the Clan Registry—a friend of my wife. I must confess I did pull rank. Successfully this time. Emeli agreed to open up the office for me and helped me find what we need. She did all the work. When I praised her efficiency, she told me it was easy because it was the second time someone had come to research Viliame Bovoro's ancestry recently.'

'Really? Someone from Tanoa?'

'Well yes, but it was Vili himself. Emeli showed me the record book they keep of visitors' enquiries, so his interest in his descent is verified. To cut a long story short, Vili's grandmother and great-aunts were the last generation of the clan before it was declared extinct because there were no male descendants. Just chance that only females of that generation survived. Two of them married in Tanoa, but the others ended up in other villages. Most of their land was not used for agriculture, being remote and hilly, but there was a large area of government mahogany leases. These, along with the land itself, reverted to the chief, who was Ratu Osea's father.

'Now, this sounds shonky to me, but Emeli insisted that it was usual practice. Nothing illegal. Nevertheless, these days, the younger generation often feels resentful when they find out such things. Influenced as they are by Britain and America, they are keen to feel cheated and to express that. Their own Fijian customs can seem strange to them.'

'What's your conclusion, sir?'

'As this extinction and reversion was not illegal, there's no motive for the chief to murder Vili. No crime for Vili to expose. No reason for the chief to fear exposure. Don't you agree?'

'Logically, yes. We have to consider Ratu Osea's personality, too. He's reserved, as expected of chiefs. But he has an odd intensity when he talks about his pet project, today's ceremony. Like an obsession. He seems far more concerned with that than with either a village murder or a young woman's disappearance. He's quite calm about those. Don't Tomasi's claims justify us cancelling the ceremony and questioning both Ratu Osea and Ilai immediately?'

'Your assessment carries weight with me, Joe. You know that. But we need evidence. I can't agree, based on what Tomasi's given us to date. You'd be bringing a landslide down on your head. We wait until after the ceremonies and then question them both. I bet we get nothing out of either of them.'

'Yes, sir.' Horseman was disappointed, but understood the super's decision was prudent.

'Sir, my second request is to fingerprint everyone in the village today. It's the only way of finding who the watcher is. Not until after the ceremonies are over, goes without saying.'

'Joe, the grounds are not sufficient. Whoever used that hideout may not have killed Vili. I understand how keen you all are to crack this one, but you're getting ahead of yourselves, rushing in...'

'Where angels fear to tread, sir?'

Navala shrugged, one corner of his mouth creased. 'Did it myself last Friday night. We all do it sometimes. That's why I'm here. To stop you repeating my mistakes.'

38

She lay before the simple cross at the front of the church, arms outstretched, in the black blouse and gathered skirt she put on for the funeral of her beloved. A livid mark circled her neck, abrading her skin in places. Surely the silver chain still around her neck could not have done that? It was quite fine and would break. Beneath her was a fine pandanus mat, newly woven for the special service later today. There was no blood.

Kelera's mother had found her when she came to arrange the fresh flowers she'd picked herself. By the time Singh crossed the footbridge, Pastor Joni was waiting to tell them his daughter was found. She had returned to them.

Singh's heart lurched. She had failed this good family. Failed to protect this young woman whom she admired and liked, failed to save her from evil. Mere was right: evil had once again killed good. Singh had failed to recognise the human face of evil, although she must have seen him, spoken to him, perhaps shared a cup of tea with him and smiled.

When she entered the church with Pastor Joni, Mere and the younger children were sitting on the floor around Kelera, eyes closed, weeping. Singh waited in silence for a minute. She grasped the pastor's hand. Would he understand?

He held her hand and met her eyes. When he spoke, his voice shook as he repressed sobs. 'You have a most important job to do. We depend on you, Susila. Mere and I both know that.' He released her hand and went to his wife, put his arm around her shoulders, and spoke softly. Mere got up and took Singh by both hands. When she looked into Mere's beseeching eyes, she could not speak; her lips trembled. Mere pulled her into a hug and rocked her gently. The older woman's soft body, convulsing quietly, gave Singh resolve.

Singh wriggled out of the hug. 'I will find who did this, Mere. I will seek out this evil. Kelera was the finest of—' She bit her lip hard.

Mere nodded, trusting her. 'You are too, my dear.'

Singh forced a deep breath. 'Have you moved her?'

Mere shook her head. 'We know that's important.'

'I'll ask you to move further away from her in a minute or two. Constable Musudroka and the other constables will take a good look around the church, if you don't object. Then, it would be best if you sat by the wall while we examine the area around her, or you may leave the church. It's up to you.'

The pastor put his arm around his wife's shoulders. 'Thank you. God bless you in your work. We'll pray here until you wish us to leave.'

'This new radio equipment is a blessing. I'll contact Inspector Horseman now. He'll send in the specialists.'

Mere and the pastor nodded. Their children wept.

Before she left them to their prayers, Singh had to ask, 'Does Ratu Osea know about Kelera yet?'

'Yes, I told him straight away. I thought he might still be in Suva with our special guests, but I found him in his house. Apparently he returned to Tanoa last night. It must have been late, because I didn't see him pass my office window while I was working there after dinner.' He paused, looked up as if trying to recall the question.

'Where was I? Yes, Ratu Osea was as shocked as I. He enquired whether I could conduct the church service today and I replied that of course I could. What could be more comforting than worship with my family and congregation?'

'Many thanks, pastor. We'll start our work now.' She signalled to Musudroka and gave him instructions.

When her personal radio failed to get through, she returned to the vehicle where the more powerful transmitter connected right away.

'Bad news, sir. Mere Tora found Kelera dead in the church this morning. Looks like she's been strangled. She's arranged in the same posture as Vili. Exactly the same.'

'Poor, brave Kelera. Thank God for this radio. Has Ratu Osea arrived yet?'

'Yes, Pastor Joni told him. He apparently returned late last night. The ceremony is going ahead.'

'Hmm, can't really call it off now with the VIPs already on their way, can they? Susie, we have to know when Kelera died. It's a shame Matt Young's away, he's the only doctor I trust for an accurate opinion.'

'Can we get him back, sir?'

'I'll look into it. We can't leave Kelera in Tanoa. I'll find the best available doctor. Ash will organise a team from SOC and Forensics.'

'It's Sunday,' she reminded him.

'We must respond as if it's Monday! Do we let the killer get away just because it's Sunday? Sorry Susie, I'm just frustrated. I'll let you know when the team leaves. What's your plan now?'

Still shocked, she had to wing it. Never her preferred way. 'Tanielo and the uniforms are starting a preliminary sweep of the church right now. They'll expand from there if they can. The church service will go ahead, but I'll ask Ratu Osea to hold it somewhere else. Kelera's parents want to help, so I'll talk to them some more. Ratu Osea and Ilai are my priorities for questioning. I'll do my best, but I don't hold any hope of full disclosure there.'

'Neither do I. Probably one of them is our killer, but this is the worst day for forcing their hand. The super says there's not enough evidence to bring them in, nor to fingerprint them or the whole village. He's right. We'll get that evidence today, though.'

'Sir, I've talked to everyone the last few days, because of the search. They're quiet people, but cooperative. I can't imagine any of them committing these horrors. Someone did, however.'

'As I told Tani last Monday, this killer is clever, organised, and bold. He holds the police in contempt.'

'Mere would say evil holds good in contempt.'

'Yep, the devil disguised as an angel. Keep an open mind, Susie. We can't dismiss anyone without a proven alibi. Ratu Osea and Ilai are the front runners, but really, we know so little about Tanoa. '

'Agreed. Out.' She felt like a fraud. Completely inadequate to fight evil, no matter how good at heart she might be. And she wasn't even confident of that. But the boss and the others would fight for her, she knew. Horseman's immediate reaction was focused on solving the problem, not fussing about whether he could cope or not. She must be more like him. Singh took a deep breath, bracing herself for her greatest challenge yet. She would just do it.

39

What a total idiot he was! He should have foreseen the worst and been prepared for it! Melissa had offered time after time to postpone her holiday because this bizarre case needed 100 percent of him. Why had he stubbornly refused to listen? So vain he thought he was superman? But, the job being what it was, he'd been afraid. It would just keep on being postponed until one or other of them, or perhaps both, would cool off. In the end, they would decide that such a long-distance relationship was doomed and do the sensible thing. Remain friends. That had happened to him before, and it wasn't how he wanted it to be with Melissa.

At this very moment, Melissa was leaving Suva with the other guests, travelling to a village where a murderer had killed twice in eight days. Yesterday he had the creepy feeling that he was a fly lured by a cunning spider. So today, had he flung Melissa into the web? Effectively saying, 'Take her instead of me?' He was disgusted with himself and frightened for Melissa.

And what about Susie? The super said she was capable of running the Tanoa scene and so she was. But he was IO. He was responsible, and he would not lead from behind, feeding his troops to the enemy. He must get to Tanoa fast.

He phoned Matt Young, who was lazing at Paradise Island resort. Dr Young could be at Suva hospital to start the post-mortem at three o'clock. He suggested a pathology trainee who lived at the Fiji School of Medicine campus where there was an equipped Land

Cruiser. Luckily, Dr Krishna agreed to leave for Tanoa right away and also to transport the body back to the hospital. No problem.

Ash wasn't happy about being called from home on Sunday, but he promised to rally his SOC team together and set out within the hour. The super left in the middle of his church service to coordinate from the station. He commandeered extra uniforms and a detective constable, who piled into Horseman's vehicle. They hit the road at eleven o'clock.

40

When Kelera's family finished their prayers, they moved aside and sat next to the wall. Singh knew it would be better for everyone if they returned home, but she couldn't order them to leave. She wouldn't. They sat and watched the police begin their thorough search. Mere Tora was mesmerised by the process of measuring, taping, labelling, dusting for fingerprints. Suffering from deep shock after days of anxiety and fear, she seemed in a daze.

Suddenly she leapt up and swiped a brush from one of the constables.

'I can do this, you know. I'd like to help. You'll finish quicker with more helpers. Come on, children, Joni. We can all do this!' She got down on her knees and started sweeping a square of floor, numbered B4.

Pastor Joni quickly followed and touched her shoulder. 'Mere, this is a job for the police. I don't think we're allowed to help, are we?' He looked at Singh.

'You'd probably do a better job than me, Mrs Tora, but your husband is correct. Perhaps it would be better if you went home now.'

'Bring our children home, Mere. This is not the place for them.' The pastor held her shoulders. She looked at him as if surprised to see him there.

'Io, Joni. Come children.'

The family walked to the door together. As the pastor opened it wide, Mrs Tora turned around. 'How about a pot of tea for you all? You'll be ready for it soon, I bet.'

'That's very kind of you and would be most welcome, Mrs Tora. But only if you're making it anyway.'

'Oh yes, my dear. I think we need a cup of sweet tea. Kelera's sister will help me.'

'*Vinaka vakalevu*, Mrs Tora.'

The family held their hands together and bowed before they left the church. Were they bowing to God or to Kelera? Singh got a bit confused about the different customs of the various Christian churches, but she had the notion that Methodists did not bow or curtsey to God. That was the Catholics. They must be paying their respects to Kelera.

Ash and the SOCOs wouldn't be here for another ninety minutes. She'd supervise her team in the church for another fifteen minutes, then Musudroka could take over. Then tea and a talk with Pastor Joni and his family. They were going through hell, but they had their faith to see them through. Singh thought it would.

Her next priority was to speak to Ratu Osea and Ilai. Would they consent to that? The super had got nothing from the chief. Horseman had got nothing, apart from tea at the Fiji Regiment Club. She had no choice but to try.

She took Mere's overloaded tea tray back to the church for the men to help themselves, then returned to the pastor's house. Pastor Joni was on autopilot. He sliced bread, spread it with jam, cut it into neat triangles, arranged it on a plate which he placed on the table. His wife poured mugs of tea and passed the sugar to Singh. She seemed to have recovered some of her competence.

'I've asked you this before, but I must ask again. Did you notice anyone watching Kelera, looking at her in church, choir, or anywhere?'

As always when she asked them this question over the last two days, Kelera's parents looked baffled. 'No, not in any unusual way. We want to help, we wish we were more observant. But in a small village, there's not a lot to notice. The people don't change, life's routines don't change,' Pastor Joni said.

'Both of you are just too good for this world. But you believe in evil, and the man who killed Vili and Kelera is evil. I need to share with you some evidence we have found. It may help jog your memories. It is strictly confidential. Please, you must not tell anyone.'

Kelera's parents nodded. 'We will not tell, my dear,' Mrs Tora said.

Singh told them about the lantana hideout, and the suspicions of the police.

'The watcher in the hideout rolled his own cigarettes from tobacco bought in a store,' she added.

'Neither of us smoke, we're not likely to notice these fine points,' Mrs Tora answered.

'At least half the men smoke, and unfortunately, some of the teenage boys too,' the pastor added.

'Perhaps you could make a list for me of all the smokers. It doesn't matter if you don't remember everyone. It will be a great help. If you do it together, I'm sure the names will come to you.'

'Oh yes, we can do that, my sermon is ready. It's brief, but I will deliver it in English so our guests can understand,' Pastor Joni said. He reached behind the table and picked up an exercise book and biro from a shelf.

'I'm sorry, but I will need to seal the church as a crime scene, until the specialist team give the say-so. I'm off to tell Ratu Osea about this now. Can you suggest an alternative place for the service?'

The pastor reflected. 'In the open, on the *rara*. In view of her school. Kelera would like that. If it rains, we can move over to the school shelter shed.'

'I'll let Ratu Osea and Ilai know as soon as I can get to see them.'

'Thank you, Sergeant Singh. God bless you.'

She opened the door, but stopped at the pastor's voice. 'Please don't think I'm Ratu Osea's puppet. I respect the chief, but I am

God's servant, not his. It does not matter to Kelera whether the chief's day of reconciliation is cancelled or not. She is with God.' His voice shook and his wife took his hand. 'I will not permit my daughter's murder to be swept under the mat today. I will pray for her during the service and include her favourite hymn. All the villagers will be glad of that.'

Except one, Singh thought. But maybe the killer would join in sincerely. If he watched for her hour upon hour, he could believe he loved her, in his own twisted way.

'*Vinaka*,' she said. 'I'll drop by to pick up the list when I can. Again, let me say I'm so sorry.' Her eyes welled. That was not like her. She turned and went down the steps.

***

Ilai stood on the verandah of the chief's house, looking through binoculars towards the *rara*, which villagers were transforming with finishing touches. He was dressed in a dark *sulu*, jacket, and tie. '*Bula*, sir,' she called out politely. He lowered the binoculars and looked down at her.

'*Bula*, sir, I've come to speak to you and Ratu Osea. The matter is urgent, as I'm sure you understand. Is the chief here?'

'Yes, ma'am. We're leaving in a minute to await the arrival of our guests at the bridge. We expect them very soon.'

'I understand. However, I need to speak to Ratu now, before the guests arrive.' She felt she was shrinking beneath his cold gaze.

'I'll check. Please come up, Sergeant.' Ilai went inside. He had not invited her in, but she took off her sneakers anyway, placing them neatly on the top step. Act positive.

Ilai reappeared. 'Please come in. Ratu Osea can spare you a few moments.' He held the door aside.

The chief was in his anteroom, also dressed formally. He shook hands courteously.

'*Bula vinaka*, Sergeant Singh, I regret that we meet again under such tragic circumstances.'

'I do too, Ratu Osea. Thank you for seeing me.'

Neither man invited her to sit. 'First, I want to assure you that the police will do their utmost to find the killer of these two fine young people of Tanoa. Inspector Horseman is on his way with the scene of crime and forensic specialists, and additional officers. A doctor should get here before them. I'm afraid I cannot move Kelera until the doctor has examined her. The church will be sealed until the specialists have completed their search.'

'Thank you for notifying me, Sergeant. I understand these procedures are unavoidable.'

'I'm grateful, Ratu. I've spoken with Kelera's parents. The pastor expressed a wish for the service to be held on the *rara*. Should it rain, he thinks the school shelter would do.'

Ilai and the chief exchanged glances. 'You may advise him of my approval, if you see him before I do.'

'Thank you. I'll ask him if he needs anything from the church. I can get those items processed as a priority and leave them outside the church for his helpers.'

'Thank you for your consideration, Sergeant Singh. Now we must be going.'

'Gentlemen, may I beg you both to urgently consider who could have killed Kelera?'

'I will certainly do that, Sergeant,' Ratu Osea replied. 'However, Tanoa has been filling up with visitors from around the district and beyond for several days now. The criminal is probably not one of us. What do you say, Ilai?'

'*Dina*, probably not, Ratu.'

'Please let me know straight away if you notice anyone or anything suspicious, gentlemen. I will need to talk to you after the ceremonies are over.'

The chief nodded. 'Please excuse us now, Sergeant.' The two elders paced down the path ahead of her. She felt ineffectual.

She walked a little further up the slope and looked back to the bridge where more than a hundred people had assembled. The bright colours of floral garments splashed over the grass as more people made their way to join the crowd clustering around the bridge.

Singh returned to the church where the three officers were still examining, bagging, and tagging. She flipped through the box of tagged evidence bags, but nothing grabbed her attention at first sight.

She went over to Musudroka. 'Tani, you've been working with the villagers for a few days. Can you write me a list of all the men who smoke?'

Musudroka frowned. 'I haven't spent time with many of them.'

'That's okay, Tani. Just write down the names of the smokers you know. That will give us a start. Please take a break from the search and do it now.' Musudroka looked surprised by her insistence but obeyed, squatting down by the nearest wall. He pulled out his notebook and turned to a new page.

The men had finished the tea, so she picked up the tray to carry it back to the pastor's house. She hoped she hadn't put too much pressure on Kelera's parents.

The pastor opened the door and took the tray from her. 'Come in, Sergeant, you are a blessing.'

Astonished, Singh sat at the table again. How could her questioning during such suffering be anything but a rude intrusion? Mrs Tora smiled at her. 'Yes, my dear, you are indeed. Giving us this task is helping. I did not believe I could come up with a single name. My soul is stricken, but this task has made my mind function again. That is a blessing. We're getting on quite well with the list of smokers. Not finished yet, though.'

'My wife is right—we didn't know where to start at first. Then it occurred to me: a good method would be to take each house in turn, and ask ourselves, "Who smokes in that family?" Write the names and move on to the next house. Mostly, we can do it. If we are uncertain about anyone, we don't write their name. You can rely that our list is correct, even though it is not complete.'

'Pastor Joni, you're a scholar. You would make a great detective. Mrs Tora, too.'

'Oh no, no, no, I found my true calling,' he said, but looked pleased all the same. 'Did you speak to the chief?'

'Yes, he approved your proposal to move the service to the *rara* or the school shelter.' The pastor nodded, satisfied.

'Where are your children?' Singh asked, suddenly alarmed by the silence.

'Oh, they'll be alright. They went with their young friends down to the bridge to meet the guests. It's good for them to be outdoors, under God's sky.'

Singh was a bit surprised by their easy confidence in their children's safety. 'I'll go down there, too. I'd like to check they're okay.'

'We will remain here until it's time to go to the *rara*,' Pastor Joni said.

A low murmur from the unseen crowd reached Singh when she came out of the house. She hurried off, hoping Horseman had arrived. As she approached the bridge, the jumble of people sorted themselves into two lines, like a funnel: children lining each side of the narrow bridge, then two widely spaced rows of adults with *salusalu* garlands ready in their hands. The others crowded behind the human barricades. The chief and Ilai stood in the middle of this central space. Singh spotted the Tora children with some other teenagers, their arms round each other. Thank goodness.

Vehicle doors slammed, and a minute later a Fijian woman led the six foreign guests to the bridge. Was it Ratu Osea's daughter, Adi Ana? Yes, as they got closer she was certain of it. The chief and Ilai walked slowly across the bridge to meet the guests. Melissa was among them. They all shook hands, taking their time about it in Fijian fashion. Singh wondered what the VIPs had been told about Kelera, if anything.

An upbeat Fijian welcome song pierced the quiet. Singh's heart lifted, as always, when she heard a Fijian choir. The guests would never guess the customary verve and sparkle was toned down by grief.

The chief led his delighted guests between the lines of curtseying children. The reception line garlanded the chief, Ilai, and all the guests with *salusalu* of fresh flowers, while the entire crowd sang another song. Ratu Osea turned left and led the guests along the riverbank towards the remains of the fort. It looked as if a guided village tour was the first item on the program.

Singh returned to the church, willing Horseman and the doctor to arrive soon.

41

Melissa sat on the mats with the other foreign guests, garlanded with sweet-scented mokosoi leaves and frangipani. She was excited to be at her first *yaqona* ceremony. Like the others, she sat respectful and uncomprehending while the Fijian speeches rumbled on. In front of them, in the middle of the pavilion, stood the carved *tanoa* which divided the day guests on one side from the people of Tanoa on the other.

In the clear space around the *tanoa*, three young men in grass skirts solemnly prepared the brew. Muscles rippled beneath their oiled skin. They poured water from a length of bamboo, swirled the sinnet bag of ground *yaqona* root through the water, and squeezed it, again and again, until the mixture was right. The same principle as a tea bag, really. The server, moving with military precision, scooped up a coconut bowl of the beige brew and knelt before the chief. He bowed his head low and proffered the bowl. The chief clapped three times, took the bowl, and downed it amid approving claps and shouts.

Once the principals on either side had been served, the solemnity lifted, and the audience chatted quietly. Then a second round began. The dour-looking headman, who had greeted them when they arrived, invited guests and the media to take photos. Melissa shot footage of guests shuffling around on their knees, careful to keep their heads lower than the chief's. She was delighted with everything.

The chief, Adi Ana, and the headman rose. The drinkers immediately hushed. The headman spoke directly to the foreign guests. 'Ladies and gentlemen, our honoured guests, you are now Tanoa villagers for the day. After our lunch and reconciliation ceremony, you will have some free time. You may go wherever you please. At the school there is an exhibition of children's work and a display by our potters. For those interested in farming, you can join guided tours of our plantations, including our spice projects. Later, there'll be a rugby match here on the *rara* between Tanoa and our closest village, Lailai.'

Enthusiastic applause followed this last announcement. The solemn headman looked disconcerted. 'You already know that someone died unexpectedly in our village last night. Ratu Osea and the deceased's family decided our ceremonies today must go ahead. In accordance with Fiji law, police officers are here to investigate. Do not be surprised if you see uniformed officers about. This is normal routine in such cases.'

The audience quietened again. 'Please stretch your legs for ten minutes while the boys prepare this space for a presentation of *meke*, Fijian traditional dances.'

Melissa was beyond impressed by how this backblocks village, which had no electricity or phone connections, could mount such a slickly organised event. Unimaginable!

And where was Joe? She expected him to be here by now. On the journey to Tanoa, Adi Ana had told them that a young woman had just died. Melissa was immediately alarmed. Was it Kelera? She said nothing to the other guests. It was probably a natural death, but what if it had been murder? What if Vili's murderer had struck again? She had her mobile, but it wouldn't be right to call Joe about this, overheard by others in the van. She'd sent a text but hadn't got a reply. Joe said he would leave by eleven o'clock. He should be here soon. She'd noticed Susie at the edge of the crowd during the garlanding. How beautiful was that? She fingered her *salusalu*, releasing more exotic scents.

But, if there had been a second murder, she needed to know. Without Joe by her side, she was a little afraid. Tanoa was beautiful, but very, very foreign.

42

Ash arrived with Alisi, the photographer, and a forensics officer Singh had not met before. She welcomed them with open arms. Figuratively, anyway. Her natural reserve with anyone beyond family and friends always escalated with male colleagues. Ash approved of their work in the church and took over from her. She allowed Tani to join Ash when he finished his list of smokers. She deployed two constables on village patrol, while the third accompanied her to the *rara*. She could see the bridge from one end of the *rara*. She didn't want to miss Horseman's arrival.

The six foreign guests, including Melissa, sat on low, carved chairs at the front of the VIP shelter. More than two hundred spectators gathered around the perimeter. The small boys stamped in first, young warriors in grass skirts and war paint, brandishing their small clubs. Their treble voices belied the menace of their advance right up to the guests of honour. The older boys and men followed, filling the space surrounded by the spectators.

Singh loved a good *meke*, and they were always good. Fijians performed these action songs wholeheartedly, not holding back on the dramatic or threatening aspects, but enjoying themselves so hugely that no one could feel intimidated. Today's performance was more subdued. And no wonder. The performers accepted that the show must go on, despite this second murder. But they couldn't perform at their best. Even if they could, it would seem disrespectful to Kelera and her family. Tomasi would have been disappointed, if he'd been here. Did he know who'd killed Vili and Kelera? If the doctor could be certain Kelera died later than noon yesterday, Tomasi was off the hook.

A constable jogged slowly up the hill. He'd struggle to pass his fitness test right now, panting like that.

'Sergeant, the doctor's arrived,' he managed to puff out.

'*Vinaka*, Constable. Where is he?'

'She, Sarge. The doctor's a lady. Dr Krishna.' Singh ticked herself off twice: first, for being distracted by the *meke* and missing the doctor's arrival; second, for assuming a pathologist would be a man. Susie Singh, who was always annoyed when men assumed a detective sergeant would be a man! Beating herself up about that would have to wait, however.

'Oh, good. Where is she?'

'Inside the church already. I escorted her there and ran straight up to you.'

'Anything else to report? Anyone suspicious?'

'No, Sarge. The pastor asked to go to his office to collect what he needed for the service. I couldn't deny him.'

'You did right.'

'Anyone who's not at the *rara* or doing jobs for the day must be inside their houses, Sarge. There's no one around the paths at all.'

'You're doing well, Constable. Base yourself up here now while I go to see the doctor. Keep an eye out on what you can see of the village, as well as what's going on around the *rara*.'

Singh made haste back to the church. She hoped against hope that the doctor could give a definite time of death. Doctors were always so cautious about that. She had previously assumed that caution masked incompetence, but the wonderful Dr Young was even more cautious than others.

She entered the church, pulled on cap, overshoes, and gloves, and approached the woman kneeling beside Kelera. Alisi was taking photos at the doctor's confident direction.

Singh introduced herself. Dr Lakshmi Krishna had dark skin,

beautiful brown eyes with blueish whites, gold-rimmed glasses, and a gold stud in her nose. Perhaps around thirty, like herself. And maybe not the wrong side of thirty, unlike herself. She squatted down beside the doctor.

'Probably death by strangulation, you could see that for yourselves. It's possible she died some other way and was strangled post, but I can't rule on that until the post-mortem. I gather Matt Young's coming back from leave to do that. I'll assist him if I can wangle it. I need more experience, and Matt's the best. Pretty hot too, don't you think, Susie? Call me Lucky, by the way.'

Singh was surprised by such instant familiarity from a doctor, but couldn't refuse. She returned Dr Krishna's friendly smile. 'I was getting to know Kelera quite well, Lucky. It's hard for me, seeing her like this. It's very important that we know the time of death ASAP. Our chief suspect for last week's murder has been in custody since just after 11:00 a.m. yesterday. If Kelera was killed after that time, he's in the clear for her death.'

Dr Krishna nodded vigorously. 'I'll see. Give me more time, would you? I've only been here five minutes.'

Singh went back outside, intending to check on Mr and Mrs Tora's progress with their list, but she saw them ahead, making their way to the *rara*. The church service must begin soon, and that would be a dreadful ordeal for them, knowing their daughter was lying dead in their church. She hoped the service would bring them comfort, as Pastor Joni had said.

She turned back to the church and here was Horseman striding along, his limp not so bad today. At the sight of his cheerful smile, she gladly shrugged off the burden she'd shouldered so eagerly. Maybe she wasn't quite ready for the rank of Inspector yet.

They shook hands. 'It's good to see you, Susie. Is Melissa okay?'

'She was with the VIPs watching the *meke* fifteen minutes ago. I came back here when the doctor arrived.'

'Great. Had lunch yet?'

'No, sir. Still in my backpack.'

'I've got mine too. Show me the scene; we'll talk with the doc, and then you can brief me over our lunchboxes. I'm sure Melissa will enjoy the traditional spread under the feasting shelters with the Weston descendants. They seemed a very nice bunch when I met them yesterday.'

43

Despite the clouds getting blacker and lower, the rain held off throughout the *lovo* feast.

The rousing melody of one of Fiji's favourite hymns, *A Mighty Fortress is Our God*, signalled the start of the service. 'They're taking quite a risk, having the service on the *rara*,' Horseman said. 'Let's go up. I'd like to pay Pastor Joni my respects. Check that Melissa's okay, too.'

Horseman walked discreetly beside the rows of singers towards the front. He spotted Melissa's back in the front row, among the Weston guests. Ratu Osea, Adi Ana, and Ilai were all there. Horseman stood at the end of the third row and automatically joined in. Not to do so would attract attention. Steadily, the music overpowered the subdued people who gave the final chorus their all, in four-part harmony and full volume. Just as if one of them had not killed two of their own young people in the last seven days.

When the congregation sat, Horseman went to stand at the back with Singh, beside the media reps. If Melissa turned around, she'd see him. She was safe, he could do no more right now.

Pastor Joni brought his hands together to pray. Horseman glanced at Singh—they couldn't leave yet. The pastor's voice quavered at first, then like the hymn, strengthened as he thanked God for the gift of Kelera, beseeched Him to receive her with mercy, to bless her mourning family and all the people of Tanoa, and to guide the police in their investigations. Horseman pronounced a firm and sincere amen to that.

At the end of the prayer, Horseman bowed to the pastor and left with Singh, heading down the slope to the church.

He gave in to a rare urge to share. 'I think Pastor Joni has restored all our souls a little. With the exception of the killer's, maybe. The hymn and prayer did me good. Renewed my purpose.' He stopped, embarrassed.

'Me too. We can rely on God's help now Pastor Joni has prayed for us,' Singh replied.

Was she being ironic? 'Do you believe in God, Susie? Sorry, I shouldn't have asked you such a personal question. You don't need to answer.'

'That's okay. I'm not sure. I only go to the Sikh temple in Nadi for holy days if I happen to be visiting my family. But on the whole, I think there's got to be something greater than humans. I believed just now, during that song and the pastor's prayer. Don't know how long that will last.' She smiled.

'Now I'm stronger. Is that psychology or God? I'll go for God.' He smiled at her. 'Let's see if Dr Krishna can exclude Tomasi yet.'

'Good timing. Here are the first drops of rain.'

Ash and the SOCOs were fingertip searching the area between the church and the neighbouring buildings.

'Got anything yet, Ash?' Horseman asked.

Ash shook his head. 'We're bagging everything, just in case. Nothing has struck me as significant yet, I'm sorry to say. Doesn't mean we won't pick up on something when we get the lot back to the lab.' Horseman tried not to look disappointed.

'Any cigarette butts?' Singh asked.

'One. Everything's very clean, swept for today. It's likely that one butt was dropped during the night. My thinking is, even if there's a print that does match the one we've got from the hideout, that's not conclusive.'

'Not in itself, Ash, but every little piece of circumstantial evidence can help build a case. You SOCOs are invaluable. Is Dr Krishna still inside?'

'Sure is. Not what I was expecting, sir.'

Horseman was puzzled. 'Why?'

Ash shrugged. 'You'll see.'

When they entered, the doctor was packing her equipment away. Kelera lay on a stretcher, wrapped in a green sheet.

Horseman offered his hand. 'Good to meet you, Dr Krishna. I'm grateful you were on the spot at FSM up at Tamavua Heights. That saved forty minutes travel time, at least.'

'Call me Lucky, Inspector. A shame we meet in these circumstances but what a pleasure to meet Joe Horseman! I'll call you Joe, shall I?'

He was a bit put out. He really preferred to keep things formal at work. But it would be churlish to reject her friendly gesture.

'Of course, um, Lucky. You know the time of death is our top priority with Kelera. Can you help us with that?'

'Well, I really don't want to pre-empt Matt Young, Joe.'

'I understand, but we need something now. If it turns out to be way off the mark later, so be it. I know you can only indicate a time range at this stage.'

'Well, as long as you won't hold a mistake against me. I'm not fully qualified as a pathologist yet.' She looked up at him over her gold-rimmed spectacles. 'Well, considering the appearance of lividity and the degree of rigor mortis, I would estimate she died more than twelve hours ago, say between mid-afternoon and midnight yesterday.'

'Not twenty hours ago? Before 11:00 a.m. yesterday?'

Dr Krishna rolled her eyes. 'Well, now you're pinning me down, Joe! Not in my opinion.'

'*Vinaka*, that's very helpful.'

'Just hope I'm right! I need to impress Matt Young to wangle the registrar's position!' She winked at him. Horseman looked at his watch to cover his surprise at her open sharing of her naked ambition with a stranger.

'Susie, can you get two constables to carry the stretcher to Dr Krishna's vehicle, please?' Singh hurried out.

'Can you escort me to the truck, Joe?' Dr Krishna asked.

'You'll have to excuse me, Lucky. DC Musudroka can give you any help you need. I've got to get back up to the *rara* right away. You take care now, and drive safely. Many thanks.'

***

'Susie, let me go through my conclusions again. For each point, tell me if you agree or not.' They sat on the floor at the back of the empty church.

'If Lucky's time-of-death estimate is right, Tomasi has a watertight alibi for Kelera's murder. It's highly unlikely there are two murderers in Tanoa, so that means there's next to no chance Tomasi killed Vili.'

'Agreed, sir.'

'That leaves us again with the chief and Ilai as our only suspects. The only ones with a possible motive.'

'As far as we know, sir.'

'Sure. As for means, Tomasi claims he delivered the club to the chief's house, but it was Ilai who came out to the porch and received it. Wherever it was stored, both Ilai and Ratu Osea could get it whenever they wanted, presumably.'

'I agree.'

'Opportunity. The chief claims he was in Suva when Vili was killed, but we only have his staff and Ilai to confirm it. I don't trust him. The pastor says the chief returned here last night, within the time frame Dr Krishna indicates. Ilai freely admits he was here both Saturday nights.'

'They both smoke, too,' Singh added.

'Ah yes. Our watcher. Not necessarily the murderer, but probable. Was it Vili or Kelera he was spying on, or both?'

Singh continued. 'And why? Was the plan always to kill Vili? In which case, was he simply waiting for the right moment? Tomasi stole the club three weeks before Vili's murder.'

Horseman pondered. 'If he was fixated on Kelera, the watcher might have killed Vili to get him out of the way.'

'True. But Kelera?'

'As I've said before, the chief strikes me as obsessive about today's ceremonies. So he could nurse other obsessions, too.'

'I agree. sir. But somehow I think he's less likely than Ilai to carve out a hideout in the lantana and keep watch for hours on end. However, that could be due to my prejudice that such behaviour is the opposite of chiefly.'

'True, Ilai gives away even less than the chief. My gut feeling is he's the better bet.'

'Mine too. We can go in hard, but I wonder if either will tell us anything after the ceremonies. My guess is they won't.' Singh sighed.

'If we're right about Ilai, why did the chief want the club? It can't have been to kill Vili, unless his murder was masterminded by the chief. Always possible. But if Ilai was acting alone…'

'Tomasi talked about the village shame, and wanting to remove the club from public view. Don't you believe that was the chief's suggestion?' Singh asked.

'I think it's what the chief told Tomasi. But I'm sure there's more. The timing of the theft is relevant—plenty of time before today for another try or two if the plan didn't work the first time. The chief is fixated on the apology ceremony. That club has a role to play today, I'm sure of it.'

Horseman got up, propped open the nearest shutter, and looked out. 'That sprinkle of rain is getting heavier. People are moving off the *rara* now. They must have decided to use the school for the reconciliation ceremony.'

'Do we go up there now?' Singh asked.

'Yes. That's where the action's going to be.'

She looked at him, her green eyes clouded. 'I don't know how the Tanoans can keep going with all this.'

'They're the same as us. They keep going because they have to. Duty.'

Singh looked down. 'I keep seeing Kelera, strangled. I'm afraid,' she whispered.

Any response would be crass, but he couldn't pretend he hadn't heard her fear. He touched her shoulder. 'That's because you don't know what's coming. None of us does. Let's go up to the school and face it. Then you'll be fine, Susie.'

44

Horseman and Singh grabbed umbrellas and hurried to the school. Butting up against a classroom, the shelter shed was open on three sides. The rain machine-gunned the corrugated iron roof. Mist crept in, enshrouding the garlands of yellow allamanda and purple bougainvillea. It was damp and chill.

In the front row of the seated audience sat Pastor Joni, Sasa the teacher, and Melissa. She flashed Horseman a happy smile as he entered with Singh. Uniformed constables hovered at the back and the sides.

The Weston descendants stood in a line at right angles to the wall. Facing them about two metres away was a line of Tanoan elders. In between the rows stood Ratu Osea, in tailored *sulu*, white shirt with Fiji Regiment tie, formal pinstripe jacket. In front of the chief stood a metre-high wooden bracket, its fascia carved with the word *Destroyer* in Fijian. On the bracket rested an old war club. It looked like the club which crushed Rev Weston's skull a hundred and thirty years ago, and that of Viliame Bovoro eight days ago. It was the same shape, but Horseman couldn't see the detailed carving. He couldn't know. He couldn't seize the club and wreck the ceremony. What if it was a balsa-wood mock-up like the *meke* props?

Two older boys came in, carrying a firepit made from a 44-gallon drum cut in half and fitted with wooden carrying poles. It contained smouldering coals. The boys added kindling, then more wood as the fire got going. The warmth was welcome. A thoughtful, hospitable gesture.

Ratu Osea began to speak, but he was hard to hear above the hammering rain. Horseman only caught snatches. The chief spoke in English, addressing the Weston descendants directly.

'...tradition to name the finest chiefly clubs...when Destroyer killed your worthy ancestor, it also destroyed...my village...never again...our children...the sins of our ancestors...God to forgive us...your forgiveness. To prove our sincerity...witness the end of Destroyer.'

'What? That was what the fire was for?' He turned to Singh. 'Tell the nearest uniform to be ready to seize the club if it goes in the fire.' Horseman had a word with the other constables. So he missed what the chief said next. Ilai approached Ratu Osea and knelt. The chief solemnly picked up the club and laid it in Ilai's spread hands. The atmosphere was electric. Ilai approached the fire, lowered the club.

Horseman and two constables edged in. Ilai froze for just a beat, then straightened up and held Destroyer aloft.

'No, no, Destroyer shall not burn! Never!' Ilai's bull's roar cut through the drumming rain.

'Stop, Ilai, I command you!' the chief ordered.

'Our ancestors are angry! Hear their drums of war! I obey our ancestors!' the headman shouted. He whirled the deadly club around his head, suddenly lunged, grabbed Melissa, and knocked Sasa flying as he tried to pull her away. The arc of the whirling club was huge, rising and falling at Ilai's will. Stunned, people reeled away. Those on the fringes ran, those in the middle dropped to the mats and rolled. Women and children screamed. A constable tackled Ilai from behind, but the club whacked him as it whirled, leaving him sprawled on his face. Ilai cleared a path with the wildly looping club, headed out the side of the shed, dragged Melissa down the slope, one arm pinning her to him from shoulder to waist. She stumbled and lost her foothold. Ilai cuffed her, lowered his arm to her waist, half-carrying her. Melissa did not cry out.

What had he done? Lured the woman he loved to her death? He had failed her. But Ilai could not harm her, would not win.

Was Ilai making for the bridge and the car park? Perhaps the murderer didn't know himself. He could only give chase. 'Tanielo, get ahead and cut Ilai off at the bridge. He mustn't cross. Constable, go with him. Singh, radio the SOCOs and get them on the chase. Then arrest the chief. I'm going after Ilai.'

Fear drove him, fear for Melissa. His body must obey. His knee must work. He hurtled after Ilai, who was slowed by dragging Melissa and wielding the weighty club. Musudroka was already ahead of them. Go, Tani, man!

Damn the wet grass! He slipped, ended up scrabbling, then rolling. He managed to stop, pushed up to his feet, gave chase again.

Tani and the uniform reached the bridge. Ilai read their tactic and veered off to the right well before the bridge. How terrified was Melissa? Ilai gripped her so tightly she must be in pain. He hoped she could faint—she wouldn't feel the pain and Ilai would have to carry her full weight. The chasers and the quarry were equally handicapped by the infernal downpour and slick, treacherous surface. Where could Ilai go? He knew every clod of his land. Horseman had no chance of predicting his destination, if he had one.

Ilai forced Melissa along a route roughly parallel with the river bank. There were no more structures, only pig pens further up the hill. Horseman glanced behind. Some of the villagers had picked themselves up and joined the chase.

Ilai suddenly veered again, stumbled but regained his balance, sweeping Melissa up and tossing her over his shoulder. Had she tried to trip him up? Do *not* be brave, Melissa; he could kill you if you anger him!

But Ilai had veered on purpose. He now headed back to the river, to the steep cliffs past the bridge. Would he jump off? Throw Melissa onto the rocks far below? No, that wouldn't get him anywhere. She was a hostage, a means to an end, a lever.

Horseman gradually closed the gap. He was about ten metres behind Ilai when he understood. Ahead of them was the ruined fortress. Ilai intended to hold out in his ancestors' bloody keep. He would hold the high ground, literally.

Horseman paused to take in the field. Now he could see Musudroka and the constable moving quickly along from the bridge, keeping below the top of the cliff. The SOCOs were still way off, running along the main street, but they'd catch up in a few minutes. Did they have a few minutes? Horseman gestured to Musudroka, now just a few metres behind him. Pointing up at the fort, he signalled him to approach the fortress from the river. Just like attackers in the days when Destroyer was young. Was the club the original Destroyer, then? Ilai must believe so—he wouldn't defy the chief to save a mock-up.

Now Ilai climbed up to the fortress, the stones black and streaming with rain. His bare feet were sure. Destroyer was his prop now. Melissa no longer struggled.

'Ilai, there's nowhere else for you to go. Stop there and let's talk.' Hard to sound calm when shouting.

Ilai gave no sign he'd heard. Louder. 'Ilai, where are you going? Stop, we can talk.'

When Ilai was at the top, beside the topmost boulder, he turned. He let Melissa down from his shoulder, pinning her to his body with one arm, so tight she gasped.

'Ilai, have sense, man. Melissa can hardly breathe. Let her go. She hasn't offended you. Please, let her go.'

Now Singh was beside him. 'Ratu Osea wants to speak to Ilai, sir.' Horseman couldn't take his eyes off Ilai. 'A few seconds, Ratu. That's it.' Ilai had defied his chief, why would he listen to him now?

'Ilai, please release my guest, Melissa. Remember your duty as my headman, as a host. I command you, as your chief.'

'You betrayed me, all of us. How could you cast Destroyer into the furnace? You are the destroyer, Ratu!' He raised the club, held it aloft, shaking it before the gathering crowd below. Horseman inched closer while Ilai eyed his audience.

'Ilai, God will forgive your sins if you repent. You know that. Do not harm this innocent. Please, in Jesus' name, let our guest go,' Pastor Joni said. Horseman was at the top of the earth rampart now. He smiled at Melissa. Her eyes implored him, but she managed a faint smile.

Yes, what he'd been waiting for! The top of Musudroka's head appeared above the lower battlement behind Ilai, who was now warming to his audience, gripping Melissa tight against his body.

'Neither God nor our chief will help us!' He whirled Destroyer.

Musudroka's head edged from one side of the fortress crown. Melissa looked up. Ilai felt her movement, whipped his head around.

Horseman hurled himself up, arms outstretched. He grasped Ilai's ankles, jerking them out. Musudroka forced Ilai's head back with one hand, seized his neck in a chokehold with his other forearm. But Ilai did not let Melissa go. Blindly, he swung the club behind him, but Musudroka avoided the blows—he must have squeezed into a niche. Ilai's strength seemed superhuman, and his hold on his hostage did not weaken.

But Ilai had to break the chokehold or he couldn't hang on much longer. He transferred Destroyer to his left hand, ramming its length against Melissa's body. His right hand punched and pried at the arm squeezing his throat, but Musudroka managed to tighten his hold. It was a weird tug-of-war, with Horseman's weight dragging on Ilai's ankles and preventing him from kicking, while Musudroka rammed the man's head against the stone battlement.

Soon the choke sapped Ilai's strength and he fought for breath. His right hand fell from his throat. A beat later, he dropped Melissa, and Horseman caught her to his body, breaking her fall. Two constables dashed forward to grab Ilai.

Horseman wanted to hold her forever, despite the torrent, despite pain, despite everything. She didn't return his grasp. He feared she was unconscious. But after what seemed an eternity, one hand reached round his waist and held him. Thank God.

'Say something, Melissa. How are you? Can you stand?'

Eventually she whispered, 'I think so, Joe. Try me.' He gently lowered her until her feet were on the slick rock, his arms round her. 'Yep, I think I'm okay.'

Horseman had no choice but to release Melissa to an insistent Mere Tora and her motherly friends who scrambled up the fortress, helped her down, and took her away.

Musudroka had hoisted himself over the fortress crown, ready to subdue Ilai. But Ilai sat bent over on the rock, heaving as his lungs demanded more air than he could take in. Musudroka laughed in relief as Horseman joined him and they shook hands.

'Great work, Tani. You can have the pleasure of snapping the cuffs on our prisoner.' Ilai said nothing as Horseman recited the caution and Musudroka cuffed him.

'I want one of you to hold each arm at all times. Don't let go,' Horseman instructed the two constables. They led Ilai down from the fortress.

Elated, Musudroka laughed. 'All my practice as a kid scrambling up waterfalls, sir!'

Ash and his team rushed them. 'Fantastic, you two. Tani, you did good!'

'Yes, he did. Hang on, where's the club?' Horseman asked.

Singh stepped forward. 'Got an evidence bag on you, Ash? It's still lying behind you, up on the rocks. I've been watching it, but as I've got Ratu Osea in custody…'

'Got it.' Ash scrambled to retrieve Destroyer.

Horseman had almost forgotten the chief. 'Ratu Osea, *vinaka* for trying to intervene with Ilai. Sergeant Singh will escort you to Suva for questioning at the police station. I need to search your house as well as Ilai's, with your permission.'

'You do not have it. Not without a warrant. I wish you to remove my handcuffs, Inspector. You have my word I will not try to escape.'

'Not possible, I'm afraid, Ratu. I wish it were, but…' Horseman replied.

'I need to return to my house to pack some things.'

'Not possible, again. A constable will escort Adi Ana while she packs some things for you. Don't you have all you need in your Suva house?'

The chief glared, but he walked quietly between Singh and the constable towards the bridge and his uncertain future.

'Ash, plenty for you SOCOs to do. Photographs here and up at the school. Collect any evidence. Seal the chief's house as well as Ilai's.'

'Right away, sir. Alisi got quite a few shots of the action. Don't forget the *Fiji Times* and *Fiji One* are here too.' The so-called action had fired up the patient, methodical Ash.

'Good Lord, I completely forgot about them. Too late now.' He knew what the super would say when he saw the afternoon's events on tonight's TV news and in Monday morning's paper. 'Sergeant Singh, radio Superintendent Navala please, tell him about the media. Can he get them to hold the story? Press could jeopardise the trials.'

Now for Ilai. 'Tanielo, lock Ilai in the vehicle, keep the two constables on guard. Do not permit them to speak to Ilai under any circumstances, no matter what he does or says. He could trick them. I've got some things to do here before I leave.'

He tracked down Melissa in the pastor's house, smothered in the ample bosoms and hearts of Mere Tora and her friends, who plied their patient with hot, sweet tea, just like his own mother would have done. No way would they release her into his arms, so he didn't try. They reached for each others' hands.

'How are you, Melissa?'

'No bones broken. A few cuts and scrapes. Maybe some bruises tomorrow.' Her smile reached her blue eyes this time. 'Unlike you, I won't need physical therapy.'

'Me?'

'Rock injures ribs and muscle when you throw your body at it, Joe. You've got a bunch of cuts, too. I guess you're running on adrenaline right now. But one leg's carrying most of your weight and you limp badly.'

'Well, maybe if the therapist is Melissa Martini, I can be persuaded.'

He turned serious. 'I'm so relieved you're…' His voice seized.

'I was very scared, Joe. I've never been so scared in my life.' Serious again. Was she reproachful? She had every right to be.

'Melissa, I am so sorry I got you into this. I'm to blame for everything. It could so easily…'

'What nonsense you talk,' interrupted one of the ladies. 'You may dominate a rugby game, but you can't control much else! Ilai put Melissa in danger, not you! You saved her. Be sensible, Josefa Horseman!'

'*Io*, Josefa,' said Mere Tora. 'And I know you would have saved my Kelera, if anyone could. Are you sure Ilai killed her?'

'No, not yet, but probably. We've arrested him. Sergeant Singh and I will question him properly in Suva. Did any of you suspect him?'

The ladies shook their heads. 'He's always been a quiet man. A hard worker, devoted to our chief,' Mrs Bovoro said.

Another spoke up. 'You know, since his wife died, and even more this year, I noticed he would disappear, often for hours and hours, couldn't be found. I thought it was odd, but I assumed he was just getting older, and liked to be by himself more.'

'He never got over the children settling in New Zealand. Sometimes he spoke bitterly about them,' Mere Tora added.

'*Io*, Ilai spoiled what was to be a wonderful day. No one will want to see our pottery now.'

'Vili would have been proud to have visitors tour his spice project,' Mrs Bovoro said.

Mrs Tora said, 'I think God didn't want the reconciliation ceremony to happen. Everything went fine until then. He just put His foot down after Kelera died. "Enough!" he said.' She broke into sobs, muffled by a shoulder as her friends hugged and patted her.

Horseman felt awkward, unable to express his admiration and sympathy. '*Vinaka vakalevu*, ladies. Now, I need to take Melissa back to Suva.'

'We'd love to keep her with us, but I know we can't. We must get back to the descendants of Mr Weston. What will they think! At least we can give them tea.'

After prolonged farewells, they got away just as the rain was easing. Melissa was correct, his right knee couldn't support him. He made a supreme effort to hide it from her, but failed. Someone passed him a stick and he hobbled to the vehicle.

45

Singh switched on the recorder at half past five. As the twin tapes started to spin, she announced the date, time, and the names of those present in Interview Room Three.

'I understand you have declined to consult a legal representative, Mr Takilai,' she said.

'Yes, I have,' Ilai answered. 'I have no need of advice from foreigners.'

'I can arrange a Fijian solicitor to talk to you, if you wish,' Horseman offered.

'No, that is not necessary. I have decided to answer your questions.'

'Very sensible of you,' Horseman said.

'There is nothing to hope for any longer. My chief has betrayed me.'

'Tell us about the theft of the club you call Destroyer from the Fiji Museum,' Singh began.

'Ratu Osea did not consult me.'

'Does he usually consult you about his plans?' Singh asked.

'*Io*, very often.'

'Why didn't he consult you about this matter?'

'I don't know. Maybe he wanted it to be a secret, but he knows I would never talk about any of his plans unless he wanted me to.' Ilai sounded aggrieved.

'What exactly did he tell you about the theft of the club?'

Ilai's account accorded pretty well with Tomasi's statement.

Maybe Ilai was going to tell the truth after all. His mad rage was apparently gone.

'Was stealing the club a good idea, Ilai?' Horseman asked.

'I don't think so. The apology and reconciliation ceremony for the Weston descendants was enough. The descendants sincerely forgave the past sin of murder. They did not want to see the club burned. They had no knowledge of it whatsoever. Even I did not know it still existed until my chief told me. To destroy our history, the strength of our spirit, was unwise, in my opinion. Just to make a dramatic show. I could not let it happen.'

Horseman privately agreed. 'When did you learn this was the plan?'

'The day Tomasi brought Destroyer to Ratu Osea's Tanoa house. When Tomasi knocked on the door, I went out to receive the club. The chief did not need to talk to Tomasi, so he went away.'

'What reason did the chief give for stealing the club from the museum?'

'He said it belonged here, was rightfully ours. He didn't like visitors gawking at it. I agreed with him, as I did most of the time.' Horseman glanced at Singh to take over.

'Why did you use the club to kill Viliame?' Singh asked.

Ilai glared at her, suspicious. After a few moments, he said, 'It was fitting. A young man, so impatient and ambitious, so full of arrogance. He needed a lesson from tradition. Destroyer was the right instrument.'

Horseman said, 'You didn't give him a chance to learn from that lesson, Ilai.'

Ilai snorted. 'He had many chances. He came to clan meetings with proposals, written out in some modern, meaningless way. I thought he meant well, we all tolerated him, even granted him some land to use. He didn't do too badly. Then he looked into electricity with the government in Suva. None of his business; he had no permission to act as Tanoa's agent at all. Same story with the Henny Penny shed. HP require an electricity supply. We successfully farm to feed ourselves with some to sell. We have mahogany, and when that is harvested, we will be rich enough. We were polite to Viliame, but all his actions flouted our custom. The chief and clan elders are the ones to make decisions. Not young men! How dare he?'

Ilai's anger was flaring again. Best to defuse. 'How did Ratu Osea react to Viliame's schemes?'

'He felt the same as me. But I knew he would never act. He hoped the NLTB would transfer Vili so he couldn't get back to Tanoa so often. But after years of hassling and arguments from the boy, I'd had enough.'

'I can understand how you felt, Mr Takilai,' Singh said. 'But this is not enough to make you murder someone, is it? A respected elder of a chiefly clan, like you? I don't think so.'

Ilai's eyes narrowed. 'You bring a woman's intuition to the matter. You may be right. I discovered he was violating our respected pastor's daughter. Every time he was here. In the spice gardens, like pigs. In the vanilla curing shed. Another example of his contempt for custom and, in this case, what is holy!'

'How did you find out about Viliame and the pastor's daughter, Ilai?' Horseman asked.

'I'm observant. As the chief's deputy, it's my role. They would leave the spice gardens together, then split up and each would return to the village by a different path. Yet their houses are not far from each other. There's only one conclusion to draw when a couple try to stop people seeing them together.'

'Maybe so, Ilai. But why did that anger you so much? They would make a suitable young couple, wouldn't they?'

'She was a pure virgin until that arrogant boy set his sights on her! They both deceived their parents!' Ilai's anger flared again.

Horseman sought to calm Ilai. 'I'm sure that has happened before in Tanoa, Ilai, because it happens everywhere else. Parents get angry at the time, then the couple marry, and all is forgiven and forgotten.'

Ilai lifted his eyebrows. '*Dina, dina.* But she had a lovely innocence. He destroyed that. I killed him for that.'

Singh asked, 'Did you make an observation post for checking on Viliame and Kelera? Our officers found a neat hideout in the lantana between the upper and lower paths to the spice gardens.'

Ilai looked less hostile now. 'Well yes, that was a good place in daytime. At night it's not easy to see faces, even in moonlight. However, I know everyone in the village by their shape and gait.'

'Did you wait there for Vili last Saturday night?'

'No, I waited just off the lower path, which is the one he used most often. Ratu Osea was in Suva, so I borrowed the club from his house. Two clean blows, that's all it took. I carried Viliame to the church and arranged him in a posture submissive to God. I cleaned the club and returned it.'

'Why Kelera?'

'I felt increasing distaste for her. No, disappointment, really. She displayed excessive emotion after Vili's body was found. I thought perhaps Viliame did not force her. She could very well be a willing partner in sin, maybe an equal partner. My heart broke, that I had been so wrong about her. I heard you, Sergeant, talking to her at the school. She freely admitted she was his lover but he didn't want to marry her! Then it came to me, how Fijians treated widows in the old days. Do you know?' Singh shook her head, although she was well aware of the pre-colonial custom.

'They were strangled, and not efficiently. But I was kind. It was quick, with strong sinnet cord.'

Singh looked appalled. Horseman said, 'You'd better tell us all about it, Ilai. When and where.'

'I need to explain, Inspector. Simple questions like "when and where" won't let you understand the full truth. I kept watch over Kelera for a long time, especially after Viliame died. I wanted to protect her. She and her family are from Kadavu, you know, not even from Viti Levu. Young Tanoa men might take advantage of her, just like Viliame did. Her parents are very devoted to church work, and not watchful enough over their children. They knew how much time she spent working in the spice gardens, but did nothing to rein her in.'

'Perhaps they approved of her work there.' Singh understood why Ilai's sons had all migrated to New Zealand.

'Well, I never wish to make a nuisance of myself. However, I did unavoidably run into Kelera quite often. I used to check that she was safe in her classroom where she liked to work after school and in the evening. I wanted to know when she was going to the river, which can be dangerous. When she saw me she would greet me politely, even the time I sneezed while I was sitting against her classroom wall and she came to the window and looked out.'

His voice softened. 'She said, "*Bula vinaka*, Ilai". *Io*, a few times this last week she discovered me watching over her. I think Viliame's death affected me as well. But I had hope. With Viliame gone, my secrecy was not so important, I believed.'

A tender half-smile played at Ilai's mouth. His obsession with Kelera was not driven by hate.

'What did you hope for, Mr Takilai?' Singh asked.

'Well, she's a serious young woman, well-educated, hard-working, not frivolous. Even though she sinned with Viliame, I could forgive her that. It was he who tempted her to sin. Therefore, I hoped that she might make me a suitable second wife.'

'Please continue, Mr Takilai.'

'Last Thursday after school, Kelera dropped her basket at her house and hastened across the bridge. She started walking along the road. I followed, but she was out of sight when I got to the car park. I got into my ute, soon caught her up and offered her a lift. She wanted to go to the police station to make a phone call. She was subdued. I said I had business in the next village and could give her a lift home in an hour. She said the call would be quick. I thought it was probable she was going to call one of you detectives, and when I asked the constable when I returned, he confirmed she had done so.'

Singh had suspected the Kumi officers had not told all they knew about Kelera's visit there. Now it was obvious their loyalty was to the ruling families of Tanoa, not to the police, not to the law. In short, they were spies for the chief. She would get them all transferred if she possibly could. 'Did you meet her on the way back?' she asked.

'I did, but she's a fast walker and was near the river when I came along. She said she would continue on foot, but I drove along beside her, just to make sure. I soon realised she didn't like that, so when I parked my ute, I told her I needed to check the engine and waited five minutes until she entered her house.

'At daybreak on Friday morning, the day of Viliame's funeral, I saw her through my binoculars. She was dressed in black, ready for the funeral, but she carried her school basket up to her classroom. She is a most conscientious teacher, you know.' He sounded like a proud uncle.

'Instead of hiding out of sight, I entered her classroom where she was marking the children's exercise books. I told her I could forgive her mistake with Viliame. I realise now I timed it badly. She asked me to leave her alone, but I needed her to understand. I tried to explain again how I was looking after her, and would continue to do so. Why was she frightened? She tried to walk past me, but I couldn't let her.'

'Why not?' Singh murmured.

'She may have told her parents, friends, the head teacher, anyone. She may have accused me falsely. I think she might have complained to you about me. That phone call she made suggests that.'

'So what did you do?'

'She panicked, forcing me to restrain her. I stuffed my handkerchief in her mouth, led her to her cupboard, where I found adhesive tape to seal the gag and cord for her wrists. I wanted to take her to the vanilla curing shed in the spice gardens to think about our situation. That would have been meaningful. But I realised she would be missed at the funeral, so she had to go.'

'Go, Ilai?'

'She had to leave the village. So I marched her out the door, down to the bridge. There were few people about, and no one looked at us. I held her arm firmly, she couldn't cry out. She complied, actually. I did need to show her my knife, unfortunately. I put her on the floor of my ute, tied her ankles, and off we went to Lailai village back down the road. I took her to a shed on a relative's cattle project and made her secure there. No one would be going there that day because of Viliame's funeral.

'When I returned after the funeral, I brought her some dalo and a bottle of tea made from soporific herbs. She was thirsty by then, so she drank the whole bottle. While I was engaged in the afternoon search, I kicked myself for acting impulsively. I now had no chance of Kelera agreeing to my proposal. She would report me and I would lose all respect in the community. The people's ill-will would mean I could no longer execute the chief's wishes. My rightful position would be lost and with that, the customary hierarchy that enables Tanoa to function. In effect, I had set in motion a landslide to destroy our community.

'After dark, I brought more food and tea to keep her quiet for the night. She begged me to let her go, said she would never complain about me to anyone. But she refused to become my wife, ever. I had to think.'

Horseman thought, *Why Kelera? Why did you do that? If you'd agreed, he may have released you. You could have left the village and never seen him again.* He glanced at Singh. She looked as dismayed as he felt.

'I spent last night tossing and turning, praying, coming to the same answer over and over. To save Tanoa and our traditional chiefly values, Kelera had to go. She claimed to be a good Christian, yet refused to sacrifice her own desires for the higher good of the community. She looked on the traitor Viliame as her husband. So, let tradition claim her as his widow, by strangulation.

'I couldn't risk leaving her in the shed any longer. After you took Tomasi away, your constable called for a break from the search and I went back there. Kelera was quite weak. She was very thirsty and drank two bottles of tea. Soon she was asleep again. The sinnet twine was quick. It did cut into her perfect neck, though; I am sorry for that.'

'And then?' Singh's voice was soft, sympathetic. Horseman admired her ability to do that; she must detest Ilai.

'I carried her over the rough paddock to the ute, which I drove back to the Tanoa car park. Everyone went to bed early last night, tired out from the search and the celebration preparations. It was quite late when I retrieved Kelera from the ute and brought her to the church in my wheelbarrow, covered in a tarp. I was lucky to miss Ratu Osea returning home from Suva. I had just finished in the church when I saw his torchlight outside and heard his heavy footfalls on the path. I waited for a while, had a smoke, and crept home silently. I'm practised at that. I have good night vision, too.'

'I don't believe you, Ilai,' Horseman said.

Ilai registered shock, as if he'd been insulted.

'What! I have confessed!'

'Not everything, Ilai. You are loyal to your chief, an admirable quality. So loyal, you have left out his part in this dreadful tale. Just as Ratu Osea plotted and ordered the theft of the club, he also ordered Viliame's death, didn't he?'

'No, I've told you what happened.'

'What happened, maybe. But not why. You murdered Viliame on the chief's orders. He just wanted the young upstart out of the way, didn't he?'

'No, um, yes, he wanted him out of the way, but he wished he would just take himself off. He did not order me to kill him! The idea is repellent!'

'Oh, I don't know. You want to return to tradition, the time before the missionaries, before the British. The chiefs' role certainly included punishing wrongdoers and killing off threats. And it was your ancestors who carried out the chiefs' orders.'

'That is true of the past. But not here, not now. Do you think me incapable of making decisions and acting on my own?'

'Not at all. When Ratu Osea is away, you are effectively the chief, aren't you? You run everything.'

'No, when Ratu Osea is absent, he is still the chief. But yes, of course I can manage village business.'

'We'll prepare your statement according to what you've told us, Ilai. You can read it through and make any corrections necessary. Police investigations are still continuing, but as it stands, you'll be charged with murder, kidnapping, imprisonment, and assault.'

Ilai Takilai, headman of Tanoa, said nothing.

46

'I had to escape, Susie. I couldn't breathe. Ilai's version of tradition suffocated me.'

They sat at a tiny table in the corner of the eighty-year-old warehouse that housed Arabica, roasters of Fiji's highlands coffee beans.

'Know what you mean, sir. What really surprised me was how calm he was. Only hours after a rampage with a deadly war club and a hostage!'

'It's often the way. There comes a point when a criminal accepts defeat. Then it can be a relief to tell their side of the story, and at length.'

'Do you really believe Ratu Osea was behind the murders?'

'I don't know. Perhaps we'll never know. The super's questioning him. He's more likely to cooperate with a senior officer, and a Fijian of pure stock, unlike you and me.' He grinned, but Singh frowned.

She said, 'You see, Ilai has a much stronger motive. To Ratu Osea, Vili was annoying, arrogant. He could even have hated Vili as time went by. But for the past two years, the chief has been focused on today. Ilai, on the other hand, was obsessed by Kelera, he loved her. He murdered Vili out of jealousy and Kelera out of a twisted love. It's simple, when you leave out all the red herrings.'

He pondered, nodding. 'You always make sense, Susie. Yet I keep seeing Ratu Osea's face, his eyes focused on something beyond. He's obsessed by his idea that today's ceremonies would save the village's future. I guess that's abstract, quite different from being obsessed with a woman who will never love you back. That's more likely to drive you to murder.'

'Glad you see it my way,' Singh replied, smiling.

'I need another espresso. Make it two?'

'A latte, please.'

'Don't know what you see in latte, myself. All that milk drowns the coffee.'

His phone buzzed. Melissa. '*Bula*, Melissa, how are you?'

Singh went to the counter to order.

'I'm okay, Joe. A few scrapes, which the nurse has dressed very nicely. The doctor wants me to stay for four hours, because of shock. Your sister Eva is here, she wants me to stay too. But you're the one who's hurt. How about you, honey?'

He was pretty sure he'd cracked a rib; the pain when he moved was on the high side. From chest to waist, he was a throbbing mess. But he'd taken worse pummelling on the rugby field. 'I'll survive. When I pick you up, I'll let the medics do their worst. Does that satisfy you?'

'Yes, Joe. Perfect. I'll wait till you come. Any idea when?'

'You've already been there one hour. So, in another three?'

'Okay, I submit. Maybe a nap would be good. Joe?'

'Mm?'

'You are one very brave guy!'

'Nonsense, call of duty, darling. Don't think you got preferential treatment!' he teased.

'Oh no, never! Ciao, babe.'

Singh brought their coffees when he ended the call. They sipped in silence. The waiter delivered coconut shortbread. He wondered how different he would have felt if Ilai had grabbed Elisa, or Mere Tora. He decided his actions would have been the same, but had to concede that the terror that gripped him would have been less intense. He could live with that.

The phone buzzed again. Navala's greeting sounded sombre. 'Super? Any news?'

'Ratu Osea maintains he's cooperating, but who knows? He denies any knowledge of the murders, but eventually owned up to asking Tomasi to steal the club. Says his motive was to reclaim his own property, which he wanted to destroy in today's ceremony as an act of sacrifice. He is obsessed, Joe! You were right, I'm sorry I doubted you.'

'It's hard to imagine, until you meet him.'

'*Io*. You won't be happy about this, Joe. His expensive solicitor has taken it higher, and I have no choice but to charge him with procuring the theft, then releasing him on bail to his Suva home.'

'Hell! Hardly surprising, though. What about searching his houses, both here and Tanoa?'

'Working on it. Solicitor is fighting that, too. But no problem with Ilai's house. We can search that tomorrow morning.'

'That's something.'

'When I say *we*, that does not include you, Joe. Tanielo's reported on this afternoon's highlight. You're ordered to the hospital for a check.'

'Fine, sir. I promised I'd pick Melissa up when she's discharged in three hours. Singh and I are having a coffee, perking up now. We'll be back at the station in fifteen minutes. I'll have time to file my reports.'

'Alright, I was going to order you to hospital immediately, but I'll compromise in return for those reports. I'm sorry Melissa has had such a terrible introduction to Fiji. I'm ashamed, in fact.'

'Me too, sir. But she assures me she enjoyed everything until Ilai grabbed her, and that lasted less than half an hour. I hope she'll be okay.'

'Thirty minutes of terror can have a big impact, Joe. We're all very concerned. I'm confident medical opinion will support my decision to put you on one week's sick leave from tomorrow. That can be extended if a doctor recommends it. You won't need to take your rec. leave. Recover and do some serious PR work for Fiji on Melissa. I won't have you leaving her alone. Singh and the team can handle the mopping up.'

He was about to protest, but stopped himself.

'The super is right,' Singh said, smiling. 'We're all ashamed of what Ilai did to Melissa. You're the only one who can make up for that. I don't like mopping much, but in this case… I'll try to do as good a job as you, sir.'

Tears came to his eyes. Partly pain, partly gratitude. Sometimes the captain needs to go along with what his team wants.

'*Vinaka*, Susie. I know you will. The others, too.'

His hands on the table, he pushed himself up from the chair, paused to find his balance. The adrenaline was subsiding. He straightened gingerly, head swimming. No one was indispensable.

Singh suggested they call in at the pharmacy just down the street. Horseman didn't know why this hadn't occurred to him. He downed several ibuprofen capsules on the spot and they got a cab back to the station.

47

His head swam as he mounted the stairs, but he eventually made it to the CID room. The constables' reports were on his desk. Musudroka was the only one still there, labouring over paperwork. Fair enough, it was still Sunday.

Horseman, Singh, and Musudroka sat together and set to work. Although there was a great deal to report, Horseman's rule about completing paperwork daily made the job manageable. As the ibuprofen kicked in, Horseman found he could get to his feet, carefully. He checked the unoccupied desks for papers that needed to go in the case file. On a table pushed against the wall, there was a pile of books and a stack of manilla files. Ah yes, Musudroka and Taleca had hauled this lot back from the USP Library. That seemed like a lifetime ago now. When was it—Tuesday?

'Did you read this lot, Tani?' Horseman asked.

Musudroka looked wary. 'Hmm, I started on the photocopies, sir. Pretty much heavy going for me. Didn't get very far. I've been at Tanoa most days, then we had the NLTB files to check…'

Horseman grinned. 'No need to be evasive, Tani. What did you read?'

'DS Taleca gave me a report on Rev. Weston's murder. It was interesting, but that old English confuses me a bit. I couldn't see how it could help our case, after all this time.'

'You're wrong there, Tani. The past can reach through the years and land a punch on us today. Especially in Fiji. It can pay to find out what we're dealing with. But after your sterling service today, I'll let you off lightly.'

Musudroka grinned. '*Vinaka*, sir.'

'Is everything you got from the library here?'

'Except that report I started reading. Do you want it now, sir?'

Horseman needed to sit down again. He hobbled back to their table. 'Sure, can you bring the whole lot over here, please? I've got time to get an overview before I leave for the hospital.'

Singh brought him a mug of water. 'You look like you should drink this. Can I help you with the reading, sir?'

'*Vinaka*, Susie. You and Tani, both of you head off home. It's been a long and eventful day, to say the least. You're due for some rest.'

Without further ado, Musudroka gathered his things and said goodbye.

Singh stayed where she was. 'Not for me, sir. Not yet. I'm still too hyped. Reading old documents might be just what I need.' She smiled cheerfully, but her eyes were troubled, probably with concern for him. He got the feeling she did not intend to leave him alone.

'Okay, I know better than to argue. Here, take half the folders. I'll check through the books first. Hope they have indexes.'

After forty minutes, Horseman had marked about a dozen pages from three of the books with torn scraps of paper. 'Could you copy these for me please, Susie?'

Singh took them to the photocopier. Horseman saw she was making good progress with the folders; the stacked pages to her right bristled with purple and green sticky tabs.

He picked up the folder Musudroka had started on. It was a report to the new British Governor, Sir Arthur Gordon, from Ernest Smith, the District Officer sent to investigate the murder of Mr Weston. As he read the pages of copperplate handwriting, the turbulence of those early days of Queen Victoria's sovereignty over Fiji hit him. Old enmities smouldered, especially among the hill tribes of Viti Levu, at times flaring into secret raids and open battles where heads and slaves were taken.

Nevertheless, Ernest Smith and his Fijian constables trudged up to Tanoa and investigated the Weston murder as thoroughly as they could, even retrieving some long bones and the chief's ceremonial club, Destroyer, alleged by proud Tanoans to be the murder weapon. Sifting and piecing together the accounts of both the survivors of Mr Weston's party and those of the chiefly spokesmen of Tanoa, Ernest Smith came up with mixed motives for the killing. One factor was envious opposition to the Christian Bau chiefdom, recognised as paramount by the British. Another was perceived insult to the chief by Mr Weston. Five Tanoans admitted proudly to ambushing and attacking Mr Weston's party after they left Tanoa, but three of them claimed to have wielded the fatal blow. Horseman wondered if Ernest Smith understood that implementing a chief's wishes was an honour worth competing for.

At any rate, the three men who confessed were brought to Korovou to appear before the Magistrate. However, justice was not served. After a few days in the lock-up, all three succumbed to high fevers and died within a week. Rev. Weston's murder was overtaken by the calamity of the measles epidemic, which wiped out 20 percent of the population.

Despite the perfection of the copperplate, the digital photocopier had not coped with the varying pressure of Ernest Smith's upstrokes and downstrokes. Horseman could only guess at the unfamiliar names of the confessed Tanoan murderers. But what did it matter now? Mr Smith wisely referred to the three accused as "probable culprits". Horseman wanted to know who they were.

When Singh returned with the photocopies and a bag of rotis to share, he asked her to read Ernest Smith's report while he marked up the photocopies. Their significance seemed peripheral now he had the report.

Sunday rotis were never as good as Saturday's, probably because they were Saturday's leftovers. But lunch had been a long time ago. He demolished two while Singh nibbled one as she read.

'Susie, I accept what you say about Ilai's motive for the murders being stronger. Maybe that just made it easier for him to kill Vili at the chief's bidding.'

'You heard the super. You're excused from mopping up. You're due at the hospital in twenty minutes and you're on leave tomorrow.' He was surprised at the edge to her voice.

'Susie, I know you'll understand. I can't take a holiday without following the names in this Smith report as far as I can. I bet you feel the same.'

Singh sighed heavily. 'I know. Good luck, sir.'

MONDAY

48

'*Vinaka vakalevu.*' The Pacific Collection librarian smiled warmly at Horseman as he delivered the borrowed books. 'Not too many borrowers return on time these days. It's getting so bad we're considering stopping loans altogether. But the rare items shouldn't be exposed to the photocopier flash, so what's to be done?'

Good, a chatty librarian.

'I wonder if you could help me with interpreting this photocopied report, please?' He leant his crutch against the counter and placed the Smith file between them.

'Oh my word, please take a seat, Inspector Horseman. I'll come and help you.' She pointed her chin at the readers' tables.

'*Vinaka*, I'm actually more comfortable here at the counter.' The heavy-duty painkillers he'd got from the hospital enabled him to stand comfortably enough as long as he didn't stress his two fractured ribs by bending.

'Certainly, up to you,' she said cheerily. 'How can I help?'

'As you can see, this copy is rather blurry and some bits of the letters are missing. I can make sense of the narration, but I'm having trouble with the names—these in particular.' He turned to the page with the highlighted names.

'*Io*, this is a very poor copy, because the original is handwritten. I think we should transcribe this one. But let me fetch the original for you. Sure you don't want to sit down?'

'*Vinaka*, I'll stay here.' While the librarian was hunting, he thought about Melissa, who had been sleeping deeply when he left her at nine o'clock. It had been dark by the time they got home from the hospital last night. He told her what he wanted to do today and she readily agreed, admitting she could use a rest day or two before setting off for their island adventure.

'Here we are, Inspector. The original 1875 report by Ernest Smith.' She turned the pages, spattered with brown fox marks, with gloved hands. 'The names are much clearer, despite the foxing. Looks like Wau, Matai, and Bati. What do you think?' She handed him a magnifying glass.

'*Io*, I agree.' Horseman jotted the names on his copy of the report.

'I'll prioritise this document for transcription. The original won't stand much more handling.' The librarian frowned as she carefully restored each page to the protective envelope.

'Do you keep records of the copies you make for readers?'

'*Io*, Inspector, this is a library. Do you need to see them?'

'Just for this document, please.'

The librarian disappeared again, returning with a single sheet of paper. 'That's it, we've made five copies so far this year. Readers fill in the details, then at the end of the year we enter the totals onto our spreadsheet. We don't keep these running sheets, we start off fresh each January.'

Horseman recognised none of the readers who had requested a copy this year. He thanked the librarian, picked up his crutch, and left, glad of the lift. He grabbed a taxi and headed downtown to the Clan Registry Office. He explained what he wanted to Emeli, friend of the super's wife. Emeli reminded him of Mere Tora: round, cheerful, efficient, maternal. A lump came to his throat as he pictured how bereft Mere would be today, as shock subsided and reality hit home. The reality that her precious child was murdered and gone forever.

Emeli beamed. 'I'm very glad to help you, Josefa Horseman. However, you've got the wrong end of the stick. It won't do you any good to start with these three names and try to find a connection to

Viliame Bovoro. We must start at the present and work back. Fortunately, I already traced a few generations back with Superintendent Navala on Saturday. Just watch me closely and you'll soon get the hang of the procedure.'

The procedure, involving different card indexes and microfiche, bewildered Horseman at first. However, by the time they were back to the early 1900s, he had indeed got the hang of it.

'This is where it gets tricky, Joe. The registration system before 1900 was different. Let's see how we go.' She was eager, in her element.

'For 1875, we need to go back to the Evidence Book, compiled from statements, sworn by the chiefs, about genealogy, social status, and land. The first census, if you like. But far from complete in 1875.'

Emeli spoke to an assistant, who brought several large blue-bound volumes to the table. She seemed to find her way easily through the data, tracking mostly backwards but sometimes forwards, making diagrams like a family tree.

Eventually she looked up and smiled. 'We are in luck today, Joe. One of these three names you've given me is Vili's great-great-great-great grandfather. He already had three children when he died in 1875, but only one son is recorded in the 1903 Clan Register. He's our link.'

'I'm impressed, Emeli. His name?' Horseman asked.

'Oh, it's Bati—Warrior. His status is also listed as warrior.'

'*Vinaka vakalevu*. It all fits. Have there been any other enquiries into the Evidence Book for Tanoa?'

'I know I haven't handled any. Let me get the records and ask around. Do you want to come back in half an hour?'

Fatigue was catching up with him. 'I'm happy to wait, if that suits you.'

He examined Vili's family tree going back to 1875, then let his mind drift while he waited. The drifting led to dozing before Emeli returned. He snapped awake when she coughed softly.

'Success again! There have been two requests for that volume, both in March last year. Both by Ratu Osea Matanitu.' She handed him a yellow Post-It with the dates. What a wonder she was.

'*Vinaka vakalevu.* I'm extremely thankful, Emeli.'

'An absolute pleasure, Joe. Here, take this tree template too. I've filled in the direct descent line. Like you, I'm just doing the job I'm paid to do.' In spite of her demurs, she beamed with satisfaction as they shook hands.

49

'What are you doing here, Joe? Disobeying orders again?' Navala glared, but one corner of his mouth twisted up. 'I've been listening to you hobbling up the stairs on that crutch for a whole minute! You're supposed to be lazing on some island resort!'

Horseman grinned. 'Melissa said she'd like a day or so to recuperate here before we go, sir.'

The super frowned. 'Oh, how is she? Nothing serious, I hope?'

'*Vinaka*, the hospital gave her the all clear. She's just tired. I left her sleeping.'

Navala nodded. 'You're still on leave, Joe, whether you're in Suva or the Yasawa Islands.'

'Have you read my report, sir?'

'*Io*, all satisfactory. I spoke to Singh before she left for Tanoa, so no need to debrief.'

'Ah, the warrant for Ilai's house came through, then?'

'*Io*, it did, but Singh and the team can handle it. Before you ask, no joy with warrants to search Ratu Osea's properties. He's back at his Suva house now.'

'Yesterday evening Singh and I looked through the material Keli got from the USP Library. When I returned it this morning, the librarian showed me the original Weston murder report of 1875. Three Tanoan men confessed to the murder but died of measles before being tried by the magistrate.'

'Oh? And?' The super managed to look both interested and disapproving.

'I took the names to your friend Emeli at the Clan Registry. What a capable lady! She found that one of the accused, Bati, is Vili's direct ancestor.'

'Hmm, warrior. Is Bati his name, or is that his class?'

'Both, sir. According to Emeli.'

'Interesting, but why are you telling me this?'

'Ratu Osea is the only one who's requested that particular Evidence Book volume in the last two years.'

The super sighed. 'Where are you going with this, Joe? I'm not surprised. We know the chief has been researching the Weston murder and everything relating to it for the last two years.'

'Sir, Ratu Osea is obsessed. He wanted to burn the club, to sacrifice it, to atone for the murder. What if he wanted to sacrifice the murderer too? This Bati? Or, the next best thing, to sacrifice his direct descendant, his great-great-great-great grandson, Viliame Bovoro? So Ilai kills Vili on the express wishes of the chief. That's my theory. Probable, don't you think?'

The super lifted his eyebrows. 'I would say possible, not probable. But even if that's the way it happened, there's still no evidence. Neither man will ever admit that. The fact that Ratu Osea consulted relevant historical records proves nothing, especially in the context of the reconciliation ceremony planning.'

Horseman was winded. Of course, the super was right. He'd allowed himself to get carried away by the look in Ratu Osea's eyes as he spoke of righting the wrongs of the past.

'You've done a good job as IO, Joe. Go home and look after Melissa. Yourself, too. The present and the immediate future. That's all any of us can do.' He smiled gently as he shook Horseman's hand.

EPILOGUE

TEN DAYS LATER

Musudroka and the other volunteers had done a good job while he was away. The Shiners were up against Raiwaqa High School next Sunday, and he estimated they had a chance. Raiwaqa were not nearly as strong a team as Marists. He chatted to his scrawny boys as they bolted their dinners after Thursday training.

His idyll with Melissa in the Yasawa Islands was over. They had blissfully lazed in the shade for the first few days, made love very carefully. From the fourth day, they snorkelled the beautiful reefs off the resort and were content. Melissa's inner physio had insisted he begin gentle exercises, however. He had complied, and now he'd given up his crutch and knee brace and was walking normally, more or less. Well, a bit less, but he was nearly there. His ribs still screeched if he forgot to keep his torso straight.

Neither of them had initiated any discussion of their future together. After all that had happened in Melissa's first weekend in Suva, he felt he had no right to express his own wishes, much less demand she speak of her own.

'Miss Melissa, *bula, bula, bula*!' Tevita yelled out, signalling his unique status as the only Junior Shiner who had been introduced. Horseman turned. Ah, here she was walking across the oval from Ratu Cakobau Road, while he was keeping a look out along Victoria Parade. She waved happily at him, or was she waving at Tevita? No matter, she looked happy. Matt Young was beside her. And a dog on a lead. What had she been up to this afternoon?

'She remembers you, Joe!' Melissa sounded proud as the dog sat at her command, gazing at Horseman with pricked ears, her head on one side.

'What is this, Melissa?'

'This is Tina, honey. Don't you recognise the mother dog we fed in Ratu Sukuna Park two weeks ago?'

'Hardly, she must have had a bath! What have you been up to, Melissa?'

Melissa shared a complicit grin with Matt Young. 'Okay, I'll come clean. That Monday you were at work, I told Matt about her. He came back from his island on Sunday to do Kelera's autopsy, remember? This starving mother was troubling my conscience. Matt advised me to go to the RSPCA. Such good folks there, babe. Anyways, one of them came with me to find Tina and her puppies—four weak little things, eight weeks old. I paid for the RSPCA vet to do what he could while we were in the Yasawas.'

He loved her for her practical kindness, but feared where this story would end. 'Melissa...'

'Great news today, Joe. Three of the puppies survived and are thriving. The RSPCA will place them in good homes. It turns out they have some favoured genes—border collie, Australian kelpie, probably labrador, among others. Intelligent, loyal, and placid when they grow up. Tina's been spayed and had her shots, she's filling out. Isn't she looking gorgeous?'

Tina held Horseman's eyes, thumping her tail and wriggling in anticipation of his orders. He thought gorgeous a gross exaggeration, but her black and grey stippled coat was glossy and thickening, her eyes shone with intelligence and devotion.

'Did you know *Tina* is the Fijian word for mother?' he asked.

'I didn't, the vet told me. What a surprise, my second name is Cristina. A lovely name in any language, don't you think, Joe?'

'And the RSPCA will find her a home?' he asked.

She looked rueful, shaking her head. 'They say middle-aged dogs like Tina are hard to place, honey. I want to give her to you. She'll look after you for me.'

She knew he didn't want a dog, couldn't look after one. Was all this about the dog, or him? He wished he could penetrate the intricacies of her manoeuvres. 'I can't, darling. As you know, I'm staying with Matt for now, and with my hours, I can't exercise her, feed her at the same time every day, all of that.' He trailed off feebly.

Matt Young butted in. 'Mate, I've been thinking for a while I'd like a dog, but never got off my arse to get one. We can share looking after Tina, and she'll have the maid for company in the mornings. I reckon she'll work out great.'

Horseman recognised a conspiracy when he saw one. He shrugged. Tina kept on beating her tail on the grass, her gaze steadfast. She was Horseman's dog and no one else mattered.

'You can think of me every day, honey,' Melissa said lightly, handing him the lead.

'Emotional blackmail,' Horseman complained. He rubbed Tina on the head and smiled at Melissa as he took the lead.

ENJOY THIS BOOK?
YOU CAN MAKE A BIG DIFFERENCE.

As an indie author, I don't have the financial muscle of a major world publisher behind me. What I do have is loyal readers who loved my first book and took the trouble to post reviews online. These reviews brought my book to the attention of other readers.

If you enjoyed *Death by Tradition*, I would be most grateful if you could spend just five minutes posting a short review on Amazon, Goodreads or other book review site.

I also encourage you to sign up for my newsletter on www.bmallsopp.com. You'll be the first to hear of new releases, snippets about Fiji and everybody's favourite, free offers.

ACKNOWLEDGEMENTS

This book could not have been written without the willing help of many people. First I owe many thanks to Mr Waisea Vakamocea, retired senior officer of the Fiji Police Force, who patiently answered my questions. Responsibility for errors relating to police procedure in this book is all mine.

Second, I am most grateful to the expert professionals who transformed my manuscript into a real book. Editor Irina Dunn gave me much perceptive advice. Proofreader Deborah Dove found hundreds of errors in what I considered my polished final draft. Polgarus Studios designed and formatted the interior with flair and Maryna Zhukova of MaryDes drew the map and once more created the cover of my dreams.

I am humbled by the generosity of so many readers of my first book, Death on Paradise Island, who volunteered to give me feedback on my final draft. Not only did their enjoyment of this story reassure me, but I have implemented many of their suggestions.

Finally, I thank Peter Williamson for his advice on radio protocols, his enthusiasm for my story and constant support.

ABOUT THE AUTHOR

B.M. Allsopp is the author of the *Fiji Islands Mysteries* series. She lived in the South Pacific islands for 14 years, including four in Fiji, where she taught at the University of the South Pacific. She now lives in Sydney with her husband and tabby cat. Please visit her at her online home: www.bmallsopp.com

ALSO BY B.M. ALLSOPP

Death on Paradise Island
A Fiji paradise saved. A girl's body torn on the reef. To find the link, Detectives Joe Horseman and Susie Singh must drag to the surface secrets that have no place in paradise. Dive into the fragile beauty of the Fiji islands today!

Read the first few chapters here now.

PROLOGUE

SATURDAY

A crested tern swooped down to the edge of the fringing reef, attracted by the flutter of white in the water lapping the exposed coral. But the tern flew away disappointed, for this was no fish, just a scrap of cloth. The cloth was torn from the uniform worn by all the Paradise Island staff for the marine reserve celebrations: tailored white tunic patterned with black coconut palms and rugby balls, worn with a black *sulu*, the Fijian wraparound skirt.

If the tern investigated the white flapping further, it would find the cloth scrap still partly attached to the tunic and the girl wearing it. She had washed in from the sea and was caught by the jagged shelf below the coral overhang. The delicate coral was merciless, abrading her golden-brown skin as the waves tossed her back and forth until the tide retreated.

So it was a small hermit crab who first discovered the dead body of Akanisi Leletaku, who had so proudly arranged the floral decorations for the festivities. The crab picked its way over her uniform and scuttled into her open mouth, where it began to feed on the soft tissue.

1

SUNDAY

SUVA

Detective Sergeant Josefa Horseman gazed down from the Twin Otter aircraft heading to Suva, Fiji's capital, from Nadi. At 7.30 am, the deep valleys were giving birth to clouds; white wisps growing as they rose. Some, reluctant to let go, clung just below the mountain peaks. The plane cleared the highlands, descended towards the broad patchwork of the Rewa Valley and the floodplain smallholdings, whose inhabitants were already going about their work.

Now he could see the silver meanderings of the Rewa river, his thoughts descended to life at ground level. The new bridge at Nausori, already overdue when he left Fiji a year ago, was still not in use, although it looked like the roadway was finished. Traffic was still crossing the rickety old bridge. As the plane banked before straightening up for the runway approach, dread of returning to the routine frustrations of police work gripped him.

The eight passengers stepped down from the plane. Horseman's body violently protested against his native climate. He was suffocating, drowning in steam. But a few laboured breaths seemed to jog his lungs' memory and he limped across the tarmac to the small run-down terminal. A few minutes later he had his luggage, was through the exit gate. A gleeful welcome party of relatives rushed him.

'*Oi le*! Joe, Joe! *Bula*!'

Huge smiles and wet eyes greeted him. His bags were taken from his hands. He embraced his mother and bent his head to accept the sweet-smelling *salusalu* garland she tied around his neck. Hands reached out to pat him, checking he was really there in the flesh. He was wearing six *salusalu* when they'd finished, and on his face tears mingled with sweat. His mother took his arm.

'Now Josefa, I'll tell you what we've planned. If we leave now, we'll get to the village in good time for church at eleven. The boys are preparing the *lovo* pit and the whole clan's busy with the feast. It'll be extra special, all your favourites! How much leave have you got?'

He wanted to do what they all expected, he really did. 'Probably none, Mum. I assume I'll be reporting for duty tomorrow. I'll call headquarters from the airport police post before we leave.'

'What? I can't believe you haven't got leave after your long journey, all your study, and surgery, rehab. . .'

'Mum, as far as everyone in the Force is concerned, I've had a very privileged holiday, and I owe them heaps.'

Mrs Horseman drew herself up, ready to battle the entire Fiji Police Force, if necessary. He recalled with a smile how formidable she had been in his childhood when confronting wrongdoing, usually his own. His easy-going father had left her to it.

'Excuse me, I beg to differ, Josefa. You wrecked your leg bringing honour on the Police rugby team. Not to mention our national team, the Sevens and two World Cup tournaments. If that's not the line of duty I don't know what is. Five premierships in a row! The commissioner was basking in glory as if he'd scored all those tries himself! How's your knee now, by the way?' She cast her professional nurse's eye at the right leg of his jeans. 'I'll need to have a proper look at that later.'

'Coming along well, Mum. I should be fine for next season.'

'Wait a bit, now. Didn't the specialist say—

'Detective Sergeant Horseman. *Bula*, sir. Sorry to interrupt, sir.' A sweating uniformed constable stood at attention.

Horseman turned to him with relief. '*Bula vinaka*, Constable. He glanced at the badge. 'Peni Dau. Stand easy, Peni.'

'Message from the Deputy-Commissioner, sir.' He handed Horseman an official brown envelope.

He read the message. Once again he was going to disappoint his family, and there was nothing he could do about it

'Mum, everyone, I'm so sorry, but I've been ordered to report immediately to the Deputy Commissioner at CID. I haven't a clue what my orders will be after that, but I'm afraid I can't go back with you now.'

His mother's mouth trembled for an instant, then clenched in a straight line. 'And what right has that young Rusiate to destroy your homecoming? Why, I was at school with his sister. He was ten years our junior—always sneaking off to our secondary school compound to hide behind his sister and tell tales on his own classmates!'

Her righteous indignation made them all smile again.

'Mum, I've told you that as far as the Force is concerned, I've had a whole year off.'

'Well, we'll all go to Suva, and I'll give young Rusi my opinion about that! Your cousin Seru brought the twin-cab utility. We'll all go in that. After this meeting with Rusi, there'll still be time for us to get to the village for lunch.'

'I'm afraid the boss has sent the constable to drive me. I'd better go with him or he'll be in trouble. Whether I'll have free time after the debriefing, I don't know.' He shrugged. 'I'm sorry, Mum.'

'We'll wait outside HQ until you come out of this meeting, Joe.' There was a hint of a twinkle in her eyes. 'Don't worry, I'll try not to embarrass you, son.' The return of her playful tone was a relief. He patted her shoulder.

Horseman waved to the constable, who was standing a discreet distance from them. He immediately returned. 'Ready to go now, sir? I'll bring the vehicle around.'

'No need, Peni, I'll walk with you.'

They got in the car but Constable Dau made no move to start the car. He looked as if he was steeling himself for an unpleasant duty.

'Anything wrong?' Horseman asked.

Constable Dau's gaze was on the steering wheel. 'No, sir. Just wanted to say, sir, it's an honour to meet you. You know, me and my friends are so sorry you won't be playing rugby any more.'

'Where did you hear that, Peni? I expect to be back next season, or maybe the one after. Now let's get going. We can't keep the Deputy Commissioner waiting on a Sunday morning.'

***

It was still only 9.30 a.m. when Horseman arrived at the CID headquarters on a hill high above central Suva. The building looked just the same, but across the road, the expanse of bitumen car park had disappeared. The footpath was now fenced in plywood sheeting, behind which scaffolding rose a good twenty metres skywards. The caged structure within looked to be about four stories, already taller than most buildings in Suva. To his astonishment, work was in progress on a Sunday. A towering crane slowly hoisted a concrete panel and swung it to the waiting workers who eased it into position. Dangerous work, even with the flimsy-looking helmets, and work most builders in Fiji would not be much experienced in.

'They're getting on very fast with the hotel, aren't they?' Constable Dau commented. 'They say it'll be finished by Christmas, all ten stories, and the ground floor shops and cafe will open in August.'

Horseman watched for a moment, wondering where the workers had come from. Perhaps returned from working overseas, lured by big bonuses? It did happen, but few citizens who departed for greener pastures ever returned permanently, except in defeat. 'This way, sir.' The constable led the way to the stairs.

'Is the Deputy Commissioner still on the third floor, Peni?'

'Io, sir.'

'Then I know my way. Why don't you let the duty sergeant know you're back.'

Constable Dau looked unhappy, but he'd have to wear it. Horseman wanted to tackle the stairs unobserved. He climbed to the second floor without difficulty, but his reconstructed knee rebelled against the last flight. He used the balustrade for support and maintained an even tread, weight equally balanced on both legs, as the American therapists had taught him. He paused at the top to catch his breath before approaching the only door to the right of the landing. It was open. He tapped on the glass panel in the door. His superior rose from his desk and strode across.

'Ah, Detective Inspector Horseman, come in, come in. *Bula vinaka*. Welcome home.'

'*Vinaka vakalevu* sir.' Horseman ignored what could only be a slip of the tongue regarding his rank.

'How are you, Joe, how are you? Knee must be improved, eh? Listening to you coming up the stairs, your steps sounded quite normal. Perhaps a bit slow, eh? We've had reports from the rehabilitation people in Oregon, of course. They think you can be returned to the front, as long as you follow the instructions they've given you and keep up the exercises. You know all about that.'

'Yes sir. Surgery was successful, and I've trained hard with the rehab team since. Hope to make more progress here.'

'An athlete like you, no stranger to training, eh? I have no doubt at all you'll stick to it and make a full recovery.'

'Yes, sir. I can't wait to return to the field for Police.'

The DC nodded and smiled, a paternal, indulgent smile. Irritating. 'All in God's good time eh? But I'm advised the new knee should do fine for police work. All our glory days come to an end, eh? But you're still young and can expect a good career ahead of you in the force, Detective Inspector. No doubt your family met you this morning?'

What was it with the DC? Getting senile? He'd not have been confused about anyone's rank a year ago. 'Yes sir, quite a crowd came, ready to whisk me back to my mother's village for church and

a *lovo*. They were pretty cut up when Constable Dau arrived to bring
me straight here. As a matter of fact, they'll be waiting outside now,
hoping I'll be free to go back with them after our meeting.'

The DC frowned. 'I'm sorry about that Joe, but my letter to you
last week expressly stated you'd be required on duty as of today.
Usual shortage of officers, eh?'

'Sir, I'm sorry, but I didn't receive your letter before I left. I had
to leave Portland the day before yesterday in order to catch the
morning Air Pacific flight from L.A. Perhaps that's the reason.'

More paternal nods. 'Ah, that may be. My secretary followed up
with an email when I didn't hear from you. Surely you got that?'

'No sir. My temporary account through the Oregon Police server
was closed the day before I left—security protocol. So it must have
been flicked back to you, or. . .' Horseman trailed off lamely,
thinking through the possibilities.

'Never mind, Joe, I don't care about the technicalities, I have no
ambition to understand IT, that's one reason you were sent to the
Portland course.'

'Yes sir.'

'In that case, you won't have seen the latest Gazette, either, eh.'
This was a statement.

'No sir, I, er, was wondering. . .'

The DC interrupted. 'Why I'm addressing you as Detective
Inspector? And I was wondering why you didn't acknowledge your
promotion. Do you realise this mix up wouldn't have happened in
the days of telegrams?'

'*Vinaka vakalevu* sir. I'm taken by surprise, and honoured.' This
was an extremely bad time to beg for the rest of the day off, but he
owed it to his family. He tried for a light-hearted tone. 'Sir, this will
give them even more cause to celebrate. I'm afraid my mother
simply will not hear 'no' about today. If it's at all possible for me to
resume duty tomorrow, or even this evening. . .'

The DC puffed his round cheeks out, let the air out very slowly.
'Joe, you don't seem to realise the extent of the privileges you've been

granted in your career so far, because we needed you on the rugby field, winning the premierships for Police. We're always pleased to free up any officer selected for the national team too—goes without saying. You've been protected from the real life of policing because of that, to an extent. All in our self-interest, I know—'

'Sir, this is too much. One player can't win any match on his own.'

'Let me be frank, Joe. Plenty of brilliant players in Fiji, but few can be relied on for a whole season, much less year after year. You're consistent, strategic, determined to win. You were the one we all wanted to be. You're a leader. Now it's time for you to direct those qualities to your career. You're a good detective, otherwise you wouldn't have been promoted. But you can be a much better one now you're off the field. I expect you will be.'

'I'll do my best for the job, sir. When I'm back on the field, too.'

Horseman thought further remonstration would be less than helpful at this point. Strategic? The DC was the master of strategy—manipulative old fox! He waited. The DC opened a slim file.

'Call came in last night from the manager of the resort on Vula Island. They're calling the resort Paradise Island now—did you know that? So silly! Surely the name *Vula* is easy enough for any foreigner to pronounce? Anyway, the manager there's a Kiwi. Big day there yesterday, lots of pomp and circumstance for the opening of a marine reserve. Chiefs, press, scientists, the lot. Body of a young maid found on the reef at low tide. Probably misadventure, but keep an open mind. Ratu Ezekaia's a mate of the Commissioner, they've already talked, so there's a bit of pressure to clear it up. Couldn't get anyone from CID out there last night—humiliating.'

'Do we know who discovered the body, sir?'

'Yes, Dr Vijay Chakra, guest for the ceremonies who stayed overnight. D'you know him? He's got a private practice here in Suva. My wife's a patient of his. What we've got so far is in the file.'

He handed over a large official envelope.

'Your promotion notification, new ID, mobile phone, et cetera. Sign these papers and you're away. The rest of the paperwork can wait.'

Horseman signed.

'You'll be driven to Navua. The Paradise resort boat will pick you up at 11.30—none of our boats are available. Another embarrassment. Detective Sergeant Singh will be waiting for you at the landing. Two constables went over to Vula or Paradise at first light. I'm trying to get a detective constable assigned to you also, but no luck so far. Expect him when you see him. Be prepared to stay the night, if you need to. The resort will look after you—it's in their interest to help the police, after all.'

'Has Dr Chakra reported on his examination, sir?'

'All in the file, Joe, all in the file. When you get back report to Suva station. Superintendent Navala there will keep me informed. Where's your luggage?'

'In my cousin's twin-cab, with my family.' Horseman answered grimly. 'I'll retrieve it and stow it somewhere until I get back.'

'Do that—you won't need much. Hope you've got a *bula* shirt. I hear they're compulsory at the resorts!' The DC chuckled at his joke. In fact, the *bula* shirt, Fiji's abstract version of the Hawaiian shirt, was as popular with the locals as with visitors.

The DC continued. 'Well, the least I can do is explain things to your dear mother. She was my big sister's best friend at school, you know. Least I can do, eh, Detective Inspector? I'm still in time for the ten thirty service up at Central Methodist.' Gracious in victory, the big man picked up his well-thumbed black Bible and ushered his new Detective Inspector out.

2

TO VULA LAGOON

Horseman sat slumped beside Constable Peni Dau. The car cleared the urban fringe villages of Suva and picked up speed along the Queen's Road. Horseman was hardly aware of the passing scenery, a blur of green and dazzling blue beyond. He'd imagined he would be craning his neck, eagerly imbibing the glittering light, the colours, the earthy smells of his land. But now he was here, he didn't care. He hadn't done a single thing of his own volition since he'd got off the plane. He'd been transported, escorted, promoted, refused, assigned and packed off. So far, his return to his islands had brought only disappointment and much wasted effort to those who had wanted him back so much—his family.

He raised his hand to acknowledge the customary waves of the pedestrians they passed: single men, family groups, small bands of young people, all scrubbed and clad in Sunday best. They carried their Bibles. Some were sheltered by umbrellas, others went bareheaded in the merciless sun. They smiled and waved when they were enveloped in dust by an unknown police car on their way to church. Not for nothing were Fijians awarded the title of 'the friendliest people in the world' by the tourism industry's public relations writers. Horseman thought they might well be the most put upon.

'Like some Fiji bananas, sir?' the driver asked, pointing ahead.

Here the road skirted a beach, its white sand bisected by a band of flotsam: seaweed, fronds, bits of wood, coconut husks, scraps of nets, bottles, food and indestructible foil snack packets. A couple of dogs and a small pig were picking through it. The sharp tang of sea underlain by earthy decay pricked Horseman's senses.

'Why not? This stall's been here ever since I can remember.'

The constable bought a couple of ripe hands from the makeshift stall and returned to the car.

'Like to have a few now, sir?'

Horseman remembered he hadn't eaten since the previous night on the plane. He got out of the car and the two men ate their bananas in silence on the tussocky grass at the edge of the beach, their faces to the breeze that always blew here. Despite their size and cosmetic perfection, American bananas lacked the intense sugariness of the short, slender Fijian ones with black-blotched skins. He ate another, then another. He started to feel better.

Shattered cartilage and bone had changed his life. Just for a year or two. Medical science was unbelievable these days. He didn't know when, but he was sure he'd be back on the rugby field before too long. Now he had to focus on his CID work, and his unlooked-for promotion gave him a challenge. Stop resenting the routine and procedural frustrations and put his heart into it. One of the secrets of his rugby success was that he played any first round game as if it was the grand final. Psyched himself into it. He'd do the same now. He would investigate the resort maid's death as if it were the death of the President himself. He didn't know who she was yet, but he knew she deserved that.

***

Constable Dau parked on the roadway adjacent to the riverbank landing stage. Horseman got out and walked along the bank but couldn't spot anyone who might be Detective Sergeant Singh amid the bustle of the landing. However, he could now identify the sleek white Paradise Island launch rounding the bend in the creek. The boats were already two deep at the landing. This could be interesting. At least he could get his bag and be ready.

When he turned back to his car, he saw a slim Indian woman talking to his driver. She wore grey cotton trousers, short sleeved yellow blouse, sandals. Black hair scraped smoothly into a tight bun. He smiled to himself. What would his mentors in Portland say if they had caught him making gender-based assumptions? Quite rightly, they would say he had taken a shortcut, not considered all the possibilities, and therefore neglected a fruitful and ultimately correct line of enquiry. Hadn't the DC told him to keep an open mind? He went up to her, held out his hand and spoke in English.

'Good morning, I think you might be Detective Sergeant Singh. I'm Joe Horseman.' The woman nodded formally and shook his hand briefly. She looked seriously at him from behind large sunglasses.

'Pleased to meet you, sir. I've got a crime kit bag for each of us.'

'Thanks. The Paradise boat's just come in so let's get going. We'll go through the file together during the crossing.' He turned to Constable Dau. 'What are your orders, Peni?'

'Back to the station, sir. I'll bring your bags down to the landing first.'

Horseman smiled. 'No need. By the way, thanks for the bananas. Just what I needed.'

At the bottom of the landing steps the Paradise deckhand, spruce in turquoise polo shirt and navy shorts, was waiting for the two detectives. The launch was berthed midstream, tied alongside two fishing boats.

'*Bula, bula ovisa.* I'm Maika. We shouldn't be rafted up to other boats, we'll push off right now. Come this way, please.' They clambered across the sterns of the fishing boats, took the skipper's outstretched hand and hauled themselves up to the launch deck. Horseman was annoyed to realise that he needed the support. They introduced themselves to the skipper.

'I'm Jona. *Oi le*, I had no idea I was bringing Josefa Horseman to

Vula Island—or Paradise, we call it now! What a privilege to meet you, sir. But the circumstances are tragic, tragic.' The flesh of Jona's dark face hung slackly from his bones.

'We're here to investigate what happened, Jona.'

'*Io*, sir. But why the police should be so concerned with a tragic accident, I don't know.'

'Why do you think it was an accident, Jona?'

The skipper shook his head slowly. 'Akanisi's body was found on the fringing coral reef at low tide. She must have drowned when the water was higher. There's no other explanation. Please take a seat while we cast off.'

It would be impossible to discuss the case on the trip. Although they were the only passengers, Jona was skippering from an auxiliary wheel in the cabin, so privacy was impossible. As the twin outboard motors roared to life, Horseman smiled at his sergeant and shrugged. He took the file out of his bag, sat down and started to read. Taking his cue, Sergeant Singh retrieved a purple plastic file from her backpack and followed his example.

Horseman's file held the transcription of the manager's telephone report of the discovery of the body of the eighteen-year-old maid, Akanisi Leletaku, on the reef at low tide. In addition, the local chief had provided a summary of her background to his friend the Commissioner. She'd been born and raised on nearby Delanarua Island, much larger than the tiny coral island now called Paradise. He was gazing at the foaming wake, speculating about how an island girl, who probably swam like a fish, could come to drown, when the sergeant held out her own file to him.

'Sir?' she yelled.

'*Vinaka*,' he said, accepting it and handing the DC's file to her. Good to see she had initiative. She wasn't a time waster, either. In addition to copies of the reports he'd already seen, the sergeant's file contained a printout of several internet pages detailing the protocols of the new Vula Marine Reserve, a double-page spread from this morning's Fiji Times reporting yesterday's festivities on the island,

and another download from the resort's own website.

'Great!' he yelled back, and settled to read the papers in detail. Singh must have already read them herself, as neat patches highlighted in either fluorescent yellow or pink scattered the pages. He turned to the newspaper article first.

Vula Lagoon Marine Reserve has Ratu's blessing

Exclusive Paradise Island resort, in Vula Lagoon off the south coast of Viti Levu, yesterday hosted unusual numbers of visitors to celebrate the inauguration of the Vula Marine Reserve. The crowd of around 100 included villagers from the lagoon's islands and guests from Suva, including diplomats from Australia, New Zealand and the United States, delegates from the university, Fiji Institute of Marine Science (FIMS), environmental NGOs, tourism and media organisations. Ratu Ezekaia Tabualevu, chief of the lands and waters of Vula Lagoon and keen proponent of the reserve, travelled from his home on Delanarua Island by the resort launch, together with his official party. When they arrived at 10.30 in the morning, resort staff garlanded the chief and VIP visitors with exquisite salusalu while the staff choir sang traditional songs and hymns. After a formal kava ceremony of welcome, Ratu Ezekaia formally proclaimed the Vula Marine Reserve, then the visiting villagers entertained the crowd with lively traditional dances on the resort beach.

The Paradise resort cooks surpassed themselves with a magnificent buffet of Fijian delicacies. Ratu Ezekaia explained the importance of the new reserve and the rules which now operate.

'Fishermen have been too greedy and now our stocks are depleted. From today, no one can take any species from the waters inside the outer reef. We all know there's very little there now anyway. Beyond the outer reef there are no restrictions at all. I know we will stand united in support of the reserve so our lagoon waters will brim with life again,' Ratu Ezekaia said.

To cap off the day, Ratu Ezekaia and Methodist minister Rev.

Mosese made a ceremonial circumnavigation of the island in the flower-bedecked dive boat, representing the circle of protection which now applies to the entire lagoon. Rev. Mosese prayed for the success of the new reserve in replenishing marine life. On their return to the resort beach the boat steered close to the shore while Ratu Ezekaia demonstrated the goal of the reserve to the waiting crowd. One by one, he held aloft live creatures of the reef waters: an octopus, a bêche-de-mer, a parrot fish, and a giant clam, then released them into the waters. But, just as the chief raised a turtle, his boat suddenly listed dangerously towards the beach. Villagers at the front of the crowd immediately rushed to the boat and succeeded in righting it. Ratu Ezekaia and Rev. Mosese were borne ashore on the villagers' shoulders to the delight of the cheering crowd.

Horseman was intrigued and wished he could have witnessed the last scene. He wondered if the dead maid had been there. One of the press photos showed the chief beaming, his dark face framed by abundant crinkled white Afro hair, dark formal jacket, white shirt and Fiji Rugby tie. It was heartening to see an older chief leading his people to combat a threat all too common in their little nation of islands.

He turned to the print-out from Paradise Island's website, amounting to twenty illustrated pages. Of particular value were the Paradise People pages. Their skipper Jona turned out to be the head boatman, a key position on an island resort. Deckhand Maika didn't warrant a solo shot, but he appeared in a photo of the Vula Voyagers, a string band of three men in pink *bula* shirts, flowers in their hair. The dead girl wasn't identified, but perhaps she was somewhere in a group shot of smiling staff.

He was still immersed in the file when Maika tapped him on the shoulder and pointed ahead. Horseman stepped over to the windscreen. They were heading towards a green smudge on the horizon.

'Paradise Island?'

Jona nodded. Sergeant Singh joined them. As they watched, the smudge resolved into a scrubby hill, which a few minutes later acquired surrounding green flats. Soon they could see tall waving palms, a fringe of bright sand, a breakwater, moored boats and a tall white flagstaff. He forgot his assignment for a moment, and surrendered to delight. How magical this approach must be for the executive from Osaka or Houston! Now he could make out figures on the jetty. The boat slowed as the water shallowed.

Horseman couldn't resist going up on deck for a better view and Singh followed. Her curiosity was another promising quality. He caught a glimpse of a thatched roof and reed walls through the trees beyond the flagstaff. The boat slowed further as the bottom shelved. Jona steered a careful course, avoiding the coral boulders strewn below. But this welcome party wasn't smiling and singing. Horseman wrenched himself back to his mission and went back inside to get his things. The cabin seemed dim after the brilliance outside. Sergeant Singh was rummaging in her backpack, her sunglasses pushed up onto her head. He handed her the purple file.

'*Vinaka*, Sergeant. You've done a great job getting that background information so quickly.'

His sergeant continued to rummage. 'No problem sir. You can hang on to it. I've got duplicates.'

She zipped her bag and looked up at him. Her eyes were the clear green of sunlit shallow water over sand. He tried not to stare.

She smiled. 'Call me Susie, if you like.'

Buy: http://www.bmallsopp.com/books